To Olivia,

Hmm... someone's daughter too!

[illegible]

A Field in Arlon

Marek Nowina

AuthorHouse™ UK Ltd.
500 Avebury Boulevard
Central Milton Keynes, MK9 2BE
www.authorhouse.co.uk
Phone: 08001974150

First published by AuthorHouse 9/29/2008

ISBN: 978-1-4389-2402-1 (e)
ISBN: 978-1-4389-0757-4 (sc)
ISBN: 978-1-4389-0758-1 (hc)

Library of Congress Control Number: 2008907166

Printed in the United States of America
Bloomington, Indiana

This book is printed on acid-free paper.

With thanks to Michael Cretu for words from Cross of Changes.

1

Cornwall braced itself for a motorized human deluge and, with only two roads to Penzance, Melly Cheval wasn't taking any chances. It's as though, oblivious to the ease of international mobility, England had claimed the solar eclipse of 1999 as its own, exclusively, and the Southwest was to reap the rewards and headaches as millions moved down country to descend on the peninsula for the summer. A rarity for the UK, this event was more frequently experienced in mainland Europe, but without all the excitement and without all the panic.

Melly toyed with the idea of shipping his car over to France and then selecting a location on a line anywhere between Dieppe and Belgrade. He enjoyed driving; he enjoyed going to new places; he could cope with sleeping in the car. Every so often, he'd pack a toothbrush, a quarter ounce of smoke and a change of underwear, put on his combat jacket, get behind the wheel with guitar in hand and hit the highway; he'd claim the open road.

Such a romantic, Melly, he'd grown up playing the blues and, now, the refrains of countless broken-hearted hobos gave him all the justification he needed to head anywhere away from home. He'd go farther a-field each time, as if he wanted to get lost, as if he was looking for *something*. He didn't know what that something was but he was sure he hadn't found it. Every time he ventured out he'd return despondent, disillusioned, and unfulfilled. He needed a challenge, like being dumped in the middle of nowhere, penniless, and having to find his way home. He needed a direction; he needed a purpose.

Melly once talked with friends about wanting to 'do Amsterdam' but met their looks of resignation, which suggested they felt it might be a final fling for them. As the idea lingered in his head, general interest in it subsided. His generation had assumed the reins of power, of influence and of responsibility and, now, had little free time to indulge in long benders. Holidays were strictly family affairs; a long weekend was not something that was easily predicted or planned for, let alone something that would coincide with the free time of others. *His* work with delinquent juveniles was finished for the year and, now, *he* had time on his hands. He was looking for a friend who would not only join him for Amsterdam, and not only extend it by a few days to include the eclipse, but who was also prepared to slum it with no frills and go where the mood took them.

Spontaneity! That's what he liked.

"I can't do it," said one. "I'm running the show while my boss is away this month,"

"I'm off to Portugal with the kids on Sunday," said another.

"I can do 'Dam," promised a third, "but I can't do the eclipse."

This was no longer his wife's idea of a good time either. Jean had experienced luxury and found it very much to her liking; there was no going back! They agreed amicably to plan and take holidays separately unless there was common ground between them. And, more importantly, smoking disagreed with her.

⁂

Melly had met Jean in his Second Year, at the University of Surrey Christmas Ball of 1973, and it took only thirty-seven minutes of their drinking from one another's eyes for him to be absolutely convinced that she was to be his forever. He'd experienced tempestuous love before; in fact, he had just freed himself from a relationship with a fresher from Newcastle whose insecurity in the world of the clear-spoken, well-heeled south-east made her easy prey for his Bohemian attentions. But *insecurities* are not the easiest of signs to read for a young longhair whose goals are limited to racking up sexual conquests and bragging to his mates about suppressing both daytime and night-time squeals of delight. Before Melly knew it, the Geordie was declaring her love for him, and devotion to him, and begging him to move in with her. Too fast, too close, and too inhibiting; he wasn't prepared for her. Nor was he particularly impressed by her threat of suicide if he didn't swear his love for her in return. It was fortunate that he was able to deftly introduce her to a friend of his who showered her with a touch more sanity, sensitivity and, hell, just security, plain and simple, and who, winning her over, took her out of his life.

Freed at last, Melly went to the Ball a loose cannon, out to try his luck again, and off to dip his wick the way Oz magazine had instructed: "*...just go up to a girl and ask for a screw. Society ought to cast off the shackles of propriety,*" it said, "*and make sex as natural and easy as, say, scrounging a cigarette; a refusal indicates only an unwillingness with no hard feelings...if you don't ask, you don't get; if you don't ask, you don't want...*" At least that was *his* interpretation of the article.

The first opportunity on this rebound was Jean. She was a tall, dark, and full-chested Sociology graduate, ten years his senior. Senior, indeed, but very young at heart – some would say quite immature emotionally. Jean had a succession of broken relationships behind her, including a failed marriage to one of her college tutors. Melly had heard his name mentioned once, somewhere; he was a considerably older conservative man who, on their wedding night, according to Jean, demanded she not use a contraceptive because he wanted to exercise his right to sire. While he desperately wanted children, Jean was dead-set against the idea. She wanted to wait until after graduating, until she got settled into a job and knew where she stood, like in a place where they might allow her to take maternity leave. But the old man grew impatient in his wait for children and, in his frustration, took to drinking heavily and becoming abusive. He rapidly got to patronize his younger wife to distraction, holding her up as a fool; a naïve child to be mocked and, worst of all, the one to blame for the downturn in his own fortunes.

But Jean was no fool; she may have been a late starter but she had ambition and wanted to gather qualifications while still in the mood. She realized, very soon into the marriage, that respect for the intellect does not necessarily equate with love, and that neither a nightmare vision of screaming babies in squalid conditions nor the ideal of sedate coffee mornings in a spotless home with toddlers playing in the nursery were for her. She simply enjoyed a faster pace of life and was desperate to resume a life closer the edge; to find her feet again and run with the best.

It's debatable whether Melly was the best; more than likely, he fell far short. He was already falling behind with his coursework; Divinity was the easiest course onto which to be accepted, yet the hardest on which to stay focused (and focused he was not). He was always penniless, investing heavily in amphetamines and grass, and being far too generous as a dealer. It was the classic trap for students who, in no time at all, lost control of a meagre grant. It was the inevitable outcome of bad financial management, but his decision to deal dope made of him a known figure in the Union bar; someone to be sought out; someone, for better or worse, attractive, if only because he was the disreputable rogue about whom all mothers and, especially, fathers, issued stern warnings to their daughters. He was *just like a Rolling Stone*, and the girls loved him for it.

In truth, he was not the cleanest of men; living as a squatter in a derelict warehouse in Guildford left him with no option but to wash infrequently and only at the times he managed to co-ordinate the bringing of a fresh change of clothes, a clean towel and toiletries to the showers at the university sports hall. Indeed, Melly was one of those rank individuals who typified the kind of student dropout broadsheets such as *The Daily Telegraph* would describe as "scum" and "a waste of the nation's resources". But Jean saw only the shock of tightly curled hair that cascaded over the wide shoulders of a hollow-chested non-arse, whose Biba-mauve loon pants barely hung on narrow hips. She noted immediately that he wore no underpants. She heard only the laughter and animation that surrounded him whenever he walked through public spaces; the rapt and attentive, tear-soaked silence that draped itself over an audience when he gave impromptu renditions on his guitar in the Common Room. Oh, she'd noticed him a few times.

And, then, this man who oozed sex and the promise of sex noticed her at the Ball; as soon as their eyes met, both were lost; mesmerized, captivated, helpless and unhooked. Thirty-seven minutes later, they were making their way to an empty Union office; thirty-nine minutes later their hips were grinding in time to the distant thud of the Strawbs beating out *Part of the Union*. The question of which one of them climaxed first was immaterial because the grind continued for some considerable time; each, in turn, soared to new heights of ecstasy, and for several hours. Neither Melly nor Jean closed their eyes to fantasize about a perfect, unattainable lover; their desires were fulfilled in the here and the now.

And, in the afterglow of their passion, Melly wished for no future without her while Jean cared for no future without him. They were perfectly matched and needed to look no further for sexual satisfaction. She was to be his intellectual guide who made him consider his emotions rationally. They lived a compassionate life through those initial university days – she gave him the positive strokes that allowed him to blossom and finally make sense of Divinity; he gave her the freedom to be both stupid and clever within the same hour and within the same sentence. Her seniority was valued and nurtured so that, within a short time, she had made of Melly a stronger and more resolute man. He, in turn, had influenced and corrupted her magnificently and brought her out of herself to become the kind of woman she'd always hoped to become.

Within a month of their meeting, she was a divorcee; uncontested, some would argue she was discarded, but free.

Melly's relationship with Jean became enviable. It was uncommon. Shit, it was exciting and unpredictable. So much love yet so much space; his friends loved her; her friends loved him yet none dared trespass. This couple was indivisible; they were the new measure by which all relationships were to be judged henceforth. And even when they eventually bucked the trend and married, to the astonishment of those who'd sworn never to contemplate doing such a *straight* thing, Melly and Jean dismissed their critics by letting it be known that it was "only for the tax breaks". How clever was that? How truly revolutionary; a number of marriages in their social circle followed in suit.

Theirs worked; typically, enviably and inevitably. She was his rock-solid base, his voice of reason; he was her excitement, her window on and access to the world.

◼ ◼ ◼

"You watch yourself," Jean said. "Remember you're not as young as you used to be."

She worried about his heart and the possibility of his being the next victim of a life of near excess. She knew he liked to indulge; she also knew he grew exhausted easily. Too many hurried jobs in the house had shown how achievements in furniture-shifting, patio-laying and rubbish-removal were done on willpower alone; there usually followed a lengthy period of convalescence as his unfit frame struggled to repair and heal itself. There was one matter on which Jean did not trust Melly; it was in him to go over the top without reference to a concept known as *limitation*.

As the weekend approached Melly resigned himself to the fact he would have to go abroad alone. It was, however, clear that at long last he had a trip with a purpose and, so long as he had an open ticket for the return Channel crossing, he could wander towards the eclipse, somewhere and anywhere, in a stoned haze, and then wander back. He'd hitched across France before; it wasn't a problem. He decided to leave the car at home and reach the Continent by coach. He'd take the overnight red-eye to Amsterdam.

Melly once knew people in Amsterdam but they had now moved on. Perhaps they were still there; either way, they were old business contacts who, as Melly found out years before, showed little interest in him once he proved that he was no longer of use to them in their industry.

"You can't mix business with pleasure," thought Melly. "All those friends you think you have all over Europe; drinking partners, party animals together, dining out in top restaurants, getting the best seats and backstage passes. It all goes in an instant as soon as you're no longer under the protective, providing wing of a company expense account. No longer a player; huh, not even a *professional fan*!"

Melly was never one gifted with sound business acumen or cunning. He was lousy at politics. He never made any fortunes in music, though he had plenty of chances. Plenty! Ah, but that was long ago. Now, he would have to experience the city, not as an executive as before, nor as a partygoer as before, not even as a tourist; he was going to get wasted in a place where it was perfectly okay to be wasted but, it would have to be in solitude. That was the price to pay for wanting to go there, and then, on *that* weekend.

"Odd," he thought, "how two people being excessive is okay whereas one, *drinking alone*, is an indication of a personal malaise." He tried to avoid typecasting and he scoffed at clichés.

Jean often joked that he was tight with his money; Melly, who hated debt, chose to think of it as being careful; prudent, even. And although this was his holiday (though he preferred to think of it as *time out*), he would, as usual, not spend wildly. On Friday morning he withdrew two hundred pounds from the bank, booked and paid for the coach ticket and, unfailingly, bought his weekly clutch of lottery tickets for the following two draws. The remainder he exchanged for guilders which, he estimated, would give enough to keep him in food and lodging for a week.

Melly had stayed in many a hotel before; a high price to pay for a bed, but that's *all* it needed to be. Experience showed him he would probably spend little time there; every time he went to a lively city, he could expect to be up half the night. He'd need somewhere just to leave his baggage and to use as a base from which to soak in the city life. For most people, that meant a hotel room; Melly thought it through only as far as feeling he didn't need the luxuries offered by hotels. Just a basin and loo, really; or a shelter and the hope it wasn't raining. Unless, of course, he met anyone who offered him a bed to share…

⊠ ⊠ ⊠

Melly could get no sleep on the coach during the night. As one who would regularly toss and turn, he awoke with a start whenever he nodded off, but only because he sensed he was falling out of his seat all the time. Thus, tired but excited, he arrived in Amsterdam at 7:30 in the morning, five days before the eclipse. It took him fewer than ten minutes to glide on the subway from the coach terminus to the Central Station and across its wide plaza to the nearest of the smoke shops on the edge of the Old Town. He felt casual; he felt youthful. He had a right to be there, and he knew what he was doing.

"A bag of Sensi, a bag of Temple Balls and a coffee, please…any crash pads here?" Melly heard himself ask the question, though he did not go so far as to picture himself doing so. If he'd been more paranoid, he'd imagine the American Wild West where a deadly hush descends, the music ceases and everyone stops what they're doing to gaze at the intruder. There was little chance of that happening in Amsterdam. A couple of guys shuffled groggily around a pool table, one end of which they used as a joint-rolling surface. Music played loudly from speakers in all corners of the bar. No one could hear him anyway. Those who *might* listen and watch saw a late forty-something man in an early twenty-something bar asking the unlikeliest of questions.

He was directed to an adjoining hotel where the charge was eighty guilders a night – way out of his range. He decided to go deeper into the network of alleys and paths that made up this poorer part of town. If he was lucky, he might just strike up a friendship with a local and be offered a floor. Ever the optimist was Melly.

It was looking increasingly unlikely he'd find anything really cheap until, while he stopped to eat breakfast at a shabby hotel deep in the Red Light district, he was summoned to hear word of a cancellation.

"It's not much, not even a bed. Just a mattress but you can have it half-price," chirped the Dutch receptionist, sizing up Melly. "Pay by the day. Upstairs - Room 101." She passed him an allocation ticket to give to the cleaner.

"Yesss! Sorted! It's only 11:30 a.m. and I'm paid up and I'm sorted! Survival!" Melly whooped and congratulated himself on having secured a mattress for three nights. He could have got it for longer but that would have meant abandoning it halfway through the fourth night to catch a train, and he was too frugal for that kind of unnecessary expense.

"Anyway," he thought. "I might be having too good a time by then and not want to get to bed at all. Hmm, actually," he remembered, "I was sorted by 7:40 a.m. but that's the story of my life, isn't it?"

⁂

There was particular significance in that, with his first dormitory joint, Melly hot-rocked the newly laid sheets on his bed. Just like his tee shirts and his trousers, his car seats, and the wooden floor at home, there lay behind him a trail of devastation and the telltale signs that heralded a committed smoker. He lay on the floor in Room 101, thinking. Earlier, the cleaner had turned over his mattress to hide a widely spread, fresh stain.

"Arse-end of the world, huh?" mused Melly, looking out through French windows to the street below. "Well, this is Shit Corner and I'm sitting on it with a perfect view!"

Crack addicts outside staggered as though blind, resting their heads on railings that overlooked the canal. Perhaps they were throwing up, but it's not as if there was any food in their bellies. Melly *chose* to be here. He *wanted* to watch it. But what did he want to make of it all? Did he want to despise it or did he want to identify with it? Was he relieved that he hadn't plumbed those depths himself…?

"After all," he thought, "how did these people sink this far? Just how easily is it done?" There was, inside him, a tinge of regret that he didn't really know how they felt about their condition, nor about their situation; not yet, though he really *did* want to know.

Melly felt incomplete. Despite his age, he also felt immature (or was it *unseasoned*) and still not able to get it *quite* right. There was definitely something odd about him. He kept getting life wrong in all sorts of ways. He was unfortunate in thinking, for example, that when you wanted to buy a barman a drink it meant *just that*. Earlier, whilst looking for a place to stay, he'd walked into a hotel looking the worse for wear and talked to the barman about finding work to pay for lodgings. The guy, from Dundee, took him to be an itinerant and advised him accordingly.

"There's a hostel round the corner," he said. "It's twenty-five guilders a night but you have to do duties like collecting all the rubbish. And over the canal, to the right, there's a laundry. You work there and live upstairs."

Melly had gone back to report that he was now fixed up. He wanted to show his appreciation to the man for having given him useful advice, but he didn't fully understand the mechanics of 'tipping' a barman. Not at that moment, anyway. He couldn't rally his thoughts around a tip; huh, a *drink*. He thought about saying, 'I'll have a beer…and one for you'. That would do it.

"Yeah, thanks man," he opened disarmingly, "I wanna buy you a drink. What are you having?"

"That's okay, thank you," said the barman.

"No, no," Melly insisted, keen to drink a toast with him. "What are you having?"

The man walked to the other end of the bar before replying. With his back thus turned, Melly heard his voice as no more than a distant mumble. He came back to within earshot. "… And keep your money," was all he could make out.

Too stoned to fully appreciate the significance of this or, indeed, any response, Melly called for a small beer then closed his eyes and listened to the music, which pumped from large speakers above him. It is small wonder conversation after that was light. What especially upset the barman was seeing Melly pull out a wad of hundred guilder notes to pay for the drink. To the barman who had, himself, recently landed in this city and who had to make the running alone, this represented wealth and Melly was clearly taking the piss; to Melly it was all that he had to play with in this city and on this occasion. Melly found himself suddenly abandoned by an embittered man who felt absolutely suckered.

⁂

He got it wrong with Katryn, too. Perfect, petite and private, she sat on a stool outside a bar on the street along from the hostel, gazing at passers-by, one of whom greeted her by name. Melly, who was out exploring, wondered about finding an excuse to talk to a prostitute. He fancied having her give him the come-on. He felt challenged to handle a hooker's proposition. Wow, what a laugh that would be!

"You want a drink?" she purred unexpectedly, sounding Californian.

"Yeah," he replied, taken by surprise. It was all too sudden; he'd said the wrong thing, and too quickly. Embarrassed, he walked straight past her and into the bar.

"Small beer," he called as he entered. He didn't want to buy *her* a drink just yet, and he panicked at the idea he'd be thought of as a punter. A glass of beer was ready by the time he reached the bar. After paying just enough, that is, with no tip, Melly carried his effete tipple outside and chose to sit directly across the street and opposite the woman, just a girl, really, to observe how she conducted her business.

And so he sat, and she sat; they faced one another; he curiously and coarsely, she cautiously. Katryn continued to gaze at passers-by and, every so often, would stop herself from looking in his direction. She was such a fine shape; her curves accentuated by the clinging black top and tight jeans she wore. A shock of blonde curls tumbled from her head; Melly could quite imagine losing himself with her, and in her. After a while, she rose to buy a sandwich from a deli a few doors away and returned to sit inside the bar, in a large picture window. Piquantly, large letters both obscured her and gave her refuge from Melly's undressing eyes. Still he gazed. He would ask her when she came out; he would ask all the questions he ever wanted to ask.

Soon, she came out, not to sit down on her stool and tackle punters as Melly has imagined, but to ask a couple who sat outside the bar what they cared for.

Uh...Melly had got it wrong again. So *that's* why she wouldn't look his way. Had he taken just a little more time to consider; had he given a moment's thought to recognizing a waitress instead of making his own assumptions. Those damned assumptions! Clearly, Melly had shown himself to be a Wally! Here he was, after all, in Amsterdam, in the Red Light district, and typecasting.

It's important to understand Melly was feeling hazy and a little red-eyed. This was an excuse he often used to explain irrational behaviour. It also partly explained why he always kept very odd hours. No overnight sleeper, he rarely went to bed before 3 a.m., and survived on three or four hours sleep. Amsterdam was, for him, the perfect place to be; like New York, it never slept. Melly returned to his hostel and dozed in short measures to recover from the coach journey. Around him, in the darkness of Room 101, as everyone slept, he rose quietly and went out into the night to explore.

⊠ ⊠ ⊠

There was little to separate the colour of the dark trousers and the ragged trainers the girl wore to that of the pavement on which she stood in the five o'clock morning while Melly sat on a stone step, skinning up. Her head lowered, she looked intently at the dirty nails that poked out of her torn, black cocktail gloves.

"You got any change?" she asked. She didn't go as far as to propose a trick – she could see Melly didn't have much money. "I'm so tired," she said, blinking hard.

Melly shook his head. "What's your name?" There were only the two of them in the chilly pre-dawn mist. He felt he had the right to ask. He hoped she would answer.

"Talish," she said, dropping her shoulders. Melly sensed she had unburdened herself at that moment and shared something of herself that few knew or cared to know. He cared; it mattered to him, a bit. Perhaps he might come to understand what she was doing there and if she was there by choice.

"Want a pull on this?" He offered her the spliff.

"Oh, uh no." she replied, "I gotta keep my head together. I'd fall asleep."

"You got work to do?" suggested Melly, not quite sure what he meant.

"Yeah…" her voice trailed off round the corner as she continued on her beat.

He finished the spliff and walked the length of the street and back again, window-shopping. The prostitutes he saw didn't particularly impress him nor was he especially turned-on by them.

"Why are we, all of us sad buggers, here?" he thought, once back on his mattress and gazing out through the window that separated him from the world outside. "Red lights at night have it in them to be mocked. In the daytime it all begins early, even on rainy mornings. Costume-dressed, the hookers hold quiet conversations with one another across open windows and doors. Whom do they finally attract? Is it those who are intent and single-minded or is it those who are challenged and egged on by their mates? So why do the men here not carry an easy smile; why do they look so sad?"

He lay through the hours and watched the streets fill with people.

"Come to my corner and spit," thought Melly, cursing the addicts and tourists as they crossed the canal by the bridge just outside. And they did spit, unashamedly, in this arse-end of the world.

Melly's attention was caught by the politics in the dormitory. Tony, a Cornishman, suddenly proclaimed, "It's very significant that at eleven past eleven, on the eleventh, the world goes dark!"

"Strange," sneered Wolfgang, a Bavarian, "so it won't be so bad when it goes dark, where I live, at twelve thirty-four!" It seemed everyone had their own agenda.

"This moment has been foreseen and feared for generations. The end is upon us," chanted a voice in Melly's head.

And then, back to normality. Presumably, as so often before…

Melly lay stretched out on his mattress with his arms folded comfortably like a corpse, very happily stoned on Sensi. He came to with a start and was aware of voices in the dorm referring to him as *that geriatric fucker in the corner, in need of a Zimmer frame.*

"Oi, Frank Zappa!" a voice growled its way into Melly's head.

The bullying had started but he ignored this barracking. He'd seen people die defending their honour but he was no fighter. He chose not to be. He could cope with words. That was his job, after all: deflecting the insults of those who had too little self-esteem and who took it out on others whom they regarded as the weaker.

But in every hellhole there are virtuous things. Like Caroline. She was such a sweet, young thing – too sweet to be looking for cocaine. Still new to Amsterdam, she spread her Mid-West openness like butter melting into warm toast, befriending all the wide-eyed, wide boys in the dorm who said they could help her. They wanted her body but *she* hadn't realized. Shit, none of the female travellers here seemed to anticipate the abruptness of three Scousers who held court in the dorm that day. Caroline had the sense to introduce herself as travelling over from Madrid with her brother, a young blond American who just happened to be laid out on the adjoining bunk. She and 'her brother' had given the lads the last of their money to go find some white powder, and were alarmed to discover they had brought back crack-cocaine.

"I don't want that!" she protested as she lay on her bed, tripping.

"Too bad," they jeered as they proceeded to smoke it themselves, alone and corruptly. "Railroaded!" they laughed and turned to ignore her.

"Tell you what, my Caroline," said the loudest at last, "I'll go to the bank tomorrow and I'll extend my overdraft. I'll pay you back. That's you and me, Cassie, tomorrow!"

He nudged his mates "When I shag her, she'll feel better about it, I tell yer," he whispered.

But the following day they packed their bags in the early morning while everyone slept and left without a backward glance. Only Melly was awake to witness this. Only Melly, the wise old cynic, fully expected this inevitability. Brash and brawny, they had dominated and intimidated the dorm. Like so many others in their early twenties, their wives were no longer giving them sex and they were desperate for some relief. One claimed to have been with four hookers in quick succession the previous day, but it wasn't enough. He wanted sex with affection and that, as Melly suspected, was just not possible. Not here and not now.

Melly looked up. Caroline lay on her back, asleep on top of her bedding, dressed in short shorts. She looked peaceful, vulnerable, and tantalizing. She was hoping the air might now clear of the boys' callous intent. He was hoping his lust for her was not too immediately obvious. She and he had exchanged a few words in passing but he could tell by her dismissive tone that he, at least, was not on *her* mind. He turned his attention to a crossword in order to clear his head.

While young travellers arrived and left, Melly continued to lie in through the early afternoon, reflecting on his first day and began to focus on Talish. He *so* wanted to take her home, have her climb out of her filthy underwear for the last time, and step into a shower. He *so* wanted that she should snuggle up under his arm and sleep; sleep like the dead, and sleep in safety; then to dress in fresh clothes, to eat, to drink, to sleep, and to rest. To manage a smile or a glint of contentment. A fresh start. *"Just one more go at life. Promise I won't take any more crack. Just get me out of this hell!"*

He wanted her to think this – it settled him to imagine she might, just might…

⊠ ⊠ ⊠

Melly needed to experience Amsterdam again – revisited after ten, twenty and thirty years. Wasn't this the place where the revolution of '69 had fermented? Wasn't this where the very best smoke could be found? Alas! The revolution had long-since passed. Yes, the children of the Sixties had become the elders of the Nineties. Their fight for libertarianism was over. It was won, as evident in the enlargement of civil rights and government by radicals. Except, now, the next generation was roaming the streets and there was no peace in *their* eyes. Now it all seemed so shallow, unmotivated, and without direction.

And the smoke? Melly pulled on some Temple Balls. Nope. They had no effect of any worth. He had become immune. Was there one more high? A trip, maybe? His mind wandered, unable to fix on one thing at a time.

"So," Melly reasoned, "why *should* 1999 be like 1969? Shouldn't people and things have moved on? They moved on hugely between 1939 and 1969, and that was thirty years, so why not now?"

Melly looked around to see there were no signs of an ongoing revolution in Amsterdam. There was no counter-culture that he could see and, in any case, Melly had never quite known how to deal with that. He was too suspicious of people's motives; he was far too cynical. He had never really understood it, anyway. Now, he took to comparing London with this place. Amsterdam, too, was a city full of young people, but not everyone carried a mobile phone at their ear. Amsterdam was a city full of blacks but he heard no gangsta rap and saw no *attitude*. These were Tunisians, Somalis, and Lebanese Africans; their agenda was completely different to that of London's Afro-Caribbean population. Amsterdam was a city that remained full of smoke and hallucinogens but no flowers or paisley motifs were to be seen anywhere. Those badges of the Sixties had no place in this place. There were plenty of football strips, though; this was the true mark of the Nineties and Melly was severely out of step. Never one to enjoy playing the game, never picked to join in a playground kick-about, he was the geek who rolled his eyes upward whenever the other guys in class wasted everyone's time chanting "Come on you Spurs" and "Arse-n-all", and slamming their hinged desk-lids in unison during double-French. He steered clear of aligning himself with any teams and, so, never tasted life in a gang; never experienced the rites of passage into adulthood in the company of men's men. He had done it all alone and, perhaps, missed out on something. But, at least this way, he didn't need to justify himself or his loyalties to others. This way allowed him to watch, critically and dispassionately. Anything, but anything, to steer clear of the mob; any excuse to rise above it all. Oh yes, he thought he was a better man for it; he was, after all, independent and freethinking.

Melly thought he had people skills; he liked to meet and make new friends. How was it, then, that after thirty-six hours in the city he had befriended no one? Was the look in his eyes too hungry for women? Was his manner too aloof for men? Was it neither of these, or was he unable to hide either well enough? He was, by far, the oldest of those in the dormitory. Who was he and why was he there? What the fuck did he want from them? Was there good reason for people to be wary of him or was he just another sad old man?

"I'm an observer," he told himself, "I'm watching. *Leave me alone.*"

⁂

The giant, plush and expensive Grand Krasnopolsky Hotel on Dam Square has the most expensive rooms on the sunny, south side that faces a quiet, narrow canal. On this same canal, 400 metres further along, a mattress was home to Melly in Room 101. For him, it had been a long fall from grace, begun at the Grand some twenty years before when he'd tried, with no apparent subtlety and certainly no success, to score with his boss' mistress. He now felt correctly placed. He was now able to laugh about such misfortune. Other instances were less humorous.

"Shit," Melly remembered, "I've got it wrong again."

There was a time, in his teens, when he sat comatose on Hampstead Heath and failed to notice a dog cock its leg and piss all over his back. Many years later, Melly sat down against a large advertising bollard to eat, in a quiet corner overlooking a canal in Amsterdam. The broccoli and apple salad from the European deli looked too spit-filled and tasted too bland to generate the required 'yummy' response so he took himself off to a Taiwanese takeaway for an alternate flavour.

As he peered at the fare by the crowded counter, it occurred to him that someone close by had pissed themselves. He looked askance but saw no one who looked as though that's what they did normally and, as he moved across the shop, the smell stayed with him. It then became apparent to Melly that he had, with the back of his shirt, wiped the stains of a thousand urinations from the bollard. He would have to get back to his room quickly, but it was already too late. By the time he got back to the dorm to change and wash the discoloured shirt, everything had soaked through to his skin. Piss-stained skin! The tattooist, booked to etch a mandala on his back that afternoon, would have to wait.

⊠ ⊠ ⊠

Melly sat on his mattress counting his money and drew up a list of comparative prices. These were stark choices indeed, should he choose to make them:

Two coffees or a ready-rolled Sensi,
A glass of beer or a ready-rolled Nepalese,
A McDonald's burger or a bag of Colombian,
Two bowls of Thai noodles or a fresh Fly Agaric,
A mattress for the night or a hooker in the daylight hours,
A collection of mementos or a hooker in the hours before dawn.

He wondered whether it would be cheaper, in the long run, to stay on a perpetual high where food played little or no part in a daily routine. An attack of the munchies would mean devouring a packet of chocolate biscuits and that was fine except he hadn't had that kind of craving for a long time. It was more likely he'd end up wandering among the smells of fresh bread, the aromas of frying steak and hot coffee, or the fragrances of apples and cheeses in the open market, just taking it all in. Feeling and looking gaunt, his would be an act of denial, the supreme sacrifice - resisting food.

He decided to go window-shopping again in Amsterdam, only this time, he was not interested in *livestock*. He wandered in to a porn shop to see what was happening in the world of sex-aids – maybe some little something for someone...

"You never know until you find it," thought Melly.

"Something for the gentleman...," minced the lean, tightly clad man in black, "...or something for the lady?" he continued as he set about explaining, in detail, the full delights of an *I-can-stimulate-three-places-at-once-o-tron*. His sales patter changed direction effortlessly as he picked up a weighty latex moulding.

"This dick is so lifelike," he drooled lovingly, "hand-painted, you know."

Melly was at a loss as to what to say in reply. "Hmm, good," he said and moved into the back of the shop where the videos were stacked high in racks.

The genial, helpful owner was upon him immediately. "We have men, teen, lesbian, fist-fucking, splash, animal, shit-lovers, huge dick, fat bitch, all-comers, two in one..."

Melly moved away again.

"These penis enlargers are so good. Good grip, you control the air supply just *so*. Excellent for masturbating. Here's a cheap one – still very good."

Melly didn't need one, yet he felt a tinge of regret that there never was a queue of women throwing themselves at his endowment as the magazines and videos that surrounded him now suggested they would.

"Fiction, pure fiction," thought Melly. "That's what it is."

He cursed the countless fucks going on around him. He wasn't even a part of *that* world. He thought he'd console himself with the eternity of an ejaculation caught on camera and yet he knew the moment was fleeting…not to mention the baggage that came with it. He found it all *so daunting.*

"How's it done? All this instant and joyful fucking between people!" he thought, forgetting the sum of his experience, "or does it only happen between those who trust each other? And doesn't it take time to build up that trust?"

Back home, *his* friends agreed that sex between long-standing couples improved as they grew older together. He always wondered what they were talking about because *he didn't know* and was unlikely to find out what was meant by *a fulfilled sexual relationship*. Melly loved to get his rocks off every now and again but he didn't want an *affair*; he just wanted an uninhibited, consenting adult. An affair was, after all, too contrived. He could never knowingly allow that to happen and it never had. That's not to say he'd resisted the opportunity to fuck whenever it arose. And at this point in his life and in this place, he felt demoralized by the notion that the opportunity had not arisen in a rather long and frustrating while.

"Thank you," mumbled Melly as he went to leave the shop. The owner was shocked, aghast and, fortunately for Melly, penned in by the counter.

"Why don't you say something like *I'm not buying*," he said, sounding hurt and looking petulant, "having me follow you around like that?"

Melly felt very sheepish and backed out of the shop. As he sloped off to his bed in Room 101 he wondered how a dynamic man, sober and self-assured, would have handled it.

"He wouldn't have been in the shop in the first place," he concluded bitterly, and closed his eyes on an unsettling second day.

On the third he awoke at 5 a.m., alerted by the chiming cathedral clock across the canal. He planned to visit Katryn and apologize. He'd need to be relaxed, sober and alert; clear-headed enough to hold a decent conversation, quick-witted enough to deal with any unexpected challenges, and sufficiently dynamic to be just the slightest bit *appealing*. So he smoked, and strolled, then went back to bed to lie in until breakfast at eight. It was a simple continental; full of old bread, stale cheese and small, strong coffees yet he ate everything set before him. It made sense to fill up on food while it was there. Then he showered and had another smoke before lying down again. This was his preparation; he was *chilling* and focusing. Maybe? Probably not.

At eleven he was ready to seek out the girl and looked through his window up towards the bar where she worked. In the street below, he noticed Talish was sifting for food on the litter-strewn pavement. His spirits rose, yet he was touched by sadness. He wanted to believe she didn't belong there in the gutter. He wanted to intervene. Something, somewhere deep in his subconscious was nudging him in her direction, as if she had been put there to test him.

"Why the fuck does she matter to me?" Melly shrugged his shoulders and resisted any temptation to reschedule his next move. In a moment she was gone, having disappeared into the grey-brown cobbled streets like a chameleon. He would find her again, no doubt, later. He let the safer of the two options warm his shoulders and very soon he was nodding quietly to himself.

Looking his best (shaved and not too immediately stoned), Melly made for the bar where Katryn worked and resumed his seat at the table outside. No sooner had he sat down than she was at his side. He turned to find her no longer dressed provocatively in black but in a simply restrained pattern top and jeans. At close range he could see she needed glasses.

"Coffee, please," he said assertively.

On her return, she advanced closer to the table to set down the drink.

"Look, I'm sorry about the way I was watching you yesterday…girl in a doorway and all that, you know…" The words spilled out helplessly and stupidly.

She blinked awkwardly and managed a hesitant "okay" before moving away. Melly considered how she must detest him.

"This guy's so weird," he imagined her thinking. "I've gotta stay right out of his way!"

He didn't blame her at all for this notion. He could have done it so differently; he could have been charming, relaxed, and affable; he could have drip-fed her with witty asides and snippets of conversation for hours; he might have made an intelligent play for her the way older men set about wooing younger women.

"Then again," thought Melly, "they don't. Younger women make a play for older men, not vice versa. And that's because older men either have the wealth and the power that is desired by some, or they replace a significant father."

Melly was neither of these. But he *was* much older and he was out of his depth. Here he was, considering playing a young man's game while not being interested in playing any games. He didn't want an affair; he didn't want to engineer or construct a relationship with any depth, or meaning, or permanence.

"What the fuck was all that about?" he thought. He looked and felt very foolish; and having made a complete fool of himself, left quickly and quietly.

Melly returned to his mattress to hide his embarrassment under a sheet and to indulge in some re-evaluation while he allowed the world outside go by. This world wasn't moving very fast; in fact, it was dragging its heels and, with the evening's approach, he was soon bored. While time raced as the clock outside struck seven, then eight and nine, nothing at all happened in the street outside. Every movement was slow and deliberate. It just seemed so sluggish and unexciting. His thoughts turned to his leaving the city during the next couple of days to go south to see the eclipse. It seemed an occasion good enough to seriously consider ceasing his dope consumption completely.

"And if that be the case," he thought, "then how's about one last journey to hell! What is it to be?"

He need not stray far from his room and, this time, he set out to a shop he'd visited earlier for hallucinogens. They had stock of herbal and fungal concoctions guaranteed to make him trip. There was even a space at the back, laid out with scatter cushions under diffuse lighting, where he might lie down to curl up and die, if he so fancied.

"What's the strongest you've got?" Melly had asked during an earlier visit.

The reply was not something he recognized apart from the words, "Strongest mushrooms in the world…smoke this and get a mind-fuck for twenty minutes…fifty guilders."

Melly did not fancy chancing a hefty part on his money on a pleasure that needed the secure company of a friend to experience. He had turned it down. *Right now* he was ready, but it was Sunday night and the shop was closed.

"Well then," he thought, "a glass of milk; I really fancy a glass of milk."

As soon as he entered the Space Cafe, a laminated menu was shoved into his face. It was a long list of smokes, followed by the fare 'Space Cake' and 'Space Tea'. It sounded good! He sat down to partake of this excellence, sandwiched between ready-made joints of Northern Lights and Red Colombian. But it was all to no effect; no effect at all, and not anymore. Sitting alone, nursing a glass of milk and nibbling his cake, he looked across at huddled groups giggling mindlessly. He wasn't in a group and he wasn't giggling mindlessly. He was absolutely and begrudgingly sober.

Disheartened, Melly rose abruptly and left the bar, taking his solitude with him. Outside, the brightness of yellow and red neon lights, the competing rhythms of neighbouring clubs, the grey-blue haze of char-grills and burning weed, the dense atmosphere oscillating between tastes that were sweet, bittersweet and foul, and the sea of bodies into which he launched himself, should have collectively blinded all his senses. They didn't. He walked like a lost soul, looking for someone to recognize, and anyone he hadn't yet pissed off, until he reached his mattress again. There, his legs gave way much too easily.

When he awoke his eyelids ached like they had gravel in them and his face felt waxed but, even though he looked rough, his mind felt clear. Melly was unhappy with his appearance. The long curls he cherished throughout his life had long-since all but fallen out and he'd had to compromise with a Number 2 head-shave on what was left. He would often hear echoes of 'gay' resounding in a crowded background and would begin to feel *misrepresented.*

"These gays, they all smell of bananas…!" Wolf had laughed with the others.

Melly wondered about the light vanilla perfume Jean had given him to wear during his last night in London. People said he looked like the actor, Richard O'Brien. He never objected before; he resented it now. It was as though there were no bald people in Amsterdam apart from the shaven heads he'd seen in the Gay Pride parade earlier. He found himself deflecting the advances of men whenever he stopped to stand around and to observe. A shaved head was a gay statement in this city. It irritated him to have got it wrong again.

Melly looked round the dormitory, wondering if he shared common ground with anyone, anyone at all. *He* used to travel, *he* used to hitchhike, looking for sights and eating the native food. Now things were different.

"How times change," he thought bitterly. "It wasn't always this way. Back-packers used to search the world for culture and stimulation."

In Room 101 things were different. Dennis, a wild-eyed hiker from Oakland said he'd seen it all before; the crack and the crack heads.

"I can handle all that shit, and it *is* shit," the American said. He'd also never been outside the US so this European trip was the big adventure, starting with three days in Amsterdam. Dennis found himself joining sixteen others in the dorm laid out on his bunk, immovable and tripped out, day and night. Some culture! Not all travellers were like this but, in that dormitory, there was common purpose. They knew their dope; they had the knowledge. So did Melly, only he was exhausted by it and felt only complacency.

Melly could feel now it in his bones. The desire was in him to stop. He could come down from orbit after a flight that had lasted thirty years. Clearly, he was now unaffected by it all. Being stoned was no longer a thrill. The argument over whether cannabis was addictive or not had raged at home for several years. A user since his college days, he had sampled and favoured amphetamines, LSD, ecstasy, mushrooms and cocaine. What he enjoyed most of all was Bahamian grass and opiated cannabis resin - it could get him so terribly mashed! He once spent the night locked out of the house. He'd lain down on the concrete floor of an outhouse and imagined his nineteen-year-old head as a bag of blood. The more he moved his head, the more the blood sloshed around; it quite wore him out. In the morning, his mother found him in a sorry state and chilled to the bone, blabbing incoherently. She made him promise to her never to do it again. Melly had actually enjoyed the trip and continued to indulge; only now he kept getting panic attacks about her uncovering the deception.

Through the Seventies, friends who travelled to India and the Caribbean established connections and he was able to get absolutely and fearfully mindless, often hallucinating in ways that made him think he'd found the answer to life's big questions. Inevitably, 'the answer' was total bollocks (not that he'd ever managed to write down this answer; everything rushed too quickly) and, too, he heard more music in his head than he could hope to play. Whenever he replayed recordings of himself playing while high, it sounded self-indulgent and technically weak. His audiences were none too impressed either and his performing days petered out.

As the years progressed, he smoked more regularly but had sufficient control over his habit to be sober by morning and ready for work. 'Sober' meant 'not recently partaken'. He, nevertheless, remained slow-witted and worn-looking. *Totally sober*, he might have made greater progress in his work, not that he particularly wanted to aspire to great heights professionally. He had been in touch with kids all his life. He had a way with them, and seeing all these kids growing over the years, high on one thing or another, he understood how solvent abuse led to sulphate and then onto crack. He'd witnessed how *havin' a reefer* had become *smokin' a joint* and then *bunnin' a zoot*. In most cases, smokers remained smokers until they stopped whereas users of chemicals ran helplessly down a road to self-destruction. It gave him some consolation to know he had remained a smoker, but…what of it?

With the passage of time his intake increased and he was now getting through an ounce every month; that's six or seven joints a night. What did it do for him? Increasingly less, that's what, despite his having found a dependable source that made sure he rarely got less that the highest quality resin. Melly had long forgotten how one joint could be made to last an evening. The ritual of building a three-skinner was central to his addiction and the particular taste that held so much promise was what he craved most. His evenings had become marathon-smoking sessions as he indulged in his pastime; only he never got any higher than the level reached by the first joint of the evening.

He also worked out how much money he'd spent over the years; the figure was staggering; enough for a small apartment; enough for an annual holiday abroad; enough for an updated wardrobe; enough for a lovely car. However he looked at it, his priorities obliged him to wear hand-me-downs, to drive simple, functional motors and take low-cost excursions. Yet, somehow, he still needed a badge. He needed to 'fly his freak-flag high'. The hair gone, he still wore a gold stud on his left lobe, just to warn people he was unconventional. He yearned to remain a player even though most of his contemporaries had withdrawn from the game. And although a sizeable section of his generation continued to smoke, his own motives for wanting to play were that it kept him in touch with youth, and youth in touch with him. He enjoyed being the old sage yet he wasn't getting anything new from it. He no longer lost control. Now, it was just plain boring.

He just needed a suitable occasion, like a milestone. He felt one coming and, provided he timed it just right, could promise himself a final fling with what he had left and prepare mentally. He could set a feast in the run up to the eclipse and go in on this challenge with a clear conscience; with determination and resolve.

With his four remaining cigarettes he put together two spiffs of Temple Balls, a fat Sensi and also one with what had come very highly recommended by a guy in the dorm and which he had traded for a smidgen of Temple Ball. If the joints from counter sales were weak then his own were guaranteed for content. They were crammed full of every last crumb and every last shredded leaf from his diminished supply. Today was to be his last. Today he would stroll and chill for the last time. No more that his stools should stink of cannabis. No more the reek of nicotine in his skin, or on his clothes. He was to be reborn – after just one more day...

⊠ ⊠ ⊠

"There is a very fine line," thought Melly, "a defining moment when we move from having the wherewithal to solve a problem rationally to being frozen to inactivity through panic."

That moment came for him when he realized that he could barely afford a hot meal or a bed until the end of the week when a coach was booked to return him to London. He had plastic, but that wasn't the point. He had gone with a cash limit and wanted to exist within those limitations. It made his quest for answers so much more a journey of self-reliance, of self-discovery, and of denial of the trappings of luxury. He needed to feel raw; yet, here he was at the start of that week, with no more than the price of eight cups of coffee; call that two light meals; call that something small from the supermarket. There are those who would, given such a situation, hibernate; would forget about the world for a few hours and would fast-forward time. Melly lit up the first of his Temple Balls and closed his eyes to await *later.*

He was awoken by the shadows of the castellated gables opposite that were thrown across his face by the setting sun. Outside his window he saw the crack heads with their odd stagger, rocking on their heels. With each small crystal burned, they studied one another's movements and, like hawks, looked to see if any rocks had fallen out of their pipes. Continually and studiously, they peered at the ground. Some placed coats over their heads as the pipe passed around. Each whiff of smoke was sacred and not to be missed. As one smoked, another would hold him down, as if the head might separate from the body with the intensity of it all. This was their blinkered existence, hour by hour, day in, and day out.

Melly felt there were parallels to be drawn with his own existence. He felt empathy. They looked pathetic... Melly felt pathetic. He was not really any different to them in their single-minded addiction.

"Time," he thought, "time for a second Temple Ball."

Melly thought he'd seen Talish once or twice during the night but there were so many look-alikes; there was something Middle-Eastern about them. Was it the olive skin? Was it the brown curls or the imperfect American English they spoke? He'd seen one of them secure a fresh-faced student for a cheap blowjob or, maybe, a fuck, and disappear down a dark alley. Now, in the warmth of a new, sunny day, he knew it was *her* because she made to approach him in a busy shopping mall wearing ragged socks and carrying dripping trainers. Talish had the topmost button of a stiff leather overcoat undone. What might once have been a leopard-skin cocktail dress hung by a few threads over a lean collarbone. She recognized him immediately and they spoke briefly.

"You wanna buy me a drink or something?" she said.

He wanted to, yet he knew that 'a drink' would drain him of any loose cash he had. Didn't she realize that a beer was half a meal or was two litres of milk? Did they need to *share a drink*? Could he not just buy a loaf and a block of cheese with some guava juice from the supermarket for less, and sit on a doorstep somewhere? He would have to defer until the morrow when the supermarket was open. And, as with the helpful barman, words and meanings had their own key and their own legend... What did *you want to buy me a drink* actually mean?

"I'm looking for a hotel I used to go to a long time ago," he said, stalling. "I'll catch up with you later."

She might be dead from hunger 'later'. *He* was determined not to be.

"I'm out on the streets myself tomorrow," he offered, half in jest. "I've got to hang around until a train at five the following morning. Then I'm coming back in the evening for a coach to London at ten-thirty."

The words spilled out as if he *needed* to let her know he'd be around for just *so* long. Talish smiled while they spoke but it was a guilt-ridden smile. The kind that felt it had no right to be seen crossing her grubby face.

"That face," thought Melly. There was something unnervingly familiar about it. "Where? Who? When?"

None of these questions had answers. He couldn't even begin to think of an answer. But the questions nagged him. They nagged him enough to make him want to run away from her. They nagged him enough to make him want to come back for more; but not just yet.

Melly lay down with his penultimate joint – the one with the highly rated cannabis and reached a plateau rarely reached; the kind that told him, 'I'm wonderfully and warmly stoned.' It was intense, enveloping and enjoyable. It was also short-lived, so regrettably short-lived. He felt his eyes cooking under closed lids and lay, Zappa-like, immobile and listened to the sounds around him. In the dorm, fresh travellers related old and new experiences. He suddenly felt embarrassingly stoned and unapproachable. As so often before, he felt huge regret that his role, at times like these, was non-participatory.

He rose to do one last circuit of the Red Light district in his old guise of dope-head. He decided not to hanker after Katryn; it would be wiser to leave her alone. She was young, possibly nineteen, and not a hooker; he would not lust. He had no right to interfere in her life; he could not benefit her in any way.

He lit the fourth joint, his last he kept telling himself, as the clock struck midnight but it was no longer the same. It wasn't as good as the previous one. He felt only dulled and recognizably, if not identifiably, stoned. It made him feel self-conscious and stripped him of the confidence to look people in the eye. They would know he was weak and could dismiss him; they would not take him seriously.

Standing on some steps outside his hotel he suddenly realized that at no point during his time in Amsterdam had he broken into sweat during sleep and that, despite his huge intake of drugs, the tips of his fingers and toes were unusually warm and did not have the deathly chill that Jean had come to fear whenever he stroked her face or neck. Overheating and over-cooling had plagued him for years and he regularly moved between having clammy, sweaty hands to that of being likened to a cold fish; what element in his existence, missing right now, had caused this change? Melly felt a wave of nervous anticipation wash over him. He was going to leave all this shit behind. He was starting afresh. No money and no more dope; no place to stay after tonight. He would awaken tomorrow to live the first day of his long-forgotten life and look for the person he had neglected to become. He had thirty-six hours until the eclipse and he was going to face it entirely sober. This was the contract he had made for the new dawn. He could feel positive about this.

Turning to return to Room 101 for the last time, he stepped in and slipped on a pool of saliva and stumbled forward, landing heavily on the littered cobbles. Sweeping towards the ground he put his arms out, closed his eyes and turned away as he braced himself for the collision. Among the debris was a small, unburned rock of crack cocaine. It made contact with his temple where it crushed into the skin and anaesthetized the nerves there, killing pain locally and immediately. He didn't feel a thing.

Ruffled and dazed, Melly picked himself up and returned to his mattress. He was lucky; he might have been killed. But the more he thought about it, the more it felt like he'd missed an opportunity. He would prefer to have died because, just then, there was nothing he could think of that was worth living for; nothing to shout about enough. Taken to task, he would think of plenty but depression is a condition that is based on selective thinking. This day, the selection was light and biased towards the life-death struggle. The eclipse was tomorrow!

⊠ ⊠ ⊠

Melly awoke feeling surprisingly clear-headed. He showered, ate breakfast and cleared his things out of Room 101. Ahead was the long wait until the train took him south. He walked and wondered what kind of memento could summarize or reflect his experiences.

The hookers were still in their windows at ten that morning, perched on stools. Tired and worn, they fought off sleep. As soon as a punter showed, they perked up and looked on, alluringly.

Melly had until five the following morning. Only nineteen hours to go. What temptations could he, or should he, deflect? Just now, he was content to sit at the canal-side with the hot sun playing on his back. He had been to the supermarket and had bought bread and milk for breakfast!

By the afternoon, the rain began to fall and Melly found himself seeking shelter close to the bar where Katryn worked. An *even prettier* waitress told him it was Katryn's day off. In his condition – sober and alert, he talked to her easily, or so he thought. She, on the other hand, found his questions to be searching and disarming and withdrew from his attentions at the first opportunity.

Melly nursed a cup of coffee while a feeling of bitterness overcame him. As he sat looking through an open window at the clouds of sweet-smelling weed, refusing to succumb to its pleasures, he tried very hard to remember *why exactly* he had decided to stop smoking. As with any vice, the moment's pleasure, he remembered, was to be gained at too high a cost. He wanted to be off the treadmill: wanting to get stoned, regretting getting stoned; wanting to withdraw, wanting to participate. He was not going to act like a reformed smoker and broadcast his new message – the message of the convert. He knew that people would always seek their own form of simple pleasure. He did not object to that... he objected to the new disciples of healthy lifestyle.

With every passing hour and with every coffee, his demeanour soured and he began to dwell on other things he found objectionable...like the English travellers he met, virtually each and every one of whom displayed the same shallowness. In a world filled with images and clichés, he noted that every contentious situation was dealt with by their answering with a meaningless excerpt from a long-forgotten movie. It did not answer the question nor did it express an opinion. Instead, it filled a pregnant pause; one that begged a response. With this bullshitting, it was possible (maybe) to side-step the question and stall for time. He had heard it so many times during the last week, the last month, and the last five years. He was sick of it; he was embarrassed on behalf of his nation abroad and it made him wish for a more independent identity; it made him feel better for choosing to be outside of it all. But was he really outside?

Alas, making fools of themselves was not exclusively the domain of the young English. Melly called to the waitress.

"Tell Katryn that the wanker says he's sorry for being a wanker," said the wanker. Then he left to pace the streets again.

⊠ ⊠ ⊠

Melly imagined - no, he philosophized - about the eclipse now under twenty-four hours away. There were two extremes to consider. It was to be the portent of massive evil; as the moon's shadow tracked across Europe and Asia, it would cut a swathe of destruction fifty kilometres wide, sucking up all in its path and spitting it out, shredded and deformed. Alternately, it would imbue all that lived with a wonderful power, a regeneration to all and everything that lay in its path. It was going to be a very ominous time, particularly for those frustrated by their solitude. Melly wondered whether those who would come out to bear witness would dance around quite naked. Would couples set themselves the target of copulating so as to conceive within the shadow cast by the eclipse? And if there weren't couples, would there be a mad scramble for a partner, *any partner*, as the idea gathered momentum and the fateful minutes approached?

As much as had been talked about this event in London, Amsterdam was largely quiet and unaffected by it. No one spoke of it. It was just another day in the infinity of time. Melly shelved the thought. There was only one true mission. He was not smoking. He would not…

He suddenly thought about leaving a living will; one that anticipated a situation where, for whatever reason, though still breathing he might one day be unable to make a rational decision about his fate. Should he become a burden to those around him, he would wish for a termination that was speedy and effective. Wandering the streets, he had an uneasy feeling about how much closer that might be than he imagined. Here, all around him was vibrant life. He had elected not to participate; he could no longer afford to drink coffee or beer, eat, catch a show, wear clean clothes or take a shower. What business did he have here? And if he didn't belong in the gutter and he couldn't belong anywhere higher up the scale because he had chosen to disassociate himself from that stratum, where on earth *did* he belong?

Melly desperately needed a friend to be with him. He could not bear to face this day alone. He claimed the right to solitude yet detested its insularity. He'd considered taking acid, or mushrooms, for the eclipse, just to see what it was like but, without the steadying hand of a friend, he might step out over the edge of sanity, voluntarily or accidentally. It was as though the eclipse alone was not enough. Yet he was stopping all *this*…

And then he recalled why his eyesight was so bad. He remembered lying in the garden at the age of ten screwing his eyes up at the sun. It was quite good, as he remembered. With tears welling up in his eyes, he half-closed until the light diffracted through the pool, filling him with a yellowish-white brilliance. He didn't do it just the once. He did it many times. He remembered looking away afterwards and seeing everything through a pronounced green disc that floated across his field of vision. It all seemed fairly innocuous at the time but the damage was done, then and there. He *knew* the power of the sun; he also regarded those effects as piecemeal and accumulated. He was aware that looking at the corona during the eclipse was going to be entirely different. The contrast between the darkness and the brilliance of an emergent sun, post-eclipse, was too great. He would not play *that* game. He would not be one of those new victims of blindness, with seared and melted corneas. For Melly, the eclipse was to be his communion with Nature.

He was due to arrive in Arlon, in Luxembourg, an hour before totality. This would give him time to climb out onto the highest ground and seek out a west-facing panorama with, perhaps, trees for cover. He wanted to take a series of photos of the shadow plunging his vista into darkness. He was sufficiently far north of the centreline to be able to see, if he was lucky, an area within the panorama that was also outside the shadow. *That* would make for a series of shots the stuff of which memories were made.

He wanted to see the eclipse on the ground; shafts of light falling between the leaves of trees would leave small impressions of the sun's relentless disappearance. He wanted to hear all living things suddenly go quiet as surprise overtook them. He wanted to hear all living things shriek in panic. He wanted to be there. If he were tripping, these real effects might be lost on him. He abandoned the idea of getting wasted and returned to reality; he returned to await the end.

⊠ ⊠ ⊠

Talish was standing alone on the bow of a moored canal barge outside Room 101 when Melly approached. She was pleased to see him; he was pleased to see her.

"I've got bread and milk, if you want to share," he said, sitting down on a bollard. She did not need to be asked again.

She would not drink from his milk carton. Instead, she found a discarded plastic orangeade bottle which she filled and sealed tightly once but then unscrewed and quickly emptied down her throat. The bread, slice after slice, she fumbled and dropped on the pavement with numbness and in the excitement of the moment. With each drop, she picked up the grubby piece and forced the gritty, tainted goodness into her mouth.

"I don't eat very often," she laughed when they got up to stroll together. As their conversation progressed, she became more animated.

"Let's do window-shopping!" she said. "Let's see what there is to eat."

They walked through Chinatown and Talish drooled over the ready-made foods just out of reach over in a display case. Melly saw that she was starved through and through. As she rummaged through her clothing, looking for pockets, he could see holes under her coat that revealed a skeletal frame. Occasionally, and downwind of her, he became aware of the smell that emanated from her feet, her clothing, and her entire being.

Restaurateurs were unwilling to let them both in to share a plate so, finally, Talish pointed to a plastic tub full of spaghetti bolognaise and called for two forks.

"Can we have ketchup on that?" she asked.

"Ketchup on *this* or ketchup on *anything*?" Melly wondered and considered ketchup as a mark of luxury and of poor taste.

They perched themselves on top of some rusted sewer pipes that lay piled up between the canal and the road, and tucked in. There are two ways to eat spaghetti; one does not stand on ceremony. While Talish scooped a fork-load and snapped off a mouthful, Melly tried to wind a length around his fork. His efforts were largely unsuccessful and long strands fell off onto the pipes. She, very purposefully and deftly, leaned over and picked up all his dropped food, rust and all, and ate it. They joked about how only hygienic, clean living required the individual to take care over what they ate.

"Street people don't have this problem," she laughed.

"Yeah," said Melly, "and I bet if you were to have a bath, you'd lose all the protection and catch bugs in no time! I've eaten enough; the rest is yours."

It began to rain hard and Melly ran for cover to sit by a wall on a patch of dry ground. Talish saw he had moved but stayed her ground and ate on alone. Eventually she came down to join him and took off her shoes and socks to examine her feet. They looked white and unnaturally wrinkled, like when skin stays too long in the bath. They were covered in bunions, bruises, sores and open wounds.

"How long you been in Amsterdam?" Melly asked.

"Two years," she replied.

"What are you doing," continued Melly, "Running or hiding?" He wanted to know what had brought her to Amsterdam.

"Look," she said, "don't think I'm all perfect and innocent. Fifty percent of it was my fault..." She finished every last scrap of food.

"Sorry," she finally announced, "but now it's time for my smoke."

A dealer, a ragged-looking man, was standing close by but, on seeing Melly there, grew hesitant and shifty. Talish did not have a pipe of her own and she was short of money.

"You got five guilders?" she looked at Melly.

He rummaged deep and found one last large coin, which he pressed into her palm. He was prepared to fund her habit a little longer but would not be drawn for more. The dealer refused to share his pipe with Talish, claiming that she 'would make it wet inside'. While he continued to put obstacles in the way of an easy connection, another addict joined them, looking to score. Talish knew where to go to another, alternative source and led the way. Melly felt it was time to give her some space and walked a step behind. She looked around at him as they crossed a bridge.

"I used to be the best dealer," she claimed indignantly. "I was dependable, I would give it out cheap, and I would give it out for free. I was the fuckin' best."

Melly imagined he understood the logic of that last assertion. By expanding her client base, she could guarantee sales later. It was immoral but, hell, it made good business sense. Melly didn't labour the point.

"We've known each other a long time," she suddenly announced looking around and fixing him. "I know what you want."

Melly *did* want but he wasn't sure what he wanted. It pleased him to be in her company. He wanted that, at least. Eager to hear the end of the statement, he trailed along behind her as she quickened her pace. He saw, though, that he was hindering her progress. There were immediate priorities and a chat with Melly was *not* one of hers. He made his excuses.

"Catch you later," he said.

Talish gave him the kind of look that showed she knew he was in town until late. The Old Town was small enough for them to find one another again later. Melly shivered and headed for some warmth.

Having considered just *some* of the options, Melly succumbed again, and easily. It was early evening. He'd not had a smoke for over eighteen hours; enough time for him to get to think and see clearly. Now, he was thinking *very* clearly. He was thinking about the top quality smoke he'd had the previous day, the one that had come highly recommended.

"That's it, I've found it. The ultimate smoke!" he thought but, for the life of him, he couldn't remember what it was called. Nevertheless, he set out to find it. He dismissed the memory of his feelings of isolation. It was the warmth, the envelopment, and the elevation of his mind to a place not here, and not present, that he wanted.

He returned to the smoke shop visited at his first arrival four days before. In a glass display box more than twenty different kinds of cannabis, marijuana and fungus lay weighed, bagged and labelled, nestling prettily in shredded yellow tissue. He tried to remember. He knew the colour - light brown; he knew the cut - a thin flat stick; he knew the smell - sweet with no hint of alcohol. He didn't see it. It wasn't there.

"Look," said Melly plaintively at the guy at the bar, "It's the best; the very best. Really trippy."

"This one's really good. Depends on what you want." The man was not a connoisseur, he just worked there.

Melly settled for the promise in the name, *Super Afghani.* It stank in a way to which he had grown accustomed; in a way that he had come to resent as an intrusion on any kind of equilibrium he might have. It was dark, sticky and stank of camphor. He sat down and hastily put one together. Surely, *one last high* before the appointed hour? Any excuse would do...

It was *not* the same. It was sensorial; it was sensual!

What was it about the smell of down-and-outs? The smell of the unwashed is not the smell of urine and faeces. It is the smell of very old sweat; navvy sweat and more. He had not touched Talish but merely sat in close proximity. Now, alone in the bar, he could smell her all about him; a lingering presence. It was the kind of smell that clung, like a bad fart. Was it that, having sat out for some time in the rain in only his tee shirt, he had now come to smell like her? That's what the homeless do; they acquire the smell of the street.

It was to be a while before he reached a bath. This thought gnawed at Melly's subconscious mind as he drifted into a haze of fantasy. His mind scrambled; he took out a pen and began to scribble in a notebook. He turned pages rapidly and wrote eloquently.

Melly's Trip

The night had quietened and any sound was echoed in the enveloping mist. There was still an hour until the train station opened. Melly had perched himself on some steps and was huddled into his knees. The air was still but, in this hour before dawn, a chill had descended and Melly was in need of some warmth.

"What you doin'?" Talish's voice stirred him.

"I'm off to Arlon to see the eclipse," Melly replied.

"You coming back?"

"Yeah, later on. Next train. I'll be back at about seven. Then I got a bus to London at ten-thirty."

"You want me to come along?" she said. "I got some rocks for the day."

"I don't want rocks," said Melly, "I got smoke. They won't let you on the train and I've no money."

Talish looked saddened; a kind of ugly, wretched sadness that showed pain in her eyes.

"You want, I give you a blowjob?" she said suddenly. "Ten guilders."

"Talish." he answered angrily, "I don't...no. No!" The thought had crossed his mind once, earlier. He carried her odour already. Any closer contact and he would have to throw his clothes away. He could never live down this kind of lie. Jean would surely recognize him instantly as a faithless sinner and a disgusting one at that. He gathered his thoughts together.

"I gotta go," he said. Desperate to get out of the situation he had done nothing to stop developing, he picked up his rucksack.

"Here, have some bread," he said, pushing the rest of his fruit loaf into her coat pocket. "Take care, girl."

He peered one more time into her tired eyes. Talish stopped chewing the gum she'd been using to clean her teeth throughout the day and pushed it under her upper lip. It made her look curiously ape-like. Looking to the ground she turned abruptly and walked away out of sight.

Melly's walk to the train was slow and deliberate. What was he thinking of? What was he doing? Why was he so uneasy about Talish? Did she remind him of someone, once; someone to whom he owed a huge debt of gratitude? Did she really know him as well as she'd said?

Despite all the hype Melly had seen in the papers the previous month, there was no mad exodus from Amsterdam that Wednesday morning at five. A few backpackers were aware of the Special laid on – it was the only train in the deserted Central Station. There were also a few anoraks, armed variously with small foldaway chairs, cameras and binoculars.

"Why is it," thought Melly, "that enthusiasts all look the same, everywhere?" Tightly belted coats with high collars and a bobble hat, they looked like skiers who'd forgotten to bring skis. Melly settled in to a compartment, alone, and reckoned to catch a few hours sleep.

He awoke with a jolt. The sun was well-risen and shone brightly and warmly against a fresh blue sky. Tidy clouds billowed in the west. Melly felt smelly. The smell of that girl had hung onto him again. He opened a window and leaned out into the wind. The hills of southern Belgium surrounded the train.

He needed a leak and took a walk along the carriage. He sensed there were down-and-outs on the train somewhere. They'd been to the toilet; that much was clear. There, on the floor, he saw the tin foil they used for burning rocks. He'd come to recognize the smell of burning crack and it was there, with him, on the journey. It would be good, he thought, to leave all this behind and finally get back to the safety of London and the bosom that was his beloved and oh-so-tolerant family.

At long last, the train pulled in to Arlon. Set among hills, it was a small town nestled in a pass. The railway had come to this place long after people had settled. The train emerged from a tunnel in a hillside overlooking the town and Melly could see there were no factories here to throw up fumes and haze. Arlon looked very promising.

Melly headed up the hill and over it to the west side; he could tell this by the position of the noonday sun. He knew he had a few minutes to wait and then an hour before the return journey. He found the west side of the hill partially forested and turned off the road into a pasture that looked out on a magnificent plateau that stretched into France. From there, he could see the path that the moon's shadow would take.

He rolled an exceptionally well-stocked joint of Super Afghani and lay under a tree in the dry grass. He looked up at the sun. It was noticeably eclipsed; it wouldn't be long now. The smoke made him want to close his eyes; this would be safer than staring at the sun. They would, he thought, remain closed until he sensed it was pitch-black and cold and then open them to see, on first sight, the corona that everyone had told him to expect.

He heard her cough first. Had she stood upwind of him, he'd have known sooner; at least have got paranoid of smelling so much of the street himself.

"Talish...?" Melly uttered the words quietly, to himself. It seemed like a dream. The Afghani was working well. He felt immobilized and did not care to open his eyes. He didn't care to say anything either. This was, after all, not happening. The cloud of a good smoke shrouded him and allowed him to blot all reality from his mind. It was to be like so many other times: nothing to do with him if he ignored it hard enough.

He was, however, aware of someone there. There was a rustling of paper, of clothing, of a lighter being flicked. Melly felt uneasy. It was the kind of unease that made him sweat under the arms, in the elbows, in the palms of his hands and in the soles of his feet. He felt a cold chill pass through him, like someone had walked on his grave.

He was also aware of a taste in his half-open mouth as he lay there; a taste he had never known before. It was sweet, it was warm and it filled his face. The more he breathed, the more acute the taste became. He was aware that Talish was sitting very close to him.

Melly's head reeled. His brain shivered and sent a spasm down his spine like broken glass tearing at his back. The muscles in his temples twitched as warmth rushed through his shoulders, down his arms, warming the ends of his fingers and down his legs to his toes. He felt unable to move a muscle yet his heart pumped furiously and blood rushed through his veins at what seemed impossible speed. Then his brain deserted him, leaving an ice-blue void, and resurfaced in his groin. In his cracked haze, Melly remembered a time in his teens when he'd tried grass for the first time and had got such a hard-on, he had ejaculated into his pants while listening to Santana. Now, all Melly's body heat went to his penis. It seemed like all his blood had gone there too; he had never experienced such an erection. He was helpless with it. The glans tingled furiously and acidly. He had to feel it and bear witness to its ponderousness. He cared not that Talish might see him do this; he just had to hold it.

He put his hand down to his flies and was surprised to feel Talish's hair. She had his penis out already and was unbuttoning the top of his trousers. Gathering his balls in her hands she caressed them carefully and expertly. She took a gentle bite out of the side of his erection and then, with both hands, gripped his dick firmly and drew down the foreskin. So fully, so nakedly and so vulnerably; so far down that the skin strained.

Melly could not look but he could feel. God, how he enjoyed this feeling! He could expect to feel her mouth closing over his helmet at any moment.

"Oh, bliss!" he thought. Then he shivered. "Come on, Talish…"

He felt her lips closing over the tip of the penis and, then, it was as if her tongue had disappeared. Further and further in Melly went until he felt he could go no further. This was no blowjob! Talish finally come to rest, kneeling astride him. He was fully accommodated.

Her vaginal muscles gripped him gently, relaxing and tightening in turn. She made no movement, up or down, nor sideways. She caressed him internally, her juices flowing out onto his pubes. Melly caught his breath and felt a light that had illuminated his world extinguish and a chill cross his brow. He opened his eyes.

There was blackness; pitch-blackness unlike any he had seen before. Everywhere, the world was enveloped in an eerie stillness. He saw Talish's head silhouetted against the most violent of colour mixes he had ever seen. Melly felt disoriented, he felt humbled and he felt scared. He had seen many things but this was unearthly.

In his bliss, and in fear, he pulled himself up, brought his knees up against her back and gathered her up into his arms. But his arms did not feel a part of him. The two of them managed only to collapse into a helpless embrace.

The next minute was eternal. Inside her still and gripped tightly, he felt inseparable from her. And she responded totally to his embrace. She pulled his tee shirt up, as well as her threadbare cocktail dress, and slapped her thin body onto his hairiness. He felt united absolutely with her; so at home, so very, very and rarely contented, and so helplessly euphoric.

"Oh, Talish, Talish," he cried as he felt his semen gathering, "no, no, no…" He did not want this to end; not yet. She relaxed her muscles and let herself off quickly. Gathering the bloated dick in her hands she wrapped her mouth over the head, chewing the lip of the helmet while continually pulling the skin back, one hand after the other, and sucked strongly and deeply. His pounding heart felt as if it were about to slip its moorings.

Melly came; he came copiously. He came until he stopped coming. But Talish would have none of it. She did not let go and she did not stop. She now wanked him strenuously and perfectly. Melly came again, quickly. His testicles began to feel fragile. He had lost much of his erection but, still, Talish would not stop. She fed his penis into her mouth, sucking on it like a straw. Further and deeper inside her until her nose nestled against his stomach.

Melly felt his life sink down her throat. He'd been here before. A girl had once made him ejaculate twice in quick succession. He had been able to draw away from her; his glans had become so painfully sensitive; every slight movement made him twitch. But this was different. Here, he was enslaved!

His head spun and the muscles in his left arm ached. Through his closed, ecstatic eyelids he could see a bright light, welcoming him, and enveloping him. With one dying breath, he swelled and shot his last; his very last.

Then Melly sobbed uncontrollably. He had reached a state of total bliss and, now, the moment was passing. He imagined how perfect it would have been if all should now cease, completely and forever. Their lifeless bodies would be found before the day was out, set, some would think, quite romantically.

But there was another reality. As he came to his senses quite rapidly, he looked at his clothes, badly stained and discoloured and reeking of copulation and of her. What on earth had he done? He felt disgusted and totally wretched. He had no business being here and he had no business being alive. Melly wailed aloud and mournfully. He wanted to run and to hide; to leave all this, now. Now!

He grimaced and fancied that what he really had to do was run; run blindly back up the hill, to feel closer to hell with every step. Soon he would be at the entrance to the rail tunnel. He so wished he could rush in towards an approaching rumble to embrace his damned fate.

Talish looked at him. He could see her eyes were moist with tears. He felt his brain banging around inside his head, rolling like a pea in a whistle. He wanted his Mummy; he wanted the innocence of his infancy; he wanted to die yet he wanted to guarantee this bliss. He wanted to experience Talish again and, yet, he felt repulsed by her. And he struggled to understand why he felt such extremes, and why the feelings of incompleteness, and of insatiability, had come quite so suddenly.

Talish lit a rock and threw her coat over his head to share the fumes with him. Melly felt better immediately; so very much better. Shrouded and cocooned by this new experience, he stopped to consider his next move. Amsterdam was a good place; a place to return to. Talish was good value; she gave good sex. Making only a passing reference to these thoughts was all he could manage. As he was unable to focus on any one thought, he came to no conclusion; taking just one step at a time and without touching the ground.

They shared yet another pipe before climbing aboard the return train. By the time they reached Amsterdam, Melly had resolved to trade his return coach ticket and stay a while longer. He reasoned he could always get a job and earn the money to get back to London. Wasn't that right? But first, he had to go find some rocks. He peered intently at the cobbled road and thought he saw something.

By ten o'clock, Melly finished writing and decided it was time to invest in milk for the morning. In his stoned stupor he walked the dark Amsterdam streets again. Time and again, he'd seen this urban scene, so much like Greek Street and Old Compton Street in Soho, but without the cars. People here were less boisterous than in London and less intoxicated with alcohol. Everywhere in the Red Light district was placid. Marijuana hung in the air; even the children of tourists kept a low profile, numbed by the images they saw and by what they inhaled. Such a dreadful place was this; an almost single-minded sale of debauchery. Yet, as much as it offered, Melly felt immune to the icons around him. The pictures were explicit, certainly, but of squeaky-clean people photographed with care and precision. It was rarely like that in reality. He had seen enough.

The hookers, too, had got used to seeing him on the street. They knew he wasn't buying. No longer did they offer him the come-on. One did give him a quizzical look as if wondering, "Who the hell is that guy? What does he want, hanging round here all day?"

No-one walked alone. Those who did looked aimless and lost, much like Melly. Couples and groups had purpose. They were having a good time; they had someone off whom to bounce ideas. He missed the friends who didn't make it for his trip; people who could make him feel good, *doin' the Dam*.

It was after midnight and Melly felt sickeningly bored; bored with waiting, bored with still having no-one to share with, and sickened in the knowledge he was not trying to meet anyone. As an observer, he could only watch; he could not participate. Quite possibly, he had forgotten how to. He tried to while away the hours by sitting in cafes, nursing cups of coffee but the caffeine made him impatient and wired, and he decided to walk across town to the coach station, something he might have to do the following day if his money ran out and he couldn't afford a bus to his coach home.

He looked at a roadside map of the central area, blinking hard in the sodium dimness and figured on following the main ring road.

A passing refuse collector had pointed, "Straight down there. It's a long way."

A long way later the road had meandered and divided. Instinct had told him where to go but, now, he was confused. He stopped a passing cyclist who told him to go in a direction completely unexpected. Offering his thanks, Melly crossed over to a bar out of which had tumbled two burly men.

"It's a long way," they both slurred.

Melly decided that he had walked far enough. He also figured that he'd covered half a circle and might as well cut back across the centre. Unbelievably, within a very short time, he was back on his old canal and standing outside his old room. He would need to look at the map again properly or, simply, opt to jump a train.

He returned to a pissoire he'd come to use regularly, just opposite a row of hookers' windows. The same women as were there earlier that morning were still touting for business though he could see they were no longer trying, just coping with a stream of hesitant and drunken men.

Melly looked forward to a sandwich, a chance to rest, and some warmth. The streets were emptying and the bars were closing but some people were still sitting at tables out in the street. Melly sat down and was soon spotted by a waiter.

"Coffee," said Melly, "and bread and cheese."

"No coffee. The machines are now cleaned," replied the waiter. "No food either. Sorry!"

"Beer," ordered Melly, ruefully. In truth, the ale had a depressing taste and was so chilled that it gave him a headache. He could have sat out the hour but chose to leave sooner in order to look for a hot coffee.

"Hi."

This monosyllabic greeting was the least expected and most welcome interruption he'd heard in what seemed an eternity.

"At last," he thought, "someone, somewhere, wants to talk to me. *Me*!"

He turned to see Katryn walk up alongside him.

"Want to come back with me?" she asked, looking at him directly.

Melly felt a disorientating hot flush sweep over him. He smiled apprehensively. His heart beat faster and he started to shake. Katryn the sweet, Katryn the young, Katryn the desire was actually *propositioning* him.

"Uh, fine, great," he answered, his head reeling in ecstatic anticipation.

Within a few paces, they reached a short flight of steps that led down to a basement. Katryn unlocked the door onto a sparse bed-sitting room. An unmade single bed stood against a wall under a huge poster of a lone red tulip. She threw the duvet back into shape over the mattress, plumped up the pillow and turned to him.

"Thirty guilders," she announced suddenly and harshly. "I'll give you a *good* fuck for thirty guilders."

"My bluff's been called," he thought, panicking, "Fuckin' hell. Fuck, shit. Dammit."

Melly looked at Katryn and wished he'd not had the beer. She stood, legs slightly apart, arms folded and watched him fumble.

"I haven't got that kind of ca-."

"Twenty guilders for a blow job. You can come in my mouth." The muscles in her cheeks softened and she licked her upper lip. Her eyes widened and rolled. Melly thought for a moment. He'd wanted her, all that time. Now she was there and was his for the taking.

"Damn the food, damn the hunger, damn tomorrow," he thought.

"Yeah, okay," his voice deserted him and he managed only a whisper.

He went through his pockets one by one and found a couple of notes and some loose change.

"Twenty," he said, passing it to her discretely. He had a way with payments for services; he never liked to make it too obvious. He found it difficult to accept cash payments for any work he'd ever done. Money was the kind of commodity where simply the way you held it showed a great deal about you. Katryn carefully and deliberately counted his then placed it on some clean underwear in the second drawer of a tallboy. From the top drawer she took a condom and tucked it under her sweater then looked in a mirror over a small, unused fireplace and applied a swift line of lipstick.

"Undo your trousers. Lie on the bed," she ordered, matter-of-factly.

Melly undid his belt and let his trousers fall to his ankles though he kept his briefs on. He wanted her to...*find him.* He lay on the bed feeling nakedly foolish and vulnerable. Katryn kicked off her shoes, undid the buttons of her jeans, peeled them off and then pulled her top up over her head as Melly looked on, hungrily. In her skimpy underwear she was every bit as inviting as clothed, even more so now he saw there was no padding and no corseting; just raw, tight, young body.

She sat down by his side, with her back to him, and prodded the flaccid lump in his briefs. She then stretched backwards over him, her breasts hovering above his eyes, and took out a pair of surgical gloves from a bedside table. Putting them on, she returned to focus on his underclothes and surfed with both hands under the waistband. Katryn let out an audible sigh when she found him.

Melly raised his head and looked over at the hair, which fell loosely on her shoulders, covering the straps of a pale blue brassiere which looked as if it had been in a coloured wash once too often. As soon as he felt his member located, he instinctively reached up and curled his hand around her waist, sliding it up towards her ample breast, somewhere, out of view. She stopped suddenly and turned to him, pushing his hand away.

"Don't touch," she barked, giving him a severe look.

Melly felt suitably reprimanded and, laying back down again, closed his eyes. He heard Katryn sigh as she played with him, attempting to inspire an erection. Melly lifted his legs to readjust himself and curled his right foot under his left knee. The leggings of his trousers turned inside out, caught on his shoes and bound him, tangled and powerless.

Katryn reached to her bra cup with one hand and pulled out the condom. Gripping the sachet in her teeth, she pulled off the wrapping and, pinching the teat, rolled it down over Melly's flaccid penis.

Behind his closed eyes, Melly felt detached. He felt like a piece of bacon, wrapped on a butcher's counter and handled by a gloved assistant in the *most hygienic* of conditions. He felt as cold and limp as that piece of bacon too. He needed to know there was some bond of hot flesh and blood between the two of them. He reached out to touch her thigh; maybe her inner thigh. He so wanted to do something for *her*. That, in itself, would turn him on. She elbowed his palm sharply.

"I told you. Don't fuckin' touch me," she repeated. "You're not allowed to touch me."

Katryn's words fell like an avalanche and suffocated Melly's hopes. She gave him a wry smile, a mocking look, and returned to study her work at close quarters. Melly saw her head bobbing and turning above his groin but could feel nothing. No surges, no passion, no excitement, and no anticipation. Just mild warmth as she chewed him like a sweet. Not a boiled one; rather, a soft-centre.

"You're not enjoying this, are you?" she hissed after a minute.

"I, uh…I need some control..." he replied, rubbing his temple with his left thumb. "I got to be able to…to hold you."

She sucked a moment longer, then stopped and pulled off the condom.

"It's not going to work, is it?" she said, turning to him and rising to her feet. Perhaps a bonus in working as a hooker was the range of dicks she got to see but, substantial or not, this punter was going nowhere. He wasn't going to get it up and, for once, that was a shame for it might have made her change of heart to Melly more worth the while. She felt a mild disappointment at not seeing him full-grown and, to a greater degree, a feeling of disquiet that she had failed *professionally*, and failed in her objective. Normally, it wouldn't have mattered but, on this occasion, she would have preferred a result.

Katryn peeled off the gloves, straightened them and put them down. Melly *knew* it wasn't going to work. He looked at her standing in the room; by all accounts, a very desirable girl. *Everything he saw was on offer, at a price. Yet, none of what he saw was available, at any price.* He envied her boyfriend. He *really* envied her boyfriend.

"You got a boyfriend?" asked Melly, pulling his trousers back on.

"You got a girlfriend?" she replied ruefully, and gathered her clothes.

Melly thought about the hopelessness in his question and the meaninglessness of her reply. It was small talk; there was nothing else to talk about, nothing else for Melly to discuss on this unfulfilling occasion except, perhaps…

"Any chance of, uh, a small refund?" he bleated pathetically, picking imaginary fluff from the back of his wrist...

He did not wait to be shown the door but moved out of her life, swiftly. Katryn's light was out before he got to the end of the block. *She* was going to bed. Melly went off in search of a corner for himself and hurried through the tacky, cold streets, feeling them stick to the soles of his shoes. He needed to forget about Katryn now, and immediately. Passing a large drum from which a telephone cable unrolled into a shallow trench at the canal side, he jumped in and squatted down to roll a joint and collect his thoughts.

With his eyes moistened by the sheer humiliation of his experience, he clasped the sides of his head and let out a moan of regret. And then, Melly sobbed bitterly in that trench until the echo of his despair bounced off the surrounding houses and brought him back to earth. He checked himself.

"What the fuck am I playing at?" he observed finally and climbed out of the trench and up onto the street to shake himself down.

And so he returned to his perch on the steps next to his window at Room 101 with the church clock in view. This spot, like it or not, was now his home.

⁂

Melly was startled and awoken from a light sleep by the sound of railway carriages being shunted into position and readied for work. His waiting almost over, he wondered where Talish had got to. For once, he missed her; missed her in a way like he felt he finally had someone to talk to and, now, that person was not there. He felt so lonely; he wished he could weep just a bit and, at least in part, for losing out to Katryn.

Within half an hour, the crack heads had begun to congregate in large numbers at the canal bridge at the foot of the stairs. This time,

Melly did not hear their chatter; rather their nervous asides as they looked furtively up at him while he rocked on a doorstep, clutching his heels close to. He would need to move aside to allow life to carry on normally. *Normally* meant there was no room for loiterers without any purpose. It seemed everyone here did have some purpose and some immediate objective. How Melly hated watching in empty space and friendless, especially in Amsterdam. It was with mixed feelings for this memorable city that he left for his train.

The 5:15 to Arlon that morning was packed with all sorts; old and young, rich and poor, Dutch and foreign. It was going to be a crowded trip and especially so since, at every stop, more passengers climbed aboard. As the train rolled south, daybreak heralded a thickly overcast sky. A flicker of disappointment spread itself across Melly's face. All shadows would diffuse; it would be so much darker, and the eclipse would seem so much woollier. The anticipation grew. As the train threaded its way across Belgium, every road it crossed glistened with rain-soaked cars jammed end-to-end in the rush to reach the shadow line.

God showed great omnipotence to Luxembourg that Wednesday morning. No sooner did the train arrive in Arlon than the sun broke through the clouds; at first in patches, then more dynamically. A rousing cheer went up from the alighting crowd. Each group of people had their own destination. Some stayed at the railway station; they had, after all, reached this place that was the cross on *their* map; some took to an imposing church, high up on a hill, with commanding views. The thought of sharing this experience in the company of an unpredictable mass was anathema to what Melly was about. His experience of life was always, by design, as solitary observer. He wanted the raw, unblemished experience of what was on offer. He hated to be influenced by the reaction of others to events that none had any control over; that's why he rarely read or believed the words of journalists. Those he'd spoken to always seemed to have some axe to grind. He did too and he didn't want anyone getting in his way, of spoiling his fun, or of cramping his style. In this place, he wanted to face it alone. He walked a few hundred metres and was soon out of town. He settled in a west-facing bank of tall grass, overlooking a distant forest. With his camera, he would snap the incoming and outgoing shadow using eight exposures each and snap the halo with the middle eight. The time was right for breakfast of bread and milk; his communion with nature…

Melly took stock of his environment. This was undulating country; he could hear birds in the trees close by, chattering wildly and singing; he could hear crickets in the tall grass. The air was quite still with hardly a breath of wind. On a narrow road close by cars passed every few seconds and disturbed the calm. Meanwhile, the train station had grown quiet. It was pleasant here in this patch of blue and yellow flowers. A bee took nectar from a buttercup next to him. Someone was playing pitch pipes in an adjoining field. The eclipse was nigh.

Melly lay in the grass and gazed at the sky. To say it was overcast would have been, he thought, too simple. Over the celestial panorama, large areas of blue sky were visible but shifting banks of cloud conspired to hide the sun for much of the time. He could see three layers of cloud, each one higher than the other. Those closest to him were patchy and blew west. Higher up, a layer that blew south while, higher still, he could see it blown northwest. Seen together they appeared to swirl like an inferno. If only, thought Melly, these patches would coincide once more to reveal the sun clearly.

And, then, they did, and the sun *did* shine clearly but, largely obscured by the moon, only with the intensity of a low wattage bulb. Even though it shone (and he dared not look up at it), the light was dismal indeed. The air grew chilly. As the seconds passed, the sun ceased to illuminate and the world grew eerily stark. On the ground, green remained defiant while other colours seemed to fade lifelessly to grey. And as clouds once again obscured it, though clearly visible through the diffusion of one layer, the sun all but disappeared.

High above the clouds, a jet was seen heading west. Melly knew that it flew into the moon shadow when its long white vapour stopped trailing and the airliner itself, visible as a silver arrowhead, suddenly disappeared into the dusk.

The eclipse was sensational. Melly did not need to close his eyes nor avert his gaze. He did not even have to rely on instinct to let him know what was happening because the crowd in the town hollered their approval, yelling wildly with every continuing phase. The sky cleared enough for only the thinnest of veils to cover the sun. Suddenly, the whole landscape died a complete colour death. Melly snapped at the closing darkness, the battery straining to keep pace recharging his automatic flash.

And as the sun disappeared, the sky around it cleared once again. Obscured entirely by the moon, the sun was replaced by just a halo of light in an otherwise dark, starry sky. All around him had gone an unhealthy, mournful sea green. He could make out the distant horizon but it was so ugly and so uninspiring as to make him feel this was no place for humanity. It was plain to see why prehistoric peoples had been petrified by this kind of event. Melly knew it would last only a minute yet the loss of sunlight dragged for an eternity, and a very sorry-looking one at that. It was maddeningly sad, and Melly felt an incredible sense of loss. A deep chill mesmerized him and had his soul crying out for warmth, for colour, and for life.

Then, over the topmost lip of the moon, in a brilliant diamond flash, the sun reappeared. Melly was already snapping the parade that advanced from the distant horizon. The crowd cheered again but it sounded more like a collective sigh of relief. The light streamed back into the world and all living and non-living things re-acquired their vitality and vibrancy.

Melly felt humbled; he felt incredibly small and insignificant. There, and at that moment, he found good reason to worship the sun and to be grateful for all the life that it brought. Something primeval in him stirred. The world had been returned to him and to others, intact. Church bells rang out in Arlon at that moment and fireworks burst triumphantly overhead. The crowd surprised itself with the intense sincerity of their rousing cheer; none of this seemed to have ever been a part of their experience. As champagne corks popped and glasses clinked, they were grateful indeed for preparing such a welcome and for being equipped and empowered to give such thanks.

Were the animals quiet? Did they shriek? Did flowers close and open? Did a momentary glimpse of night confuse the natural order of things? Melly had no idea. Everything had happened so suddenly and he didn't care. *He* had survived the eclipse. He looked around. The world looked good from where he stood; only time and future reports from around Europe would confirm any changes and any unusual occurrences. But eclipses occur frequently worldwide and there had been no evidence of strangeness during or after the last few. Melly had survived and so had everyone else; nothing had changed. It was all just preoccupation by the masses. Some might call it hysteria, others would call it a focus; Melly was undecided on the matter. Part of him wanted the world to end, another part wanted to buy the tee shirt and wear it with pride...*I was there, man...I made the effort...I came out the other side!*

The journey was not yet over, of course. Back in Amsterdam, a late coach to London was waiting and the organization behind the ride back seemed, to Melly, in danger of collapsing. All Europe had travelled to a spot somewhere along a path fifty kilometres wide and thousands more in length. Getting people there, and wherever, was easy; it was clear where they needed to get to and by what time. The return was not so straightforward. Thousands of travellers crammed onto all the platforms at once and then shuffled about, deciding whether or not to get onto whichever train pulled in. Two alarmingly over-filled trains to Paris sifted and thinned the burgeoning crowd. Melly let them pass.

The station announcements did not help matters much. Too many unintelligible words clanked out over the loudspeakers and made no mention of Amsterdam. He looked pitifully at a man dressed in a railway uniform and, sounding mid-European, said, "Amsterdam?"

Sweating under a stiff cap, the man gestured to the left, pointed to the right, and honoured him with a stream of Walloon. On seeing the blank expression, he stopped and said, "*Ellefn, ellefn*," but Melly remained unconvinced. In broken French and in broken English, Melly asked other passengers what route *they* were taking and on which of the many trains that now shunted through the station they fancied their chances. Their answers seemed to conflict; no-one knew and no-one seemed to be going his way. He'd been told a departure time when he first bought the ticket; an efficient clerk had written it on a scrap of paper. He now grasped that paper firmly and, at the appointed moment, pushed his way on to a train that was about to leave, someone said, for Brussels.

Melly got no further than the inside the carriage door and spent the next five hours pushed face-to-face with others while standing among large items of baggage. And at every stop, another few passengers and their luggage would force their way on and find room to squeeze in. Melly felt, at times, that it would have been easier to embrace fellow passengers so that, as two became one, there would be more room to breath, to uncurl his legs and to adjust his poise.

The nicest thing about this close proximity was the ease with which he could scrutinize the apparent sophistication of French women. They may have been a mother with young teenage daughter but they both looked wonderfully chic. The mother was long and lean, dressed casually in white tee shirt and dark slacks, standing barefoot on slippers and reading a book. The elegant rings on her graceful fingers cast her as a woman of distinction. Her daughter, meanwhile, looked enviably and traditionally French: sunken, brilliantly piercing eyes, a perfect complexion, the sweetest, coyest smile and the kind of travelling clothes that fourteen-year-olds in London would only ever wear when dressing for a night out.

What struck Melly was that, of the people he'd seen while travelling, most were well behaved, controlled and decent; now he could see national character showing through. To his reckoning, the Danes were dorky and, seemingly, naïve. For them, everything seemed a new and exciting experience. Maybe, Melly considered, it was the sound of their language that let them down. The Germans were intense; they studied all around them very seriously, documenting much and commenting on everything. The French were impetuous, short of patience and quick in temper, hence found to be cynical and confrontational for much of the time. The Dutch were laid-back, confident and accommodating, perhaps among the more self-assured of the people he'd seen. The Belgians, uh, the Belgians! Melly found them withdrawn to the point of apology. Britons, however, were prominent as sloganeering louts with little of interest to say other than clichés remembered and recited in mimicked regional accents; Melly found it pathetic. Then again, theirs were the only conversations he could understand. It might have been different if he understood every utterance in this Babel and heard everyone else was like this too. However, their insincerity and lack of restraint gave them away. Thus, these multi-national sardines approached Brussels where they were disgorged to a variety of platforms, which radiated to northern Europe.

"Ah, platform 11…to Amsterdam." concluded Melly.

⁂

It seemed to Melly, as he finally stepped off the express at Amsterdam Central Station, that he could no longer have an active part to play in this city; he was now quite penniless. That he had money in his bank account to draw on was not the point; he had spent his allocation which meant *this* trip was over. It was time to go home. With a subway fare of three guilders to find, he paced the cobbled streets around his old haunts, eyes fixed desperately to the ground. If Amsterdam's streets were ever paved with gold then, surely, the crack heads had got there first and found it. And if *they* hadn't, it was because a little electric road-sweeper, which came around every evening, had scooped up all lost coins. He would have to jump the train for the coach station and, on a network built with the honesty of its commuters in mind, this was going to be easy. But it didn't make him feel any better.

He wanted to take back a photo of Talish - *this* was to be his memento. There remained the nagging feeling that she looked somehow familiar; at least with a picture he might recall why he thought her so significant. And a picture of a down-and-out was far less contentious than, say, a picture of Katryn. He would not need to defend Talish or his memory of her; Jean could never consider her a threat. He crept past Katryn's bar one last time. Fortunately, she was inside at that moment, attending.

"Probably just as well," he thought. He had made such a spectacular fool of himself in so many ways and he didn't want to remind her of the joke. Someone, somewhere, would find his encounters with her hilarious but *he* was unwilling to see the funny side of it; this was one story he would not be telling his friends.

And as easy as it had been to find Talish before, she now eluded him. He began to think that she *was* there, all the time, watching from a safe distance, from behind a twitching curtain in one of the houses, or with company at a bar, laughing. Laughing at his expense? Perhaps *not* finding her was also a good thing. What could he say to her? What would make sense? Would she believe that all he ever wanted was her company? Surely she was too wise for that and would not believe him? And did she care anyway? He wanted to know what impression he'd made on her. *That's* what intrigued him most of all; what was it she 'knew' about him? He felt that now, penniless and footless, he was no better than she was. In fact, she was better, so much better, at survival.

Melly, heavy in heart, slipped past the subway security guards and arrived at the terminus. All around him, travellers stood waiting for coaches to European destinations. Each and every one of them was below the age of thirty; each and every one of them was red-eyed, doped up and sated.

"There but for fortune go I," he thought.

Borrowing from his own account to buy more cannabis was never on his agenda; he had dope at home and a reliable supply, should he need it. But he was not able to buy any of the last few items that would make this journey tolerable. He estimated that a coffee and spliff at home with his own bed awaiting his long sought-after crash was but twelve hours away. Deprived of sleep and hungering for juice and stodge, he spent his one final guilder on a Kit-Kat. And, in the absence of tobacco, he felt justified in tearing open a small pouch of shag he was bringing home for a friend in order to light up his first cigarette in six hours. He hoped he would be forgiven; he felt quashed and deflated.

It was not only the lack of heating on the coach, it was also the defective overhead ventilators which insisted in blowing cold air at his sparsely covered pate, that conspired to make him feel even more miserable. Sleep was, once again, not one of his options. Food was something only others could consider. Melly felt very much the crotchety old codger who detested this feeling, as if youthful zest had been unceremoniously ripped away from him and been replaced by old age; cantankerous, mealy-mouthed, impatient, short-sighted, narrow-minded, embittered old age. So, when a stowaway joined them at one of their scheduled watering stops, it was a mean-spirited Melly who alerted the driver. The driver did a head-count, was satisfied that the numbers tallied and drove on. Somewhere in Belgium, a backpacker suffering constipation searched fruitlessly to rejoin a coach home that had long gone.

Melly wanted to continue thinking as he had thought during his time in Amsterdam but this was a return to reality and he was no longer enjoying himself. Deprivation of sleep left him chilled to the bone; he could find no comfortable way to close his eyes. Perhaps, in the Chunnel ahead, he could grab an hour or two before London. It was there that Melly realized that fate had done him a good turn. The French customs officials on duty were taking no prisoners. Him, they waved through; he was, after all, a comparatively older man, older than the other passengers and an unlikely smoker. Yet, they might so easily have picked on him in the way they now tormented one poor unfortunate from the coach as they looked in any concealment and every stitch of his clothing. The coach was delayed some considerable time. Melly would have brought back the cream of the crop had he ever re-discovered it but, as the transport moved on without one passenger, he was reminded that smuggling was a risky business.

Melly was hoping that this trip might have buried some ghosts for him and might have got Amsterdam out of his system. He had reached plateaus, both sensorial and intellectual but he had also sunk to new, lower depths. He had been confused and clear, purposeful and aimless, sated and starved. He had secrets to keep, to add to those accumulated throughout his life and secrets he would to take to the grave.

Was this trip really any different to all the others? Here he was, returning home again. Dejected? Most certainly. Disheartened? Absolutely. In sum, he was despondent. Thinking he'd find answers, he asked far too many questions and did not like the sound of any of the answers. He'd left with a spring in his step and returned with his head hung low with the weight of failure; a social outcast, clearly disillusioned with his view of himself and of the world as perceived through his own eyes. And, definitely, he was unfulfilled; he didn't get his rocks off, he hadn't shagged anyone, and he hadn't tripped out. He hadn't really had a good time. Yes, he was, quite definitely, unfulfilled.

The eclipse had come and gone; the world had not ended and it seemed unlikely that anything, anywhere, had changed significantly. He wasn't mad for a smoke but, then again, he always knew that he *couldn't resist* smoke. That was all. If it was there, he had to smoke it; if it wasn't there, it wasn't there; period. In any case, he knew nothing was ever given up; it was only ever suspended, perhaps indefinitely, but still only suspended until the next time. He needed to moderate; this much he had learned. And he had a notebook with some mad, scribbled fantasy about Talish and the eclipse.

As he jumped one last train, a short hop on the Northern Line to the suburbs, Melly licked his lips and found the annoying spot that had begun to grow on his mouth. Was it an ulcer brought on by lack of nutrition, a cold sore due to a lowering of his resistance to illness or was it a wart? He thought to blame Talish and tried to think back to what incident had put them in such close contact that he should catch *this* from her. It made it impossible to forget her; that was good, because he had no intention of doing so.

Melly sat, regretting the closing of this period and wondered if there was anything he would have done differently. He wondered if he had wasted his time, or whether he had not used his time effectively. *Effective use of time*; that very 90's phrase which made every moment precious was anathema to his entire approach to life. First Thatcher, now Blair, marginalized and berated the unproductive in society; every action needed planning; every outcome required some insane documentation as if, for ever, even in death, all would be held to account and judged as if everyone had to justify their existence. This was not *laissez-faire*; this did not allow for spontaneity. Yet, oddly, spontaneity was still in evidence in London. Modern, streamlined society had no use for anything that would ruin the line of their clothes or anything that would make them bulge unnecessarily; no-one took their litter home, they simply abandoned drinks cartons and lottery tickets where they stood.

Melly returned home filled with words, filled with memories and filled with the ideas and ideals released by *Melly's Trip*. His word processor switched on, he rolled a big joint from his tin and began to write furiously and imaginatively, as if refusing to let go his time in Amsterdam, and refusing to let Talish go. He was no longer sure what she looked like, but that didn't stop him writing.

2

Melly kicked aside an assortment of paper cups, sweet wrappers and polystyrene cartons and picked up a discarded newspaper. Pictures of the eclipse reminded him of those indelible minutes in Arlon, the real and the imagined. It could so easily have been a good trip; so good, he imagined that he might soon return to Amsterdam with a mate; any mate, so long as he was able to experience those highs again in sympathetic and dependable company. He still wanted to try out the mushroom he'd missed out on. He wanted to reconnect with that singular smoke that had hit the right spot for him.

Reading through the article, he noticed how the emphasis had shifted. All those who prepared for Cornwall, be they visitors or locals, had scared themselves into inactivity. There were, however, only a few traffic jams in the peninsula over the period simply because everyone, fearing the worst, had stayed away. The entire Southwest was overcast on the day, making viewing conditions so impossible, there were those who would now seek compensation from anyone to whom blame could be attached. It seemed that even Nature was accountable. Matter-of-factly, the paper then reported the eclipses upcoming the following year; eclipses that would be visible in Southern Europe. Melly wondered just how many readers had been taken in by the tabloids and forgotten that there was life outside the UK; perhaps even, a better, honest and more open life.

It occurred to Melly to check the Lottery numbers for the previous day. He had a particular system. Whatever numbers he chose, and it didn't matter which ones they were as long as they were mostly between 32 and 49, he wrote out five duplicate tickets. That way, if his numbers came up and six tickers were found to share a six million-pound jackpot, each would get a million. He could count on five of those winning tickets being his, giving him five-sixths of the prize. He hated the thought of a huge prize being halved, and the thought of a huge amount versus a goodly amount made him salivate.

He compared the numbers against those he always carried. Melly rarely won anything on the Lottery; a tenner here and there over the years. The standing joke was that if you ever wanted to win, then any numbers other than those he picked would be dead certainties. For once, however, things looked promising. *Promising indeed.* Melly made a spontaneous decision. He called in at his home briefly. Jean would be at work; his son, Peter, might be about but he wasn't and he could see the place was a mess. Not a filthy mess, where every crack was full of grease and grit; rather, the kitchen table was covered with a number of empty champagne and wine bottles and half-emptied glasses. What looked like the remains of a take-away lay scattered on plates.

"Par for the course, really," Melly thought. "She's been entertaining again. She's obviously in a good mood."

Jean no longer depended on him for a good time. Apart from the people they knew together, she kept her own circle of friends, mostly colleagues from work. They loved to drink together, to gossip and talk shop. He normally left them all to it whenever they came over. This was the pattern their lives together had traced. *Exceptionally close and harmonious*; that's how they were seen. *Enviable and exemplary* in their even-handedness. Theirs was a love that was a yardstick by which all others were compared. They were good for one another; they were excellent companions or, maybe they were simply seen to be so well-matched. They had learned, over the years, to make allowances for one another and to make compromises. He needed to drink from her eyes; her startling green eyes that gave him strength. She needed his calming intelligence and wise counsel. He needed her liberal accommodation for all his hair-brained schemes; she needed the excitement of his spontaneity, always just *so* close to realizing the big-time and the generous reward of success. They were independent spirits who didn't walk in each other's shadow and who gave one another room to manoeuvre. Inevitably, they began to lose touch but hung on in their quiet complacency. And what was love if not companionship; blind, tolerant companionship? They no longer argued and they no longer cried. Their passion was now gone, leaving an easy-going, time-devouring void. And as time continued to be thus devoured, Melly began to panic. There was a great deal of life he hadn't experienced and, more to the point, there was a great deal he wanted to experience yet again. Theirs may have been an open relationship from his point of view but it wasn't seen quite that way from hers.

He pulled out his dirty washing from the rucksack, threw it in the laundry basket and packed another couple of tee shirts. He had a shave, changed his underwear, pulled on a new top, put another toothbrush in his back pocket and scribbled a hasty note: *Left something behind. Back in a few days. M.* It would be okay; he still had a couple of weeks before starting back at work and the usual list of domestic chores which, this year, was still short, would have to wait a bit longer.

Melly paused and checked himself. It was as if he felt there was no need to aggravate Jean on this unnecessarily. He screwed up the note and tossed it into the bin. It would be as if he hadn't yet got back.

Turning to leave the house, he noticed his old 12-string. He hadn't played it for a long time and dust choked the tuning keys. He hadn't written a song for even longer but maybe, just maybe, he might get some inspiration. There were snippets of poetry and prose he wrote now and then, inventing, or so he thought, new clichés. There was no guitar case - that was sold off years ago. His *ol' gitbox* wore the scars of battle; it had been sat on twice, each time snapping the neck. He'd dropped it the first day he bought it and cracked the seam, and the finger plate was gone, leaving a patch of encrusted, dark adhesive.

"What the hell," thought Melly. Picking it up, he threw the guitar over his shoulder and closed the door, packing the rucksack into his car. His dope tin sat in among the potted plants on the kitchen dresser, untouched. He never thought about it; it clearly was not *that* important to him, not when he was excited.

Melly jumped into his Volvo and drove off to collect his winnings. Knowing that one shop alone would not hold enough for a full payment, he visited five different outlets en route to Dover and collected £116.23 from each, amassing in total of £589.95. He wouldn't tell anyone. He was like that; secretive, and tight.

He'd often talked with Jean about how he would cope with a massive win.

"I wouldn't tell a soul about it," he said, "not even you. Not for a while, anyway."

He knew that a huge amount would change his life forever; he knew that any new people he met would be fair-weather friends who were only after his new wealth. He also disagreed fundamentally with Jean about how to spend it.

"If I won six million," she said, "I'd give you a million to keep you quiet. I'd put half a million in trust for Peter, put two million away and give a load to each of our friends who could really do with a helping hand. Then I'd blow the rest on a fuckin' great time."

That sort of distribution agitated Melly. "I don't think our friends would know how to relate to us if that happened," he argued. "Do you not think they'd forever be beholden to us? I think many of them would up sticks and go away, abroad. I don't think our friends would stay here. You would be paying them off and losing them."

Melly's way would be quite different. He'd put it all away in a high-interest account and ask the bank to pay out in measured amounts: a hundred thousand in the first year, two hundred in the second, four hundred in the next, and so on, doubling the amount each year. Melly reckoned this was an ideal way to get used to big money. It would take five years to pay out three million and, by that time, the interest on the remaining three would pay a handy three hundred thousand every year. Forever. Melly didn't want yachts and fast cars. He just wanted things to remain as they were and just have his life made easier; so he wouldn't have to work anymore, not at his job, anyway. He was spent and wanted out. Six hundred pounds was not a lot to shout about. It would not be enough to change his life. Melly decided that it was a bonus; a godsend, free to fritter, waste, squander, and indulge, and to blow on a return to Amsterdam. Going with a mate no longer seemed important. It was Talish he was returning for. He wanted to find out more about her. He got to thinking he wanted to help her out.

At the Channel tunnel, he loaded up with muesli bars and Lucozade and drove apprehensively onto the train. "Here we go," he thought, struggling to cope with a rush of adrenaline.

By the time he drove into Amsterdam it was early evening. Wide-eyed, he shook with nervous anticipation. The car had got him to the city in good time but he had no further use for it. It might be useful as a place to get out of the rain and, maybe, a place to stay overnight. It might come in handy to carry him away to another location but, right now, he wanted to leave it somewhere fairly safe and go into the centre on foot. He drove to a suburb on the eastern edge of Amsterdam where he parked in a quiet, unassuming street. Pulling out his guitar, he filled the pockets of his combat jacket with the remains of his snacks and a pair of briefs, and walked the remaining two kilometres towards the Old Town.

The foreign exchange kiosks in the Central Station at that time of day had their rates pegged at 3.41 guilders to the pound.

"Nice," he thought, "Very nice. That's a good rate."

Melly walked out into the piazza clutching seventeen hundred guilders and, slipping them into his back pocket, set out to look for Talish. Amsterdam looked different.

"Different in a way," Melly thought, "like when you buy a car and it's a certain colour, you soon find many identical cars on the street."

Without his rucksack he was no longer a traveller; backpackers in the city were no longer so obvious. He did not feel himself identifying with them. They were just tourists but he was here on *business*. His business was to seize Talish and regenerate her. He'd seen down-and-outs at King's Cross, some newly-arrived in London. They were lost; they were easy prey to the pimps and pushers. He'd always wanted to get in there, snap them up and give them a roof over their head for long enough for them to dry out, clean up and rethink their quest for the bright lights in the big city. He'd had lodgers live in his house before; they were always grateful for his and, especially, Jean's generous hospitality. If he could only offer a firm foothold to one lost person...

Melly gave himself the luxury of a baguette filled with a cheese and ham salad, served up in a small sandwich bar behind Dam Square. The sharp colours glistened invitingly under the bright counter light; the cheeses had already darkened and curled under the heat, but he liked hard Edam. He washed it down with coffee that was strong and sweet, and then took himself off.

Melly wondered where to start looking and opted for a position at a table outside a smoke shop. She was sure to pass by, sooner or later.

"Beer," ordered Melly, "and what have you got rolled up?"

"Sensi, Northern Lights, Panama Red..." came the reply.

"Panama," said Melly immediately, remembering the legend of songs past. This was going to be just fine, he figured. He was no longer waiting for an eclipse, days away; he was no longer waiting for a train, hours away. He was in Amsterdam with a purpose; he had a good reason to be there. He didn't feel out of place. In fact, he belonged. He belonged in the way he belonged twenty years before. Okay, so he didn't have an expense account as before, but he did have money, and money gave him power; it gave him authority. It *enabled* him. He felt confident, self-assured and uncommonly relaxed.

He lit up the joint of Panama, pulled deeply and drank on some beer. It wasn't long before Melly had become like numerous other visitors to this part of town: red-eyed and silenced into submission. But it didn't matter to him because he knew what he was doing here and he was doing that now. He was looking for Talish.

"Yo…M…Melly? Is that you?" The voice sounded hesitant.

Melly turned to look. An older, greying man, rotund, bearded and spectacled, had come with another, much younger, to sit at a table behind him.

"Come, again," Melly rubbed his brow, nervously.

"Wasn't sure it was you until I saw you in profile! Drijs. Drijs Van der Wejden."

"Fuckin' shit…Drijs!" exclaimed Melly, his face brightening. "Wow, good to see you. How's it going?"

"Hey, where's all the hair gone?" Drijs grinned broadly.

Melly knew Drijs from Munich where they'd met often many years before and again at parties in Baarn, a wealthy town outside Amsterdam. He worked as a lighting engineer for touring bands and was, for them, a connection for serious cocaine. Melly and Drijs had lived through sessions together; they'd become matey but, like ships in the night, their friendship was brief, directed by the commercial politics of the day. What Melly especially remembered about Drijs was his knowledge of *this* city. Having spent his teenage years growing up among the hookers in town, he had befriended many. He had stories to tell; hilarious, bellyaching stories. But that was then; now was different, and a different era.

Drijs lowered his eyes on hearing Melly's coarse language and looked across at his friend who muttered something in Dutch.

"This is my partner, Ton," he said proudly.

Melly shook hands with them both. The two old acquaintances spent a minute or two swapping details about where life had taken them since the mid-seventies. Drijs had, like Melly, abandoned the music industry and was now running his own restaurant in Berlin. He was back for the weekend, visiting friends.

"So you don't live locally any more?" asked Melly.

He could see Ton tug annoyingly at his partner's sleeve under the table.

"Ye...uh...no. No I don't," answered Drijs, glancing back at Ton. "What are *you* doing in the Dam?" he asked.

"I dunno," said Melly hopelessly, "I'm looking for a girl called Talish. Don't suppose you know her?" There was no reason to suppose he would.

Drijs thought a moment then let out a raucous laugh. "What, Talish Thorensen? Titi, the prick-teaser, if it's the same girl? Unusual name; I've only ever heard of one Talish. Young thing, brown, curly hair. Same profile as you, actually. I never forget a profile. She's a tease, or was, last I heard. She used to come in to my place to eat."

"When was that?" asked Melly.

"A couple of years ago," said Drijs coldly.

"What do you mean 'a tease', Drijs?" asked Melly.

"All I know is she don't fuck nobody. Had them dyin' at her feet, spending all their money, but she wouldn't give."

"What's that? Spending money on *her*, or *she* spent their money?" asked Melly. Drijs wasn't being clear.

"All I know is," said Drijs looking patiently at Ton, "she got expensive tastes. Expensive tastes and no fanny! Ha, ha!" Drijs chortled. "That's what they say about Titi. I don't know what she's doing now. Probably a nun! She in trouble or something?"

This was not the same Talish and, even if it was, there was a world of difference between the person Drijs described and the one Melly was looking for. If he only knew, he wouldn't mock so. Then again, Melly did not remember Drijs well enough to know what his reaction would be to her current status. He might laugh more heartily, more dismissively, and more cruelly.

"Why you looking for her? Why here?" asked Drijs.

"Hey, I'm lookin' everywhere!" replied Melly quickly and defensively. Talish was *his* project, *his alone*, and he didn't need anyone to divert him from his mission.

Ton was shifting uneasily on his chair. Melly picked up the signal.

"Look, I gotta go. Drijs, Ton?" Melly looked at them both. "I'll see you again, yeah? Say, you got a phone number or something?" He shook hands with the pair again.

Ton glared at Drijs. "No," he replied, the resignation apparent in his voice.

Melly moved away. He was not ready to hear all this about *his* Talish. He wanted to get out of range of any defamatory remarks. He didn't know Talish at all yet there was something, uh, more honourable, about her. At least he wanted to think there was. He walked back to the canal bridge outside Room 101. A couple of shabby men sat on their haunches smoking crack. Melly closed in. One went to move; the other gripped his arm, nodded and shook his head. The second recognized Melly as one who'd walked the street a lot in the last week and looked up to acknowledge him.

"Crack-cocaine, Ecstasy, Viagra," he said, hopefully.

"Yeah," said Melly suddenly, "Give me a gramme of crack; give me two tabs of E and a Viagra. How much?" Melly felt hot under the collar. He'd never bought any of these before. He had no idea of the cost; he'd have to play it all by ear.

"Fifty for the rocks, twenty for the E and fifty for the V," said the man.

"I'll give you one hundred, the lot," said Melly. It seemed the pusher wanted a lot. Melly was sure he could bring the cost down by haggling.

"No, no. One-twenty." countered the man, a weather-beaten African. He screwed his eyes up against the sunset, now pouring an orange glow into *his* corner of the street, and gnashed his teeth.

"Forget it," said Melly, turning to go.

The man looked at him quizzically.

"Tell you what," said Melly, stopping. "Make that two grammes and I'll give you one-fifty."

"Yeah, one-fifty!" The man felt good; a load of cash was rarely turned down, whatever the sale.

Melly felt for the notes in his back pocket - he knew them to be fifties. The dealer searched an inside pocket and held out a small handful of pills. He selected a small blue diamond shape and two round white ones and passed them to his friend to hold. He then pulled out a batch of small watchmaker's envelopes and pulled off two. He poured out a number of small white crystals onto his palm. Melly peered into the shaking cupped hand and told him to put them all into one bag. The deal done, Melly looked at both men.

"Seen Talish?" he asked.

"Yeah, she don't hang here some time," the man spoke Pidgin English.

After a moment's reflection, as the words they'd exchanged merged into what might best be described as a purpose, the man looked at Melly. A broad grin creased his face and he shook his head, knowingly.

"Problem?" asked Melly. Obviously there was. He guessed what the man was thinking, nodded slowly and left, clutching his purchases. Drijs may indeed have identified Talish for him.

Melly wondered why he had bought so much dope. All he needed to do was buy a single rock for Talish but something inside him urged to stock up and to prepare for a lengthy meeting with the girl. The Viagra was not wishful thinking; rather, it was the first time he had been offered it. There would be a time to use it, somewhere, eventually. The Ecstasy was for him and Talish. He knew it to be a great leveller. He knew it was trippy; it brought contentment and made telling lies really difficult. Or was it that it made telling the truth very easy? And the rocks?

"Hell," thought Melly, "If I'm in for a penny, I'll go in for a pound!"

He called in at a tobacconist's kiosk and bought a short pipe for small change, together with some chewing gum, and hit the street nervously. He was aware he had an addictive personality yet he was armed with enough to really foul up if he chose to or if circumstances took a turn for the worse. And what if he was to be busted by the police? Melly blinked, resigned to an unknown fate. He was stepping into dangerous territory; he wondered about the price he'd have to pay for this indulgence.

Melly wandered through the narrow streets, along quiet canals, and in and out of bars. At long last he found one, which stocked Panama Red. He didn't need to smoke. Not habitually, anyway, and he knew this. The last two or three days demonstrated to him that he didn't physically depend on it. This was just a relaxant; a bit like having a drink only that, like an alcoholic, he couldn't bear to look at a half-empty bottle. While it was there, it had to be drunk. Melly knew he didn't need to get stoned. He also knew that with smoke in his pocket he would most likely remain stoned until it ran out. The time was not yet right for him to book a hotel for the night. With money, he had a choice of many places to stay. He was in no hurry to sleep, not tonight anyway. He'd keep looking; he'd keep his eyes open.

By three in the morning, Melly had walked a long way, mostly in circles; he had drunk a lot coffee and was beginning to tire. Outside the Red Light district, across Dam Square and towards another side of town, there stood a car park, several storeys high and open-sided. It looked like a good place to curl up for a couple of hours. Melly picked a large cardboard box from a pile of rubbish and carried it up an echoing staircase to the top floor but one. There were only a few cars parked. Melly found a corner that looked out over a small sector of the Old Town. Below, he saw it was a quiet area; some building work was going on in an adjoining block and a row of tall warehouses stood opposite, shuttered and empty. They overlooked a short stretch of canal, one of many that linked the Amstel River to the canal arteries that encircled Amsterdam. Melly broke open the box, laying it out flat as something to insulate him from the cold concrete floor and sat down with his guitar by his side.

Within only a few minutes, some movement below caught his eye. Despite the darkness, he saw Talish was standing waist deep in the shallow canal. Melly felt gripped by a shiver, helpless to the knowledge he'd found her. He watched as she fumbled with her jeans and pulled them down; he watched as she splashed and swilled the cold waters through the garment, periodically reaching down to rub her crotch. Melly felt vaguely queasy, like when he saw fresh blood or cut flesh. He'd watched many an act performed but he was unprepared for seeing people defecate in a canal. This was a bad time to break his silence so he decided to keep quiet.

Talish pulled her jeans back up, climbed gingerly out of the water and shuffled uncomfortably to retrieve her coat from a bench nearby. Leaving his guitar, Melly rushed down the stairs and ran to the canal side. Talish was gone but he soon located her wet foot-steps; small puddles, betraying her route. They led to an alley where he found her, slumped on a pile of broken cartons behind a large skip. Above her was an illuminated window with an extractor fan. Warm air, stale with the smell of a greasy kitchen, blew her tousled hair over her face.

"Hi," said Melly, trying to look and sound surprised to find her among the shadows.

Talish looked up and, on seeing Melly, curled herself up into a ball, her knees tight up at her chest. "Uh? Oh fuck off…trash." She blinked hard; the words came out as a moan. She was distressed and, clearly, displeased to see him.

"Say, what?" Melly, taken aback, shifted his weight nervously from one foot to the other.

"Fuck off. Leave me alone," she cried to him, hiding her face in her elbow though Melly had already noticed dark lines under her eyes. She let out a loud, hoarse cough.

"You okay?" he asked, moving towards her.

"No. No thanks to you, fucker. I got the shits since the cow's milk you gave me. Crapping me pants…bastard." She sounded exasperated.

"Are you hungry?" he asked, rather thoughtlessly.

Talish reared up. "Fuck off and die," she spat. "Fuckin' makin' me sick like that. Go on, fuck off." She grabbed a handful of litter and hurled it at him in one movement.

Melly stepped back and felt suddenly drained of colour, of optimism, and of his jaunty step. "Hey listen, I'm sorry, Talish. Let me make it up to you."

Talish made no answer. Melly knew when to ease away from a rabid dog. It was enough to know she was alive.

"Pity her sorry state," he thought, "but she'll only get help if she wants it." He turned to leave.

"You got any change?" Her voice had softened after the angry tirade; she was now looking at his ankles yet through them and rubbed a temple with her thumb.

"If that's all you want, forget it," he declared firmly, "You want to talk to me, you come and see *me*. I'm up there." He pointed up at the car park. Without a backward glance he walked away and left Talish to ponder, if she might.

He returned to his guitar and his cardboard groundsheet and started to roll a joint. Very soon, he was nibbling on some crumbs from a muesli bar. He wasn't particularly hungry, just disarmed. He needed to compose his thoughts. He felt he was getting it wrong again. Meeting Talish again was not as he'd expected.

"And yet," he thought. "how should I have expected it? She's been laid up, having to lie low. I should have reacted more positively."

Melly lit the joint and was wondering on how to re-approach Talish when she emerged from the dim darkness that was his car park. He smiled warmly.

"Good to see you," he said.

She moved close slowly, eyeing him carefully, and sat down on the farthest edge of his marked territory, just out of reach. Immediately, the dry card darkened as it soaked in the dampness of her soggy clothes.

"You go to see the eclipse?" she asked.

Melly looked across at her and passed her the joint. "I did. It was really scary. Good, but scary and ominous. I was thinking about you."

Talish looked at him defiantly. "Trash. Yer lying! That's so much fuckin' trash," she sneered and re-arranged her legs. She took the joint from him and pulled deeply on it. The smoke caught her by surprise, as it does a novice smoker. She heaved and held her breath, looked at him with panic-stricken eyes and, suddenly, erupted into a fit of coughing. Melly watched her patiently and impassively until she subsided. He passed her a small bottle of Lucozade. It was half-full and the fizz was gone. Talish took a sip, breathed out, took a larger one and then quaffed the remainder. She dried the tears of strain from her eyes.

"Fuck you," she grinned. Just as quickly, a frown overcame her and she hunched up, whimpering. A breeze caught and scattered a waft of fresh diarrhoea from within her ripe, lived-in clothes.

"It's okay," said Melly quietly.

"Whaddya mean, it's okay." she retorted angrily, "It's not fuckin' *okay*. It's fuckin' shit! *You* give me the shits."

"What are you saying?" asked Melly patiently.

"I'm saying," she said, rolling her head, "I can't smoke because of you. I get ill - I don't smoke. Simple… I want a smoke but I'm ill and you, you're the man fucker. See?"

Melly turned away and rested his head on his elbow. He was making little headway. "*You're* trash," he muttered to himself.

Talish launched herself at him immediately and dealt him a blow smartly across the cheek with a clenched fist.

"Don't talk to me like that," she screamed, "you got no right to talk to me like that!"

"Tell me about it," said Melly feeling his face for traces of blood or swelling. He could feel her stench clawing away at him; a stink that was now deeply impregnated in the skin tissue where she struck.

"No-one talks to me like that," repeated Talish.

Melly paused to reflect. "Well now," he said philosophically and at last, "what can *you* do to make people *not* think that way?"

His question arrested her. "I mean," he continued, "what is it that *makes* trash?"

"Trash…?" Talish thought for a moment then stopped thinking further. "Huh, I haven't got time for this, I gotta clean up again."

She rose to go. Melly seized the moment and leaned forward. "Do you want me to help you clean up?" he asked.

Talish glared at him. "Whaddya wanna do, lick my ass clean? *Arschloch!*" She sounded incredulous.

Melly shuddered at the thought. "No, straight," he said, "I get a place and you clean up."

A shiver passed through Talish, like someone walking over her grave. "No, man, forget it...." she said and turned to go.

"Look," he said, lifting his hand and flattening out his palm, "I'm not asking for anything. I just thought you might want to rest up some."

"Yeah, well who the fuck do you think you are? God or something?" she said nervously.

"Huh! Yeah!" he said, "Look, it matters to me, it matters to you. I'm just saying I can make it happen. *Your lucky day*, if you like."

A silence descended on them both. Talish wondered about Melly and his proposal. She looked him up and down suspiciously. He seemed harmless enough; she'd escaped tougher and rougher men and he was, after all, a lot older than her; old enough, she reckoned, to be her father. She could beat him off, if need be, and she could outrun him. His offer was not the offer of someone penniless. He had kind eyes and she liked his smile; he was a soft touch, she concluded.

"Who are you?" Talish asked finally. She was exhausted.

"I don't know," said Melly. "Well, I do but I don't, if you know what I mean…"

Talish didn't, or maybe she did. Either way, he wasn't making sense.

"Let's talk about this later," said Melly. "Have you got any gear?"

Talish had her hands in her coat pockets. She lifted them both up. She and her clothes were all there was. Melly was astounded.

"Is that it?" he asked, "you and the street…?"

"I got all I need," she said quietly and hopelessly.

"Are you cool," he asked. "I mean, can you handle it?"

"What are you talking about?" she looked irritated.

"Tell me," he asked, "What did you do before living on the street?"

Talish looked him straight in the eye. "I lived in a big house," she said impassively, "three cars, servants and a do-"

"Cut the crap," Melly cut in.

Talish laughed. "Yeah, okay, okay," she said. "I'm cool. Don't worry 'bout me. What you got in mind?"

"We'll start with a hotel," said Melly, picking up his guitar. He wandered down the stairs; Talish trailed behind, her wet leggings rubbing together noisily. At a phone kiosk he dialled a number. It was 4 a.m.

"What's that," asked Talish, her face brightening, "Krasnopolsky?"

"Hello, Sonesta..." Melly looked at her, turned his eyes heavenward, and shook his head. He adopted the tones of the executive he had once been. "Look, just into town. You have a room, immediately?" He'd need to smuggle Talish in by a back door or through a ground-floor window. "...And don't put me upstairs, I get terrible vertigo." Melly put the phone down.

The Sonesta Hotel was a few streets away and opposite The Koepelkerk, a seventeenth century church now used for conferences. A shopping arcade with covered market stalls separated *it* from Dam Square. He'd stayed there before and he knew how it was laid out.

"This was the place I was looking for that time we met in the mall," Melly said.

He led her to the back of the hotel by a quiet, east-facing backwater, and left her waiting with his guitar while he went round to the front to check in. After a few minutes, he appeared on the canal-side at a ground floor window which he opened, and quietly summoned Talish to come forward. Talish groped her way though the darkness towards the unlit room and knocked the guitar into the window frame. The *ol' gitbox* resounded noisily; Melly seized it to deaden the sound. With one kick of her leg Talish was over the sill and into the room. Melly stopped her there.

"Talish," he said gravely. "Getting you sorted means getting you out of this stuff you're wearing and into some clean clothes. It means you get into a bath for a soak, so you soak forever. It means you start getting healthy again. What do you reckon?"

Talish looked over his shoulder into the darkness of the room. It was a typical four-star with en suite. Her eyes fixed on the twin bed. She sighed and pursed her lips.

"Hey!" he interrupted her scan of the room. "I know what you're thinking-."

"You ain't gonna touch me…" she asserted, thinking aloud.

"I know that," he said, almost reassuringly. "I'll give you all the space you want. But I aim to be here, watching you get better, so don't you be going off. Is that okay with you?"

"I'm listening," she said, looking around her. "I'll let you know if it's not okay. Or maybe I won't. Why are you doing this?"

"Hmm," said Melly, thinking out loud, "I'm doing it for you 'cos I hate to see you on the street and I'm doing it for me 'cos I've always wanted to try this out."

Talish stomped and turned to the open window. "Well fuck you," she said, "What am I? Some fuckin' experiment, some fuckin' ego-trip for you or somethin'?"

"Yeah," said Melly angrily. "It's an ego trip. I'm getting off on it, big time! Don't we all do things for our own benefit, all the time? I'm just being up-front and admitting it to you before you work it out for yourself. Something wrong with me trying to help you out?"

"Did I fuckin' ask for you to help me out?" Talish looked at him severely. "I don't remember saying *sort me out*. You said it to me."

"So why did you come with me, then?" he asked. "What are you doing standing here? Do you want this or not?"

She turned back to face him. He looked at her directly; her tear-filled eyes reflected a lone, distant light.

"I feel like shit," she said. "I gotta lie down…"

"Well then," he said, "tell me you'll stay a while." Melly wanted her reassurance.

"I'll stay till I go, alright?" she said at last.

"Fine," he said, relieved. "Now, empty your pockets." he ordered.

Melly could not see the facial expression in her response. She took a couple of coins from one pocket, a bottle of pills, a couple of tampons and a flick-knife from another and, from inside her coat, a cassette tape, an identity card, and a passport. Talish set them on a bureau.

"Is that it?" Melly maintained his composure. In the darkness, he saw her head nodding. She did not see his look of incredulity.

"Is that your life?" thought Melly to himself. "Is there anything else you're carrying?" he asked. She shook her head. "Right; so, give me your coat." He offered to take it; she obliged and he set it down on the floor where she stood, like a mat. "Now…" he said, "take all your clothes off. All of them. I'm going to throw them all away!"

"And you?" she asked. She was suddenly unsure.

"I'll run you a shower to start," he said, matter-of-factly. "Later, I'll run you a bath."

He went to the bathroom and ran a shower, testing the water until it seemed right, and came back. Talish stood where he had left her.

"Well?" said Melly.

Talish had not stood naked in front of a man or anyone, for that matter, for a long time.

"I don't want you to look at me," she said with a deliberation that, more than shyness, suggested she was nursing wounds she did not want him to see.

"Hey, it's dark," he joked, "I can't see much in the dark! Tell you what…" he said and moved the coat to the bathroom. "There you go; try that." He sounded more reassuring. He would have liked to put a reassuring arm around her but that would have made him filthy too. She, in turn, would have liked a reassuring arm around her but no-one had done *that* for her in a long time and there was no reason to suspect it would happen now. She *did* feel repulsive; Melly found her repulsive.

Talish went into the bathroom and closed the door behind her, locking it automatically.

"Don't lock the door, please," said Melly.

He knew she shouldn't lock herself in. There was no telling what might happen to her. She knew this too and unlocked the door immediately. After a few minutes Melly went in himself and groped for the stinking, discarded heap of clothes on the floor. Talish was busy having a shower and did not hear him. She had not switched on the light but in the dimness Melly was now accustomed enough to gather up all the rotting garments in the leather coat and take the bundle to drop through the window to the outside. He then climbed out himself and carried the pile at arm's length round to some rubbish bins wherein he tipped the clothes and wished them farewell. The coat, he brought back and hung outside the window on a hanger to air.

Talish spent a long time in the bathroom and in the darkness. In truth, she didn't even want to see herself in the mirror. She knew that she could look better, as she had once. She knew it would take time for her to 'regenerate' and get the grime off her skin, the dirt from under her nails, to sort out her hair and build up fat and flesh on her thin frame; to have her innards working properly again and her external wounds heal. She hated to see herself just now. She hated herself all the time, always. Ever since…

From behind the shower curtain, steam poured forth, tempting her, and threatening her with cleanliness. Her chilled body had not been warmed for a long time, neither by hot water nor by love, nor even by respect. She felt she had no place here and began to back out of the bathroom. As she did, she sensed her soiled thighs crumble with the encrusted dirt and realised she needed to make an effort.

Talish placed her foot into the stream of water. It seemed very hot, and then it seemed blissfully hot. She accustomed herself to the unusual sensation and allowed her knees in, then her bottom. As soon as the water washed over the cheeks of her buttocks, the most glorious fire warmed inside her, urging her to envelop herself more completely. She backed in further until her shoulders caught the full power of the spray. Down the centre of her back and below both shoulder blades, what little fat she had responded to the heat and began to soften. Warmed adipose tissue, warmed kidneys, warmed buttocks; there had been nothing to rival this feeling of well-being for many months. It was only a matter of time before she was able to put her head under the shower and lose herself completely. She wept; she wept with joy and with delirium. She wept for the loss of a life that was once so much more comfortable.

The shower sprayed relentlessly into her face, filling her mouth with its clarity and dribbled out over her lower teeth. Talish washed the slime and the scales from her tongue and gums. She could trust this water; it was safe to swallow; it was cleansing, life-giving and kind. Even as she stood in the warmth of the steamy, curtained enclosure, a cold tingle spread up her back, over her head and came to rest on her brow and she sensed she was falling asleep with contentment.

Looking down at herself in the steaming blackness, she could feel the caking of several days of incontinence dissolve and free itself of her. Talish shamelessly let go any additional fluids from within her bowels and washed herself down as best she could with the small bar of soap she found in the tray; she knew there would be some. She finally felt clean enough to come out and emerged into the bedroom wrapped in a large towel.

Melly sensed her wafting in. "How you feeling?" he asked from within the shadows.

"That was good," she said quietly.

Melly passed her a small cup of honey and warm water he'd mixed from the complimentary tray. She drank it quickly.

"Bed!" he announced, pulling back the covers. He moved to sit at the bureau.

Talish fell onto the bed on all fours then burrowed her way under the duvet and stretched out.

"Who invented bed?" she mumbled cutely. "Mister Bed," she answered herself. "Thank you, Mister Bed!"

Silence descended on the room. Talish fell soundly asleep, breathing rhythmically and deeply. Melly went to the bathroom, closed the door behind him and switched on the light. The stench of stale body odour and soured guts was overpowering. An extractor fan switched on automatically with the light and he set about mopping up splashes and wiping down surfaces. The bath housing the shower and its curtain were in need of a thorough swilling. All around the floor were a number of discarded tissues stained with puss and blood. When he had finished cleaning, Melly shaved and showered himself, washed his socks and hung them over the towel rail and then dressed again. Switching off the light, he padded barefoot to his guitar and sat down in a chair with it.

He plucked the strings randomly, forming simple chords and stroking them with his thumb. A couple of strings needed re-tuning. With each incidence of perfect pitch, the guitar grew more resonant and more assertive. Melly felt the urge to *kerchang* out a full C. He stopped himself. Talish was asleep; he would play later.

He sat on the floor by the bed and leaned up against it to sleep. Looking over at Talish, he reached out and touched her brow with the back of his hand. She was cold to the touch; he wondered about what he might buy in the day that would make her feel better.

⊠ ⊠ ⊠

Melly was awoken by Talish shifting uncomfortably in the bed. An untidy mop of curls spread over the pillow and stuck to her face. He saw she was sweating heavily, her brow glistening in the mid-morning sunlight, the pillow at her head damp and stained. Talish unconsciously reached up and scratched her scalp.

Melly rose, pulled in the leather coat from its hanger outside the window and closed the curtains. He left the room and the hotel and took the coat to a dry cleaner there in the arcade. Shops were already opening up for business; he settled the bill immediately on the promise the coat would be ready later. He then went to a pharmacy and bought things he thought might help Talish in her recovery. Diacalm was first on his list; St. John's Wort and Echinacea he bought optimistically.

"Maybe if she takes them long enough, she won't need much else," he thought.

For the immediate future, he bought a large bottle of high vitamin fruit extract, effervescent vitamin C tablets, multivitamins, coal tar soap, tampons and a fungicidal cream for her feet. Finally he picked up a pair of white woollen socks from a market stall. They were to play an important part in his plan for Talish that day.

This was local shopping at its most convenient; convenient also for Katryn, who sat impassively by a window, waiting to have her hair conditioned in a salon there. She noticed Melly pass. He seemed more strident and more confident than the piteous man she'd failed to stimulate a few days earlier. He looked purposeful and interesting. She watched him walk toward the eastern end of the arcade and turn toward the Sonesta. She watched until the morning sun blinded her.

Katryn thought about this man. He meant no harm to her. He could have been nasty, he could have been violent and, naturally, she was glad he hadn't been. She wondered what business he was in. She had seen him from inside her coffee bar or out on the street at all times of day or night during the previous week looking increasingly desolate and, yet, he now looked enlivened; even distinguished. Katryn was sure she had seen his face before, long before; like he was famous or something.

Melly was away from the hotel for no more than ten minutes. He returned to the dining room to eat breakfast of corn flakes and fresh milk, fried ham and light rye bread. It filled a void he, only then, realized had come into existence. A couple of guests sat with their back to him. Melly slyly, though confidently, strode to the breakfast bar again and helped himself to toast, pads of butter and a handful of mini-jars of honey. He poured out two large cups of coffee, a glass of orange juice, threw on some slices of lemon and a banana, and carried the lot back to his room on a tray.

Talish was still soundly asleep when he returned. There was a distinctive, foul smell in the room when he returned. It smelt of Talish as he had grown to know her; stale, stained Talish, street Talish. He pulled the curtains apart to reveal the open window and placed the fruit in the fridge. Then he picked up his guitar and started to tinker again.

Melly wasn't a professional musician and never had been. He simply didn't consider himself good enough. He'd played coffee bars a few times and busked a bit during his university days and in lean times. His repertoire was small and simple yet he always managed to earn just enough for a chicken dinner. He liked the way words fell together and found it easier to compose his own songs than try to interpret the work of others. If he had any fans, it was the girls who were the subject of his compositions of love and lust. He hadn't written one of those in a long, long while. Melly strummed hesitantly.

"Wake up, Talish," he thought. He so wanted to strum out loud.

Talish shifted and wiped a film of perspiration from her brow. Her stomach ached. She opened her eyes and it took a moment for her to realize where she was; she felt so comfortable. She saw Melly hunched over his guitar. This man was a kindly man. He reminded her of her grandfather; the shiny, ruddy pate surrounded by short, grey tufts of hair. He used to tell her what to do and how to behave; he was wise and she adored him. But, now, he was dead.

"Good morning," announced Melly, like a holiday rep. "Care for toast, orange, lemon tea?"

"No, no," she moaned, "my belly hurts."

Melly quickly prepared some Diacalm and gave it to her.

"In that case," he said, "here, have some medicine. Wash it down with this."

He passed her a glass of warm, honeyed water. In the clear light of day and, against the white sheets, she looked grey.

"Are you up for a shower?" he asked.

He went to the bathroom and turned on the shower. This time, he switched the light on. He unscrewed the top on a complimentary bottle of shampoo, unwrapped the coal tar soap and set them on a face towel. He placed a toothbrush in a glass tumbler by the basin. A white Terry bathrobe lay folded on the vanity counter; he hung it up.

Talish was not one to lie around in bed. She fell asleep quickly and she woke quickly. By the time Melly returned, she was sitting up on the bed wrapped in the towel again.

"How are you feeling?" asked Melly.

"A bit weird," she said, "I'll be okay."

She shuffled to the bathroom sipping on the honey. Medicine always made her shudder; it was always *horrible*, however it tasted. She was out of the bathroom after only a couple of minutes, clearly no cleaner.

"What's happening today?" she asked.

Melly looked at her severely. "Talish," he said, "I want to take you out to buy some clothes today but I need you cleaner than that. I want you looking good, smelling good. Wash your hair, use the soap…go on!" he encouraged.

"Yes *Bapu*," she said, mimicking penitence.

"Come again?" said Melly startled by the name. He wasn't sure what it meant; it sounded like some European version of *Papa*.

Talish rolled her eyes secretively and backed into the bathroom while Melly returned to his guitar.

"So, I'm mothering her," he thought contentedly. "That, or fathering her!"

When she emerged some time later, it was with her hair towel-dried. There was a lot more of it now that much of the grease and grime had been washed out and it was freed for release to the air. It hung in long curls and reminded Melly of his younger days when his own hair would look like that. She also had deep, brown eyes; they were pained brown eyes and though she looked fresher and radiant, she still had dark rings under them.

"Better?" he asked.

"Better," she replied. She looked trustingly at him.

"Sit on the bed," he said, "I'll do your feet."

He took the cream and spread it over her wounds. Her feet were a good shape though they were in poor condition and the toenails needed cutting. They still smelled of the bacterium that was Athlete's Foot and they felt cold to the touch. He took them carefully in his hands and massaged the cream into every pore and crevice, and into every cut. He then pulled the woollen socks up over her toes and bagged her feet.

Melly went to wash his hands again and again in soapy water while Talish nibbled on plain toast washed down with vitamin C. It was all that he would set before her. She looked around the room and saw the guitar.

"Play for me," she called out to him.

Melly came out and quickly picked up the guitar, *kerchanging* a C chord, loud and proud. He put the guitar down just as quickly.

"Later," he said "We gotta go out soon…how you feeling?"

Talish looked at him with a look of disappointment. "I like it here," she purred, nestling into the bathrobe.

"Come on," he said, "We're going shopping!"

Talish stood up and tied the cord tight round her waist. Melly moved to adjust her collar. She stepped back momentarily and then relaxed to allow him to come in close. He collected all her personal effects and put them in his jacket pockets.

"Ready?" he asked.

She reached in to one of his pockets to retrieve the bottle of pills and a tampon. She went into the bathroom and emerged a moment later, smiling, and put the pills into the pocket of the bathrobe.

"That's better," she said. "Ready!"

"What are the pills for?" he asked, going back into the bathroom. He looked around for traces of her having been there and systematically eliminated them all. He took the pills from the bathrobe. It would not do to be thrown out of the hotel just yet.

"Antibiotics," she called out, "they keep me clean."

He wondered briefly what the antibiotics were for, but his main thought focused on the idea that she would probably not be touching alcohol for a while. He found something distasteful about women, or anyone for that matter, who drank a lot. Alcoholic intoxication made for a different human animal; one that was insincere and liable to unpredictable and violent outbursts, and vulnerable. He was looking forward to talking some sense with Talish. Dope made people talk nonsense but at least it was sincere nonsense. He was glad she wouldn't be drinking.

Melly looked around and checked the room. He took a red pansy from a bedside spray and slipped it into her hair, balancing it behind her ear.

"We won't be out long," he said. He could feel her initial stiffness softening.

"Good." he said, "You climb out of the window and wait for me. I'll be round in a moment." Talish giggled mischievously and nervously.

On his way out, Melly told the concierge he would be staying another night. When he got to the back of the hotel he found Talish hunched over his window, looking in. She looked troubled, holding up her collar to shield her identity.

"I can't do this," she said. "People I know on the street; they'll see me. They'll wonder what's going on. I don't want to talk to them just now."

Melly reached into his jacket and took out a pair of wide sunglasses.

"Try these; you need to look so famous that no-one recognizes you," he said triumphantly, placing them on her nose. "Or, if they have a hunch, they won't dare come and ask, just in case it's not who they think it is. Dark glasses are so separating. Shall we go...*my child*?" he added in a mimicked tone.

He offered his arm; she took it and they walked out toward the arcade. With every step closer, Talish grew more anxious and held into him more closely. By the time Katryn saw Melly re-appear, on his arm he carried a young, lean model who appeared to hang on him, craving his indulgence. He, in turn, seemed unconcerned; so strong and so perfectly in control.

A girlfriend who'd noticed her in the salon as she walked by joined Katryn. Darla was working her way through the summer before returning to university in Cologne. She was on the game too and, like Katryn, was free of the control of any pimp. She would discretely visit lonely men in their hotel room, taking them unawares as Katryn as would have done Melly.

Katryn had already shared with Darla the joke about the man who remained forever limp; now he was here, on parade. She sought to analyze and place her client.

"What is the power he exerts over this young *starlet*?" she wondered out loud, recognizing her as such. "Is he *that* rich? Surely not. Well then, he has connections. Or, maybe, he's a brilliant lover." Katryn could see the starlet was besotted with Melly, even if a touch hazily and unfocussed.

"Only people infatuated with new love promenade in their socks and a bathrobe," she said to Darla, ruefully. "This *thing*, hiding behind dark glasses, has his attention while I missed an opportunity to exploit him!"

Katryn was fed up working at the bar and she was unhappy about having to take tricks for extra cash. She wanted out and a new start; anything more varied and more exciting. She wanted to travel further because she knew the world was waiting for her, if only she were to get the right breaks…

"Who is this man?" she asked Darla but addressing herself. "Is he the break I'm looking for? What was that he asked me… *did I have a boyfriend*? Why did he ask that? He wanted to know if I had any ties, I know it! And he didn't answer when I asked him if he had a girlfriend. What must he think of *me*?"

Katryn felt sick to her stomach. "Oh, shit!" she said, "He's been wanting to see me all this time. He *must* be someone famous; I'm sure I've seen his face before. He wanted me for something. I bet he's in films." Her head spun with anguish. "And I played him like a punter. I pushed him away and now he's gone off with someone else. She's in *my* role; *I* should be there."

She felt cheated. No-one had told *her* who he was. But, she figured, she could match the starlet, anytime. She knew she could, especially now that her hair was done. She got up to leave; Darla rose too, without having uttered a word. She was accustomed to acting as a sounding board to this talkative *wannabe*.

Talish hung on to Melly's arm, looking out from behind her shades at anyone she might know, and at anyone who might recognize her out of character and out of role. Feeling cleaner and warmer was a good way to be. She hoped this time spent with Melly was not to be short-lived. It didn't matter how long it lasted, just so long as it didn't end just yet. She was out to buy clothes and that was an experience untried for far too long. She clasped her hands as they continued to walk together and looked forward to dressing finely with eager anticipation.

"Right; do the biz," said Melly outside a lingerie shop. nderwear!"

Talish closed her eyes and thought for a moment. "Silk, oh, I love silk," she said suddenly.

Melly stopped in his tracks and turned to her. "No." he said quietly and firmly. "Clothing, not fashion. Nothing fancy." Talish petulantly loosened her grip.

In the shop she fingered her way through a rack of panties and pulled out a pair. Melly took them from her and collected a second. They moved to brassieres. She found a black size 34 C.

"I used to fill these," she laughed sadly; she sounded tired.

"You reckon?" said Melly, pulling out a 34B.

"I'm there!" she grinned, "Well, I used to be! Will be, too."

"I'm looking forward to that," said Melly quietly as he looked away.

Talish heard the aside. It pleased her, quite unexpectedly, that anyone should care. No one had really cared for ages; now someone was trying to tell her something. This man was, actually, quite *nice*. Talish wondered again about his motives. He hadn't made a pass at her and that was unusual because every man she'd ever met wanted to grab at her. It was refreshing not to have that happen, yet it unsettled her. Was it her fault or was this man not interested in her at all? Maybe he was gay, except that he didn't act at all gay.

"Yes, it must be me," she concluded, "and I don't blame him."

Melly walked away towards the sock counter and selected two black woollen pairs, half-length and returned to collect Talish. Outside, he led her through the arcade to a group of stalls selling jeans, tops, and trainers.

"Feet!" Melly spoke like an automaton. "Size?"

"Forty-one," she replied, pained.

Melly picked out a rugged pair of trainers; Talish found herself approving the selection. It seemed to her that she had little choice in the matter. The man was taking control and she felt too weak to want to fight it.

"If he wants to be sugar-daddy," she thought, "he's got a weird way with presents..."

The excursion had taken them no more than fifteen minutes - they were noticed by only a handful of observers who each thought the way Katryn had thought. It seemed to matter to Melly that Talish begin the regenerative process immediately and that meant *looking* healthy.

"*You* don't think I'm gonna make it," said Talish sharply as they walked back.

"What do you mean?" he asked.

"This cheap stuff. You're getting me clothes for the street," she said, "Why not dresses and perfume?"

"Why? Where are you going?" he said, "I just want to see you in fresh clothes."

"That's what I mean," said Talish, "*That's all.* This is just simple clothes. This is not goin' out stuff."

Despite her recent emergence from hideously soiled rags, Talish felt cheapened by the simple, unflattering clothes she was now expected to wear. She had loved her leopard halter-neck dress and her long gloves. It was her last remaining link with a previous life, her life before Amsterdam. Now, this man had thrown them away, had severed all the links from her past, and was putting her in common clothes. She was better than that. She wanted to feel better about herself and he might have been able to help.

Melly stopped and looked at her. "What you do with your life after I'm gone is up to you," he said. "I'm putting you in at square one. I'm not saying I'll put you back in *your* world, just back in *the* world. The rest is up to you."

She reined him in and sidled up. "How long you staying?" she asked.

"I really don't know," he said, momentarily remembering his other life; his life with Jean, and his life in London. "You want me to stay?"

Talish did not answer. She dared not answer. She'd had such bad luck; it wouldn't do to tempt fate with giving voice to a plea for something good to happen for a change.

At that moment, Katryn stepped out of the salon and saw them standing close by, talking. Melly might have acknowledged her but, unable to rid himself of the feeling of humiliation he suffered at the hands of this temptress, he looked away, averting his eyes to Talish, and turned his back on Katryn.

Talish noticed Katryn approaching behind Melly, heading towards him intently; she saw her hesitate and noted how her expression developed a scowl. It frustrated Katryn to be thus avoided; she looked at Talish scornfully, and decided, there and then, to make an impact and to undermine any *progress*. Relaxing into a saunter as she passed Talish, she held her hand limply and wiggled her little finger at the starlet. Melly saw Katryn's action reflected in a window and, looking back at Talish, flushed and felt dizzy with embarrassment. He reached for her shoulder to steady himself, and tried desperately to pretend he hadn't noticed Katryn and that he was oblivious to the display.

Talish knew of no reason behind Katryn's actions but concluded that she must know Melly. Talish, herself, recognized the blonde;

she'd noticed her start work a month earlier in the bar that spilled onto *her* street. As Katryn walked away towards this bar, her locks shimmered brilliantly in the sun, and she spun round to face Melly, walking backwards a couple of paces before turning around again. Her hair caught in a breeze, blew up and billowed like a golden veil. Melly saw *that* clearly; Talish did not. He was quite mesmerized for a moment; mesmerized and confused.

"Why is she doing this? What does she want from me?" he thought, "I don't owe her anything."

"I'm feeling tired," said Talish, breaking in to his thoughts. "I want to go back now."

"Yeah," said Melly. He had lost the thread of their conversation and said nothing for the remaining few steps of their outing. Talish took his arm again and also walked quietly but unsteadily. She was quite exhausted and wanted to lie down again and curl up in a warm place.

They returned to the hotel, he entering through the front, she from behind, to find the room had been cleaned. The short journey had not only tired Talish but had also brought her up in a mild sweat; enough to have her body odour change significantly. Melly immediately ran a deep, hot bath, filled with all the oils and salts that the hotel provided. He also poured her a glass of water and gave her some pills and vitamins, together with a spoonful of honey.

Talish watched quietly and took her medicine unhappily. She didn't know about this man. He knew the blonde; that meant *other* people knew him. That meant he wasn't *hers* alone. She had to share him, which meant he wouldn't be staying with her. This thing wasn't going to last and she wanted out. Now was the time for her to go; or, at least, it was time to find a way to close her mind from these awful conclusions.

"Bath!" said Melly, "Soak!"

"I need a rock," Talish suddenly said.

"Why?" asked Melly.

"Don't fuckin' ask me why I do. None of your fuckin' business why I do. You said you give me money. I gotta have a smoke." She began to fidget nervously.

"No you don't," said Melly, "You don't need a rock. You just wanna get high; I've got some Panama. It's really good."

"No," said Talish, her eyes misting. "It's gotta be crack-cocaine. I just gotta go find some…" she grabbed at the jacket he was wearing, coaxing him to give her some money to score.

"If you go out to find some, you're not coming back here," he said firmly, "I'm taking you out of this very soon. Don't go back to it."

"Fuck you," she spat and moved to leave.

Melly knew how she was feeling. He knew she had fixed on the idea of a rock and there was no stopping her. He knew how that felt. He groped in his jacket pocket and pulled out the small envelope.

"Look at what I got," he teased unkindly and gave her a rock, a lighter, and the pipe. She grabbed at them gracelessly and prepared to smoke. At her first inhalation, she choked and coughed.

"Shit," she moaned, "Not ready for this. Shit, shit, shit." She stomped her feet on the carpet.

"Here, let me help you," said Melly, "I'll give you a blow-back."

He took the pipe, lit the rock, took a small mouthful and blew it slowly at her mouth. The taste was harsh and sickly and clung to his tongue and palette; the smell was like that of burning plastic. It was vile.

"Take it really slow," he said.

Talish took as much as she could, inhaled carefully and deeply, and closed her eyes. He could see the frown disappear from her brow.

"Another?" he said sympathetically and kindly.

"Uhuh." She relaxed completely and he did the same again. Talish gathered up all his exhaled smoke and lay backwards onto the bed holding her breath. Once down, she let the smoke out slowly and lay motionless for the next few minutes.

Melly waited until she came to. "Now," he said, "bath?"

"Now," she said, offering her arm to be helped up.

"Teeth?" he suggested.

She entered the bathroom dreamily and locked the door behind her.

"Door!" he called. She unlocked the door.

Talish found herself in the bathroom with the lights blazing unforgivingly, and the extractor fan whirring quietly. She brushed her teeth as well she could. The new bristles attacked her fragile mouth and very soon she was spitting blood from torn gums. It was not the hardness of the brush that caused the problem but the weakness of her gums. A diet such as hers, which lacked calcium, made her teeth loosen in their sockets and any trauma was bound to draw blood.

She stood back and looked at herself in the mirror. Slowly, she untied the loose belt on the bathrobe and waited to be disgusted by her nakedness. This was not how she remembered herself; she remembered a good-looker that used to attract the attentions of many admirers, even though she always gave them short shrift. She rubbed her hollow belly and wondered how long it would take for her to fill out again. She wondered what it would take for her to rejoin society. She knew she was misplaced; she knew she didn't really belong on the streets. And, furthermore, she had the opportunity to escape it all but only if that man outside the bathroom could take care of her just a little longer; if only long enough to see her well again.

"At least," she thought, "he's got rocks!"

She wondered about this man again. There was something vaguely odd about him. He looked at her in such a strange, searching way, as if he was out to identify something about her. It almost made her feel he was undressing her with his eyes.

"No," she thought, "Not undressing me from my clothes. He's searching deeper into my soul; that much I can feel. He can see a deeper side to me." Talish wondered how much about herself she might reveal and how much of herself she might give. "Well, he's going to want nothing of me if I don't clean up," she considered finally and stepped into the warm pool of bubbles. "How long is it since I had this kind if luxury?" she thought.

She knelt in the bath, swirling the water around her and onto her trunk, growing accustomed to the heat and found herself ready to pray for a change of fortune. Prayer, however, was not something she ever did or had done willingly; her convent schooling had done enough to steer her far away from the faith. It only seemed appropriate, though, to have the idea flash through her mind.

"And what is prayer, anyway," she thought, "if not an appeal to a higher authority?" Talish was the highest authority she knew, so she prayed to herself. Then she relaxed fully.

Melly sat down to unwrap all the clothes he'd bought and laid them out on the bureau. They had cost over 350 guilders and he began to wonder how he could make his money last longer. The room was, after all, costing him 120 guilders a night.

"We can't stay here forever," he thought. "It was never in the plan to do so but, well, creature comforts, they exist."

He knew he was exploiting an expensive hotel – he also knew that as long as he showed he had money, the staff would respect his privacy. It made him feel secure to be so empowered. He also knew this expensive pose could not last long. It was important not to get too settled and he reckoned they would have to leave the following day.

"And anyway," he thought, "I'm just passing through. I don't have forever."

He was very happy at home with Jean and wasn't about to throw all that away.

"I can leave at any time," he thought.

He wondered what more he might do for Talish. So far, he had given her a bed and a few hours sleep. She'd had a bit of medicine, some clean food and a wash. And now he had a fresh set of clothes for her.

"But what about *her*?" he thought. "What does *she* want?"

It worried him that she was desperate to have crack-cocaine so suddenly and with such menacing demand. And yet, he understood how fixing on an idea could be an obsession. He did it with smoke. He could live without it, but when he wanted it, he simply had to have it. Yet, Talish did not seem to be part of the group of down-and-out crack-heads on the bridge outside Room 101. She didn't have their shell-shocked demeanour. Hers was more alive; she was more assertive than other down-and-outs; somehow, she seemed more independent.

"Yes," he concluded, "It would be great to shag her when she's together again and when she's clean. But how long can I get her to stay? I gotta find out more about her, like, whom she belongs to."

Melly picked up his guitar and started to strum idly. He turned phrases over in his mind, phrases that encapsulated some of his experiences during the past week. Nothing gelled and nothing sounded right. He settled, instead, on running through some of his old songs, the ones he'd written long before. Several times he forgot the chords and had to correct himself, searching for the right key changes. The words linked the disparate music. He never forgot his own words. He sang each verse with more emphasis, with greater clarity and with good range and control.

Talish lay quietly at rest in the bathroom. She had stopped splashing about in order to listen in dreamily. After a while, the playing stopped and a chill filled the quietness. Her arms felt cold, as did her face; she took a deep breath and submerged herself in the warmth of her bath.

Outside, in the bedroom, Melly took off his shoes and socks, jacket and sweat-top, and knocked on the bathroom door. There was no answer so he walked in. Talish lay underwater, buried under a mountain of bubbles.

"How's it going?" Melly asked.

Talish surfaced and sighed contentedly.

"Do you trust me?" he asked. "Do you trust me to help you wash?"

"Don't know." she replied quietly. "Try me."

Melly sat on the edge of the bath and pulled both her legs out of the water and onto the rim of the bath. Carefully and gently, he washed the grime from the pores, from between her toes, and from her heels. Melly was no expert nor was he a reflexologist but he understood how a massage might improve circulation and health. He played with each foot, mindful to avoid tickling the arch under her soles. All too often in the past, sensitive and magical moments such as these had been cut short by a fit of giggles and a hastily withdrawn foot. When he did touch the arch, it was with a firm clasp and a massaging thumb. He placed her feet back in the water.

"Sit up. I'll do your back," he said.

Obediently and with ease, she sat up and offered her back. Melly took a sponge to her and was amazed at how much of her dark flesh tone was, in fact, grime. He washed only where he knew she wouldn't easily reach and included her neck, which he saw was too grubby to leave alone. Her hair was already wet. He poured shampoo onto it and started massaging her scalp.

"Okay, okay," she stopped him. "I'll do this."

He watched her blind herself with lather and grope for a showerhead with which to rinse but, on not reaching it, submerged herself completely.

"And again," said Melly when she surfaced.

Talish washed and rinsed her hair a second time. The water that washed off even after this second wash was still markedly discoloured. In truth, she was filthy. She had lain in the bath for close to an hour, softening her skin in the bath oils and introducing a fresher scent to herself. But in the bathroom, despite the extractor, an unhealthy odour hung. Melly reached into the murky depths of the bath and, unceremoniously, pulled the plug.

"Rinse cycle!" he said, turning the shower on. Cold water cascaded onto Talish, shocking her. She let out a squeal and made an attempt to hide under the disappearing bath water but soon emerged to flick some water at Melly. As the shower warmed to its pre-set temperature, she lay rubbing an imaginary speck on the rim of the bath and looked up at him. For a moment she hesitated to say something. The spray had cleared much of the froth from her and she lay increasingly exposed. Melly felt a hot flush and scratched his head. He pulled the shower curtain smartly and left her to finish alone. Soon, Talish emerged wearing a fresh bathrobe. Melly ordered her into bed.

"You," said Talish, "you like control, don't you?" she said, climbing under the fresh sheets.

"Not really," said Melly, sitting on the edge of the bed. "I don't think anyone can be controlled unless they want to be controlled, especially not you."

She looked at him angrily. "You think I want to be controlled?" She demanded to know and she sounded resentful.

"No," said Melly, "but I think you want this to happen and you're letting me set the agenda. But I also want to give you room to breathe. Listen, you're gonna have to tell me if I'm closing in too much and too quickly."

"What do you want from me?" she asked, looking at him.

"I'm glad you asked that," said Melly, looking for a way to avoid having to answer. "You said a couple of days ago you knew what I wanted. What was it you know?"

"I thought I knew," she replied, "But I'm not sure now."

"Yeah?" said Melly.

Talish looked at him and nervously drew imaginary pictures on the duvet with her finger. "I thought you were looking for crack," she said. "Cheap crack. I thought you wanted to share a rock with me. I thought, oh, I dunno. Maybe you were from the mission." She swept non-existent crumbs off the bed. "You are, aren't you?"

Melly was taken aback by the nature of her assessment. Talish was clearly not dumb; she had the capacity to think clearly and intelligently and, perhaps, more intuitively than he did.

"Talish," he said, "You're so right, but also wrong. No one sent me from a mission though I do work with people in that way. I'm not from the church. I'm here by myself. I'm doing this for you, honestly, because I think you might appreciate it. But, really, I don't know what the fuck I'm doing. I don't want crack 'cos I don't use it, so you're wrong on that one but I reckon it would be good to pull you off it."

"Me and crack?" she looked at him defensively. "I got no problem with crack."

"You were desperate for a hit!" said Melly.

"Listen, fucker," she looked at him severely, "Why you smoking so much? Do you have a problem with smoke? You take it sometimes, you leave it sometimes. You can handle it. I have crack sometimes 'cos it's a great buzz. But I don't have the money for it. I've seen the others fall apart and I don't want that. I've kept pretty clean, you know."

"So what the fuck you doing in Amsterdam?" sniped Melly, eager to determine his next move.

"Yeah, whatever," said Talish dismissively. She sounded tired. "So, what's next?"

"I want you to stay in bed today," he said. "I want you to take your medicine. I want to see you get some of your strength back."

"Yeah," she said. "And then what?"

"Tomorrow," he said, "we leave here and go to another place. I can't afford this hotel. We'll go elsewhere, maybe leave this town. You got anyone here?"

"What you sayin'?" she asked.

"This is your town, right?" he said, "You got friends here, looking out for you?"

"I know lots of people on the street; they've been good to me," she said, "We help each other out sometimes. But I can go. I can go anytime, if I had a way of getting there." Talish looked hopelessly out of the window at the sunlit world outside. "Give me anther rock," she said.

"Let's get some food inside you first," said Melly, changing the subject. "Are you hungry?"

"Yeah," she said, "I could do with some food."

Melly picked up the phone. "Can I have fried ham on brown bread with toasted cheese and a pot of coffee?" He looked to her as he spoke. She nodded approvingly.

"How are your guts?" he asked.

"Holding." she smiled.

"Fancy an E," asked Melly, "Give you the chance to chill out some?"

He was desperate to get inside her head. Talish seemed too strong and complex a person to speak easily about herself.

"Okay," she said matter-of-factly.

Melly took the tablets from his jacket and, without hesitation, they both popped them; there would be an hour before the Ecstasy took effect. He went to the bathroom to brush his teeth and was aware of a flurry of activity as he re-entered the room. Talish was sitting half out of bed; the envelope lay partially hidden by the dressing gown. She looked embarrassed.

Melly held out his hand. Talish picked up the envelope and put it back in the jacket pocket on the chair and an uneasy silence descended on the room. Melly dissolved a glucose tablet in some water and gave it to her. As she drank, he sat down and rubbed more cream into her feet. When he finished, he rolled the new woollen socks onto her feet to work as a bandage.

"So you don't want the rocks for yourself?" she asked at long last.

"No," said Melly, "the rocks are not for me. They're for you, but later."

"Later...now...who gives a shit?" She was surly.

"I give a fucking shit." Melly snapped back. "How many rocks have you *not* smoked because you're ill? Two, three, four, five? I dunno. But one rock's a fucking shoe."

He picked up one of the trainers and waved it at her. She snatched it out of his hand.

"Don't you get all fuckin' high and mighty with me," she snapped. "You can keep yer fuckin' shoe." She threw it at him. "Fuckin' man trash. Cunt."

His reaction was instinctive. He swung out and slapped her hard across the face. "No-one has *ever* called me a cunt," he yelled.

She shrieked and threw herself at him like a cat, her nails attacking his face. Melly grabbed her wrists but she resorted to elbowing and kneeing any part of him she could reach. They tussled and bounced on the bed. Melly would not strike her again; he made only to restrain her.

Talish quickly realized he would not fight her. She relaxed for a moment and Melly loosened his grip whereupon she quickly yanked her wrist free and scratched wildly, catching him on the throat. At this point Melly snapped. He backed off, keeping hold of her other wrist and ordered her out of his life. He would have none of this.

"Get out; just get out of here!" he shouted at her, pointing to the window.

Talish thought. The envelope was still in his jacket pocket; she *had* to get the rocks. She looked around and, seeing the pipe on the table, grabbed at it. Melly got there first and snatched it away.

"Go on, fuck off," he said, trembling. He shouldered her away from him and walked out of the room.

"That's it," he thought. "If there's one thing I can't stand, it's malice. Vindictive malice. And there it is, as plain as day!"

He walked to the lobby in a daze and sat down in a deep sofa. It felt too comfortable; he was twitching with rage and confusion. He *had* to go back, to smooth ruffled feathers, and to regain some control over his own composure.

Outside his door he met the waiter bearing a tray. Melly took it from him and walked slowly into his room. The scratch on his throat prickled as a draught caught it. Talish was deeply in bed, her eyes wet with tears. Melly set the tray down and sat down with her.

"I'm so fucked up," she sobbed.

"Why do you hate so much?" Melly put an arm around her and tried to offer some re-assurance. Talish felt very light and very thin. "Why are you so angry?"

Talish was shaking but, finding a niche under his arm, relaxed into his protective embrace. "I don't know. If I knew, I'd tell you."

Melly reached over for his paraphernalia and prepared to build a joint.

"What are you doing?" she asked, "Why are you rolling up?"

"Dunno," said Melly, "Guess I'm trying to numb the pain and forget; I like the taste," and stopped rolling. "She's asking *my* questions and I'm giving the answers I'm hoping *she'd* give." He thought about this reversal and continued rolling.

"Light me a rock," Talish said. Melly looked at her, knowingly. "I wanna forget too."

"Is that what you do? Smoke to forget?" he asked.

"It gives me comfort..." she replied.

"…keeps the cold out," he continued. "I wish I'd never started using smoke. Like, I wish it never existed."

"Yeah?" she seemed to agree.

"I love it," he said, "I love the buzz. But I also get these huge guilt trips about it. Like, standing outside of myself and tut-tutting. You know, pointing the finger at yourself and saying *'arsehole, fucking arsehole'*. You spend your life looking out from within; doing what you do and, suddenly, you got this conscience thing berating you for doing it. And I know it's right. In the scheme of things, it talks sense."

"So why don't you do something about it?" she asked.

"What, like stop?" he said. Talish nodded.

"I dunno," said Melly. "It's like, it's central to my existence. Gotta keep my freak-flag flying and all that. It keeps me in touch with young dope-heads. It makes sure I never forget how kids are feeling when they're off their faces. The work I do; it allows me to cope with people without pre-judging them. I'm into second chances."

"What's that?" Talish cut in.

"Making up," he said, "starting again; having another go; getting it right. Saying, *"do it, but don't fuck me about. I think I know part of where you're coming from.""*

"Who you talking about?" Talish looked confused.

"Them," said Melly, "the kids. Why? Did you think I was talking about you?"

"I dunno," she said. "I heard what you said about calling myself an arsehole and lost it"

"How do you mean?" asked Melly.

"I was thinking about my father… well, he wasn't *my* father… making me feel bad about myself. Fucking bastard. Fucking, fucking bastard." With each word Talish's voice wavered and she grew closer to breaking point until she erupted in a burst of tears and rolled onto her side sobbing. "Give me a rock; I wanna rock."

Melly took the pipe and re-lit the half-burnt rock within. He bent down and blew the smoke into her face. Her arm came down over his shoulder and guided his head closer to her mouth. Melly gave her a second blowback, long and slow. Talish gazed at him briefly and closed her eyes, as she slipped out of consciousness. Melly did not inhale; he would not inhale. Nevertheless his skin crawled in the fumes. He rose to the bathroom to wash the taste out of his mouth.

Suddenly, he had a crazy notion. He decided, there and then, *that's* what he must do. There was a memento from Amsterdam he had in mind and he had to get it *now.* He could count on Talish being comatose for a while. He also wanted a walk; the afternoon was sunny and there was clean air out there, outside the hotel. He left her a note saying he'd be back later.

Melly returned after an hour or so. He was getting rushes of warmth and delirium from the Ecstasy. He needed to lie down on the bed or on the floor; anywhere would do. As he walked in the room, he saw Talish on her knees, on the bed, crying bitterly. His notebook lay closed in front of her. It was obvious that she had found and read *Melly's Trip*, the fantasy he'd scribbled a few days earlier in the smoke shop. Melly walked round the bed quietly and lay down in the available space next to her. She looked down at him.

"Get away from me!" she spat. "You're a fraud, you're fucked in the head," she said. "You're a disgusting pile of bollocks. Where have you been?"

Melly rubbed his temple with his thumb, penitently. "I went out."

"What? To go see some whores, I bet. That fuckin' blonde?" she sneered.

"I went out," he muttered

"When did you write this?" asked Talish, holding up the note-book. "Are you this Melly guy? Is that who you are?"

It occurred to Melly that Talish did not yet know his name.

"What the fuck do you think I am? You think I'm a whore, don't you? You fuckin' hate me; don't you fuckin' hate me?" Talish was screaming at him.

"Whoa! Stop, stop," said Melly rising to his elbow. "None of that happened, did it? It's a fantasy. I was tripping when I wrote that. Remember, I only met you twice before. Twenty seconds of chance conversation, that's all we had. I found I couldn't stop thinking about you. It's only my imagination. Are you saying I can't think things?"

"Hey, think what you fucking-well like," she screamed, "but don't you *dare* write it down 'cos then it's all there in black and white. Go on, deny it; you just think I'm some slapper. There's nothing about *me* in there, how I might feel. It's just you. You and your fuckin' dick. Fuckin' man trash." Talish beat the notebook heavily on the bed. "It's just about how much you get off on it. Your dick rules your head, doesn't it, and fuck everyone else. Fuckin' dicks. Shit! Shit!" Talish was moaning desperately. "I see that man's fuckin' dick waving in my face whenever-"

"What man?" interrupted Melly.

"My *father*!" Talish burst open with the word and stopped speaking. Reddening with shame, she leaned over and buried her head in Melly's chest and nuzzled him, looking for a dark corner in which to hide.

Melly gathered her in close and squeezed her. "Tell me about you," he coaxed gently.

"What's to tell?" she said. "I'm nothing. Everything I do is nothing. You watch; I'll make you into nothing too. No," she paused and began to shake. "You must go - *now.* Go while you can."

Talish sobbed and gripped him tightly, her fingers clawing at his flesh. "Ah, it always goes wrong. I'm trash," she cried.

"Nothing's going wrong," he said, "Nothing's going to go wrong."

His words tumbled out. Melly didn't think they were insincere but he could see no reason to feel pessimistic. And yet, as he sat with her, it occurred to him that this girl was working her way under his skin and into his affections. It made him feel uncomfortable to think this might be another case of someone who might want to contemplate love for him. He recognized the danger signals. It was only a matter of time before he would bring the shutters down and forbid himself from getting closer to her, and forbid her from getting closer to him. That is what he normally did. He wondered when to stop yet, helplessly, he encouraged Talish to continue.

Melly felt unusually protective toward her while, within him, a demon waited to bask in some form of glory. The Ecstasy was freeing up her demons; his, too, were stirring.

"Tell me about you," he repeated. "Where are you from?"

Talish composed her scattered thoughts and spoke slowly.

"I lived a lot of places," she said. "My mum was Greek; we lived there sometimes when I was little. Sometime we lived in Zurich. That's where my dad worked. But he wasn't my dad, see. Mama was married to him and she had me but I wasn't his daughter. He got really pissed with that and gave Mama a bad time; a really bad time. I saw him hit her a lot." Talish paused. "He… he gave me a bad time also."

"Yeah…? Go on," said Melly.

Talish lay down on the bed and looked up at the ceiling. She closed her eyes and continued recollecting.

"He hated her," she said, tears welling in her eyes. "And he would never forgive me for not being his little girl. He was always calling us trash and said we were scum."

Talish blinked hard. Melly nodded, acknowledging her pain. "He always came to me," she continued, sobbing, "waving his dick and make me play with him, telling me all this shit about how I had to suck him hard. Him and his fuckin' dick. I hate him; I hate the fucker." She recoiled suddenly.

"And you," she snarled. "You're just the same. All you want to do is have your dick worshipped. You're all man-trash."

"He was over the top, Talish," said Melly. "That's clear."

He felt a hot flush of embarrassment sweep over him. Her recollection and his own written fantasy revealed enough for him to feel, in these circumstances, rather perverted. Talish realized the same.

"I'm not waving anything at you," he said. "Um, er, I'm sorry you think I'm like him. I can't deny my thoughts."

"You wrote them," she said. "And you're wrong, you know. Wrong about me and wrong about crack. You just don't know, do you?"

"No, I don't." he said. "It's all bullshit; it's all made up. But I did think about you. I had a *desire* for you."

"That's where you are wrong," she said. "You wanted me *down there*. You wanted me to drink from you. Like *him!* Making me feel like shit."

"Hey," he interrupted, "In my fantasy, I was enjoying it and so were you. And don't forget the bliss during the eclipse. It was an act of fulfilment; it wasn't horrible, it was great."

"But you thought I was shit when you finished," she said, "You wanted to die."

"Guilt, Talish…" he said. "I'll always think of a reason to deny it, to turn away and to allow me to run from it. I dreamt it. It was okay until I started to wake. I don't want you to be important to me, but you are. But you, you're turned off men, huh?"

"Yeah," she said slowly. "They scare me. *He* scared me. I didn't know he was weird 'cos I didn't know different. But he wouldn't touch me nicely; he only beat me. He made me to do all the work on him and then come all over me, like he was saying, *"fuck you"*. He said I was trash, *man-trash*."

"And you believed him…" said Melly.

"I hate myself for doing that." Talish said. "Mama got sick and went to hospital when I was twelve. He came home from seeing her one day and pinned me to a table. And then he fucked me, fucked me hard and horrible; he stabbed into me, he cut me. I bled real bad, and he was bleeding too 'cos he cut himself on me and then he beat me around. He was screaming at me, and cussing me, and thumping and smashing me. I was hurting inside, I hurt outside."

"Oh, fuck," said Melly.

"And *then* he told me Mama was dead. He said she was dead from AIDS," said Talish quietly. "He said it was my fault she was dead. Then he walked out; he just walked right out. I never saw his face again. That's when I first figured all he said was all so much shit. That's when I realized he was shit. I mean real, full-on shit. Huh, but he's dead now. Ha!" she trumpeted. *"He* died of AIDS too, after three months! Got the fucker!"

"Wow," Melly was gripped.

"I've never told anyone that before," said Talish and paused a while. "My grandparents found me and took me home to Berlin with them and that's where I grew up."

"Do you know who your real father is?" asked Melly.

Talish shook her head. "Mama never talked about him. My *Nana* said she was hung up on him for a while but she never met him either. She said Mama never loved her husband; well, you know, maybe one time. But *he* would never leave her. He wanted her money and, fuck, he got it. But, you know, we got it back when he died, too."

"So what about Amsterdam? How did you get here?" asked Melly.

Talish sighed. "It was crack, man. I thought I could handle it but it just got too big for me. I was flying back to Berlin from a trip to Chicago a couple of years ago and, I guess, someone at the airport slipped a package into my purse. The flight included a stop at Schipol; then some guy on the plane had a fit and lost it, like, *completely*, so they threw him off. He started smashing up the seats and that, and he broke a bottle over my arm and they had to take me off the plane too 'cos it was bleeding so hard, and I needed the hospital. I reckon I lost the guy who put the package there 'cos no one ever came looking for me. Next day, I'm out of the hospital and I go looking for an old school friend; when I open my purse, I find all these rocks; hundreds of them. I guess I haven't really looked back since."

"Yeah?" asked Melly. "Did you not want to go back home, to Berlin?"

"I wasn't in any hurry to get back," she said. "I figured I could hang around and make some money selling crack here so I started putting it out and then started to smoke it myself. Well, as soon as I got my first hit, I couldn't stop. It's like that. I was always looking to get a bigger buzz than the last one. I just went through it all; giving it, selling it, and smoking it. By the time it finished, I was one big mess. I just abandoned everything; all the people I got to know and the rooms I had. I stopped washing. I stopped everything and just coasted for weeks. Do you know," she said gravely, "this is the first bath I've had all year. I'm so fucked all the time; I can't be bothered with anything anymore. I just don't give a shit."

"And you think you're not strung out on it?" he asked. "After all that."

"Hey," she stopped. "Dealing it was a fuckin' revelation. I saw all these people around me goin' under. I didn't want to be like them, stealing and stuff to feed the habit. I pulled myself off it."

"That's bullshit!" said Melly. "You still hunger for it."

"Not as much as I could," she protested. "I use it so's I can run away; I enjoy the buzz. You can't beat it! But I *can* keep away from it."

"So why are you still in Amsterdam?" he asked. "Why don't you go home?"

"*Scheisse,*" she said, "they couldn't see me like this. Not my people. I couldn't do it. I'd never live it down. I've never been in touch with anyone there about it. I don't belong there any more. It's that guilt thing you were saying. I guess I'm, I dunno, *missing.*"

"But you got clean clothes now!" Melly said.

"Yeah!" Talish thought for a moment. "But I got to get to Berlin and sort my life out. I forgot what I was doing when I left. I don't know where to start picking up the pieces."

"So that's where you want to go, Berlin?" asked Melly, glowing in the discovery of a home and destination.

"Yeah, there. Or some field in Arlon!" she announced.

Melly was taken aback. "I don't understand."

"That piece of writing," she continued, "it was getting good! I mean, I was reading it; I saw it in your pocket and I thought I'd try to find out who you were. I really liked the picture of me kneeling on top of you. I was wondering what it felt like, you know, to be in control like that!"

"So you stayed off men?" he asked.

"Look," she said, "I've never felt good enough about me to let anyone in and no-one has turned me on."

"You don't fancy guys?" he asked.

"Yeah, sure I do. Some of them are cute and that, but I've got this thing about what happens once men get a hard-on. It just takes over their mind and they get all heavy with it. No, they've never turned me on. Ha!" she laughed. "I've never been turned on, but your story turned me on. Well, it did, to start with; then it got really out of hand. You know you got it wrong about how crack hits you. It's clear you never used it. You wanna try some?"

"Fuck off, Talish," he said. "Go on, listen to yourself." Melly was finding himself having to justify *not* taking crack. "You're telling me you fell down a hole and now you're telling me to jump in it with you. I've never done crack and I won't because I've seen too many people wasted by it. It's one-way and you know it. What are you trying to do? I ain't joining your club, you get it?"

Melly was feeling panicky. He wanted to change the subject. He was severely out of his depth and now it was time for him to change direction. He had been an observer to Talish's pain, he had watched over her for a couple of days but, now, he was being offered temptations; temptations he would normally resist. This girl was tempting him. Was there anything else on offer, he wondered, other than the knowledge that he could share her plight or that he should follow her down a path to self-destruction?

They nibbled at the sandwiches and drank coffee.

"Now you sleep," he said and moved a curled lock of hair off her eye.

Talish looked at his throat regretfully and, taking one of her large sleeves, placed it on his tongue. His saliva moistened the absorbent cloth and she wiped the scratch with it.

"I'm sorry." she said, tearfully, and lay down. "Look," she said, "who are *you*?"

"I'm probably everything you think I am," he said with mock triumph. "Who do *you* think? Who would you like me to be?"

"I don't fuckin' know." Talish looked pained. "You're weird. I mean, you come here like some lost soul; you get stoned all the time and you just watch. I've seen you during the week, just sitting there, coming on like some missionary who's about to start selling Jesus. Like, you're casing the joint. I mean, why are you here? You don't belong here, you know. You writing a book or something?"

"Well, yeah," said Melly considering the idea. He felt self-conscious. "Call it research."

"That's crap," she said. "I don't believe you. Where's the book?"

Melly nodded toward the notebook.

"That?" Talish mocked. "That's garbage. That's not a book. And if it is, then stop 'cos you ain't writing stuff like that about *me*."

She grabbed the notebook and hurled it out through the open window. It slid across the narrow, cobbled towpath and stopped by a tuft of grass. A touch further to the left side or the right side and it would have sunk, without ceremony, in the canal.

"You wanna write," she stated, "then write about real life, not some perverted thing. You wanna research, then get *involved*."

"Books don't have to be fact-based," countered Melly. "They can be pure fantasy; it's called fiction."

"Yeah, well start again, okay," she said. "And don't include me."

"I *have* to include you," said Melly. His eyes began to water.

Talish looked at him severely. "Why?" she asked.

"'Cos you're the reason I'm here," he said. "You're the reason I came back to Amsterdam."

In the cold light of day, this explanation seemed very improbable, yet it was the truth, as Melly knew it.

"What?" Talish was incredulous. "Did you go all the way back to London and then come back for me? I don't believe you."

"Well I'm not going to try to convince you," he said. "Maybe I just wanted to spend some time with you. I mean, I'm glad I have. But there's still stuff I have to do. We're not finished yet."

"Hey," said Talish knowingly. "We haven't *started* yet!" She was sounding threatening. "You married?" The words intruded on Melly's conscience.

"Yeah." Melly sounded a note of regret.

"Got kids?" Her tone was insistent.

"One," he admitted.

"Well, then, fuck off back to them," she said. "I'm sure they need you. You sure as hell don't need me."

"Hey," said Melly, "that's for *me* to decide. I know I'm not staying long; I just want to help out."

"Oh, this is your God trip again," she mocked. "*I'm here to save you!* Fuck off."

"Please don't tell me to fuck off; not yet." Melly's eyes moistened.

"Listen *arschloh*," she screamed at him. "I'm not telling you to fuck off; I'm telling you *I'm* wasting your time, *therefore*, fuck off."

"No," said Melly.

"Well then," said Talish, challenging him. "Burn me another rock."

Melly sighed. It seemed to him that whenever crack was mentioned, Talish's thoughts went to using it. Unstoppably. Like, whenever cannabis was mentioned, he could not resist it either. And not only that; it seemed that whenever they'd talked about anything which brought on anxiety to either of them, using a drug became the cop-out.

"Aren't we both just a bit pathetic?" he said, a look of resignation in his eye, and then, under his breath, "There's too much running away going on here. But it's not really running away; it can only ever be hiding."

Melly again performed the ritual blowback with Talish and, very soon, she lay comatose and blissful. He took this opportunity to jump up and out of the hotel to collect the cleaned leather coat. He was confused and his ideas were evaporating. He wanted to stay longer. He *so* wanted to score with Talish. He wanted to score now, today, yet knew that this was extremely unlikely.

"These things take time," he thought. "One day, when she's feeling better; I'll have to wait for that one."

The afternoon air was still fresh in his lungs when he returned to the pungent environment that was their room.

"She's still a bit rank," he thought, looking down at her. "And wait? Wait for what?"

Again, he had only a fantasy of what she might be like, and of how she might respond sexually. She might not and she probably wouldn't.

"More likely *couldn't* respond," he thought. "Why on earth do I think she would? I'm no catch; nothing hunky here about me! Why should she even want to? Bedding her is *my* fuckin' hang-up. She's probably got so many other things to think about. Shit, I'm spending too long with her. I ought to just get out now and have done with it all."

He thought that, maybe, he wanted her gratitude. Bingo; that was it! He wanted her to *worship* him. He wanted to be appreciated, physically appreciated. But doing this for Talish and expecting gratitude in return was too much like buying her affection. He shuddered at the thought. *That* would definitely not turn *her* on.

This one...*this one was not right.* And what was more, he was getting it wrong. Wrong in the sense that he was playing with a girl's emotions for his own ends; wrong in that he was about to cast her adrift to find her own way home. He could so easily have driven her to Berlin but it would have meant meeting her people and that, he felt, was too intimidating and might incriminate him. He didn't want to get involved with her any further. He didn't want to have to explain to *her people* where he had found her, what he had done with her and, perhaps, to her. He did not want any kind of publicity that Jean might get to hear of. He preferred to remain anonymous in all such matters. Nothing, he felt, should tie him to her.

"No-one ever hears of the observer, only the participant," he thought.

And he wanted to keep Jean; she was infinitely more preferable. Over the years they had grown to suit one another well; each gave the other what they needed. Except, that is, for sex. Peter's had been an exceptionally traumatic birth which overwhelmed Jean both physically and mentally; so much so, she lost interest in sex and had completely avoided it ever since. She remained affectionate and loving, just not sexual. It wasn't made into a big thing; Melly quietly accepted the fact, knowing that arguing would be pointless. One does not confront a mental block or hope to dislodge it, or dissipate it, by yelling.

But *he* thought about sex a lot. He had *always* thought about sex a lot and, now, it was denied him; absolutely. Out of frustration he found himself indulging anywhere he could, whenever the coast was clear. He wasn't rampant, just a bit of an opportunist indulging in a bit of free love if ever he met it. And, provided it was sex alone, he considered it no threat to him or to her. Jean understood his motives but remained forever ignorant of any of his associations or any of his successes. On a couple of occasions over the years, when he found a woman who really turned his head, he saw the signs early and was merciless. Aware of his own weaknesses, he would cut her off cruelly, give no quarter, refuse to even consider the possibility of leaving Jean and refuse to get involved; he would quit while he was ahead.

The worst thing about the revolution of '69 was that sex was up for grabs and he'd never accustomed himself to it. He was too jealous a man to share his women with others. He could never read women's motives, or work out who wanted sex and who wanted a relationship. Women could be so fickle and Melly found himself missing out on his share, or so he felt.

It was all too confusing. Talish was already deeply under his skin. He felt he was being protective towards her yet couldn't touch her; like, he had no right to. He couldn't wait to touch her and, perhaps more importantly, he couldn't wait for her to touch him.

Oddly, he found her both repulsive and attractive. The tramp was cleaning up and he was growing fond of the woman but there was still some way to go before she was totally clean. Yet, along the way, throughout their short time together, she had made no move toward him; she obviously felt nothing for him. He wanted to cease this relationship before he went over the edge and allowed himself to fall headlong for someone other than Jean. His wife was precious to him. He also knew he could not commit himself to Talish. There was *not enough about her* to make him want to leave any of his life in London behind. And if there were, he was determined not to recognize it because that would have meant commitment, and commitment doesn't come cheaply.

This was beginning to look too much like pre-meditation. *Intent to seek another.* No, he didn't want that; he didn't want that at all. This was, he decided, to be his final time with Talish. It seemed he had done as much as he could. He really didn't want to get it wrong again, so he made a decision.

He walked off purposefully to a nearby travel agency where he bought a one-way air ticket to Berlin, scheduled for noon the following day, and paid cash.

"Done, sorted," he thought. "Just one more night, and it will all be over."

Showing her weathered Swiss passport for the agent, he saw the studio photo of one *Talish Thorensen,* TT…Titi! The picture showed a sullen adolescent with severely scrimped-back hair. Melly felt a chill of recognition pass through him and returned, deep in thought, to the hotel where, using the last of his Panama, he hurriedly put together a strong joint.

Lighting it, Melly looked down at Talish. She lay there, half in and half out of the bed. The dressing gown had slipped around and off her legs. She lay exposed, indiscreetly. It fuelled a lust in him.

"Fuck it," he thought, frustrated by these pressures. "I can leave at any time. If she can't handle it, well, we've only got until morning."

He took out the memento he'd bought in order to examine it. It was *the I-can-stimulate-you-in-three-places-at-once-o-tron*, a thin moulded sliver of plastic. There was a short, curved dildo designed to penetrate the vagina; another, shorter one for the anus and what looked like a lyre, a sprung clip, to stimulate the clitoris. The man in the porn shop relented when Melly returned to buy it. He explained it had been designed by women for women. Melly decided to let Talish work it out for herself. He set it down in the bathroom next to the toothbrush, and picked up his guitar.

"What to play?" he wondered, and began…

"When dawn is breaking, bring the cool, fresh air,
I look beside me but you are not there,
You are gone.

"Don't you forget me and I'll keep my own,
You can go on back, but then come on home."

Melly sang an old song of his, remembering, in brief flashback, the girl who inspired it. He tried another:

"There was a time not long ago,
In a slave market down in Rome
When emperors came and emperors went
With fair young maidens to their home.
Half a drachma, that was the price
To free the Athenian girl,

But of emperors there was only one
Rich enough to buy just her.

"Welcome release in the sunrise
Loneliness is drifting away-."

Melly stopped. Talish was shifting uneasily in her sleep. A film of perspiration on her brow coalesced into a droplet and ran down across her face. She lifted a hand to scratch her hair. She was saturated with the smell of stale sweat and it was not because she was especially unclean. It was because her body was crammed full of toxins and low quality food. Her pores now seeped this cocktail of rejected fluids.

Something John Lennon once said rang in Melly's head: *The only reason our crap smells so bad is because we eat so much shit.* He knew how alcoholics smell but he'd never met anyone whose body so obviously reeked of a bad diet. Within a couple of minutes Talish was awake, groggy and irritable.

"I'm starving," she said.

"What do you fancy?" asked Melly.

"I want food," she said. "Anything!"

"You can't have anything," he said pedantically. "There's a limit on what you can handle right now."

Talish was in no mood for speculation. "Well then, fuckin' get me something I *can* eat, if you know so much."

She had not eaten, at least had not held anything down for close to a week. Her belly felt better, her diarrhoea had ceased and she had rested, though she wasn't coughing any less. She felt almost fighting fit. She also seemed in the mood for a fight.

"Good evening," interrupted Melly offering to restart the conversation. He prepared a glass of warm honey-water.

"Just go away, leave me alone," she snapped and threw herself into the pillow. Finding that it was damp with sweat, she lifted herself in distaste and in embarrassment.

Melly knew how she felt. He suffered from the same problem. So did Peter. Sweating during sleep, and the feeling of irritability on awakening. He remembered how he dealt with it at home.

"Space; give them space," he recalled. "Don't talk to them for at least an hour. And no questions; it's too much to cope with."

Melly passed her the tumbler and went to run the shower. "We're going out to eat," he said. "Get cleaned up and dressed and I'll see you in the lobby when you're ready." He left without a backward glance.

Talish threw the glass of water after him. It bounced off the door and landed quietly on the carpet. It should have hit the man who was annoying her so much. It should have shattered into a thousand fragments to register her disquiet. But it didn't and her frustration consequently grew. Illness does that. Recuperation does that too; it leaves one with a sense of timelessness, like time standing still. Night had turned to day and back to night again and Talish had lain in bed long enough; she needed to get up and she needed to get out again. She felt the need for fresh air and for a breath of wind.

She was aware of her own odour and she knew it to be unpleasant. She rose and went to the bathroom to run a bath while the shower continued. She used it to wash her hair again and again until a thick lather choked her ears and she momentarily lost her balance. It made her want to lie down somewhere safe.

❖ ❖ ❖

Talish immersed herself in the steamy, watery cocoon behind the shower curtain and thought about Melly and the situation in which she found herself. It was unusual for her or anyone else on the street, for that matter, to be taken in hand as she had been. There were precious few strangers who talked to her, let alone got past brief conversation, so it made her feel rather special to be singled out like this. It allowed her to stop thinking about where her next meal was coming from, and about how much she'd have to hustle to get any money.

She ached from the feeling that Melly had such a dim view of her; it didn't matter to her what he said about his notebook, and how he defended it or tried to justify it; she didn't believe his excuses or his rationale. She was a tramp in his eyes; a disgusting crack-addict. And he had the gall to introduce her as someone offering to blow him off for a few guilders. She had done *this* only seven times before (she had counted) and a while back at that, when she found herself strung out on crack and needing a regular supply. With few other means of generating cash, that was one avenue she chose not to travel for long. Her need to break away from dependence on crack was greater than her willingness to prostitute herself. But she had done both, and with tragic consequence.

Artur was the first casualty, when she readily gave out freebies from her windfall bag of rocks. There were others too, among that sudden influx of new 'friends' who emerged from the shadows and gathered at her feet. But she wanted only Artur. Looking back, she was sure he was never interested in her as a person but, in those days, she wanted him so much that she gave him *special consideration.*

"Special consideration ain't worth shit when the guy overdoses and dies in a pool of vomit," she recalled painfully.

And the bag of rocks eventually became just some small scattering of crystals. As soon as it ran out she was selling tricks on the street. She knew what men wanted for she was well-schooled, but after every single punter, she threw up with the prospect that men should only want her as a vehicle to ride and as a depository for their semen.

Her education, like that of her mother's, never included anything relevant on the facts of life, particularly where it concerned whoring, so it was unsurprising when she fell pregnant by her first trick. There were no more than a handful of punters she had struggled with, and struggle she did; it struck her that the sex was a very violent act where the male dominated and determined any outcome.

One day a girlfriend suggested that in whoring, it was the whore who dominated, the whore who determined, and the whore who made the decisions. That idea ran counter to all that she was led to believe in listening to her 'father'. No-one had told her before. It made her feel so hideously foolish that she stopped immediately. She was far from ready to become a willing participant in this ritual. And she was still too green to realise she was pregnant until she miscarried at five months. She had to feel grateful for some small mercies and there were precious few in her life.

Sex was never something she was eager to find out more about; hell, there wasn't much else she was eager to find out more about either, not in her adolescence, at any rate. It's as though belief in anything was bound to lead to disappointment when it let her down. She became very wary of people and their intentions and, especially, their motives, and would not give of herself until she felt it was safe to do so. Both at school with her teachers and at play with her friends, she was a tough nut to crack; she was very much an outsider and very much a loner. She knew her stuff but could not organize herself to give definitive answers; she was always so cagey, so non-committal, and so listless. It only took the recurrence of one or two indelible memories to tip the balance between caring and uncaring, between showing feeling and unfeeling, and between being alert and inert. That made her dangerously unpredictable and it didn't win her many friends.

And this man, Melly; he was weird. He didn't even *like* her; he was just tolerating her. Talish was not sure whether she preferred that to having him clawing at her as one particularly sicko punter had; at least with him, she knew where she stood. But she didn't have a clue with Melly. All except that he kept issuing orders.

"What happens," she wondered, "when I don't like the orders he's giving?"

And while it was a relief for her to not have to deal with any sexual advances, his lack of enthusiasm in this regard made Talish doubt herself.

Bapu had not been particularly sexual. He and Nana had one daughter only and sent her to a convent school. Whatever Talish's mother had learned there didn't show; it didn't show in her confidence or in her self-esteem. And it didn't show in fidelity either, or so Nana had said. All that her mother had, it seems, was a fine singing voice.

Nana probably went to a convent school herself, and Bapu to a seminary because, even though they took her in, they could never acknowledge that she had been so savagely raped; they never considered such things possible. A hiding, in all probability (and probably well deserved for being so wilful) but not *that*. Certainly not in *their* charmed world.

Talish never spoke to them about the relationship with her father; it was only school-friends who were taken aback when she made mention of any past goings-on. There was a terribly uncertain time when she realized that there were only two of them at school who talked of *a secret understanding* with their fathers. Talish learned to keep her mouth shut; she also learned to keep her guard up.

One other thing emerged. As she grew older she came to resent her grandparents' naiveté and resolved to become independent of them, irrespective of how good they had been to her.

"Titi," Bapu would say whenever she won an argument, "you're such a rebel."

She left home at too young an age and lived unnecessarily alone. This was not solely their opinion; it was now also her own opinion too. Her allowance, paid from her mother's trust fund ceased the day she turned nineteen and would resume when she reached the age of thirty. It was designed this way so as to oblige her to make her own way in life for ten years. Through a network of contacts, she made good the deficit by working in an art gallery. But it wasn't work, really. She just had to put in the time, make the effort to be there with a ready smile and a welcoming glass of wine.

She wasn't sure about the art itself. Whatever it was, it was in vogue in the current decade; she expected it not to be in the decade following – Modernism was like that; it was so easily devalued: Mondrian the canvas became Mondrian the bedspread became Mondrian the doormat. Talish was in Chicago delivering a set of three Braun lithographs from his Gasket period when her life ended abruptly.

But she chose to end it. She was keen to escape Berlin; there were too many there who had invested heavily in her and she had not responded. She knew she was really pissing them off, so it was good to get away; even better to stay away. She wasn't welcome.

Talish lay in the bath with the shower cascading on her. The spray, chilled by its long descent, landed on her as cold droplets. She lay mostly underwater, but whenever her body surfaced, she was reminded of the bitterly cold, stormy nights during winter when there was no escape from the driving rain. A succession of local residents and tourists alike had taken pity on the friendly young girl who claimed she had not yet found a room for the night. When she added that her purse had been stolen, they offered beds, sofas and floors but this all came to an end as Talish lost her ability to charm or to beguile. And often, they would throw her out in the morning; sometimes even earlier, when she gave no sexual favour in return for their *hospitality*. On principle, she would no longer allow others to take advantage of her; both physically and emotionally, she could not bear to confront the male gender.

Dazed, confused, wearied and shamed into silence, she found warm, quiet corners among the alleys of the Old Town in which to sleep. She set up a routine where she'd sleep close to restaurants while heat was generated and beg when it was too cold to sleep. Walking the streets in the early hours of the morning kept her warmer than if she lay still among layers of cardboard. As autumn moved into winter, she acclimatised well. But reducing her crack use made her aware of the elements and she felt the cold much more easily, especially the penetrating cold of windswept rain. Sometimes it was the cold felt in bones when starved of nourishment; crack did that on its way through her system, and she felt the cold when there was no crack but her body craved it.

Talish shivered at the thought and realized the water in which she lay had cooled. Pulling herself up, she pulled the plug and rose up against the rain that fell about her. The closer she came to the source, the warmer it got until she was able to stand upright and heat her head while rinsing her hair. The heat warmed her skull and her brain, melting away her anxieties; it warmed her jaw, softening it; it warmed her shoulders, relaxing her muscles. This allowed her to breathe more deeply.

She gave a sharp cough. There was something there; she could feel a rasp and a clicking noise, if she breathed a certain way. She'd ask Melly about it. He was a clever man and an older man. He'd know what to do.

"Melly…" she thought. The water rinsed her completely and left a puddle of grey water in the emptying bath; she stood out of the spray and gave her crotch a scrub with soap. As she brought up lather, she kept rubbing against and disturbing her clitoris. It gave her an odd sensation, a bit spine chilling and a bit debilitating. She wasn't sure whether she liked it or not. She could imagine wanting to lie down to experience this feeling. She didn't have time for that now, though; Melly was outside, waiting to feed her. And the more she thought about it, the more ravenous she felt.

Talish rinsed herself again with one final all-enveloping blast and climbed out to a fresh towel and the toothbrush by the basin…

❖ ❖ ❖

Melly was struggling to complete a crossword when Talish walked in through the front of the hotel and joined him in the lobby. She was wearing his dark glasses again and was carrying her leather coat. She had put on all her new clothes and, for once, looked very good. Her loose hair cascaded from her head and framed her face in a mass of damp ringlets. The jeans fitted her, not too loosely, and the bright sweat-top contrasted well with the black leather to give her an appearance of vitality.

But healthy she was not. Her face was drawn with exhaustion as if she still needed to sleep for a week. If only Melly had the means to send her to a health farm for convalescence, or to a sauna to cleanse her more deeply. If only he had won millions, not hundreds. The voice in his head asked him if he was doing the right thing. However he answered, it shook its head disapprovingly. It knew him better than he did.

Melly was upset to see Talish carrying the coat. She had, by all appearances, vacated the room. He wondered if she was preparing to leave, and to leave him. It made him feel very isolated and fragile because he did not want her to leave.

Talish moved uneasily and seemed distracted. "I want my passport and my things," she said assertively. "Give 'em to me."

Melly sensed anxiety in her voice. "Sure," he said. "Any particular reason?"

"They belong to me," she said, "I want them back. *Now*!"

Melly caught his breath. "Are you leaving?" he asked, his voice breaking.

He didn't expect to be asking such a question before his efforts to help her were complete. She was, after all, booked on a flight home in just a few hours. Talish did not answer, and she might not have heard him, however, she stood awaiting a response. A dense cloud of sorrow descended on Melly.

"Rescue her?" he thought. "I haven't rescued her at all and she knows it. I've really fucked up here. It's done; she's had enough. Uh, come on Talish, just one more night."

He looked at her gravely, the colour draining from his face, and realized he'd left his jacket in the room.

"I'll go get them," he said, moving to go. "Are you sure you want 'em now?" he asked.

"Yes," she answered simply.

He saw no expression on her face and, through the black lenses she wore, could read nothing from her eyes; she looked ready to leave. Melly walked back to the room, feeling disconsolate, with Talish following close behind. From his jacket, he first took out her passport and identity card. She took them from him and, without waiting for anything else, retreated out of the room.

"Don't follow," she said seriously. "I'll come back soon, in a few minutes."

"You want me to do anything?" he asked, bewildered. "What are you doing? Are you okay?"

"I'll tell you later, Bapu," she said, "maybe." She hung her head and closed the door.

Melly felt the word 'later' sounded very optimistic. He didn't mind about the 'maybe' bit. She had a life of some sort and was living it. As much as he wanted to control her, he knew there were things that were not his business. At least, not yet. He wondered whether she might, indeed, have slipped out of his grasp; he still had her knife. That was enough to make him think she'd return.

He busied himself with cleaning the bathroom. It was not as badly stained as after her first wash and it didn't take long for him to clear signs of her having been there. While he tidied he wondered why Talish had not just taken her things from his jacket herself instead of scaring him like that. Then, stricken by fear, he hurriedly felt for the envelope with the crack-cocaine; it was still there. He wondered if he should he have doubted her honesty? He had, after all, little to go on. Maybe she just didn't think of it. Either way, she was not there and he wondered for how long. His thoughts were interrupted by a knock at the window. Talish stood outside, beaming.

"Can I be you're back-door girl?" she joked. Melly pulled open the curtains and, taking her by the hand, let her in. Once inside, he hugged her. She did not recoil; she allowed this.

"I'm so glad you came back," he said, smiling. "Are you ready to eat now?"

"*Now* I am," she said, "Have you got my medicine?"

"Sure," he said, feeling like a dispensary. "Here are your antibiotics. Here's another glass of Diacalm, have a fizzy vitamin C, here's some multi-vitamins, have a drop of Echinacea, have a drop of St John's Wort."

Talish took each of the potions, one by one.

"Fancy a Thai?" he asked finally.

"Dunno! I'm so full, now," she joked.

It was not Melly's intention to take her for a romantic dinner. The restaurant they walked into that evening made that assumption itself and set a table discretely in a quiet corner with a small bouquet and candles. The waiters danced round them, referring to them as "the gentleman" and "your companion". With the deferential tone having been thus set, the two of them had little choice but to play the game. To object would have been churlish. Melly claimed his right to some light relief.

"We'll have *Yao Wiraj* to start," Melly ordered, knowledgeably, "followed by *Pla Neung Manau* and *Meekrob…*" he glanced across at her, "and *Chiang Rai* with *Phad Thai*."

"Wow," said Talish, impressed. "What's all that?"

"Clear vegetable soup and then steamed fish for you, stir-fried pork for me," he said, nonchalantly, and completing the pose. "And two kinds of noodle."

"Oh, I wanna stir-fry!" she pleaded, her eyes lighting up momentarily.

"Sorry," he said, "That's too strong for your stomach right now. The fish is very light; it's better for you."

Talish looked at him kindly. "Oh, Bapu," she said. "You're so fussy."

"I care, Talish," he said, ordering a carafe of water. "That's all."

Cast into their role, both played their part with little inhibition. They gazed at one another and spoke in brief snippets while playing with their food. The flavours were a revelation to Talish. Sustenance was an even greater bonus. As soon as the soup arrived, she tore apart bread and dipped it, stuffing it into her mouth.

"Relax," he said. "Don't rush it. No one's going to take it from you. It's yours to savour. Slow down."

"Fuck," she said, "Sorry. This stuff is good, uh." and continued to gorge untidily until her immediate hunger was sated.

By the second course, she slowed and gave herself a chance to enjoy the taste. In the candlelight her brown eyes were like magnets to his attention. Periodically, she would gaze at him intently. There was moistness in her eyes; often, whenever she shifted, she would lose concentration and he found himself having to repeat things so that their conversation could continue.

Melly basked in the close attention he was getting. It lifted his spirits considerably to feel appreciated; that's all it was, Melly thought. It was not love; she had no right to love him. Not yet. Why should she? *How* could she?

He thought back to his conversation with Drijs. If Talish was indeed TT, he thought, then there would to be no sex on the agenda, not tonight and not at any time, ever. The things she had told him about her father made that outcome obvious. It relieved him to know where he stood in this matter. It meant he didn't need to try. It meant he didn't need to pitch. It meant he could relax and be himself.

"What was all that about?" he asked, "The passport, the ID…"

Talish looked at him. "I had to get more medicine," she said. "I go every week. I almost forgot. I need to prove who I am."

"Don't they know you by now?" Melly asked.

"Sure they do, most of the time, but it saves hassle to have ID when there's someone there who doesn't know me," she said. "It was like that tonight. Sometimes it takes ages to clear. Tonight was cool. Thanks."

"Thanks for what?" he asked.

"The clothes, man," she said. "They treated me fine. I forgot how it feels to be treated like a human. People can be so shit, you know; when you're dirty, when you got old clothes on."

They finished their food and Melly found Talish tapping her foot impatiently.

"What's the matter," asked Melly. "Are you looking for another rock?"

"Not right now," she said, hunching forward.

A veil of perspiration formed on her nose. She looked down towards the table and closed her eyes.

"I can't bear it," she said suddenly. "I've got to go and lie down. I gotta get out of here."

Melly wondered what the problem was; perhaps it was the chillies. Spicy food, he knew, was good for sweating out a fever yet he wondered whether Thai food was a good move on a tender stomach. Now, he concluded, it was tiredness. Her body clock was ticking strongly and she was in need of sleep. She reached out and clasped his hand with both hers. They were hot, clammy and trembling.

They walked back to the hotel quickly; it was not far away, though exposed enough for Talish to continue to wear the shades. She looked incongruous in the dark night, shielded from a non-existent sun. But this was Amsterdam and, like London, spawned international poseurs who wore sunglasses everywhere. Melly knew she was not posing (that was *his* role) but he now fully understood just one of the many reasons people take to wearing dark glasses at night, since *he* never did. She was clinging to her anonymity, irrespective of the time of day. He could see she did not wish to be recognized by anyone. The fact that her odour was no longer so pronounced was a big help. Any identification would have to be visual only. Melly thought the coat would be a give-away but, so long as she didn't actually wear it, she looked nothing like the girl he had first met.

They halted within a few paces of the entrance. To bring her though the lobby would have identified her as a guest and a non-paying one at that. They had been here before; Talish knew the drill but, for no good reason, Melly outlined her next move.

"Talish," he said, "go round to the back and come through the window."

Talish was shaken by the suggestion. She was, after all, his dinner guest.

"Am I still not worth anything to you?" she asked. "When do you get to see me as someone who's worth anything, anything at all? Can't you get a larger room? Where are *you* gonna sleep tonight?"

Melly was resolute. "What? And pay twice the price. Nah!" he said. "I'll be okay for sleep - don't you worry about me. We're leaving here tomorrow anyway."

"You cheap fucker," she mocked.

Melly returned to the room and, leaving the light switched off, opened the window for Talish to climb through. She threw down her coat in a heap by the bed, tore off her sweat-top, as if freeing herself from some kind of bondage, kicked off the trainers and climbed out of the new jeans. Then she poured herself onto the bed, curled up like a foetus and pulled the duvet up over herself. She took short, irregular breaths and was clearly distressed. She did not sound well.

"I'm scared, Bapu," she said quietly. "Come, lie with me. Hold me close."

Her voice wavered. She looked up at him and shifted to give him room.

Melly searched for all her belongings in his jacket and set them on the bureau. He also tucked the airline ticket into her passport. Talish looked up when she heard the flick-knife clunk against the wood.

"What's that?" she asked, peering at her passport.

Melly was taking off his shoes and jeans. He put his smoking paraphernalia on the bedside table and lay on his back beside her on the bed. She turned over and cuddled up under his arm, her knees bent up against her chest. He gave her a squeeze.

"Sshh," he said, hoping to pacify her and hoping to change the subject. "Okay," he continued, "time to ask you…"

"What's that?" said Talish. "Ask me what?"

"Well," said Melly, "you've eaten a bit, you've rested a bit, you've had a wash, you got some clean clothes and, maybe, you don't feel so shit. What's next? What do *you* want?"

"What do you mean?" she looked worried.

"What do you want to do now, tomorrow, next week," he said. "You got a dream? I wanna hear it."

Talish immediately let out a miserable wail and clutched his tee shirt tightly.

"No, stop," she cried. "Don't say any more. You talking about tomorrow, aren't you? I don't wanna talk about tomorrow; I wanna talk about now."

"Yeah, now," said Melly in consolation, holding her close. "Talk about now."

She was very light and, to stop himself from crushing her, he loosened his grip.

"No, no," she protested and nestled in as best she could.

Melly massaged her back, trying to warm her and felt the sharp bones of her curved spine interrupting his caresses. He kissed her on the forehead and tightened his embrace.

He started again. "Tell me what you'd like to..." He stopped. "Is there anything you want me to do for you?"

"Why do you keep saying that?" she countered. "You're going aren't you?"

"Okay, listen Talish," Melly announced, "You're going home tomorrow. There's a flight to Berlin in the morning. I want you to be there."

"You can't say that," she protested. "I can't go there; not like this."

"Not like what?" said Melly, "You're looking fine. Your clothes are there, you look good."

"You coming too?" she asked. "I don't want to go to Berlin alone. Take me home with *you* - where do you live?"

Talish thought about the hopelessness of what she'd just said and knew instinctively that the answer would seem like a resounding rejection.

"What are you talking about?" said Melly. "No, you cannot. You have to go to Berlin. You know they'll be very pleased to see you home."

"But my home's here. It's here with you," she protested.

Melly looked at her. "Bollocks," he said, "You know it isn't. Get real!"

That was it. He recognized the nature of what she was saying. He was glad she was flying out in the morning.

"You know," he said, "I really want to stay, I want to stay a long time, but I can't do you any good 'cos you need a doctor, and you need a home, and you need warmth, and you need help. I can't give you that. Just let me point you in the right direction. I want you to get better; I want you to get away from Amsterdam. Don't you want that?"

"Why can't you stay with me?" she asked poignantly. "What's wrong with me?"

"Nothing's wrong with *you*," he said honestly, "You're a lovely girl, I really like you, but you must go back to your people and pick up the pieces. Your Nana will help you, she'll forgive you everything; I'm sure she will."

"Yeah," said Talish solemnly, "and what about *me*?"

"I don't understand," said Melly. "What do you mean?"

Talish paused for thought. "I wish I wasn't so scared of men," she said finally. "I mean, I want to be loved, but no man will have me if I don't fuck. But I'm scared, Bapu. I'm so scared." Talish sobbed with big wet tears. "Oh, fuck, I can't stand it."

"It's okay," said Melly. "Relax."

"It's NOT okay," she countered.

The unconnected way she spoke was confusing him. She wasn't making sense. Talish loosened and uncurled herself until she was stretched out alongside him. She turned to lie on her back and brought her knees up, her feet flat against the mattress.

"You're terrible, you are," she sighed, elbowing him in the ribs. "So clever."

"What is it?" he asked.

"You left it there for me, didn't you?" she said. "Now, *take it away.*"

She flopped one of her legs over his, took him by the wrist and laid his hand on her crotch. She was still wearing panties but, underneath them, Melly could feel the *orgasmatron*. He looked at her quizzically. This was *so* unexpected.

Talish looked up at him and smiled a flushed smile, not that Melly could see for the dark.

"You *wanted* me to wear it," she said. "You wanted to turn me on, didn't you? It feels so good, I feel like I'm gonna explode. Take it off me; release me from it. You have a wife; you know how to be kind to her, don't you? Be kind to me. Melly?"

"That's my name," thought Melly. "And where's Bapu?" he asked.

"Bapu?" she said. "Bapu is dead. He was a good man but he wouldn't be happy to see us here, like this. This is not for him; he wouldn't understand. When I look at you, I think of him. The things you do, I think of him also. Look," she said, "I've got my eyes closed – pouf, he's gone now. Will *you* help me, Melly?"

Melly broke into a cold sweat as a burden of responsibility suddenly crashed down about him, weakening him to the bone. With adrenaline rushing through his body he felt curiously detached from his immediate surroundings; his stomach churned and he started to shake nervously. So often when, as at times like these, push comes to shove, he lost his bottle. He *so* wanted to help her but, now, his own considerable store of guilt made its presence felt and invaded his consciousness.

How he longed for a smoke. At that moment, a deep toke on a good spliff would give him just enough detachment to cope with this. But he was out of smoke and there was only crack. Melly took several deep breaths. The air smelled of their combined odours though he was particularly aware of his own.

"Just a moment," he said, rising from the bed.

He had to get some movement in himself; he had to get his brain to relax and chill some. He went into the bathroom and rolled some deodorant in the pit under his arms; it might, he thought, give him the confidence he needed to stop quivering. He also ran a tap and tried to warm his chilly fingers under a stream of hot water. He was gone a matter of seconds and returned only slightly more composed than before.

Sitting down lightly at her feet, he reached under her with both hands until he found the gusset of her panties. She lifted herself slightly to free them and he slipped them slowly up, over her knees, and down, off her feet. Her knees flopped open and he saw the clever sex-aid pressed close into her, looking not unlike an ornate G-string used by girls in a show he'd seen advertised outside one of the strip clubs. He wondered if that was, indeed, what they wore.

"What a thrill *that* must be for them," he thought.

Melly picked the plastic moulding off Talish much in the same way he would pull off an adhesive label. Aware that there were three sensitive areas being addressed, he held her pubic hairs down while pulling the flesh up out of the clip that gripped her clitoris. Talish took a sudden breath and slapped her palms down on the bed uncontrollably. He gripped across the width of the double-dildo and levered it, first out of her anus and, then, followed through by pulling it out of her vagina. He lobbed it towards the bathroom.

Her relief was palpable. She took a long deep breath and pulled her knees up slightly as though giving her fanny a chance to breath deeply too. Melly took a long look at the girl's newfound serenity.

"Can you trust me?" he asked

"Uhuh," she said. "I *want* to trust you."

Melly caressed her thin, inner thighs briefly. "Yum, yum," he declared ravenously as he bent forward and buried his face in the moistened fanny.

Melly loved dining on fanny. Ever since reading Frank Harris at the age of twelve, he was alerted to the relish to be found in taste and smell. Harris was a Victorian explorer who made it his life's work to screw his way round the world; to fuck a woman of every race he encountered and write comparative notes. He came across a tribe in deepest Africa whose chieftain made him a present of one of his wives for the night. He was obliged to take her lest he appear rude and incur the wrath of his host. He wrote something like…*I was aware, in that darkness, of a most awful stench, which overpowered me into submission.* While other boys at school wailed with disgust at the mere idea, read out to excited, huddled groups during break-time, Melly looked forward to a time when he could explore female genitalia and try oral stimulation for himself. He had, since, been with Indian women. Their taste was particularly bitter;

the smell of coriander hung on them and oozed out of every pore. He had been with alcoholics; gin-soaked and gin-flavoured. And he had been with heavy smokers; sour-tasting, stale, wet ash-smelling smokers.

Talish had sweat the smell of which he found quite unpalatable, despite the number of times she had washed recently, as if she was ingrained with the smell of the street, much like the bollard he had leaned against. But she oozed other juices too, from within, which had both an uncommon sweetness and incomprehensible familiarity; a familiarity that relaxed him completely and a sweetness for which Melly developed an immediate and insatiable appetite.

He stroked, caressed, rubbed, and pinched, and licked and sucked and chewed her thoroughly and longingly. He now understood completely what Harris meant when he spoke of *worshipping at their altar*. And, as if in prayer, Talish cupped her hands over his ears and held his head in place, accepting his homage.

Talish was glad the *orgasmatron* was gone from her. It was a great experience but an almost annoying one too. At times, when she had it in place during the meal, she found she could force it in and out by flexing the muscles in her vagina. And when she did, its grip on her clitoris grew too painful, and the fear of shitting herself too real to allow for concentration or clarity of thought.

Now, as she lay with eyed closed, another pair of hands touched her with tenderness and in ways only *she* had touched herself. But they did more; they were able to do much more, and she resigned herself to the sensation. No longer did she need to imagine a lover. This was all really happening and it was not harsh, nor was it vile; there was no anger and no retribution. This was not the kind of sex she had ever experienced. She was not enslaved to this, she was free; free to be kissed in places she believed no one would ever want go; not go with her, at any rate. She was, after all, trash. She knew this kind of thing happened between people but never was her due because she was not worthy of it. Yet, here she was, with a man again, but with a different role to play.

She lay, basking in this man's selfless attention. This man, who now gnawed at her so knowledgeably, who seemed to be dining, and relishing every mouthful; and *she* was the meal. And what an *appetite* he had! A shiver of delight passed through her as she thought this; a shiver that coalesced with all the other shivers that streaked through her, shaking her and warming her. Her scalp tingled; the hairs on her legs, on her arms and on her head waxed and waned under goose bumps that rose and subsided.

She felt his mouth closing around her and instinctively flexed her vaginal muscles as she had earlier with the dildo. At that moment she felt his face draw hard against her crotch as her 'lips' sucked on his. She relaxed again to free him. Melly came up for air.

"Thanks for the kiss," he grinned.

"You're welcome, thank *you*!" she whispered, surprised at her own ability and at his recognition of her intent.

Melly resumed for a while longer, taking long, deliberate licks across her thighs and across her belly, across places where she did not expect to feel anything. But these were sensitive areas and Melly knew them well. He was not finished and would not finish until, he fancied, she could die in ecstasy.

"Please stop; stop now," Talish said weakly.

She was happy and she was delirious, perhaps, for once. She could take no more. Melly wondered if that was *it*, for he did not want to stop. He stretched full-length alongside her and embraced her. She nestled into him; her arms tucked up against her chest, and lay in a glow, exhausted. Calm descended on the room.

Talish was first to break the warm silence.

"Is that sex, then?" she asked, almost philosophically.

"That, Talish, is me *adoring* you," said Melly. "You've got a glorious fanny. I love it. I've spent a lifetime searching for a fanny like that!"

"You're mad," she said.

"And there's more," he said, pulling away. "How about this…?"

Through her tee shirt, he cupped her sunken breasts, caressing them and rolled her hardening nipples between his fingers and thumb, pinching, pulling, scratching, and gripping. She smiled contentedly. He reached down and rolled the tee shirt up over her head and left it on her arms, above her. She was not wearing the bra; the darkened nipples against her lighter breasts guided him in the darkness. He took them in turn and gave each a long, hard suck. He licked the pit under each of her arms and nibbled on her skin, biting gently into her flesh and muscles.

He was now so used to her smell that any new odour simply added to the sum of his experience, and to what constituted her overall scent. There was still clear evidence of toxins in her bloodstream; toxins that now issued through her pores, but Melly found the raw foundation of her smell and her pheromones irresistible.

"That's terrible; you're *so* perverted." she giggled.

"No, I'm not," he protested. "Do you not like it? Perversion is in your head," he continued as she nodded, "This is *you* I'm making love to –."

"*Making love*?" she sighed scornfully. "You don't love me…"

"I could," he said to himself whilst hoping that no-one was listening.

Melly licked the nape of her neck, he licked her under the chin, he licked in and around her ear, and he licked and sucked her closed eyes, her nose and her chin until he found himself face to face with Talish. In the darkness, he could make out she was mouthing something to herself, deep in concentration. He bit her lower lip gently, he licked her teeth, and he licked her gums.

Talish was thinking about how she might prolong this pleasure and how she might prolong it indefinitely. In her experience there was never a man such as this. She determined not to let him slip away, not now that she had found him. There was a prayer she had learned at the convent, concerned with the sacrifice of all worldly goods in exchange for humility and some kind of glory. Talish let go her great distrust of all things religious and promised to abandon her life in Amsterdam and leave the past behind her, if only she could stay with Melly, and if only he would stay with her. She was reciting it when she realized his lips were on hers.

Talish opened her eyes wide, clasped both sides of his head and rolled over onto him. Then she kissed him. It was not often Melly met a woman he liked to kiss or who was right for him.

"It's not training that makes it good," he thought, "it's the suppleness of the jaw, the fullness of the lips and the nimbleness of the tongue."

All of these made a difference. Kissing Talish was meant; it was meant like there was nothing else in the world, ever, that mattered or existed. In his mind's eye, the two of them floated as one, joined at the mouth, gyrating in zero gravity. It was not so much passionate as all-consuming and, quite simply, perfect.

Melly stopped; he needed to stop and to draw breath; to hold her, just hold her close and bask in the glory of it all. This was *their* bed; he had *this* woman, and she was for *him* to hold. Finally.

"Perhaps not for ever," he thought, "but, at least, for now."

⁂

As Melly lay with Talish, he began to think about what she said of her mother's illness. He wondered if she contracted HIV *before* giving birth to Talish or *after*. The virus can have a lengthy incubation, sometimes as much as ten years, before developing the syndrome of anti-immune deficiency, which cannot protect the body and prevent it from succumbing to illness and disease. Even then, the secondary ailment need not necessarily kill immediately; some suffer a prolonged illness, which brings death after many months. Melly needed to know if Talish was a carrier of the virus, be it at birth or from the time with her father, or from the punters she allowed to fuck her. Plenty of people contracted HIV without developing AIDS. As with cancers, some bodies develop them despite a healthy lifestyle while others never bear a trace despite years of stress and abuse. He suddenly considered the likelihood of Talish injecting herself with cocaine, amphetamine sulphate or heroin and sharing needles in the process. She had not made mention of it and he rested in the vain belief that she had not.

"You either get it or you don't; you either live through it or it finally gets you," he thought. It was such a lottery. But unlike cancers, HIV was highly infectious and moved on to another victim by entering the bloodstream. Melly faced a dilemma. On the one hand it meant his having to use a condom for any further exploration of her suppressed sexuality, and he had none with him, while, on the other, he had never yet used a condom when having sex. He trusted the women with whom he dallied to take care of contraception. He was, after all, only ever passing through and if they didn't realize that he would be gone and out of their lives after breakfast, if not before, then that was their problem. *Fuck 'em and flee* had always been his guiding principle.

He absolved himself of all responsibility, until now. At this moment, he lay alongside a girl who was a willing participant to his endeavours, someone who now genuinely turned him on; someone who, although but a shadow of a former self, could be nurtured back to a fuller life and to a fuller shape.

"And, oh, that she should extend gratitude, or show appreciation, *forever*," he thought with self-satisfaction.

This relationship held more promise for him than the sexless one he was in currently; here, he had the opportunity to start again, afresh, and anew. And if there was a risk of infection attached, if he were about to sign his own death warrant, then it was more than compensated by his new feeling of fulfilment. He felt fulfilled to a point beyond which he could die content, knowing that he had done Talish a huge favour. Such was the extent of his feelings and such was the blindness of his infatuation. Talish interrupted his thoughts.

"So you're not going to fuck me, then?" he heard her ask.

Melly feigned a philosophical response while wondering where in the hotel he might find condoms at the dead of night.

"Sex doesn't have to be about fucking all the time," he said, stalling for time. "There's plenty of time to fuck. What do you want? That I should just bang you, get my pleasure and fuck off? You *know* that men lose interest as soon as they ejaculate. You wouldn't want that, would you? Not yet; I know *I* wouldn't."

He believed what he said to be true. He never usually turned down a fuck like this but, in her case, things were different. He had acquired a measure of respect for this girl. He wanted to get it right, just once.

Talish looked at him mischievously. "No! I reckon you're lying," she announced suddenly, baiting him. "You're hiding something. Hmm, and a little bird tells me you got a weenie. You can't *do it*, can you?"

Melly's heart sank. "What little bird?" he asked, prepared, nevertheless, for this challenge. "Trust Katryn to stick in her two-pence worth," he thought. "Why on earth did she do that?"

"I'm talking about that girl in the arcade this morning." she said, "You know, the one who works at the bar next to the cathedral; the one where I've seen you sitting. Didn't you see her this morning? Huh, what does she know about you that I don't? Tell me!"

"You mean the blonde?" he asked, pretending not to know what had happened while his back was turned. He was thrilled that Talish should have noticed him so early on.

"She knows I don't get off on hookers," he said revealingly. "Probably just a bit sore 'cos she didn't turn me on."

"Nah, I reckon, she's right," she teased, "Come on, show me what you got."

"Does it matter what I got?" he asked defensively.

"You can't get an erection, can you?" she assumed. "Yeah, that must be it!" Melly detected the faintest hint of dejection in her voice.

"Yeah?" he sneered, "What's this then?"

He picked up her hand and placed it on his crotch. Through his briefs, Talish felt an undeniable and sizeable firmness. It shocked her into withdrawing her hand quickly.

"So why aren't you waving it in my face?" she asked.

"Do you want me to? Is that what you expect me to do?" he said smartly.

"Every man I been with wants to wave his fuckin' dick in my face," she replied. "And you. Your story; I mean, you're just like them too, aren't you?"

Melly's heart sank at the prospect of his innermost thoughts being paraded in front of him and adjudged. He grew resentful.

"Oh, really," he said sternly, "Aren't I *just* like them? Well, fuck my story; it's a fantasy. It's *my* fantasy, okay? But reality is different, you know. It can be better. Isn't *this* different to what you expected?"

"Yeah, wow, I *never* expected this," she said, perking up. "I've never been treated like this before. Look, I'm sorry. You're lovely Melly; you're so good to me. I want to keep you." she said and hugged him.

"*Keep me so that I can worship you*," said Melly. "That's a great job. I like that. Let's sleep on it. C'mon, we got things to do tomorrow."

"Like?" she asked.

"Like going to Berlin…" he replied.

He still had the option of cancelling her ticket and driving her home to her grandmother in his own car. He chose not to reveal the confirmed booking to her; at least not until the morning. He might want to change his mind though this did not seem likely.

They cuddled up close and fell asleep quickly, breathing in unison, rhythmically and contentedly. Talish did not sweat that night. Whatever stress it was that had caused her to sleep uncomfortably before, was missing now. Melly did not sweat either. He too, for his efforts, was awarded a peaceful sleep.

Talish awoke first and hid deeply under Melly's arm, shielding her eyes from the light of an incoming morning. Not for a very, very long time had she felt so secure and so wanted. Her mother had been the last to show tangible affection, what with both Nana and Bapu being somewhat less tactile than most Greeks. She wanted to keep Melly and wondered how she might get him to stay with her and not return to his wife. This was a catch too good to let slip.

Talish knew Melly's fantasies; she knew he wanted his dick sucked. He hadn't said so, but she knew he'd appreciate it.

"Men do appreciate it, don't they?" she thought.

That was all she ever heard about. *Cocksucker* was part of the vernacular. It was expected. It was the only sexual act she knew how to perform, though some of the things Melly had introduced her to seemed worth pursuing further.

Through his sleep, Melly had garnered his strength and a morning boner was developing. Talish could feel it growing beside her. Soon he'd wake; she half-expected him to start waving it around and demanding relief just like her 'father' used to. But Melly? Melly was different. *He* didn't hate her. He had been particularly good to her, and respectful. He also smelled different to her father. She had grown to hate *his* smell and his unwashed penis wiping across her face. To think that she had been obliged to pay homage to *that*?

Talish felt unusually comfortable with Melly's odour and concentrated her mind on a winning move. She had not had sex *willingly* with a man for a long, long time. Could she remember what to do? Did she recall the fine line between pleasure and pain? So often, her father would slap her hard across the head or claw at her cheeks and temples or pull her sharply by the hair and berate her for being too brutal or too insensitive. She wondered why she had not seized an opportunity to slice off his dick with a carving knife and have done but, she thought, "When you're a little girl, you don't know and you're so, so scared." She thought back to Melly's story and tried to work out how *he'd* like it. Throwing caution to the wind, she put her hands inside his briefs and pulled down his foreskin. With her eyes closed and fearing the worst, she wrapped her mouth around him. Melly awoke with a start.

"Talish, stop." he said, struggling to gather his other senses. He was still tired and under-slept. "Stop. You don't *have* to." He pulled himself free of her.

"But I want you to *want* me," she said, confused. "Don't you like this?"

"I do," he said, "believe me, I do."

He was not lying. He both liked it and wanted her to continue; sometime, though not just at that moment.

"Just don't feel you *have to* any more," he said. "Only when you *really* want to; when you truly enjoy it, the way I enjoy you."

Talish sighed a long, relieved sigh and lay back in his arm, grateful that he understood her so well. Still, the memory of the *orgasmatron* haunted her; she was prepared for an alien body inside her and wondered if Melly had any intention of being that alien. She looked around to see if the dildo was close by but it was out of sight.

"Why are you carrying Viagra?" she said finally. "I saw it in your pocket."

Melly reflected. "I dunno," he said. "There are a lot of weird things in this world. I made you a present of one with the stimulator. Seems to have helped you a bit, what do you reckon? I don't know. I've never used it. I just, er, got it. Picked it up 'cos it was there."

Talish reached over to his jacket and found the blue pill in a pocket.

"Try it," she said. "I dare you to take it."

"Dare?" he said. "You want me to get a solid erection. Do you know what that will do to me? From what I hear about people who have used it, it's life changing. Old men looking for young women like fucking studs. That's too dick-oriented for my liking. It's a fucker's pill. I prefer, uh, lovemaking. I prefer to attend to your needs rather than to have *you* attending to mine."

"*Scheisse*," she said. "What are you talking about? I know you; I can tell you wanna fuck. You want a piece of meat you can keep up for ages!"

Talish was making it sound too base, too automatic and too pressured for Melly.

"You won't enjoy it," he said, hopelessly.

"Hey, that's for me to know, and you don't," she said carelessly.

Talish so wanted to break her own resistance and Melly was her key, she was sure of that.

"You said it yourself," she said carefully. "Men lose interest as soon as they come. If you got a fear of that, then it's because you go all limp and can't do shit. You take Viagra; you'll stay stiff and stay interested! What do you think?"

Her eyes sparkled with the eloquence of her argument. Melly did not need further persuasion. He grinned and agreed to give it a try.

"So she's finally propositioned me," he deduced proudly to himself, "hasn't she? And I've accepted!"

If there's one thing Melly valued more than anything, one statement he yearned to hear over any other, it was to be *asked* to make love to someone; to be *invited* to fuck. Maybe it was because he got sex so rarely, so accidentally and so hurriedly that he never could enjoy it. But here, in these conditions, he could. She *wanted* him, she wanted to enjoy him, and she wanted him to enjoy her. It's as though his sexuality was being acknowledged, at long last, and that made him feel great, *just fucking great.*

In the breaking dawn, Melly took the blue pill with some water. Before long, he felt the head of his penis tingling sensitively as blood rushed to fill it. More tingling, more blood; he grew and grew until he felt close to bursting. Solid; indeed, his dick was solid. Implacably solid and unyieldingly stiff, it throbbed mercilessly. While his heart pumped with increasing ferocity, Melly focused entirely on his erection; he could focus on nothing else at all. He was getting increasingly restless and needed relief. His dick needed immediate relief.

Talish watched this transformation anxiously, anticipating the moment he would turn on her as she had come to expect. But Melly did not impose himself on her; instead he lay hoping to control any impulses, and shifted uncomfortably. Talish found herself with space; space to absorb, space to consider and, for the first time, she began to relax in the presence of an erect penis. She picked it out, gingerly, to examine its rigidity and to toy with it. All the while, Melly felt none of the coolness of her fingers and sensed nothing through the roasting he was now experiencing.

"Hey, you're boiling," she said, cranking it like a pump handle.

"Shit," he said, "I need to douse it in cold water. It feels like it's been dipped in acid and I'm burning up. I gotta cool it down."

Talish knew how to cool it down. Her father had, since her infancy, given her strict instructions on how to cocoon it in her hands and mouth. But Melly would not take a blowjob from her and she wasn't really ready to give one. She was, however, prepared to cocoon him inside her.

"I've got a better idea," she offered, "Close your eyes and keep still."

Melly shut his eyes and, without a visual reference to the world about him, he suddenly felt his consciousness slide from the centre of his head down his back and into the end of his erection. It split and both remained there while returning to a space behind his brow. The erection invaded his head; his strength of will lay helplessly imprisoned within the walls of his dick, not interchanged but simultaneously. His mind's eye was the penis and the penis was his mind's eye; his ability to concentrate or rationalize shattered as images of pain and lust sprang into all levels and all locations of his consciousness.

He raised his hands to his head and shielded his brow with his elbow, disoriented, helpless, enslaved, determined and ashamed. It grieved him terribly to have so little control over this situation. It was not the range of sensations he expected nor did he feel he wanted this sustained but, now that the drug was in his system, there would be no respite and not for some considerable time. There *had* to be an upside to this drug and Melly was anxious to find it.

Talish rose and knelt astride him. "Let's try out your fantasy and turn it into reality, eh?" she said and, slotting herself onto the end of the penis, let herself down slowly onto him.

Now, she was in control; now *she* was setting the agenda. Allowing a man, allowing *this* man, to enter her was a high priority. She was still quite lubricated following their earlier embraces and his passage into her depths was smooth and unhindered. And when Talish came to rest hard up against him, when he could slide no further, he reached out to massage her clitoris. She took a succession of short gasps and tossed her head back.

"Oh bliss, man," she said. "What a release. Melly, thanks for bringing me to this."

Talish moved neither sideways nor upwards. She knelt with her hips motionless and concentrated. But it made no difference to Melly what she was doing; whether she was flexing her vaginal muscles or not, for he felt nothing. His dick was unassailable, insatiable and irritable. He did *not* enjoy the feeling though he could sense her exhilaration and her excitement.

"Release!" he thought. "At least *she's* having a good moment."

He looked up at her. The bright morning sun, hidden behind her head, threw a halo through her hair and pierced his eyes with its brilliance. This reversed image of the eclipse contrasted beautifully with the apparition he'd written about in his notebook. This was a moment to remember. He fancied it might be celebrated in a new song and yet, as the words she spoke echoed around his head, he recalled the song he sang earlier and resumed the chorus; it seemed *so* appropriate:

"*Welcome release in the sunrise,*" he uttered in voice,
"*Loneliness is drifting away.*
See, I've come to pay the price
That's setting you free today.

"*No more toil and hardship,*
Slavery's a bygone thing-."
Talish interrupted tunefully…
"*The keeper's got no hold on you,*"
"*You are free you can dance, you can sing.*"

Ah, music! Music is such an evocative thing; it's been known to bring grown men to tears. Haven't peoples have gone to war over the *correct* interpretation of a composer's manuscript? Mountains have been moved; didn't Jericho's walls fall to the sound of horns?

Music has value; people will claim it for themselves and, no matter what the composer's intentions, there will always be someone, somewhere, who seizes on a tune and uses it for their own ends; to rewrite the history of the time or to write the story of the future. Creating carries a responsibility but Melly never believed he would be judged on the things he created. And, as with many of the things at which he had tried his hand, if he wasn't good enough to be excellent, there was no point in carrying on. He wasn't particularly happy with this song but it was complete and he sang it sometimes on the road. Hell, it was just another song in the repertoire of a weak folk singer; there was nothing particularly earth shattering about it.

At that moment, as Talish took up the reins of *his* song, the world stopped turning for Melly. He stopped thinking and the blood drained from his face. It drained from his shoulders and from his arms. A chill, unlike any other chill, closed in on his brain.

"Oh no; no, please. No," the voice of his conscience wailed. He wailed too.

"Can't take me, huh?" laughed Talish, her eyes closing to contain and to concentrate the bliss.

She felt good; good enough to sing out in joy, good enough to tell the most important person in her life about it.

"Oh Mama," she said, "Look, I'm free, I can dance, I can sing. Mama, release… *release in the sunrise*! You always said so. *He* has no hold on me, not anymore!"

Melly cowered back into the pillow. "The song means a lot to you, doesn't it?" he said quietly.

"Yeah," said Talish, "Mama used to sing it to me whenever I came to her, crying after *he'd* finished. She used to lull me to sleep with it. I never knew it could mean so much."

Melly recoiled, his head consumed with the recollection of the participants to his philandering life. He backed into the deepest recesses of his tortured mind, desperate to avoid the inevitable conclusions that were being drawn from the deck and which, turned one after another, now stared back and slapped him in the face. In this game, his was definitely a losing hand. He felt truly insignificant against the world and he despised himself absolutely for having come to this. He was so very disappointed in himself and wanted to run yet he lay trapped, both physically and emotionally.

An image formed in his head. It was of a painting by Goya, *the Execution of the Defenders of Madrid*, in which a man stood, held by soldiers, facing a firing squad. His bilious, white shirt cast him as an innocent; the terror in his eyes betrayed the realisation that, irrespective of how much of a contribution he still had to make to this world, his life would soon be over. Yet in the setting, the knowledge that his death would be that of a martyr made him a willing victim, one who did not struggle with his body but who, instead, tried desperately to reason verbally with his captors, the unbelievers. Now, Melly wanted to run and hide because the only alternative left to him was to offer himself for summary execution. It was inevitable; it was deserved for someone so detestable.

But Talish liked him, Talish was getting used to him, Talish now wanted him to *stay* inside her. Behind closed eyes, she savoured the moment. All that she was experiencing might have been denied her if she hadn't met this man.

But unknown to her, *this man* wanted out; he wanted out, *now*. He did not want to be there, in that hotel room. He had to fast-forward time to *later*, even though *later* would be of no consequence. It would never again be of any consequence. The future was bound up in his past and in *this* present.

His thoughts raced back through time, back to a memorable point twenty-three years earlier and a hotel bar in Rome where he met Mariella. He was at a European Music Fair over five days. Mariella was staying at the hotel too; she wouldn't say why she was there except to say that she was unhappy. Her style and manner showed a huge reserve of class yet it was she who looked at him fondly and told him she knew he would be a very important person some day. She left him wondering why exactly she *needed* to sleep with him.

Mariella was pretty; so pretty, he fancied carrying her around in his pocket, to be brought out on occasion to lie with and be gazed at adoringly. With his ego thus massaged, he quickly wrote her a song about her unburdening herself from a man she did not love but with whom she was, somehow, obliged to stay. Greeks partner for life; most Greeks Melly ever met had partnered for life. But they had affairs, and this was hers. Mariella was captivated by the song and learned to sing it and play it immediately. No-one else who heard Melly sing it afterwards took such an interest; no-one else ever wanted to know the chords.

Mariella was to remain just an opportunist's fling; the four days and nights they spent together were too intense for Melly, and he was glad to finally get away from her and return to Jean. At the end of the Fair, he left without ceremony; in fact, he fled.

So, Talish was the product of their union and it was Melly's intrusion, which had caused her husband to feel such bitterness. Melly wondered whether Mariella had planned it that way; *that* would have made for extremely malicious intent.

Melly was largely unfazed by the idea that he might be screwing his own daughter. He did not have a history of close contact with her, which would have made him, or anyone else for that matter, consider this behaviour unacceptable. She was, in effect, just another face on the street; incest and its taboo, he reasoned, was the way modern society coped with inbreeding and he had no intention of impregnating this girl, at least that's what his conscience said.

His dick, though, had other ideas; *it* was home and dry; *it* was where it wanted to be and *it* thought single-mindedly. Melly became irrational. This relationship with Talish was destined to be short-lived, and he had to keep this secret from her. He could do that if he was careful and he toyed with the idea. Though he never saw his women again, this time he had felt differently.

He dreaded to think that Jean might, one day, find out about Talish. Jean, his faithful wife of twenty-six years. Playing away from home was one thing, but to do so within two years of their marrying? He thought about how much of their life together had been a lie? He wondered if his view of their relationship was truly sincere; he wondered whether his were empty gestures, all of them, after years of continuous infidelity?

His mind trawled further back to the year previous to his meeting with Mariella, to his very first deception. He had long forgotten the name of the young Nigerian refugee who, seeking safety, had clung to him one night in a darkened room adjoining a party in Southampton. She was unwell; she said so; certainly, she was weak. She spoke only a few words of English but, for the few fumbling minutes they shared in the semi-darkness, there was no need to talk. When the darkness lifted, he found he had ruptured himself.

It was an embarrassing time for them both and he remembered laughing it off…

He'd never thought about it; people didn't then but, on reflection, she showed some of the symptoms of anti-immune deficiency syndrome. If she had the infection and had passed it to him, he should have been dead but, perhaps, he was just a carrier. It would have been too late to affect Jean; Peter was already a year old. His birth was full of complications and Jean never, ever, wanted sex again; *that* was why he was with the Nigerian; just a selfish quickie, somewhere quiet.

So, Melly reasoned darkly, he had passed the virus to Mariella who died. In giving birth, mother had passed it onto daughter. As a survivor, it was obvious that Talish too, like Melly, was a carrier but HIV negative. And the father? Her glee at his demise left open the question of whether it was she or Mariella who had infected *him*.

But it wasn't just Talish or Mariella who were Melly's victims; he wondered about all the other associations he'd had over the years and shuddered at the prospect of being the harbinger of death to so many of his anonymous lovers. How many were there who, like he, didn't know and had passed on the virus to other partners? And how long after these had partnered others did anyone notice? He imagined an epidemic with him at the centre, and the thought turned his stomach. His arms now ached and he began to sweat profusely.

Then, he wondered why he hadn't spotted the similarities earlier. *She* sweated at night, *she* had the same mannerisms, *she* had the same profile; there had always been *something* about her that troubled him. And, now, the eclipse fantasy, so much a premonition of impending doom, was becoming a reality. He had to escape this moment. He could not carry his secret alone. He wanted to tell Talish but to do so would be to destroy her, and destroy everything. Hadn't he already done enough damage? What was the advice his father had given him? *"When you got a hard-on, son, your brain's up your arse."* Never a truer word had ever been spoken.

Talish, meanwhile, was ecstatic. "Mama," she called to the ceiling, "my man has come to take me away, just like you said."

Melly groped around for his smoke. It was an instinctive reaction yet he knew there could be no other. He had to forget; he had to escape the present, the *now*, and *any* means would do. He grabbed the pipe and the lighter; a half-burned rock sat in the bowl. Melly did not stop to consider the consequences. Nothing was as important as his wish to extricate himself from the here and the now. He *needed* to be reckless.

"No, no, no," he kept repeating in his mind and crying out loud.

"Oh Melly," Talish said happily, her voice resounding with optimism, "it doesn't matter if you feel you're coming. I *will* want your baby!"

"What?" Melly cried to himself. "The poor, misguided fool. What *is* she on?"

"Titi," he said tearfully, "I'm so sorry."

"Titi?" she said immediately, "what do you know of Titi? Why did you call me that? What do you know of me? Who are you?"

"I know about you," he said quietly. "I know what you want."

Her own words now came back to haunt her. He lit the rock and inhaled deeply. Talish saw him at work.

"Why are you smoking rocks?" she asked, suddenly.

"You want some?" he answered, putting the pipe down.

"Well no. No!" she said, shaking, "We *agreed*, remember. I want to be *here* for this. I want to remember you and every moment with you. Why are you smoking rocks *now*? What's in it for you? Who are you? WHY YOU SMOKIN' ROCKS?"

Talish's voice rose in panic. This was a new style for Melly; she knew something was wrong, but Melly would not answer her.

"What's in his head?" she thought, "I don't understand him. Hell, if he's going for a ride, then so am I," and snatching the pipe from him, took a deep lug herself, held her breath and closed her eyes again.

The sickly smoke hung in Melly's lungs and his nostrils, was absorbed by his blood, and circulated rapidly to his brain. His cheeks hollowed and his body hollowed, as if he was collapsing in on himself. His brain fried, disassociating itself uncontrollably from reality. His head reeled under a crackling storm of electric blue. His heart ached; indeed, his heart felt like it would burst. Every muscle in his body felt as if it died in him at that moment, stripped of will. Melly held his breath and lay inactive until the haze cleared and he saw, with stunning clarity, his feminine self astride him.

He had to reach Talish; he had to hold her just one more time before finally casting her aside. Summoning up all his energy, he raised his shoulders to meet her and enveloped her in warm embrace. He tried to lift her but was powerless; he was now so bloated inside her that nothing could separate them. There was, also, no strength left in his arms with which to lift her off. She sat astride him, united with him by her light weight, oblivious to his trial.

He let the remaining smoke out of his lungs and was taking in air when Talish realized her own lungs could not cope with the inhalation. She, finally, jerked and coughed. It was only a small jerk but it smacked into Melly chest just at the wrong moment. Any other time would probably have been fine but today, in this instant, it was a bad call. His heart was jolted just as the muscles engaged to sound a beat and stopped pumping; just like that. Like when gymnasts stop bouncing on a trampoline by bending their knees against the bounce; suddenly, there is no more trace of a bounce.

Melly's head split with pain, his chest split with pain and he thrashed aimlessly for rescue. That's what he thought he was doing but, really, his arms just flopped helplessly onto her while she, herself, fully embraced him. He nestled his head in against her neck and a penitent tear trickled down his face. She, too, lay her head on his shoulder and, with eyes closed tightly, glowed in the belief that the nervous, lurching man she sat astride was her prisoner, climaxing, and *that* suited her fine. She let go of him and he fell back onto the pillow while she drifted into a delicious haze and flew onward and upward. She now felt complete.

Talish landed some minutes later, shivering slightly and aware that Melly wasn't doing much. He was fully inside her, still, and lay with a look of pained concentration, his eyes tightly closed, and a tearstain on his cheek. She placed her palms on his chest and felt a chill in his skin. He didn't react or respond. He did not move at all. In the brightness of the morning, he looked unnaturally pale.

"Melly?" she called to him. *"Gott hilft mir!* Melly!"

A wave of panic swept through her as she realized that her man lay lifeless. She beat him with her fists.

"Fuck you, fuck you Melly," she wailed, *"Gott erbarme Dich.* Why did you do that?"

She so nearly had him. He was talking about some future and, now, he wasn't going to be there to make it happen. And it was *her* fault, *again*.

"I said I was bad for you," she cried.

These were sobering thoughts and Talish returned to reality and the quiet of their room in the Hotel Sonesta with a rush of adrenaline. She'd been here before. She remembered Artur died on her too. Not *in* her, but in her company. It took an awful lot of explaining to the police, especially since she was incoherent with crack and inconsolable with sorrow, blabbing uncontrollably and unnecessarily. A number of principal characters and players in Amsterdam suffered harassment and arrest soon afterwards and Talish was shunned for a time while they thought to forgive her. It would *not* happen again; she would not be found with *this* corpse. She chose to flee and make her escape good through the window. But first, she had to gather her things and make like she had never been there. She had to take herself out of the equation.

Talish lifted herself off Melly's body and was surprised by the size of the distended penis that finally emerged from her and flopped onto his belly. It made her feel curiously empty to not have it inside her but at least the chilling feeling she had was gone. She pulled on her panties and her jeans, she tied the trainers onto her socked feet and picked up the other socks and panties, which lay on the floor, and stuffed them into her pocket. She hurriedly put on the bra, the tee shirt and the sweat top and, finally, the leather coat. In a few minutes she was ready to leave and looked around the room.

"The bathrobe!" she recalled and took her bottle of pills from the pocket and, going over to the bureau, found her knife, her identity card and her passport, She saw in it the air ticket to Berlin and a wave of emotions flooded through her.

"He was serious about getting me home, after all!" she thought, "He wanted the best for me but, he was such a fool. He came to me and I killed him. Oh, Melly."

Talish went over to kiss him farewell. There was something magnificent about the way the body, which lay on the bed that early morning, held such promise but was unable to deliver. Talish wished she could take it home with her, in her pocket, to bring out, on occasion, and lie with safely whenever she wished. But there were more pressing matters; Melly had money and that's what she needed. She searched through his jeans and found the wad of guilders in the back pocket; she stuffed it into her own pockets and fancied he would have wanted it that way. Perhaps he had some more; she reached into his jacket and found his wallet. It flopped open the way empty wallets flop; too heavy with credit cards and calling cards to be trifling with cash. It was Melly's lifeline to reality. She knew this because a picture of a striking brunette stared back at her from behind an acetate window; it was probably his wife.

Suddenly, she heard the sound of the cleaner outside the door. There was no time to lose; she tossed the wallet onto the jacket and, in a second, had climbed out through the window and closed it behind her. She looked around in concentration and wondered if she had got everything. Melly's discarded notebook lay close to the canal; she picked it up and stuffed it into her coat, sure there was nothing left in the room or at the hotel that might connect him with her. She would be grateful that he had taken such care to keep her presence there a secret.

Talish put on Melly's sunglasses and went off in search of a taxi to the airport. She had a couple of hours to spare but it seemed that flying out of Amsterdam was her safest option; the sooner she could get to the airport, the sooner she would escape the city. There were too many people she had upset in this town and there were none she could turn to for help anymore. Escape, after two lost years, to *do a geographical.*

The maid knocked at the door twice and, on hearing no reply, came in to clean the room. Darla noticed the smell immediately; it was like the smell of burnt plastic. She didn't recognize it but on seeing the pipe, drew her own conclusions. Melly lay lifeless and unthreatening and would have given her a shock were it not for the circumstances in which she found him. She took the time and had the presence of mind to study him carefully; it was all rather romantic and, definitely, one to tell Katryn about. She pulled out her mobile and gave her friend a call, inviting her to view before having to alert the manager. She knew it would take Katryn only take a couple of minutes to get there.

"This," she thought, "is guaranteed to get the silly bitch to shut up about him."

❖ ❖ ❖

Talish walked out from behind the hotel and made for the plaza in front of the Central Station. She warmed in the knowledge that she was going home. She'd need to call, to let Nana know she was alive after all this time. She'd need plenty of care, Melly had said so. He was right; Nana would take good care of her. She may never have understood Talish but she had a good heart and that was all that mattered now.

She dialled Nana's number but there came no reply; worse than that, there was no ringing tone either. Talish dialled and redialled but with no success. She was sure she had the number correct in her head and rang the operator.

"I'm sorry, that number is no longer in operation," said the operator.

These words struck a blow for Talish. She asked if there was any listing anywhere in Germany for her grandmother but there was none. She asked for the number of the family lawyer and was connected quickly.

"Fraulein Thorensen," said a familiar voice, "you are alive; are you well? I am sorry to tell you, your Nana died last year. There is-."

Talish replaced the receiver. She did not want to hear any more. There would be no going back to Berlin. She was not ready to face any of the people from her past yet, none except for Nana and, now, she was gone too. But it's not as though Talish depended on Melly for any decisions he might make on her behalf. She had, very simply, welcomed the opportunity to be taken in hand but, if that was not going to be, she still had herself to turn to.

Talish felt desperately unhappy. She remembered all the people she had lost, especially her mum, and all those she had let down, all those whom she had pissed off and was forever running from. She sobbed quietly behind the sunglasses. At least she still had her memories. Talish fumbled in her coat pockets, lazily at first then, in a panic. She searched each and every one of them, again and again, until the realization dawned on her that her cassette was somewhere back in the hotel room, probably in Melly's jacket. She had to return to get it; it was all she had left that was her mother's; she had treasured it for fifteen years and was not prepared to lose the sound of Mariella singing to her, singing the song that Melly had sung.

Blind with tears, Talish hurriedly made her way back to the hotel. She needed to search through Melly jacket; there was nothing else to be done.

In the distance she could see that outside the Sonesta Hotel the doors of an ambulance were being closed and, even though she hastened her step, the wagon drove away before she reached the hotel entrance. Talish walked in to be met by an ashen-faced manager; this was, after all, his first fatality.

"I've come to meet with Mr. Melly uh -" Talish had no idea of his second name.

"I'm afraid," the manager interrupted automatically, his voice trembling, "the man you come to meet is not here. You will find him at the hospital."

"And his belongings?" asked Talish.

"His room has been emptied," said the manager, "all his personal effects are with him. Are you a relation?"

Talish did not answer but left abruptly. She needed time to compose herself and staying close to the body was the best she could think of doing. That cassette was everything; without it, there was no point, no point at all; if she could only listen to it one more time, just once.

Meanwhile, the air ticket had value and she was standing outside the agency where it had been bought. She imagined that Melly would have approved of her going in to cancel and refund her seat. As she placed another wad of guilders in her back pocket, she realized she now had enough money to go just about anywhere she fancied.

"Melly has made it happen," she said to herself, "the old fool, the fuckin' silly bastard, stupid; fuck you, Melly."

She wasn't sure whether she should laugh out triumphantly or cry bitter and sorrowful tears. Her fortunes may have changed but she wasn't sure whether for better or for worse. An emptiness now filling her belly reminded her it was time for breakfast; it was all she could do for the moment and, fortunately, she felt well enough to eat. Her lungs, though, were not so healthy; she gave out a deep, rough cough and spat out a trace of blood.

Talish shook herself down and went off in search of food.

3

One of the nice things about having an adult son was that his girlfriends could be such great company, especially when they stayed over. Jean loved new blood and she liked to meet new people. She popped the second champagne cork of that particular Saturday morning to top-up Deborah's glass.

"Welcome to the house," she said, proposing a toast. This was not the second bottle in the daylight hours following a night of heavy drinking, it was the second of the day, and she'd only been awake three hours. This was her right; it was the style to which she intended becoming accustomed. A lottery win of £647,364 the previous Saturday had lifted her spirits considerably and she had been celebrating ever since. It was just too bad that eleven winning tickets had to share the £7.1-odd million jackpot. It was a blessing really; not big enough to make her the major focus of attention and the destination for begging letters, and not so small as to be practically useless in enabling a change of lifestyle. There was so much that could be done with a sum like this; all those accumulated debts could be paid off, and that included the house;

no more scrabbling around, having to juggle between treats from the supermarket deli and a new pair of tights. It was, after all, appreciating by a pound every minute, simply by sitting there and gathering interest in the bank. This was a sum big enough to solve all their financial problems; she and Melly could now both stop working and set out to explore the world. Goa, finally, Peru at long last, and New York regularly. Jean was one excited individual and especially so, because the two of them could finally spend some quality time together, long denied through the pressures of work. How she longed for the opportunity to get back to her man, and to rediscover him after many years drifting inexorably apart. Money does that; the opportunity costs of spending little amounts had them squabbling over how best to holiday, and to what extent they could entertain. Now, it didn't matter.

Jean wondered about the look of incredulity that would hang on Melly's face when he found out. It wouldn't be long now; he'd been away a week; the week that she had become fabulously wealthy. He should be back any day, probably really pissed off at coming home empty-headed again. She didn't really like him going away like that; it often took a couple of weeks for him to settle back into his normal routine and she had to work hard to bring a smile back to his face. But Melly would now be a changed man. It would be good to have him not worry about money so much; it would great to fill their time with affordable activity; to wake up to life and not get so wasted all the time. Was it boredom or was it addiction? They could both get away; maybe he would try some rehab; maybe she, herself, should.

"Ha, no more frugality," she thought, "please Mel, darlin', no more frugality."

"What's money for if not to spend, eh Debbie?" she said aloud.

Jean had been saying it all week and thinking wishfully. She deferred any decision on how it might be best put to use; she wanted to wait until she had a chance to discuss it with Melly. She valued his opinion and, on his advice, organized their finances very simply. He paid all the bills from his salary; anything left over was his spending money. She bought all the food, all the clothes, and all the presents, and kept what was left over. They lost track of who had more to spend; it varied from year to year and they bailed one another out when the need arose. If the truth be known, she could have kept quiet about the win and invested it quietly, and without the fuss. She used to joke when they first married, "what's yours is mine and what's mine is my own!" but Jean was not really like that. Everyone had to know, everyone had to share her joy and share in the good fortune. She could be so helplessly generous.

Fortunately, she was also a good judge of character and knew all about fair-weather friends; she was not interested in making new friends just yet and, certainly not while their intentions were obvious.

Deborah answered the telephone automatically when it rang and then passed it Jean with a quizzical look on her face.

"Mrs. Cheval," she said with an air of mock efficiency, "it's for you."

Jean shivered; it was unusual for anyone to call on a Saturday morning asking for her by that name. This was not a business call; it had to be something serious. She knew it was bad news.

Within six seconds of taking the receiver, Jean's grip on reality had loosened. She craned her neck and tilted her head back, her eyes filled with tears, her face paled and she whimpered emptily.

Deborah was at her side immediately, shrouding her with an embrace, and took the phone from her. She found a ballpoint an arm's length away and scribbled some names and numbers.

"Fuck you," Jean wailed suddenly. "Fuck you, Mel. FUCK YOU!" She screamed the words and choked. "Why? Why now? Not now. Not now, Mel."

Deborah watched with widened eyes as her host gesticulated feebly and mouthed words silently through a face creased with pain. She hid her own in her hands and began to bawl noisily. Jean, the widow, looked out through the window at the clear sun, searching aimlessly for a future, and tapped her fingers nervously and impatiently on the wine glass in her hand.

⊠ ⊠ ⊠

Jean flew into Schipol airport and was taxi-bound for a hospital in Amsterdam by two o'clock the same afternoon. She desperately wanted to see her man. There was no way she was going to wait until he was sent back to London in a box. She had to see him, to berate him for dying, and do so before he was completely cold; the very dead look and seem so fragile, the freshly dead can still appear to be listening. She had to curse him for leaving her like this. Everything was going to be great; fortune had smiled on them. *And he had to blow it all.* His heart; she knew it would be his heart, yet she wondered what caused it to finally give out.

Talish was pacing the forecourt outside the hospital mortuary where she'd been told the newly dead lay. She had considered going in and claiming to be a relative but that would have meant her having to show identification; none that she had tied her to him in any way, and she wanted to remain anonymous.

"Besides," she thought, "how am I going to explain how I know he's dead?" It was bad enough her fleeing the hotel room and thinking she had left no trace; she was, for the moment at least, lucky but it would be tempting fate to brazenly return to the victim of their encounter. There were times she was able to talk her way out of, or into, situations but on this one she felt completely out of her depth. She wondered if anyone was out there, actually looking for her?

"The man died on me!" she thought to herself. "I didn't kill him!" Talish felt a hot flush rushing up her back until it enveloped her head. Her singular hope was that someone would call in to identify Melly and collect his things; she would need to ingratiate herself with this person just long enough to get her hands on the combat jacket. Then it was a matter of taking the cassette tape and fleeing as she had originally planned. Yes, fleeing this city! At least, in this eastern side of Amsterdam, away from the harbour, there were no beggars, no one to recognize her looking so cleaned up, and no one to wonder why she looked so transformed.

Talish had no idea how long she would have to wait; a body had already been brought out that afternoon and loaded into a hearse and she'd run over to ask the driver to check the identity of the corpse. The answer failed to identify Melly and she grew sadder, more desolate, and completely hopeless, so she sat down in a huddle on the steps by the entrance and wept bitterly behind her shades.

"Mama," she wailed to herself, "I'll get it, Mama, I promise. I won't let them take it away."

"You okay, darlin'?" a concerned, reassuring woman's voice interrupted her sorrows. It spoke native English.

Talish looked up to see a tall, slim figure silhouetted by the bright summer sun. Looking through her black lenses she had great difficulty identifying anything other than a body; she needed to see who was talking to her and took off her glasses to reveal her reddened, swollen eyes.

"Uh, you poor wee lamb," said the woman, looking at Talish sympathetically. Her voice sounded frail, as if it were about to crack and fall apart. She sat down beside her and placed a comforting arm over her shoulder.

"Someone close?" she continued, shakily.

"Someone I knew once," sobbed Talish. "Are you here too?"

Talish peered at the stranger and was struck by her raven-black hair and wondered if it was bottled. Though well dressed, she carried the telling signs of grief; there were too many blotches in the neck and the cheeks, too much puffiness in the eyes, and too much tightness in the skin to show how she really looked when relaxed.

"Ah, me?" sighed the considerably older woman, "My man; he's dead. I've come to take him home." She closed her eyes and repeated the words again in her head; "My man is dead."

She had cried on the way to the airport, she had cried during the flight, she had cried in the taxi, and had yelled and shrieked at her dead husband as he lay on the mortuary slab. And no matter how angrily she punched him, how mournfully she caressed his cold head, or how bitterly she cried into his paled shoulder, he *still* wouldn't listen. He never listened to her!

She could not coax him back to life; now, she was spent; she just wanted to get away for a while and think about something else. She put her hand to her brow and wept again. Talish gave her arm a squeeze.

"I'm sorry for you," she said, "You miss him, huh?"

The widow laughed sardonically, "Huh, if I should ever had seen him enough. He was always going out to do something or other. This time he went off to see the eclipse. And now he's gone." The woman's words rang with familiarity.

"Mmm, yeah, maybe he did. Lots of people went south to see," said Talish helpfully, and added, "You wanna talk to me about him?" She thought the woman might want to. There wasn't much else going on. She might even know Melly…

Jean looked surprised, then grateful, for the concern the girl outside the mortuary appeared to show. She was in need of a bit of company and, having been thrown into a foreign place suddenly, felt it would be good to share her grief and spend some time with someone who might know a little about where she was. Debbie, on the other hand, had shown she was not very good in a crisis and had stayed in London to sob uncontrollably. Jean wondered whether it was in sympathy or if she was doing it because she really cared. But Deborah was such a recent addition to her life; she'd only met Melly once, so why on earth was she crying so intently? Jean decided that Debbie's were crocodile tears; the girl was not to be trusted and she'd remember *that* when she got home.

As for Peter; the longhair and his father had not seen eye-to-eye since he was sent down from university in his second year for slacking. Long hair, at the end of the Nineties was not a badge as it had been in the Sixties. In those days Melly wore his hair long as a disciple of the hippie revolution; to him, albeit naively, it represented a tolerant, peaceful disposition and the belief that the foe could be vanquished with a loving embrace. It also got him thrown out of a high school that would not stand for deviation from the norm. For Melly, this was a right reclaimed after two generations of cannon fodder had sported dutifully short back and sides. It was a statement against the servile concept of war and uniformity. By the late Nineties, there were many differing reasons for men to wear their hair long. Peace, love and harmony were not among them. Commonly, the Nineties longhair was the brash antithesis to the Sixties ideal just in the same way that the skinheads of the Sixties were fascists and nationalists whose children shaved their heads in the Nineties on their road to Buddhism.

Their opposing values and attitudes caused friction at home and Peter wasn't feeling any immediate empathy for the loss of someone he had come to detest during the last couple of years. He had a flat close by the house but stayed over sometimes when the old man was away.

"I don't want to talk about it," was all he said to his mother. Peter was hard. He could be so unrelenting; so cold and unfeeling, Jean thought.

"Sons don't pick fathers," he would say, "they're just saddled with them. A wife, on the other hand, chooses her husband." He seemed to mock his mother over her choice of husband. It was only fitting, Peter reasoned unsympathetically, that Jean alone should go out and bring back Melly.

"Peter, you're so damned unsubtle and hurtful sometimes. He's your father, damn it!" said Jean. Peter's style was completely at odds to what his father stood for; he would have so preferred Peter to have been a daughter; the more compassionate of offspring.

As a token of goodwill, Peter drove his mother to the airport. He would have taken Melly's car but they couldn't find it parked outside. It was nowhere to be seen and Jean wondered why that was because she was sure Melly had taken the coach. She'd reported it stolen in his absence but had no news back about it. The guitar was missing too, and she knew he hadn't taken it. It was too confusing to contemplate.

Jean was happy to know that the young girl had the time to give her, and to listen to her offload. And she *did* need to talk about Melly; she needed to talk about him to someone who didn't know him and to someone who, grief-stricken themselves, who would make crying that much easier.

"Thanks, thanks a lot. Yes, er. I don't know your name."

"Titi," answered Talish Thorensen, "and you?"

"Call me Jean. Thanks Titi," she continued, "You got time for coffee?"

"Time?" said Talish. "I got loads of time. I ain't going no-where."

"Oh?" said Jean.

"People die," said Talish, "and you rethink your life. I got no one now. It's me against the world. Ha!" and she began to cry again.

"There, there, now. Come on Titi," said Jean, lifting herself up and pulling the girl up behind her. "I'm hungry and I'm thirsty. Are you? Let's go eat."

"I can't, no, uh, I'd like to, but, uh..." said Talish, waving her away. She had time later but, right now, she was keeping vigil on Melly's body and would not desert her post until she *knew* for sure.

"Nonsense, darlin', why ever not?" said Jean assertively.

"I gotta stay here a while, wait for something to come out." As Talish spoke, the large doors of the mortuary closed and a series of loud clunks signified their being bolted shut as the mortuary wound down its business for the day.

"Ah, I see what you're getting at," said Jean, "They'll be open tomorrow at eight. I'm going in myself to organize to get my man home. And you, nothing's going happen now so there's no point in your hanging around here. Come on, I'm starved." She looked at Talish's slight frame under the leather coat and added, "I'll pay!"

"Are you sure?" asked Talish, amazed that she should be scooped up like this again. First Melly, now this woman, Jean; both generous in their own way. "What is it with these English people?" she thought.

"Are you from the mission?" she asked disarmingly.

Jean, clearly tickled, let out a belly laugh.

"Catch yourself on!" she said, scoffing. "What, *animal rescue*? I haven't got time for that sort of stuff anymore. I used to! No; there's more to my life than helping others. I should be too busy enjoying myself, but not now, not for a while." Her voice trailed off into the middle distance she was looking into without focus. "Come on!" she said, snapping back into reality and lifting Talish by the elbow. Talish responded by linking in with Jean and the two women strolled arm in arm aimlessly out of the district and began to talk. Before long, they were talking easily.

They talked a long time and they walked a long way. They talked about the colours in the trees that overhung the canals, they talked about the buildings they saw and how they compared to those in other cities each had been to; they joked and they laughed together. It was good; it was so good that Talish began to feel that this was too good. Jean was an exceptionally personable woman and Talish was taken, swept up in the whirlwind of an easy conversation. None of which they spoke was untrue; none of it was irrelevant and none of it felt superficial.

Jean liked her new friend. She liked her irreverent sense of humour and her deep brown eyes; her moocow eyes. Melly had moocow eyes. Jean felt a surge of tears and clasped Talish closer to her.

"He was such a silly man," said Jean. "He used to sit and watch me. Just look, and watch. And read me. Oh, he read me well." Jean stopped suddenly in her tracks. "Well, I'll be damned. It's the car; look Titi! My God! When did he...? What's he been…?" Her head filled with unanswerable, incomplete questions.

"You want to sit down and have a drink?" Talish interrupted her thoughts.

"I think so… yes," said Jean, steering them into a small bar on a nearby corner.

They sat in the window, eating cake and drinking tea, then progressed, Talish to beer and Jean to wine, and talked more. The weathered Volvo estate threw a lengthening shadow toward them until the setting sun, reflected on its bonnet, blinded them both.

"You know," said Jean, screwing up her eyes, "I can take him home myself, in the car, as soon as I get a death certificate. You know what? He wanted to be burnt in the garden with all his friends there to cheer him off. He was a pyromaniac, and always setting off fireworks; he loved noise. What do you think?"

"Is that what he wanted?" asked Talish. "If it was then do it. Send him up in a rocket!"

"Oh Titi," cooed Jean, "I wish you could have met him, he would have *loved you*."

Jean knew what her man liked; she knew what he used to like. "Fancy a drive?"

"Where do you want to go?" asked Talish.

"No," said Jean, checking herself. "Where do *you* want to take me? Where's good?" She needed a change of pace.

"I'm not from Amsterdam, I don't know," Talish answered carefully. In her own head, she had already left Amsterdam behind but she was well-known in the centre; there were people in and around the Old Town who would not take kindly to her re-emergence after illness in anything other than soiled rags. That was the price she was paying for letting them down; she felt she was no longer welcome.

"Where are you staying?" asked Jean.

"I'm not sorted out yet," answered Talish.

"In that case," Jean was forthright, "come and stay with me until tomorrow. Will you do that? I do so enjoy talking to you. Yes, we can stay at the Grand. I've never been there, but I've seen it and I like it!"

"No, not the Grand," said Talish quickly. "They're so full of shit there." It was too central for her liking. "Let's get somewhere local. It'll cost less too."

"God, you're just like my husband, bless his cotton socks. Tight," chuckled Jean. She always carried the spare set of keys for the car. "You drive," she said, "I've had too much to drink. You *can* drive can't you?"

Talish answered nervously. "I haven't driven for a while. I'm not used to it."

"Nonsense," said Jean. "Just like riding a bike; you never forget. Jump in." She pointed to the driver's side of the car by which Talish now stood.

Talish crunched the gears into a series of lurches, stalls and leapfrogs through the streets of Amsterdam while Jean, as her front seat passenger, rocked about and laughed hysterically. With all the knocking and swaying, neither of the women noticed Melly's notebook bump smartly out of Talish's leather coat pocket and into the well between the seats; then it slid and came to rest on the floor under the driver's seat. Keeping control of this vehicle with its right-hand drive petrified Talish at first but, soon, she was laughing heartily. Her lungs, however, were not impressed by the strain and she started to choke and cough hoarsely.

"Titi, listen to you," remarked Jean. "Are you taking anything for that?"

"I've been using antibiotics; I need to see a doctor," replied Talish.

"You know," said Jean knowingly, "sounds to me like you've got tuberculosis. I've been listening to you breathe. You should go."

Talish drove around until she felt comfortable behind the wheel. She had driven better cars than this; more powerful, nippier; altogether, much better. But enough was enough; she was not keen on driving or being seen to be driving through Amsterdam, close to her old haunts and those from which she wanted to get away. She stopped the car in the shadow of the mortuary where they first met. This is where Melly's body lay and it is where her cassette tape was. Somewhere *in there*.

"Let's get a room here, eh?" pleaded Talish, pointing to small hotel, "I need to rest now. I want to lie down." She felt frail and weak still and wanted to forget about the day. Meeting Jean was fine, but she was no closer her tape and her life would not, and could not, continue without it.

"You poor wee thing, you," said Jean affectionately, inebriated and relaxed.

"Two singles for tonight," Talish asserted as soon as they reached the reception desk. It occurred to her that her documents had become unusually soiled after a couple of years with her living on the street and it would have embarrassed her for Jean to see them or to suspect she might really belong in the gutter.

"Do you have any sleeping pills?" she asked Jean. She wanted to sleep immediately, and absent herself from the present.

Jean passed Talish a bottle of pills from her bag. Talish, pouring out a handful, swallowed them quickly.

"I'll see you tomorrow; thanks for today." she said and gave Jean a peck on the cheek. A familiar mustiness wafted by Jean's nose, overlaid, Jean sensed, with an unhealthy smell. She decided that Talish probably had not used perfume in a while. Any oils she might have used in the past would leave a slight trace, but none was identifiable. It smelled, rather, of masculine sweat.

"A natural woman, eh?" thought Jean. "At one with the world and its smells."

⊠ ⊠ ⊠

While Talish went off to bed, Jean decided to take some air with a walk into town, to see what it had to offer and what was happening. It was a long time since she was last in Amsterdam. It was with Melly on his fortieth birthday; they came for a weekend with friends and played to excess. The boys got unbelievably stoned while the girls drank loads of wine. That was crazy, as she recalled. Her foolish husband had even tried to send a greeting card, filled with grass, back to London. It didn't get past the first sorting office and they laughed about it. As if!!

What was on offer, as far as she was concerned, was something Jean didn't find. The Van Gogh museum was closed, as was Anna Frank's house. It was too late to weave through shoe shops, and Urban Outfitters had no outlet in Amsterdam. None of what she would have liked to do was on offer. She wished that her new friend hadn't been so tired and had come out with her; Talish's company was so enlivening; she could be so funny and Jean was able to think lightly about her Mel. But as soon as she'd wandered into the Old Town where the lights blazed intensely, it became obvious to her that this was not the place to be. A single woman ambling through a red light district can have only one purpose and, with few exceptions, the men she passed looked at her longingly, despite her age. All of a sudden, an Australian crossing a canal bridge approached her.

"How much fer a root, dahlin'?" he drawled carelessly.

Jean, shocked by his abruptness, remembered a line from a movie and looked him keenly in the eye.

"You can't afford me," she said wickedly. "I'm not for sale."

"Yeah right, Sheila," he scoffed, "come on, what's the score?" and stood in her way.

"Hey," said Jean sharply. Her entire working life spent in the film editing studios in and around Euston was good grounding for dealing with arseholes in the street and she changed her tune. "Get out of my way please. I'm not selling."

"Baby, baby, what's wrong with you?" he sang tunelessly. "Aw, gissa jobbie."

Jean stopped still, glared at him for half a second and, standing her ground, pushed both her palms suddenly and swiftly into the centre of his chest and beyond. The Australian, caught completely off-balance, was thrown backwards and fell headlong into the canal behind him. She didn't wait to see him go in; she caught sight only of a few drops of the splash as he landed heavily in the dark wetness below and out of sight. Loud laughter rang out from a group standing nearby and Jean could not resist a chuckle as she left the scene.

Jean felt out of step with this place. People were a different age; they had unwelcome motivation, and the smell was sickening. It was, with certainty, not the place to be without a friend. Jean wondered why Melly should want to come here alone. She found it quite hideous; she had left all this behind long ago, along with her youth. This was not *a happening* worthy of her time.

"Youth," she mused, "that period in life when, being unsure of our true depth of feeling or our own limitations, we pick up on whatever's going on until we decide in which direction to go."

She remembered her first husband and the world of academia to which he introduced her. And then Melly, who swept her off to an exciting Bohemian alternative. It was a lifestyle more akin to this. "Here," she thought, "it's in your face and there's plenty of choice." It seemed that anything people wanted was here. "Or rather," she thought, "the things *these* people want are here."

Jean was not impressed by *these* people. They looked so hopelessly stoned. There were a couple of dead hippies; leather-clad, tattooed, guitar-wielding longhairs who looked vaguely familiar. Perhaps it was that, in being unchanged over thirty years, they remained the familiar icons of halcyon days. One stood playing in Dam Square, breaking off periodically to advise passers-by that Amsterdam was the place to be "for eternity."

"He's happy enough," she thought, "but he hasn't moved on. Mel would have said 'leave him be'." Jean, on the other hand, had grown more critical of those who didn't progress and she was past caring for smoke or for smokers.

Turning past the Grand Krasnopolsky, Jean walked along a narrow canal until she reached a low humped footbridge on which sat a loose group of ragged people; men with their shirt-tails hanging out, dressed in corduroys; there were a couple of thin, pale women with their coats buttoned wrongly. They huddled and swayed independently under a smoky haze. They turned to see who it was approaching, and cowered silently under their coats. Jean didn't like what she saw, not at all, and returned quickly to her hotel to sleep and to close a perfectly shitty day.

⊠ ⊠ ⊠

Talish woke with a jolt, feeling somewhat queasy. She had slept so hard, and so very, very soundly. A real bed that was all her own and in her own space; it felt good. But the sun was already high in the sky and she realized she'd slept too long. Looking out of the hotel window, she saw the doors to the mortuary across the street wide open and the thought that she might have missed Melly being collected sickened her to the stomach.

Pulling her thoughts together, she picked up her few possessions and ran out of the hotel and across to the mortuary.

"Fuck, *scheisse*," she said. She had to confirm Melly was still there. "Damn," she thought, "I got to get his jacket!"

Talish ran in through the mortuary entrance and earnestly demanded of the first person she met, "My uncle Melly. Is he here, can I see him?"

A grey-haired technician trudged over to a desk and peered at a list of names elegantly inscribed into a thick tome that lay there and said, "He has been released, it says here, to a monsieur Jean Cheval." The old man took care to recite the name carefully and enunciated *John* with correct but misguided French.

"Where's he gone?" asked Talish feeling a chill spreading from her fingers and from her toes, each second bringing the ice closer to the heart.

"To the United Kingdom, I expect." said the old man. "The nationality, written here, is British."

"You don't have an address?" pleaded Talish, "Where he's been taken?"

"What happens once they leave here is not our concern," he said, "I am not authorized to give you an address. Are you saying you don't know your uncle's address?" he scoffed, "I find that rather odd, what with you being his niece. I would have thought you did have it."

Talish felt hot under the collar; she fumbled and fled the mortuary, and then wandered outside with her eyes glistening with tears; she'd got there too late.

"Ooee." Jean was locking the car and waved to Talish. She called her over. "Have you had breakfast?" She noticed the young girl's face, puffed with tears. "Did you sleep well?"

"I've got to go to England," said Talish, distraught. "I gotta catch up with someone."

"Well, I'm going back to London," said Jean, walking to join her. "You can ride with me," she said, "and you could drive; I do so hate motorways; they half-scare me to death!"

"That would be good, thanks Jean," said Talish. This *was* good; there was nowhere else to go, she might as well go to London; she'd been there once before while she worked for the Berlin gallery. London had been good to her and she decided to keep a promise to return when she could. It was all she could do to follow Melly and her cassette. Talish couldn't think straight; she would need to locate Melly's home somehow, and somewhere. There was nothing else she could do.

"Let's eat and go," said Jean and led them to a café. An hour later, they had eaten a filling breakfast and were by the car, ready to leave.

"I'll drive us out of town, then you take over, okay?" she said, remembering the stops, the starts, and the jolts of yesterday's ride.

Corpse or not, she thought, Melly was deserving of a smoother ride.

Inside the Volvo, the rear seats were already folded down and Jean's lifeless husband lay in a body bag, zipped from head to toe and covered with a blanket. His combat jacket lay thrown across this; a guitar lay alongside and a small paper bag carried some personal effects. Talish climbed in to the passenger seat and recognized the jacket and the guitar immediately. Her heart rose and sank as she looked over to Jean. The *stupid* technician had misled her; she had been in the company of her quarry all the time. But this luck was unbelievable. It was as if the generosity she came to experience at the hands of each these people was not available generally; rather, it came in small packages and this pair from London was a rare, if not a unique, event. She felt blessed with good fortune; at the same time, knew she would be exploiting the situation and felt underhand and ashamed. Then guilt replaced shame.

"I'm bad for you," she said to Jean suddenly and gripped her by the wrist.

"Nonsense," said Jean. "I really like you. How are you bad for me?"

Talish could not bring herself to answer. She figured it had to do with dishonesty and, if being dishonest with Jean was what it would take to get her tape, then that's the way it had to be. Her 'father' had taught her all about dishonesty; she could lie a bit and it upset her to do so but it was the only way she knew of getting what she really wanted. She hoped that she might get her hands on the tape soon. But Jean was such a dynamic woman and so good to be with. If only she hadn't been Melly's wife; it made getting away from her and from all this so much more urgent; she had to flee before her deception was uncovered. She was *always* having to flee.

And what of Jean? Talish wondered about where *her* tears were, and where *her* sorrow was? Her dead husband was in the back of the car, recently collected; how was she able to control her emotions so well? Had she seen Melly's condition? Did she suspect anything? What was she thinking?

Talish began to sob again. They were not the tears of one who was leaving a beloved city, and they appeared not to be the tears of one who was mourning the loss of a loved one. Jean listened for a while to this gaunt, pale thing.

"Where do you live?" Jean said finally.

"I used to live in Berlin," said Talish, "but I'm foot-loose now. I guess I'm looking for a new life. Maybe I'll give London a try for a while." London was an option, naturally, but Talish knew she would be out of the car as soon as she had her hands on the tape. She would repeat to Jean her need to reach England just as long as it suited her to do so.

"And all your stuff?" asked Jean.

"Yeah," said Talish dismissing the question, "I'll send for it when I'm settled, I think."

"Look," said Jean, "how's about you come and live with me for a while. I've got a great room and it's free right now."

"I can't do that," answered Talish quickly. She knew there was no point in pursuing that line of thinking. "I got people in London I can stay with," she lied. The car fell silent as Jean continued to drive them, along the scenic route, out of Holland and into Belgium.

"Tell me about your man," said Talish eventually. She turned in her seat and looked attentively at Jean. This posture allowed her to drape her arm over the back of the seat until her fingers caught the combat jacket which she slowly pulled towards her. Within a minute, she was groping the pockets and soon located her cassette, caught between the folds of a club flier that had been pressed into Melly's hand. While Jean spoke of how her man had been such a good handyman and had added to the value of their house, Talish did her surreptitious best to claim back her prize.

A cassette tape makes a particular sound; an immediately identifiable, plastic hollowness. It only takes the tap of a finger and it was the sound that gave Talish away.

"Ah, you found a tape in his jacket!" said Jean, pleased. "What is it?"

"It doesn't say," said Talish, crest-fallen and feigning disinterest.

"Stick it on, let's hear," said Jean.

Talish wanted to hear it too but would have preferred to do so in private; it was such a personal thing; she took her time and slid it slowly it into the dashboard though not far enough for it to engage the player.

"Okay, Titi," said Jean after a while, "Here's the motorway. It's your turn to drive."

She pulled off the road and the two swapped places. Had this occurred in town somewhere, Talish would have run off with the tape but there was little point to that. As she looked around at the flat, open, featureless fields of Northern Belgium, she bit her lip and climbed reluctantly into the driver's seat. She would have to wait until they reached a town into which she could disappear.

Jean relaxed into the journey, trusting Talish with the car and with her husband's body, and closed her eyes.

"They said he died of a heart attack, you know," she said at long last. "He was smoking crack and it got to him. He never smoked crack. He said he would never smoke crack! He was so scared of it. Why was he smoking it? Why was his car there? What's he been doing?" Jean looked pained with the thoughts that now crossed her mind.

"Amsterdam's a weird place," said Talish, "It gets to you. Maybe it got to him."

"Weird?" scoffed Jean, "Solidly weird. It's so full of prostitutes. I bet he was here for them."

"Why do you say that?" asked Talish. "Was he like that?"

"Oh, Titi," sobbed Jean, "If only I'd treated him better, he wouldn't be here looking for it; not if he was happy. He wouldn't be dead."

"Did he stray?" asked Talish.

"I don't know. Do you know, I just don't know? I *would* know if he did, wouldn't I? We never talked about. He never gave me reason to think otherwise. But I wouldn't be surprised if he had. You know, he just accepted my view and never pushed me. He was so good like that. I think about it now and think he must have been rather frustrated."

"What do you mean?" asked Titi. "What view?"

Jean turned around in her seat and looked wistfully at the heap in the back of the car. She wondered if there was a side of Melly she knew nothing about, and pondered on what secrets had he taken with him.

Jean might have answered but she caught sight of the note-book on the floor peeking out from under the driver's seat.

"Ah, look," she said, reaching under the driver's seat. "What's this? Ah, the captain's log! Here it is… *Melly's Trip*! Let's see what he's been up to…"

Talish felt a surge of adrenaline blinding her and was brought to her senses by the sounds of horns hooting and Jean yelling at her to take care as she, absent-mindedly, let the car meander across the motorway lanes.

"Are you sure you want to read that?" asked Talish, quaking with nervous anticipation. "You don't know what's in it. You might be really cut up. I mean, do you know if he wrote it for you to read?"

"What's done is done," said Jean. "He can't answer now. He would have wanted me to read it now. Maybe not while he was alive, but now..."

"I dunno. You don't know what you're getting into. Don't read it, Jean," pleaded Talish, "please don't read it. Shall I read it first and then tell you if it's gonna be bad for you?"

"That's so very good of you, Titi," said Jean, "Really, really nice of you to think of me like that. Thank you, but no. I must do this myself."

"You don't have to do it yourself," urged Talish strongly, "you don't have to read it at all. Who says you have to? I bet Melly didn't want you to read it when he wrote it."

"It's very good of you to fight his corner," said Jean, "but if he didn't want anyone to read it, he wouldn't have written it down. Tell you what," she said excitedly, "I'll read it out and you can tell me what *you* think. See if I have good reason to be concerned. Oh, now you've made me feel all excited." She stopped. "How did you know his name was Melly?" she asked slowly.

Talish blushed. "You said it, didn't you? You said it just then, reading it off the book and you said his name before," she lied. "I still don't think you should read it."

"Nonsense!" said Jean, confidently, and began to read *Melly's Trip* out loud.

"The night had quietened and any sound was echoed in the enveloping…" she began with avid interest but, within a few lines, was checking herself. Surely, this was not the man she knew.

"I always thought he was good-looking," said Jean in comment, "but he's attracting sluts off the street. Oh, good, he's turned her down. He's obviously met her before because he already knows her name. You're right," she beamed, reading on, "he did make it to the eclipse; he must have had such a good time. Did you see it in Amsterdam?"

"You know," said Talish disconsolately, "I wasn't that interested; I didn't look. It was raining and it got dark for a few minutes but I couldn't see much of the sun that day."

She was feeling sore; sore in the same way she herself had reacted on her first read of the notebook. She could not blame Jean for her comments; they were, under the circumstances, quite justified.

"Have you got a photo of your man?" she asked.

Jean fished into her shoulder bag and pulled out a picture of a lean thirty-year old longhair in denims and tee shirt; it was her favourite. She blinked at it fondly and passed it to Talish who placed it on the dashboard in front of her.

"That's him," said Jean, "before all his hair fell out."

Talish's pulse raced. Melly, she felt, had been a handsome man in younger days, what with his curly, shoulder-length mane. As his older self, he retained the good looks and the sex appeal. He wore the merest hint of the smile that she had found irresistible. And then, the *undress-me* eyes. Talish felt a flush come over her. She had been with him; she had been made love to by him. She had been with him *in the sunrise.*

With the motorway stretching out before them, Talish began to daydream to the unfolding tale of Melly's trip with her and let her automatic pilot do the driving. She knew his was a hallucinogenic trip, not a real field trip; Melly had told her so. She also knew what he had meant and what he felt.

"Bloody hell, look!" Jean exclaimed as she read on. "It's that bitch, Talish. She's got him onto crack; sneaked up on him. Oh my God, no, no."

She stopped reading and placed the book on her lap. "I can't read this; I can't believe he did this. He's disgusting; he's obsessed with sex. No. No, it's *her* fault. He didn't ask her; she just showed up. And now she's fucking him. What a whore!" She took a deep breath.

"See, I said you would find things in there you didn't like" said Talish. "You sure you want to carry on?"

"You sound as if you know what's in the book?" said Jean resentfully. "How's that?"

"I don't know what's in there," said Talish defensively, "but I do know about reading people's diaries. You never read what you want to read, and you never find out what you expect to find out. They're fuckin' private things; you should know that. Didn't you ever keep a diary?"

Talish had, herself, kept a diary and she'd had *her* privacy invaded.

"I had one for a few days as a child," said Jean, "but I didn't write anything special in it, just the things I did. I'm not very good at writing."

"It's not what you write but what you feel," said Talish. "In diaries, you talk to yourself, you argue with yourself, you spit and you swear. And what you write one day is not what you feel later on."

Jean waved the notebook at Talish and said. "Well this is not what he *felt*, this is what he *did*!"

"I dunno," said Talish with resignation and said nothing more.

Silence descended in the car as both women brooded on what had been uncovered. At long last, Jean resumed reading aloud.

"There was blackness; a pitch-blackness unlike any..."

She read well. The pause had given her time to reflect. It was a good read, despite what it said of her man. She liked good writing but this did not prepare her for the detailed experiences she was now being made privy to as she read each line slowly, word after word.

"Oh my God!" shrieked Jean, interrupting herself.

"I don't think I wanna hear this," moaned Talish, "can you stop now?"

"No, no, this is really funny," said Jean. "All this stuff about bliss, and wanting to die of it. It's all the crack she's given him. She's warped his mind."

"But there was another reality..."

Talish glanced at the man in the photo on the dashboard and tears welled up in her eyes. This was the bit she really didn't like.

"She's disgusting," sneered Jean, "I knew she was disgusting. Oh Mel, why did you let her do this to you?"

"Didn't he do it himself?" asked Talish and suddenly realized the point she made lacked tact.

"It was all *her* doing," said Jean. "He doesn't work like that. He's never wanted it."

"Wanted *what*?" asked Talish.

"Sex, of course," said Jean. "He never put up a fight about it."

"I don't understand," said Talish.

"We didn't have sex. When my son Peter was born, I ripped so badly, internally and externally, it was terrible. I should have had a Caesarean. I was in a coma for two days; when I came out, I vowed never to let another body pass through me like that again. And when I was stitched up, the student doctor got it all wrong and sewed in my er, you know, *clitoris*".

Jean hesitated uncomfortably on the word.

"I don't feel a thing now," she continued, "so I don't bother with it, but that's okay because I don't want to feel anything; not if it's going to lead to another pregnancy. But Melly, my Mel, he didn't mind. He just loved me for who I was, who I am. 'Sex is such a messy and unnecessary affair, anyway', we both used to say. Well, you can see what it's done to him!"

"I reckon he would have felt frustrated," said Talish. "Don't you think? What he wrote is what many in his position would aim to do."

"No" said Jean, assertively and defending her spouse's honour, "You're wrong there. We never argued about it, see? We just never bothered. I'm sure he was impotent, you know."

"I'm not surprised," sneered Talish, though she knew better, "and don't tell me; you didn't try to find out if he *was* impotent?"

"Goodness no! Men's privates are so ugly. Yuk!" Jean shuddered at the thought. "No, well I stopped caring for it as soon as we had Peter. One was enough." She sighed and then said, rather off-handedly, "Well at least he got his oats, if that's what he was after. It's just a pity it had to be with a *tramp*."

Talish swallowed hard. She had heard enough. "Look," she said, "maybe it was a fantasy, just a fantasy. Maybe he didn't do that at all. I can't imagine something like that happening for real." She could, though the location and the circumstances were altogether different.

Jean continued to read quietly to herself. She continued to comment as she read "Oh no, don't, no. Mel don't…you fool… No, Melly…you idiot, fucking shit… Oh, I've lost him. He became a crack-addict!"

"What?" said Talish, "What's happened; what are you saying?"

"He's thrown it all away," she said, "Look, I'll read it out."

"Talish looked at him. He could see her eyes…"

Jean read all the way to the end of the story and then looked up from the notebook. The full meaning of the piece became clearer as she reread the passage.

"Oh my God," she said her eyes filling with tears, "he wants to die; he's in love and he wants to die. Well he did, didn't he? Bastard!"

The point was not lost on Talish either. No longer shocked by the story as on her own first reading, Melly's words now spoke a different language. She now knew what he meant. The man was in love with her; he was smitten and would follow her to the ends; she knew this because he had, literally.

"Melly foretold of our affair. There's value in that," she thought.

"He must have felt terribly bad about all this, this *carry-on*" said Jean. "I think he used the crack to escape the guilt of being with her. He used cannabis like that; he was always out to escape reality. You know what I think? I think he committed suicide in that hotel room! He did it to escape her attentions, to escape the crack he was smoking! He would never forgive himself for doing that. He always swore never to take it. What do you think?"

"I don't know," said Talish exhausted. "I didn't know him. Look, can you drive now?"

"Yes," said Jean, "after we rest up and have some food."

It was early evening when they drove into a fuel stop.

"What time do you have to be in London?" asked Jean.

"Oh, that's not important," said Talish, "Whenever we get there."

Good though she was, Jean was somewhat uncompromising and Talish found it irksome. She wondered how her marriage to Melly had survived for so long without sex. She wondered about Melly's story and how it identified the man she had met in Amsterdam with the man who treated her so respectfully; the man who had released her from a lifetime of mental anguish. She was unblocked and she wondered why he hadn't managed to unblock his wife.

"She really *is* frigid," Talish thought. "Her reaction to the story is that of someone who appears not to listen to what people have said or what they feel. Everything is taken at face value. There's no subtlety with her."

Talish looked forward to the end of the journey; she would climb out in the first town, anywhere.

"Can you drive again, Talish?" bleated Jean as they returned to the car. "I haven't got the energy."

"Sure," said Talish, despite having thrown up when in the bathroom. It wasn't that she felt ill, just nauseous; a sickness that hung over her from the morning. She'd kept up the regime of tablets, pills and glucose that Melly prepared for her and was feeling stronger, but she still needed to see a doctor. Melly's words bounced around in her head. He was right; she needed help. She was hoping Jean was not right in saying she was suffering from tuberculosis. Nevertheless, she felt she ought to get herself seen to and, the sooner, the better.

Jean climbed into the car and remarked about the smell in there.

"Do you think it's the body," asked Talish, looking at the bundle in the back of the car.

"No," said Jean, her mood souring. "No, it's different to that; it smells in here like an old toilet."

⊠ ⊠ ⊠

Northern France had slipped quietly under the wheels of the car throughout the late afternoon and into the evening; Talish drove carefully and unhurriedly. Jean rested in her reclined seat and, reaching over to the player, pushed the tape home. *Kraftwerk*, circa 1978, sounded out; then other names from the same year... By the time *Nina Hagen* and *Scorpions* played, Jean concluded that this was a compilation from a distant past. She faintly recognized many of the tracks, though neither by name nor by artist. She had listened to a lot of German rock music from that period and had heard these tracks before. Melly used to play new albums from all over the world; most of the stuff she didn't care for but it was part of his work and she dutifully tolerated it. Listening to it now, the avant-garde of the late Seventies sounded curiously clumsy and pretentious. Jean wondered about Melly's contradictory taste in music, his apparent fascination with twenty year-old rock from the margins was unlike the symphonic works of *Mike Oldfield* that he usually listened to. She half-wondered why he should continue to listen to this stuff.

The tape stopped and self-ejected and, with a default to FM, the car filled with the sound of a French talk-radio station not fully tuned in. Jean scanned the dial until the bright clarity of *Radio Amsterdam* whispered confidently from the speakers.

"I read about Melly's trip again while you were in the loo," she said at last.

Talish looked heavenward and sighed. "Oh, yeah," she said, "Anything new?"

"You know, we didn't have a sex life, not at all," Jean restarted. "He must have hated me for that. He really wanted it, I see that now; he wrote about it so eloquently. But I could never give to him and we never talked about it. I can't; I couldn't. Oh Titi, I drove him to it!"

Jean started to sob again and Talish switched off, unmoved, and focused on the blackness of the road ahead. She was getting impatient and wanted to get away; she really wanted to leave Jean now.

They passed a long convoy of juggernauts, complete with trailers, heading for the roll-on terminus at Calais. With her driving position on the right of the British car and, with her window down, Talish caught the full blast of hot exhaust fumes. She wound up her window against the dusty wheels and the farting, intimidating mass and overtook them, one by one. It took a long time before their lights were extinguished by distance in the rear-view mirror.

"Don't put yourself down," she said eventually, sounding a sympathetic note. "I'm sure there's another side to this; his side. But yeah, it would have helped to talk to him about it."

"And you know," said Jean, "I never knew he could be so passionate. He must have come back to London to pick up the car. You know, I lost him before he died. He was not thinking of me when he died, I know it."

Talish, at the wheel, tried to show some compassion while, deep inside, she soared to think that this man had died in *her* arms, as *her* prize. After what she had heard from Jean, his flight back to Amsterdam to find her seemed unsurprising. Ah, flight! That's how she preferred to see it now. And she was proud of having done the right thing, for once; leaving Jean oblivious to her identity was the kindest thing she might have done. Melly had become *her* man, after all, in his final days and she felt obliged to keep his memory unsullied; he was her lover, her teacher, and her therapist.

It was something she only came to realize and to believe at that moment, for the sickness of the past thirty-six hours was leading her into familiar territory. She fancied she might have conceived with Melly and wondered what she and the baby could, would, or should now set out to achieve, or to ruin. She had the means to do it; the full implication of the Berlin lawyer's snatched conversation guaranteed that outcome; there were no relatives to argue over Nana's estate. It was to be hers eventually, all of it, and there was no-one to tell her what to do, ever again. She felt good, so very good. Talish would keep Jean company until they reached Calais and, then, decide on how and where to restart her life.

Jean picked up the plastic carrier bag with Melly's personal effects and, reaching in, pulled out the *orgasmatron*. She looked at it quizzically, turned it over in her hand and sniffed it, pulling it away from her face in disgust.

"Evidence!" she proclaimed. "I got the bastard. Look at this Titi!" She waved it at her driver. "What a shit."

"I thought you said you understood," said Talish.

"He kept *secrets* from me; he's a bastard," asserted Jean, uncompromisingly. "He's perverted. What kind of slut wears this?"

Talish chilled to the bone; Jean was mocking her liberator.

"*I would!*" she retorted, "Here, pass it over. I've always wanted one of these."

She grabbed the three-way dildo and slipped it in her coat pocket.

"You're disgusting," sneered Jean "You don't know where that's been."

"Aw come on," said Talish, baiting her, "You can't handle it, can you? You just can't handle sex can you?"

"Right," said Jean, "it's so, uh, unnecessary."

"For you, maybe," said Talish feeling agitated, "but not for me, and not for him. Would you blame him for looking elsewhere?"

"I don't want to talk about it. I don't want to talk about any more." Jean stopped talking suddenly and glared out at a middle distance. Years of inactivity had moved her attitude to an opposite extreme. Talish fought to break the uneasy silence and, mindlessly flipping the cassette, pushed it home into the player.

"The good side," she thought, "At least this will give *me* comfort."

Hard-punching chords smashed out the tell-tale riff of *Cocaine*, but it wasn't *Eric Clapton*, it was *Bo Blomman*, singing in Norwegian about 'heroin'. Talish tapped her foot and swept her elbows to the rhythm. She remembered dancing with her mother to this one, bouncing on the bed at bedtime. Mariella would play it all the time; it was *her* favourite. Talish loved her mother's taste in music and it became her own taste, set in the late-Seventies. With each pan-European track that played, she warmed inside. It had been so many hours since her last smoke and she was coping well. It was fortunate that she had no access to any because she needed to be completely in control.

Jean felt the change away from the brittle atmosphere and relaxed into her seat with her eyes closed while *Giants* strutted their macho, misogynistic stuff, guitars wailing to a throbbing bass, then *UFO, Kayak* and *Sky*; each brought the tone down until the lyrical Spanish acoustic guitar *of Paco Pena* tinkled imperceptibly, muffled by the purr of the Volvo's engine. Talish took a deep, anticipatory breath.

A young woman's voice on the tape broke the quiet, sonorous stillness in the car. *"Guck mal, mein Kleines, das ist fur Dich, damit Du Dich au mich erinnerst."*

"What's she saying?" asked Jean, "That's German, isn't it? Something *das ist fur Dich,* something? 'This is for you'. What's she saying?" The European in Jean came alive.

Talish froze as the blood drained from her fingers and toes. She clasped the wheel as firmly as she could and checked that her feet were still on the correct pedals.

"Translated," said Talish, swaying her head from side to side, "it means '*Here you are, this is for you to remember me by*'."

A guitar began to strum quietly and hesitantly; Jean immediately recognized it as a home recording. The voice began to sing strongly, yet sweetly.

"There was a time not long ago
In a slave market down in Rome
When emperors came and emperors went
With fair young maidens to their home..."

Jean smiled wryly. This one she recognized as a song Melly once wrote, years ago. It came out of the blue, just like that, and in time for Peter's second birthday. It was one of his wackier songs and it didn't make any sense, and didn't refer to anything she knew. Melly had once said, long ago, when he was on E, that very few people ever understood his songs; only the *chosen*. Jean wondered who, other than Melly would sing the song. No one ever took *that* much interest, unless...

"Welcome release in the sunrise,

Loneliness is drifting away..."

Talish felt good. Entirely good. And yet, she could not recall ever having heard the song from any other source but Mariella, her mother. And Melly knew *her* song. *He* was her man!

"He wrote that for someone else," said Jean, interrupting the three-minute dose of bliss.

"What?" said Talish, startled back to reality, "Who?"

"Melly," said Jean, "He dedicated this song to Peter; I never understood why; I bet he was lying. I wonder who this is. Do you reckon it's Talish?"

Talish was confused, utterly confused. *Her song*, her mother's comforting, reassuring lullaby, sung to her since she could remember, was now claimed by a woman who dared to sully its sacred memory.

"You're a suspicious bitch, eh?" she spat. "What the fuck you talking about?"

"Melly!" said Jean, glaring at Talish, "my husband, my dead husband; songwriter, affair-haver and liar, wrote this AND I WANT TO KNOW WHO'S SINGING IT."

The answer came sooner than expected. As the song finished, the woman's voice said very gently, *"Gute Nacht, Talish, meine kleine Suesse, schlaf Du schoen."* There was a rustle, a clunk and the recording came to an end.

"Talish, that bloody Talish again." Jean's eyes opened wide, uncomprehendingly. "What's she saying? What's he been doing? Who is this Talish? How long had he been with her? How many years had he been deceiving me?"

"What are you talking about, fuck you." Talish interjected impatiently. "Did Melly really write that song? Who sings it?"

"What do you mean?" snapped Jean, "No-one *sings it. He* sings it. It's unpublished, it's a nothing song, going nowhere and of no interest to anyone. Why is *she* singing it? That's Talish, I bet. Fucking bitch. I could kill her."

"He hasn't been having a long affair with Talish; you got it all wrong in your head," said Talish.

"How would you know?" snarled Jean, "Look, when you've been around as long as I have, you tend to recognize an affair. This is an affair. Isn't it amazing how much you find out?"

Talish really did have enough of listening to the inconsistencies of this widow and looked to leaving her behind. "All this stuff about Melly having written the song..." she thought angrily.

"That is Talish's mother singing," she yelled, "ISN'T IT OBVIOUS?"

"Steady," said Jean, seeking to placate Talish who was getting careless behind the wheel.

"Fuck," ranted Talish, "You're crazy, woman. Your man's been screwing round and you wanna kill him, you wanna kill the one he's screwing around with. No one gonna survive with you like this. You should have let him know he was never gonna get it with you; he wouldn't have stayed so long. Fuck, I'm surprised he did. He was a good man and you killed him! You killed him inside."

As she spoke, the strands of their conversation interwove and presented her with the finished plait - a plait that now began to suffocate her with the realization that Melly was, in fact, her real father. An icy hollowness filled her head and paled her face down to her shoulders, spread down to the pit of her stomach, and out over her knees to her feet. Talish began to quiver nervously and then shake uncontrollably. Melly's problem too, she reasoned, started when *she herself* recognized the tune *he'd written for her mother* 21 years earlier, way back in 1978.

"I want to tell you something," she said numbly and brought the car to a slow stop in the hard shoulder.

"No!" snapped Jean, "Don't you tell me anything. You've got no right to say anything. Who the hell do you think you're talking to here? I've got a dead husband in the back and you're telling me how I should have let him go, how I should have led my life, and how I was a lousy wife. Well damn you, I think your opinion sucks and I think you should keep it to yourself. You don't know anything about my man or how we were. Do you hear me telling you how to live your life? You think life is so straight-forward? Yeah, well then go and get yourself fucked a bit, and then wait till you're pregnant. And then go through the labour; and I *hope* it hurts you like it hurt me, and then give birth and let it *tear you apart*; let it hack its way out, like it did me! That's what you get for getting fucked. And you, you're just right into that, I bet. Yeah, screw the system, fuck the world. You're just like the rest of them; all trash, just dirty, filthy-minded scum. Is that why Amsterdam is so full of whores? Don't tell me, you're one of them. *Should have let him go*! Huh, give me strength. *Fucking trash for men*!"

Jean shook her head and felt horribly isolated and angry. Angry with herself, and angry with Melly; angry with the girl who drove her car and whom she now found irritating, and all for the loss of her illusion of the love that had buoyed them for so many years. She hadn't known about any of it and it hadn't hurt. Now that she knew, and now that it *did* hurt, she wondered whether her life with Melly had, indeed, been an illusion or whether his love, real or unreal, had given her what she wanted. Had she ever objected to his love as insufficient, or as not good enough for her?

⊠ ⊠ ⊠

Suicide is one of those odd things – the end of life, decided on by oneself. The problem with suicide and suicide notes is that they tend to be appeals for help. Numerous occasions when a suicide is prevented exist simply because someone showed up and interrupted the process; it turns out for the best for some, giving rise to a re-evaluation of life brought to the brink. Others take the decision to do something from which they know they will die, only to be trapped for the infinitely long seconds of knowing that they are past the point of no return and will not be saved, however much they feel they made a mistake, and an error of judgment.

"Oh, that it could be that quick, that thoughtless, and that painless," thought Talish. Her head spun. "Unconsidered and ill-considered."

As Jean's last damning utterance 'You're all filthy-minded scum - just trash for men' echoed in her head, Talish felt she'd come full circle and had nowhere left to explore, with nowhere to left hide.

"I've had enough of this - I gotta go," she said, straining to see through her tears. "Give the story here a second?" she demanded, "Come on, pass it over."

Jean snatched the notebook from her bag and hurled it at Talish, fully expecting her to look for some relevant reference to back her unintelligible defence of a man she did not know. Instead, she, put it in her coat, then ejected the cassette and put it in her pocket too. She opened her door and stepped out of the car to walk around to the passenger side, to confront Jean one last time. In the corner of her eye she saw the headlights of the convoy of juggernauts that rolled towards them like a dirty, diesel-belching snake. All it would take was a simple two-step into the darkness.

Jean scowled at Talish through the open window.

"There's something I ought to tell you," said Talish, heart-broken, "There's something you need to know."

"I've heard quite enough for today, thank you," sneered Jean, "especially from you, you stupid, ignorant child."

"Are you sure?" said Talish, shivering to her bones, her hair standing on end.

"Sure!" asserted Jean.

Talish pulled her passport from inside the leather coat and handed it to Jean.

"You might, then, like to work it out for yourself," she whimpered. And then she took her two steps backwards into the night.

The first juggernaut had just thundered past, the second was right behind and knocked her flat, bouncing slightly as each of nine sets of tires pinned her, ever more easily, to the concrete road. The driver wondered about the bump, the road ahead as clear as the trailer directly ahead of him would show. He radioed ahead to the leader and behind, to the truck following, but heard no report of a bump and gave it no further thought. The remainder of the convoy rolled through smoothly, ironing Talish relentlessly into the road, *back into the street*, until there was no more of her. No-one stopped, no-one saw, and no-one was the wiser. The discoloured road fell silent in a second as the thundering mass left the scene, leaving only the thick blackness of the night.

Jean blinked in disbelief and looked at the soiled passport. *Talish Thorensen. T.T. Titi.* She now saw the circle fully squared and wondered if there was any point in having faith in anyone, now or ever again. What use her newly acquired fortune if none of it could lead anywhere worthwhile, and if those with whom she interacted had any intention, or any solid, believable reason to be taken seriously? And what use without her man? Her fortune was useless to her and she now had no clue what to do with it. It was all so pointless. Life was pointless.

She sat in shock, stunned by the chain of events either side of the week of the eclipse, that damned eclipse, while *Amsterdam Radio* hummed to the New Age hippie sound of *Enigma*, a Melly favourite:

"If you understand or if you don't,
If you believe or if you doubt
There's a universal justice
And the Eyes of Truth
Are always watching you."

Jean listened, unmoved by the sentiments and wished *she'd* thought of it first; the suicide, that is.

4

"Wake up Mel, darlin'," said Jean, "I've made you some tea."

Melly stirred from his daydream, his involuntary slumber at the keyboard to the word processor.

"Haven't you finished yet?" she asked, glancing at the screen and wondering if he was still making corrections, still revising the *damned thing*.

Six months. Six months of Melly's life had passed since he came back from Amsterdam with *Melly's Trip* scribbled in a notebook, and sat down to type it up. Six months during which he was buried under a mountain of words that just spilled from his head uncontrollably and unstoppably.

Talish – he had to save Talish; that's what he wrote about. And she had to be grateful. That was the story; that was the intention, set against a background of a surprise lottery win which allowed him to rush back to Amsterdam to find her at death's door. He would sweep her up and carry her off to a hotel where her regeneration would begin. She would open up her soul to him, share her body with him, and even give up her life for him.

Melly was consumed with the image of Talish that he'd created. The more he wrote, the more he felt himself slipping away from home, away from his friends and away from Jean; not because he loved them any less but because his every waking moment was spent developing his tale. He abandoned participation in the real world and the story took precedence over any domestic issue he had to deal with; it took precedence over his conversations with Jean and, when in company, his thoughts would wander and he was often reminded that he was staring blankly at people and, often, through them.

Six months spent increasingly lovelorn, and increasingly desperate to close his story. He'd finished the story twice before, each time with a different ending: an ending that gave Talish life and left him the option to continue writing about her, and an ending that saw her die needlessly but die nevertheless. He was desperate to finish with her; killing her off seemed a good way to do it and yet, the lines he gave her haunted him; "*you wanna write, then get involved*" In truth, Melly needed to dip his toe one last time.

"Finished?" he said, "I've finished the story but there are one or two facts I need to go back over to check on."

Jean knew that once he had decided, there was no stopping Melly.

"Are you going back to see *someone*?" She glared at him with a look of desperation, "because if you are, then it's over between us."

"I have no-one out there," he said. "I have to check some things and it's easier and cheaper to go there than to phone round."

Jean had good reason to feel anxious about her man. Consumed with her own depression over getting older, enjoying life less, and feeling that, despite all the good times she had lived through, there was little that was new to look forward to. Living without Melly was not something she ever looked forward to, but he had been too distant of late and she was feeling threatened. Living without Jean was not something *he* looked forward to either; but Melly needed to experience in order to write. He claimed the right to do further research.

"No-one's got me," said Melly, "no-one's going to get me. Jean, I'm yours, always. I'm going away and I'll be back."

"I hate you going away, Mel. You know I do," said Jean, "But if you've got someone out there, I'm telling you, we're done."

Depression brings irrationality. Melly felt Jean was being irrational. Threat? What threat? He was a writer; he had things to do.

"Get out of my hair," the voices inside his head pleaded, "and give me the freedom to go. Give me your blessing and give me an open slate to travel with. Don't make me feel guilty over this trip."

⊠ ⊠ ⊠

A weekend in Amsterdam, alone, after six months. He was glad he was not going with anyone. He had work to do and didn't want anyone cramping his style. It was only a short hop; he could survive a couple of days of loneliness. He had objectives, a whole series of questions to ask of the authorities about procedure, and he had to get some names right. It was going to be quick; in and out. No-one would notice. Fuck, he wanted to find Talish and see if she was *okay.*

"OKAY?" he thought, "What the fuck does *okay* mean?

Melly sat on the coach with Barry, a young Australian with a shock of blond wool on his head. Barry worked as a nurse in Cairns back home; he knew about hospital procedures regarding death.

"…It's about a guy who goes to get his rocks off," Melly burbled by way of introducing the book into conversation, "but dies in the process. It's a bit coarse."

Barry chatted the easy way that Aussies chat and confirmed much of what Melly imagined happened in a hospital. He was happy to while away the next few minutes poring over the book, opened at *Melly's Trip*. He looked up unsmiling and unimpressed.

"So, you gonna show me round Amsterdam," he said, finally, and called over to some guys sitting in the rows behind, "Hey, Jono, we can work out where to go for your birthday. Yeah, mate, he's twenty-three tomorrow. Do you know any gay bars?"

"Uh, I guess the story's a bit inappropriate for you, then," said Melly, a tad embarrassed. Not everyone was going to like it, that's for sure.

Melly found himself leading a party that included two Welshmen named Andy, to the hostel by the canal bridge, in the shadow of the cathedral clock, and boasted about the mattress he'd got for 30 guilders back in the summer.

"We're full up," he was told at reception, "there's a party upstairs in Room 101 that's leaving tomorrow. But go to the place across the bridge; that should be good."

The place across the bridge was a hovel, it really was. Set in an alley, it was primarily a drinking den for Brits and a smoking den for others. Stained, chipped linoleum lay strewn across the floor of the dormitory and, with walls painted navy blue and mauve, Melly concluded that this was probably more the arse-end of the world than Room 101. His bunk, oddly also 30 guilders, called out to him; "*C7*", painted in fat, white ciphers on the wall, instructive in Sinclair's failed C5. With every update, they still hadn't got the car to function properly and still hadn't got it right.

"Sorry buddy," said *C7*, "like me, you're doomed to failure."

Room 101, on the other hand, now looked out on an empty and pleasant backwater – there were no crack heads to be seen there on the bridge in this winter season. Maybe they'd all gone at the close of summer; maybe they were all dead. Melly had to find Talish. He just had to.

It was 7:40 on a Saturday morning again, as in August but, now in February, it was cold; wrap-up tight cold, European mainland cold, and drizzly. Melly's sleeveless puffa-jacket was what he wore to work, over a sweat top, with thin strides and sensible shoes. He was going to interview people and felt that one wardrobe was enough. He wasn't expecting to have to get dirty though he would have preferred to look less like a dork, the kind of man who would look fine; reasonably turned out, quite stylish really except that, again, he had a rucksack slung over his shoulder. And there it would stay throughout his time in Amsterdam, marking him out as a visitor, or as a tourist. He was carrying his book, a weighty ring-bound tome; however he thought about it, the ruck' was the most sensible means of carrying it around. Perhaps he opted not to buy a padlock for a locker because *it cost*. That decision left him carrying his baggage around for much of the time; secure but a pain in the butt, and so debilitating.

His cover blown, he became the mindless foreigner who walked into a shop with a camera he'd borrowed for the trip and asked for a particular, *special* battery to fit into an orifice he'd managed to open.

"That's where the film goes, look," said the young assistant condescendingly, and deftly popping out a pair of cells from the other side.

Melly, embarrassed, collapsed into a fit of laughter, and made light of the problem by admitting to being an absolute fool. The man did not share his sense of humour and left Melly speechless with ignorance, both of the workings of a modern camera and of Dutch, in which he now resumed a conversation with another, and cast Melly adrift. You know how it is when people won't even look at you because you're such a fool; Melly felt like that, just then.

Nothing much different after six months, then; still a wanker!

Melly suspended his duties as a tour guide for a moment and ran over to a couple of uniforms walking their beat.

"Excuse me," Melly opened, "you know all the girls on the street by name?"

He posed the question to a female officer who was busy writing out a ticket for an old boy sitting upside down in a doorway. His bloodshot eyes broke into a dopey smile as he righted himself. She comprehended and nodded to Melly.

"I'm looking for Talish," he said. "She was here six months ago."

The officer pursed her lips, shook her head and looked aimlessly up and down the cobbled street.

"She's dead, she's gone. It's all over," thought Melly and something in him rejoiced.

Coming to see someone after a six-month separation can fill you with so much expectation, so much trepidation, and so much damned fear. Maybe he had come too late and the girl was dead and, maybe, she was gone; maybe she was okay and off the street. Either way, it didn't seem to matter so much any more because he wouldn't have known what to say to her anyway and he was dreading that moment. Hell, he wasn't even sure what she looked like. And now, it wasn't going to happen and that meant he could dismiss her. She was no longer a threat as far as Jean was concerned, not that she ever was, and she was no longer a threat as far as the book was concerned. Melly had spent a lot of time wondering whether the people about whom he wrote had any rights over interpretations of their lives by others.

Melly worried about Talish seizing control of the identity he'd created, and wanting a piece of the action. It would have been so easy to hide the book from her, even change her name, but this was sincerity at its most insipid. *"I'm going to make lots of money from writing about you, thank you,"* sounded lame but it was, possibly, very true. That was his plan. But now it was okay; the pressure was off. She need never know about it.

So, there were only the interviews to conduct: police, hospital, hotels, and place names. He'd have to do it today because, surely, everything closed on Sunday.

"But then again, Saturday is a long day and there is a party waiting to be shown around and pointed in a good direction," he thought.

"Strewth, did you just talk to them police?" asked Jono, incredulous. "Fuck, what'd she say?"

Melly chuckled to think there were people who would not exploit someone or something through fear. It happened all the time back in London, and it was happening here. *"Shit, it's the Feds, run."* He'd learned not to fear the police and came to understand what pissed them off and how to avoid arrest.

"It was easy, really," he thought. "Attack is usually the best form of defence, sure, except when dealing with the police. Then it's compliance; total compliance is what they want. *Nice officer, good officer.*"

"Nothing," said Melly, "I said nothing, really," and took Barry and Jono and the two Andies to the Space Café where they settled on a ready-rolled Sensi and a block of Zero Zero with a cup of milky tea. Then, each member of the party picked out some individual variety and soon, very soon, they gaped at him through pink eyes, fearing their next move. They were brainless, blinking and unfocussed. There wasn't going to be a next move for them; here was just fine for the moment.

The Zero Zero was okay; the most expensive, it rocked Melly for all of a minute.

"I'm off to do my research now," Melly suddenly announced, "catch you later, here, yeah?"

Andy and Andy, Jono and Barry looked at him with awe, and *respect*, even.

"Sheeit, you going like that? Don't know 'bout you but I'm fucked." Four voices spoke in unison. Melly, however, was used to it.

First stop was the *Sonesta Hotel*, to which Melly retraced his steps from a distant past. He walked into the building confidently and asked to speak to the duty manager. *The Sonesta* had changed in décor, and had changed its name to *The Renaissance*. He had not been inside during the summer; this time he realized it was definitely a five-star hotel; tacky in five-star terms but offering the kinds of facilities that warrant a high room rate. Company expense accounts can be so blind; business types are so easily ripped off and, so often, they were. And those using expense accounts take so much for granted as they sneer and scoff at the underlings in service. Melly remembered those times; he did not remember the gold railings, the marble floors, and the sheer opulence of it. It was, after all, standard, and he had quite forgotten the *bonuses* of five-star luxury; this place would have proved much too ugly and too expensive for his story.

A tall woman, and the Dutch are, as a rule, very tall, sat down with him.

"You have to understand; all I want to know is your procedure for dealing with a corpse on the premises," said Melly, trying to look and sound charming.

What he felt and how he appeared were two very dissimilar things. He didn't look charming at all. His face was disfigured by a sleepless night and his grey stubble was striking. He tried to make light of his concern for the grave issue he was discussing. It didn't work and she grew defensive; the kind of defence that said, "I don't know you and you're asking me ridiculous questions. Am I supposed to laugh?"

"Well, why do you want to know?" she asked nervously.

"I'm just, uh, trying to get the timing right in my story," he said, trying to sound and act like his mental picture of the archetypal North London writer.

"Let us say," she spoke slowly, "such a thing might happen, then we would see to get rid of it as soon as possible; immediately, maybe."

She chose her words carefully, perhaps wondering if it meant a quote, and perhaps not.

"There is nothing more I can tell you, goodbye." She was direct and rose before finishing her sentence.

The interview was over. Short, painless, irreverent, irresponsible, and just *so* spontaneous. Melly sauntered out satisfied that he had broken the spirit of *The Sonesta*. Behind him, the duty manager looked forward to a day without any more bedraggled weirdoes masquerading as writers, soiling the hotel's deep-pile cream carpet and lowering the tone the way this one had.

Melly's next stop was the main police station. He found the solid, stone fortress wedged into a terrace in a narrow street. There, he was met by mighty oak doors; locked oak doors and a small intercom. He pressed the button.

"Hello," he called, "I'd like to speak to a superior officer about police procedure."

"Come round to the front. Someone will see you there," the intercom crackled.

Melly suddenly felt like the fool who had returned, unable to recognize detail, and unable to scan the wider *picture*. Crest-fallen and dazed, he walked sheepishly along the street and circled the block until he found himself outside the front entrance of the police station positioned on one of the main arenas in Amsterdam. A very proud building, it welcomed all visitors with flags, lights and doors that were wide open. Melly walked in and waited by a counter. Fully-filled, well-upholstered, deep-buttoned leather sofas lined the subtly-lit walls. The place was respectfully clean. After some time, an officer emerged.

"I want to talk to someone about the procedure for taking a corpse out of a hotel," he said simply. "What happens to it? I'm a writer, you see."

I'm a writer. It felt so good to say, like, I'm a promotions manager; I'm an art-school dropout; I've worked in Saudi; Rick Wakeman bought me a drink once… Badges that make us feel good about ourselves. Not untruths, but just uttered with the accent leaning heavily on bullshit.

The officer disappeared and reappeared a long time, maybe twenty minutes, later. Judging by the number of security cameras trained on the lobby where he stood, Melly imagined that somewhere in a back room, someone was eyeing him up and down, and wondering about his motives. His motives were self-seeking and harmless. He was just a dork; you get them every now and again.

"Take this address and phone number," the officer said, handing Melly a scrap of paper, "they are open on Monday; they will tell you. Goodbye."

Melly looked to see a contact for the International University of Hospitality Management, based in The Hague; a fat lot of use *that* was going to be, Melly thought.

The interview hadn't gone as planned; he would have done it differently if he'd been sober. But *they* could see he was off his face; like all the other dope-heads in Amsterdam, his eyes gave him away with their glazed, blood-shot and middle-distant look. And the message was invariably the same: *I don't care for what you're talking about; I don't know what I'm talking about and I'm not making any sense but I'm sure if I smile enough, you'll understand what I'm trying to say and forgive me if I get it wrong. You can forgive, can't you?"* Leaving the police station had been like leaving a headmaster's study; reprimanded, belittled, looked keenly in the eye and told, "Well surely, no-one, but no-one, can take you seriously." Melly wanted to be taken seriously; he also hated having to be serious. His headmaster probably had the right idea. Then again, he may have been at the root of so much of Melly's feeling of inadequacy.

Anyway, that was it; it was all done. He was finished and free! The remainder of the weekend was his and it was not yet ten in the morning! *Going to check on facts...easier than on the phone...* Two hours into the weekend, Melly found himself at liberty to do what he had been denying to himself and to Jean; he tried hard not to feel enthusiastic but knew deep inside that, from here on, life was likely to get interesting.

Few people were about on this winter's day; the streets of the red light district spread out before him, emptied of crowds and of cars, and showed themselves to be the domain of the street-people, those who live on the street and by the street. And like a rat-run, they walked their patch of town, trudging to and fro; always seen in another street, and always passing through the same.

Melly wandered through the Old Town, past De Oudekerk, the church with the clock that had, with its tuneless chime, often woken him in Room 101, and past the windows with their prostitutes' cubicles. Each of the women there dressed uniformly in white underwear, white beachwear and white bathrobes. The ultra-violet lighting they used dulled the oils of their fake tans and gave stark contrast against the brilliance of *that* kind of white. The women truly looked like painted ladies, particularly those who purposely put on whitener and made themselves look deathly. Some people are turned on by that, seemingly. Not Melly. He walked and kept his eyes open. He was definitely going to get a shag this time; all he had to do was find someone who looked really good. Someone he could bear to be with, or be seen with, and to remember fondly.

He had a pocket full of money. He'd brought 700 guilders and they nestled in a plastic Thomas Cook pouch, very tourist-like, in the side pocket of his puffa-jacket. He really did want to be cool about it but things, well, *things* conspire to make a little seem a lot less and the important seem trivial. He didn't trust the pockets of his trousers. The pockets weren't as deep as in his denims; the money had to go into his puffa jacket, in the pouch, to identify him as a tourist every time he reached for it.

Melly recognized a couple of old boys on the street; a mad one who often yelled hard at him until he was out of sight, there was the old busker from outside the Grasshopper, and a lot of new faces he'd not seen before.

"You got one guilder, ONE GUILDER," repeated a young, weathered blonde who struggled to see through half-closed eyes, tottering from high heel to high heel, her bomber jacket inadequate against the wind-chill.

"She could so easily have been Talish," thought Melly.

He was glad she wasn't and it occurred to him that had Talish been ugly, none of this would be happening. As easy as it was to shrug off the attentions of someone unappealing, it irked him that it was only ever the *decent* ones who got a response. Yet it was the lack of appeal that made the bad-lookers the most vulnerable. Melly decided that he'd give this one some money later, if he saw her again.

Melly *never* listened. He never listened to advice; he never really listened, to the vibe. He didn't believe the policewoman. Talish was there, he knew it, waiting to be found or waiting to be *found out about*. He approached a weather-beaten Algerian who was standing his ground, marking out his territory during a police-free ten minutes, selling crack and heroin.

"I'm looking for Talish," said Melly.

No response. He went on to describe the black leather coat and the dark curly hair.

The old African, nodded. "Yah," he said knowingly, "Alex."

"Is she here, in Amsterdam?" asked Melly, wondering whether Talish was a false name, or a real name.

"Yeah, she is here." he said.

Melly tried to think it through. If she was there and he hadn't seen her then she probably looked totally different. He wasn't really sure what she looked like so he concentrated on the sorry-looking ones. A tall one that he recognized from before looked not sorry but resigned and Melly wondered who *she* was.

"I'm looking for Alex," said Melly to another African who was standing by a railing, waiting for the clients that would seek him out. He looked Ethiopian.

He pointed a long finger in the direction of a grey-blue anorak that hobbled on imperfect knees before disappearing around a corner.

"There she is." he said, but the utterance was to recently-vacated space.

Melly took off after her, careful not to exhaust himself too much; he'd feel a real twat, panting and gasping to her instead of opening up a self-assured conversation. He found her in a narrow lane discussing a deal with a young Egyptian who had the capacity to talk soberly but then take off, arms outstretched and eagle-like, playing the heroin addict.

"As long as the police think he's fucked, I bet they regard him as harmless," he thought.

The ruse worked and the dealer, Melly could see, remained hassle-free, and could loiter and make deals at will.

"Excuse me, is your name Alex?" he asked the girl.

"Yes," she replied.

“Did you ever call yourself Talish?”

“No,” she said, smiling slightly, “I call myself Alex.”

Alex was a tall girl, long and lean, with a fair complexion, good skin and a mass of dark curls that fought their way out of the quilted hood of her anorak. She was stepping from one foot to the other in good, brown DM’s with pretty legs clothed in spandex that reached up towards a tightly-tied belt on a high waist. She had large brown eyes with large eyeballs; when her eyelids fell, it made her look really sad. She spoke with a Dutch accent and a slight lisp, the kind where the tongue is annoyingly large and constantly in search of a place in the mouth to rest. Her *Alex* sounded enough like Alish to make the bogus T the possible result of a glottal stop, or a *my name, it’s Alish…Tsalish…* Melly needed to believe.

“We ate spaghetti together,” he offered, looking into her eyes.

He had seen her before, of that he was certain. Had she changed *that* much?

“No we didn’t,” she laughed. “I hate spaghetti!”

He tried to remember a laugh. Alex tilted her head to the side, coyly. He remembered *that.*

“Are you not her?” he said looking up at her, for she was taller than he.

That was different; it wasn’t her.

“If you want me to be her, I can be her,” she said, seizing the moment.

“No, you don’t understand.” Melly was at pains. “She is real, just as you are real. She wore a black leather coat, and a leopard pattern dress. She carried her trainers in her hand ‘cos they were so wet. She was so thin and hungry and you look well-fed; she was so dirty.” He took her hands; her long, clean fingers were adorned with wide silver rings. “Her hands; they were not like this, they were dirty. She was, uh, smelly. Ha, you are not."

"I keep myself clean, you know," she said, "I shower and I wash my clothes, and I eat. Do you have thirty guilders?"

Automatically, Melly reached into his pocket and fumbled around for a couple of notes. He knew he had only fives and twenty-fives; he might strike lucky and pick the right two but, no, he managed only to let her know he had more; loads more where *that* came from. Alex took the thirty and, turning to her dealer who was flying close by, called to him by name.

"Yo, Kokomo."

Kokomo flew up to her and spat a number of small polythene wraps into his gloved hand. He prodded them apart, separating the brown from the white, and the large from the small, and gave her a large *ball* of white. He turned to Melly who watched impassively. Thirty guilders was worth some knowledge on the whereabouts or the fate of Talish; it was not what he wanted to spend on himself, not from *this* man at any rate.

"No," said Melly, waving him away. "That's it, go."

It was *his* turn with this girl. Girl? She was a woman some twenty-eight years old, though she still had a very young face that was youthful but sad. Crack does that; it keeps you looking young, until you stop using it.

"You have a place?" Melly asked.

It seemed unlikely these people had places; they were *street people*, after all, and they were on the street twenty-four hours a day. He'd seen them about, all the time; but Alex was unusually clean.

"I live with a man," she said, "since the summer." Melly's spirits rose. "I was in a bad way; I had an accident a couple of years ago and I got into a mess and I was on the street all the time. And then Kenneth offered me a place to stay. He's a black man of forty-eight. He feeds me and looks after me like a daughter. He's a good man. I got my own room and my own bed. I got my clothes."

Melly marvelled at the similarities with his imagined tale.

"Do you know," he said beaming, "this girl, she was in such a state, just like you were. I really felt for her so I went home and wrote a story about her. I mean, I don't know her, just met her three times, but, you know, she reached out to me and I wrote this thing about saving her."

"You want me to read it?" she asked, smiling.

"Or, could *I* read it to *you*?" Melly pleaded, "It will only take four or five hours. Do you have the time for that?"

"You have a nice voice," she said, "I could listen to you read. That would be good. We can go to my place and you can read it to me."

Melly could not quite take it all in. He had found someone who'd lived the life of the character he imagined Talish to be, and who was interested in what he had to say. She wasn't tackling him and asking him if he wanted sex the way that prostitutes might give a come-on. She was talking to him as normal. Or maybe she wasn't. Maybe she was talking to him the way he wanted her to talk to him. Maybe she *was* prostituting herself. She hadn't asked to be paid for this service yet he was chatting to her, and she to him. He thought it very good of her to do so.

"Are you hungry?" he asked her, "Do you want something to eat?"

"A milky coffee would be good," she said and led him through the town.

But she didn't lead him directly to a coffee shop; she took him instead to a metro subway and stood with him awhile, listening to him enthuse about the book. While he talked she tried, with some difficulty, to open up the ball of white crystals. It was a piece of thin polythene tied in a knot. The half-gramme balls are easier to use; they are enough for one smoke; you just bite the knot off and pour the contents into a pipe. The one-gramme balls are a bitch, first, because you need three hands to cope with splitting the bag between your pipe and your *ash tube* and, secondly because, by having to pour off the rest into your ash tube, it makes it that much easier to be found in possession of that stash. An unused whole ball is easily hidden in the bra cup so that it's not so obvious.

Alex managed to get it together. She smoked her pipe quickly, turned to spit out the sour taste in her mouth, and slid it up her sleeve. As Melly smoked a cigarette, she carefully collected all his ash and placed it into a clear plastic tube to use later to bulk out the crack in her pipe.

"Let's eat," she said, finally.

She didn't look or act any differently for having just smoked crack-cocaine. They were about to emerge from the subway when another dealer Alex knew came down the stairs.

"Quickly," she said to Melly, all excited, "that other stuff was shit. This man is good. Have you got thirty guilders?"

Melly reached into his pocket again and pulled out a twenty-five and a ten.

"Do you want some?" she asked.

"I don't smoke a pipe, just hash," he said.

"Hmm, I wish I didn't," she said and walked off with the man into the subway tunnel.

Melly lit up the joint he'd rolled somewhere earlier but not bothered to smoke and waited at the entrance to the tunnel. They were on the edge of the Amstel River estuary, the water level slopped at knee height, on the other side of a thick concrete dike. Fat water, immense, rippling amounts of water seen from close up can be intimidating. As

Alex rejoined him and prepared another pipe, he felt quite frightened by this volume of Dutch water and he felt insignificant in the scheme of things; unlikely, if not unable, to make any impression on anything.

"Put your arm over me," she said.

He didn't quite understand. He should've asked whether it was to contain the smoke for her, or to shield her from the wind, or whether to hide her from the prying eyes of plain-clothed and uniformed police in the area. The rucksack, hanging on his shoulder made him look an unlikely suitor to the girl whose face brightened as soon as she had a puff.

"That's better," she said. "Now, let's go eat. Here's your change."

Melly was taken aback. She was *not* going to take his every last guilder; she was acting honourably, honestly, and showing some integrity. At that moment, she went up considerably in his estimation.

There was only one coffee bar Alex was allowed into; only one in town where the owner would overlook the fact she was a crack smoker, a hooker, and just a little unhinged. The bar staff at the Greenhouse gave the couple a perfunctory welcome; a table in the window gave them both a view on the world outside. Melly put down his ruck' and went for the coffees. By the time he returned, Alex had climbed out of her anorak and also out of the scarf, the gloves and the quilted jacket she wore underneath. He had left a misshapen, concealing bundle of overcoat and returned to a well-proportioned girl whose legs did indeed stretch for miles, whose crop top enclosed a lovely pair of breasts and whose midriff showed the telltale loose skin that suggested she'd carried a child. As if preparing, or answering a signal, Melly took off his puffa and slipped it over the back of his chair.

They talked easily. She spoke the longer; she spoke a lot, and unstoppably, in largely incoherent, maybe unconnected, snippets. Soon Melly had lost the thread of what she was talking about and his eyes had glazed over. He was tired, and she was beginning to bore him, but the excitement of the moment kept him awake.

She laughed. "See this ticket," she said, throwing down a red card from within her pocket, "this is my exclusion order. I'm not allowed on this part of town for eight hours. They found me smoking my pipe in the street this morning. I'm not allowed back here until later on. But, ha, here I am; no, I'm not," she said, looking closer, "look, they've marked out another area. Great, I'm safe here. You know, I get these all the time and, after a while, I have to pay a fine. See that man?" She looked across the street to a young man dressed in shorts who was carrying an empty haversack and reading the menu outside a small restaurant, "He's undercover. Doesn't he look obvious? It's winter, man! See that couple there? They're police too. I mean, who holds hands these days? They look so unlikely. Urrh!" Alex caught her jaw and began to wail about the state of her teeth. "I haven't been to a dentist for over eight years. My teeth really hurt."

"Have you got any aspirin?" Melly asked. "Better still, have you tried chewing on a clove? It releases juices that numb the tooth."

He jumped up and out to an adjoining shop to ask for cloves but there were none. Melly returned empty-handed, worrying about his pocketful of money. The jacket appeared not to have been rifled and Melly relaxed some more.

"So," she said finally, "You want to read me the book?"

"Oh yes," Melly said, alerted, "would you suggest anywhere we can go. We'll need somewhere we can just relax and chill out without any interruption."

"Like I said, you can come to my place," she repeated. "Would you like that?"

Wild thoughts entered and milled about in Melly's head. He wondered what she was offering. She didn't know his story. She didn't know it was, in parts, so explicit as to have the capacity to turn people on sexually. He wanted to be comfortable so as to be ready and able to catch any loose favours and soak in what he fancifully thought might be her released frustrations. His dick began to do the thinking for him; blind, self-seeking thinking as only a dick can.

"I would love that," said Melly, gathering his things together, and trying not to move too hastily.

Back on the street, he walked close to her and offered his arm. She took it immediately and settled comfortably into his side.

"You know," she said. "It's so nice to walk arm-in-arm with you. People don't, you know. They keep their distance; they think I'm dirty. You can see I'm not dirty, can't you?"

Melly looked across and up at her. She looked serene and satisfied. She might well have worn a big sign round her neck *"I'm sorted for the rest of the day. Don't bother me now; I'm taken!"* That occurred to him when the route to her place took them past yet another dealer she identified as Rizla 22, a good friend.

"You got thirty guilders?" she asked Melly.

Melly obliged again and soon, having got her even more set up, the pair walked the kilometre out of the Old Town to a modern housing estate on the water's edge, close to the docks. But even before they reached her apartment, Alex led him under a covered passage and asked him to shield her as she smoked another pipe. It made Melly wonder why she didn't wait until she got home. What was so important about having a smoke in the open, in full public view, when a couple of minute's walk would bring them to safety?

"What do you want to drink?" she asked suddenly.

Melly looked at her quizzically.

"Your throat will get dry, what will you drink?" she asked thoughtfully. "We've got no tea or coffee."

Melly liked Alex. She wasn't at all how he imagined a hooker to be. She even looked surprisingly like a little girl he knew from years back, only much older. Melly was pleased by what he saw; so pleased, he bought a litre of diet Coke and completely forgot about the coffee, the tea, and the cigarettes he'd need for later. And what was *later*? How much later?

Alex fumbled with the key to a door directly off the street.

"It's really funny," she laughed. "I brought a client back last week and I couldn't get the key in. I was trying really hard and then realized I had the wrong block."

The blocks did look alike. Melly fancied he could have found his way out but never back in. But what was she saying? A client? Would *he* be the client about whom she'd tell a similar story tomorrow, to the next client? Melly felt just a little cheapened and a little insignificant, but optimistic nevertheless.

She led him into her apartment; it had two bedrooms, hard, tiled floors on a concrete base, faded paintwork, and blankets up at windows for privacy. There was furniture, but it was old furniture that had been salvaged from a skip. There was a well-worn and frayed, ugly, yellow three-piece suite, and a couple of disparate chairs grouped round a low plastic table that had scorch marks all across it. Alex busied herself with clearing the detritus off the table and wiping it down with a damp cloth. She then laid out all the paraphernalia for crack smoking, pulled off her coats and boots and settled into a sofa opposite Melly who fell deeply into a two-seater settee with the tome at his side. It was two o'clock. He wondered how things might be after four or five hours with her and with his book.

Alex talked a lot, and openly. She talked a great deal about important things, about trivial things, about her concerns, and about her fears.

"Men can't stand me," she said. "After a while they want to kill me," she said. "What is it that I do that makes them want to kill me?"

Melly instinctively felt he knew the answer to that question but he was careful to put it as delicately as he could.

"You're such a lovely girl," he said. "You worry a great deal; you care, you speak of all your problems. Do you not have time to listen to what people tell you and the advice they give you?"

It had been very one-sided. He looked at the clock; she had gabbed for an hour.

"Here's a Coke," she said finally. "I hate diet Coke, it's like Pepsi. You should have got red Coke, the real stuff."

"I would have-." he started.

"Come on, then," she interrupted, "read to me!"

"If you don't understand anything, tell me," he said. "You have to understand, this is an English setting. When you get bored, tell me and I'll stop."

Melly began to read carefully and slowly. He heard himself read, and give accent and stress where he knew it had to be. He heard her laugh and he heard her sigh.

"Yeah, I been there," she said every so often.

At long last, Melly reached the point in the story where he found Talish in the alley, quite ill.

"Made quite an impact huh?" said Alex.

"You-." He stopped himself and restarted, looking at anything in trying to avoid her gaze, "She was in such a bad way; my heart went out to her. I really wanted to save her. Kenneth saved you didn't he?"

"He's a good man," said Alex, "I want you to meet him. He's an old, wise man. Everybody loves him."

Kenneth, Melly figured, probably didn't get up to much. Among the paraphernalia on the table was a massive rock of crack cocaine, maybe fifty grammes in weight and solid, like marble, washed and settled and ready for crushing. Kenneth was probably a big user and users, Melly came to understand, don't really find time for home making.

The apartment looked like any squat, like any student commune, and like any bachelor pad; it was untidy, it was unkempt, it had some books stacked in a corner, and old newspapers strewn all around the floor. There was no carpet and there were no pictures hung on the walls. The kitchen had the inevitable pile of dishes that had overflowed onto the drainer, the fridge was empty, and it was difficult to find a clean knife. But the sun shone brilliantly over the top of the blanket on the south-facing window and lit up the place to a blissful serenity.

Alex lit another pipe, and Melly rolled another joint. She eagerly shared his but he took care not to share hers.

"Why do you still walk the streets," he asked, "when you have a place?"

"I walk all the time," she said. "I cannot bear to be still. To be still means to have the time and the room for noises to come into my head, and for thoughts to invade and make me think. I don't want to think; I have to work. I have to get money so I walk all night. I was not here last night. Kenneth and I argued and I walked out."

Melly suddenly felt uncomfortable. He wondered what he would make of Kenneth, and what Kenneth would make of him. Just what was *his* relationship with her?

"He told me I was driving him crazy with my talking," she said. "Why am I driving him crazy?"

Alex was driving *Melly* crazy; she would not stop interrupting him. Revealing and welcome though it was to have her talk to him, he wasn't making progress reading through the book and that was *her* fault. It didn't bother him, though; he had read only as far as the Thai meal they ate. But she *did* go on and, perhaps, she needed to. Then he noticed her suppress a yawn.

"Sorry, sorry," she stammered, helplessly. "I'm so tired. Go on, read. Yes, read."

Melly resumed and read on to the revelations and the suicide. It was seven o'clock when he finally put the book down. He had an uneasy feeling about it; he was dead, she was dead, and it seemed a long, long way from where he was now.

Alex lay, completely relaxed, across her sofa; her long legs, long feet, her long toes, clean, firm and well used, dangled temptingly

"That spoke to me," she said. "I think the way the character thinks. I understand you very well now. That is how I feel a lot of the time. I wish I could stop using white. I wish I didn't work on the street. But you know, it has to come from inside. There are so many people, well-meaning people who come to me and tell me to stop. And I want to, believe me I want to, but I cannot. I am not ready for it, not yet.

"I remember being unwell in the summer, but I was never *that* dirty. I keep myself clean. I have a shower and I wash my clothes," she repeated. Melly listened quietly and let her unburden. "I started *poof* when I was eighteen in Rotterdam and my mother sent me out to work the streets of Eindhoven as a prostitute to pay for it." She laughed, embarrassed by her recollection. "You know, there is this thing with prostitutes and expectation. Never give the guy what he's not expecting because then it can get really out-of-hand. When I first started, I didn't know what to do so I did it all. And then, one day, a friend said to me, *No Alex, don't give them that because they will demand it.* So now, I give nothing unexpected, I give as little as I can. You cannot *make love* as a prostitute. You are there just as something to ride, for the man to climax to."

"Do you like to do it?" he asked.

"No prostitute likes to do it with clients," she replied. "The sooner it is over the better. I close my mind to it. It is automatic and with no feeling. I do it as little as possible now. I came to Amsterdam about two and a half years ago and got a window in the alley, there by the Bulldog. I paid a man for the rent but after a couple of weeks I was independent. All my money went to me and there was a lot of it. But I started to use brown and everything fell apart. I don't like the smell of brown, do you?"

Melly had never knowingly smelled burning heroin and he wasn't interested in finding out. He found the whole notion scary. The single cigarette sitting in its box reminded him that he needed to get more. His stomach rumbled hungrily.

"You want to eat?" she asked. "You want to go into town to eat or do you want to get some take-away?"

Melly hadn't seen Alex eat all day. "What do you fancy?" he asked.

She would know what was good; she lived there, after all.

"Crispy Duck," she announced. "I'll go in later and bring back some Crispy Duck and we can eat it."

Melly was receiving messages and he didn't know what to make of them. Why was she offering to extend the evening? Did she expect him to sleep over, in her bed, with her? It sounded promising and, the more he looked at her tight body, the more he looked for a sign that she might want to shower him with her favour, and want to share that well-sexed body with him, *hell, just for the sake of it.*

Alex pulled out a photo of an angelic blonde infant.

"This is my daughter," she said, anxiously looking for his reaction. "She is five. I haven't seen her for nearly three years."

Melly wanted to know why. "Tell me about it," he said.

"Well," she took a measured breath, "I was born in the Lebanon but my parents moved to Holland when I was three. Then my father went back to Beirut and never came back. But my mother, she brought me up properly: to respect people and things, to be polite, and to be decent. My grandfather died four years ago and my grandmother came to live with my mother, my twin sister, and me and my baby. The baby was an accident. I didn't plan it. It was a client; I don't know who, but I was not allowed to get rid of her. My mother and grandmother both insisted. But, you know, I was travelling to Eindhoven every day to work the street; it got too much for me. I would come home and find that they'd organized my girl's life without asking me; like, *Mummy, I'm going out with Grandma.* Yeah, well what about the plans that *I* had made for her? I just turned round one day and said, *okay fuck it, you do it; I'm going.*"

Alex wiped her eyes. "And I left, just like that. This picture is all I have. They keep on asking me when I'm going back to see her, but she cannot see me like this. I have to stop the poof first. I'll stop when I'm ready. And it's gone on like that for almost three years. I came here to work the window. I also had a room over the strip club next to the *Febo* and I couldn't afford both places and the brown. Then my nephew, my twin sister's boy, my *wonderful* twin sister; fuck her, she does everything so right, so very right; he was visiting me and we fell off the balcony into the street. I broke my back, my knee and my ankle. When I got up, I said *I've got to get back to my poof*, I wouldn't believe my back was broken 'cos it didn't hurt. The bones split cleanly, you see, and I had to lie still for a couple of months. My ankle had a pin put into it and they messed around with my knee. They say it's because I walk on it so much, it hasn't had a chance to heal properly."

There was a noticeable misalignment at the knee. It made her lose her balance sometimes, and had her having to check her step. When it got especially cold in the winter the pain would be increase. Melly figured she would soon develop arthritis.

"And being ill, not working," she said, "I didn't have the money for the rent, so I lost the flat. And I spent two years on the street with no home, just walking, walking all day and all night. And, then, Kenneth found me."

"Thank you Kenneth, whoever you are," thought Melly.

"Alex," he said, pulling himself up, "You are just the kind of person I've been writing about. I can honestly say that the book could well have been inspired by someone like you. I'm looking for Talish and I've found you instead. May I dedicate the book to you? Had it been you I met in the summer, I would have loved to write about you."

"That is a great honour, thank you," she said and beamed.

She had been beaming for the past hour. She was relaxed, content, at ease, unstrained, unworried, unhurried and cosy. She glowed in the knowledge she'd found a listening and sympathetic ear. As the muscles in her face relaxed, a fresh new range of facial expressions alighted and flitted across her countenance. She became wonderfully photogenic, the kind that, no matter how long you looked, a picture would always catch her perfect, faultless expression. Melly was enamoured. He felt like some kind of counsellor, able to bring out something in her that hadn't been touched for a long time. That, in itself, grieved him because it made him see himself in a professional capacity and not off-duty. Was *she* off-duty, or was she being professional too? The questions gnawed at Melly's conscience. He really did want to explore her body.

"You know," she said, "this is really different. I don't know of anyone who can come round to a prostitute's house as you have done and get me to open my soul like this. You have shown me your soul through your book and now you are listening to mine. That is really something. I have in you a good friend."

"Do you not have many friends then?" he asked. It was a stupid question. She laughed in his face.

"Friends?" she said, "No-one has friends here. Didn't you know? You don't trust anyone, ever, any time. No, no friends; just people I know on the street, some longer, some not so long. And don't tell me about my mother and my sister either; I don't ever want to see them, not for what they put me through on the streets in Eindhoven. They took my life."

"So there's no boyfriend?" asked Melly.

Alex looked at him severely. "I cannot have a boyfriend. Not here. Oh yes, I *want* a boyfriend, but what good to me is someone with a habit like mine. I want to break mine, not have someone else's to think about. And what, you think anyone is going to come along and take up with me? I'm a hooker. You don't touch me. I have no love for anyone; I do not love, I cannot love. I cannot give affection or be affectionate. And if there is ever anyone I like, then it's over as soon as we sleep together. It's not the same for me any more."

Her eyes were filling with tears. "I love at a distance, a very long, cold distance. I do want to be loved but I'm not ready for a boyfriend yet. One day, he will come, I know he will, and he will take me out of here and carry me to a safer place where I can start again."

Deep inside, Melly felt emotion welling up. He would help her, if only she could see her way clear to, he dared not think what.

Alex rose from her sofa to fill their glasses with more Coke.

"Do you have a second name?" asked Melly.

"My name is Alex, Alexandra. I don't have a second name." she replied.

This reply did not surprise him but it did make him feel a chill, much like the chill of disassociation.

"Come and sit here with me," said Melly, inviting her to the space next to him. It seemed a facile request that sounded really thin and insincere.

"In a minute," she said and sat back down, re-arranging herself on her own sofa.

Her face tightened just then to the way it had been before; her eyelids closing to reveal sad, bulbous, downcast eyes; it took another hour of unthreatening, easy conversation before she loosened up again. Alex was not playing *that* game.

❖ ❖ ❖

It was already dark when the doorbell rang. Alex checked the intercom and announced to Melly the imminent arrival of two good, old friends of Kenneth's; people she didn't know and had never met before.

"Be polite to them, please," she said, looking hard at him.

This was her credibility-at-home that was being tested. She wanted her guest to behave himself, and to show *her* in the best light. Melly wondered how this intrusion would affect their chemistry and wondered what would become of the evening and of the night.

When Sassy and Bernard walked in, the atmosphere changed from easy to intense, business-like and unfriendly. Bernard was a kindly, black man in his late-forties who said little except that he wished for Melly to enjoy the weed he had and which he placed on the table along with his pipe and a small bag of crack. Sassy, by contrast, was a hardened Dutch woman in her mid-thirties who had an attitude; a heroin attitude of the kind that picks an argument or a fight at the slightest provocation.

"How old do you think I am?" she tried with Alex.

"I don't know," replied Alex politely.

"No, 'cos, you see," said Sassy, "you think I'm twenty-two, don't you? Fancy you thinking I'm twenty-two! You're a damned idiot thinking that. People are always telling me I look younger, but I bet you can't guess my age."

The conversation went round in circles like this and in other circles, in Dutch. Sassy turned to Melly.

"You must excuse us speaking Dutch," she said. "You must not think we are talking about you. Some people, they find it uncomfortable."

"Dutch is easy for you," said Melly, "Talk away. I know what you mean but I'm not paranoid so don't worry, carry on!"

Now fully in Dutch, the exchanges in the room continued through various stages of antagonism and Melly sensed that Sassy was being tiresome. Bernard was seen to place a restraining, placating arm on her elbow to keep her off the boil. She turned to Melly and spoke in English.

"I'm saying," said Sassy, "that in my house, if it is mine, it is yours; if it is on the table, it is to be used. Don't ask me if you can have a cigarette, because they are there on the table to be used. My white is your white; my brown is your brown."

Melly considered how hard it is for some to adapt to the lifestyle of others in their own homes and how it was even harder to resist the temptation to impose your own lifestyle on others. For some, it was inevitable; their way was the right way, and the only way. The ensuing argument was over the amount of the huge rock that Alex was letting go into each pipe. Throughout the afternoon, Alex had been scraping dust off the rock and spreading it under a blanket of cigarette ash. A heated discussion then developed when the new guests arrived and poured scorn on Alex's preferred method.

"No! Poof, ash, poof, ash," volunteered Bernard.

"Poof, ash, poof," insisted Sassy.

"Poof, ash!" Alex stood her ground.

This was Kenneth's rock and, although she was smoking it, she was also charged with minding it. She had resolved not to see it going up in generous smokes just because someone she didn't know and didn't trust was making a determined play for it.

Melly thought about the points made. Perhaps it had to do with burning the white through a bed of ash so that it might cool down more, or might purify it through the dust, and maybe it had to do with being enclosed by ash, as in an oven, and the kind of heat generated in a kiln being quite different to that found in a furnace. A different taste, a different hit, and a different high.

"No thanks," said Melly, "I don't use a pipe."

"Oh, *lucky you*," sneered Sassy.

She was weather-beaten; she looked worn, really hard-edged, so brittle and so bristly.

"I'm stopping the brown too, you know," she said. "It's not like white. White takes five stages to come off; brown takes nine and I'm on my fourth. I'm on methadone now."

Comforting words to some? Melly didn't feel comforted. Sassy looked as if she would not last the programme, and as if she would destroy the world as well as herself, given half the chance; she was brimming with bitterness. Melly wondered where the money for all these habits came from.

Mercifully, Kenneth came home before another hour had passed. Alex immediately warmed to him and ensured he was settled comfortably into a seat with his pipe by his side and a hot mug of tea in his hand. She looked to him for signals of his needs.

"This is Kenneth, my LANDLORD," she enunciated very clearly.

Melly felt more at ease regarding his own position in this ménage. There came new messages and plenty of them.

"Be nice," Alex mouthed while looking encouragingly at Melly.

Melly stood upright and gave Kenneth his hand to shake. He felt like a new boyfriend being presented to the gruff father who needed convincing. He hadn't done this for nigh on thirty years and it felt odd. Melly knew his experience would stand him in good stead; he had, after all, developed social mobility of his own and on his own terms. Yes, he could mix with the best, with the worst, and with those in-between when it suited him to do so. Otherwise, he didn't give a shit.

Melly *did* give a shit with Alex's *dad*, though. He desperately wanted to smooth her passage through this evening, after the arguments she said she'd had with him the previous day.

Kenneth looked to be a good man; gentle, wizened and grey-haired, with a well-lined face. He settled quickly into his pipe of brown and, before too long, had caught up with the conversation. Despite their best efforts not to appear rude, the Dutch in the room did, in fact, come to discuss Melly among themselves and disagreed on some points. Alex was fighting his corner vigorously. Then they all turned to him; Sassy spoke first.

"You're looking for this girl you've written a book about," she said. "Fuck, that's an honour, isn't it? You want to know where she is. From how she's been described, I hope it's not Alex, the *other* Alex."

Slowly, Kenneth put up three old fingers and spoke wisely and in English.

"There are three people I know of who are like the girl you describe," he said, "And they are *all* called Alex."

"Hope to fuck it's not Alexis," said Sassy. "She's a bitch, so hard. Such a fucker. You should be careful of her; she's bad, and such a whore. She's high demand and high maintenance."

"She wears a black leather coat, dark curly hair-," said Melly

"Yeah," Sassy cut in, "I know her. She's got red in her hair."

"Hair colouring?" thought Melly. "How is she?" he asked.

"What's that supposed to mean?" snarled Sassy. "Why should you care?"

"I don't care," said Melly, "what I'm asking is: is she in the state I saw her in or is she better or is she worse?"

"She hasn't changed, she's worse." said Sassy and spat to herself.

"Well, I think I'll wait until I meet her before I come to any conclusions about what she's like," said Melly. "Thanks for the warning but I'll make up my own mind."

"Naturally," said Sassy, stepping back. "You'll find her down at the station, selling herself to keep up her brown habit." She turned her back on him, "Alex, did you say you were going into town to get some food and cigarettes? Pick up some brown for me?"

Alex stepped out to wash out glasses for some fresh Coke. She was eager for an excuse to flee the room and get away from Sassy. Melly followed her into the kitchen where he found her, unsmiling and wrapped up in her thoughts.

"So, you want that I should get some food and cigarettes and we will eat it here?" she asked.

"If that's what you want," said Melly.

What he really wanted to know was who was at the controls of this little affair of theirs. What meaning did it have, what relevance, what future, and what outcome? He wanted to know how much longer he still had with her, or how and when he might get away.

"How much money do you need?" he asked, scribbling a list and working out the cost. "Four guilders for cigarettes, twenty guilders for the Crispy Duck and I know you want some white so, here; here's a hundred. Get what you need but, remember, that's the last of it. I'm not getting you any more."

Alex's face remained sullen; her mood and her soul, impenetrable. Neither thanks nor regrets. She set out to change the subject.

"I'm going into town, you guys," she called out, "do you want me to get something for you?"

Another two fifty-gilder notes rose high into the air. "Get me some brown," chanted voices in unison.

Melly stood with Alex in the kitchen, watching her clean some tumblers. She was inefficient and Melly would have done it quite differently. But what struck him the most was Alex's fastidious, thorough approach to cleanliness. Melly would have begun by swilling out a glass under a running tap. Not Alex. She pushed him aside and poured an individual portion of washing up liquid in the glass and scrubbed it thoroughly, rinsed it thoroughly and went on like that with all the available glasses. She used a lot of detergent and a lot of hot water. This was disorganization at its worst, and cleanliness at its best.

"Sit here and talk to me," she invited.

He sat down on a chair at the end of the drainer and imposed himself in her personal space. She had to walk around him every time she needed to access a cupboard. He knew he was in the way, and he wondered if he should be doing this anyway. He wondered why she called him over so close. Was it so they could be alone together?

Melly looked at her. He yearned for the chance to lie with her, and to embrace her. If he'd thought about it, he would have realised her sexual liaison with him would not be of any help to her at all. There was nothing in it for her, so she wasn't going to do it and there was nothing in it for him, that's why *she* wasn't going to do it either. Melly's brain, resurfacing somewhere near his scrotum begged to differ. As close as she stood, as temptingly as she leaned over him, trustingly, Melly threw caution to the wind and, grabbing her elbow, planted a wet kiss on her wrist.

In a very controlled way, she looked at him and said, "Behave yourself."

Mixed messages, again. Melly struggled to work out whether that was an assertive *"get off, behave yourself,"* or a coy *"later, behave yourself."* It was already ten o'clock and there was no food, nor were there any cigarettes. Was he staying or wasn't he? Melly thought he'd give it a go.

"While you're down in town," he said, anxious to reintroduce the topic, "you're going on Kenneth's bike, yeah? May I take a shower?"

Alex glared at him. "Are you trying to blackmail me?" she asked.

The significance of that remark was lost on Melly, and the signals she was giving out remained confusing and mixed.

"Come," she said, "bring your stuff into my bedroom. I'm going out."

She offered him a towel but he took out his own and locked himself into the bathroom, under a shower. It felt good to wash off the sweat of travel. He changed his tee shirt, had a shave, and brushed his teeth. When he emerged, Alex was still there; she had not yet gone. She looked him up and down and saw that his dress code was, as before, *modest*, and not *loosened*, and left him in the apartment.

Melly gathered his smoking accoutrements from the living room table and took them into Alex's room and lay on her bed. But this was no bed; a single curtain lay on the floor with a small cushion at one end. The mattress, below, was no more than the linoleum tiles on a cold, hard floor.

"It's good for my back," she had said.

Melly knew about solid floors. Noble they might be, but he found they put him in a bad mood. They never allowed for sufficient rest or sleep. He lay down, corpse-like, Zappa-like, and hoped to catch a few minutes sleep while she was gone; he hoped he might wake in the morning to find her by his side.

Eventually, Alex returned and began to heat up some leftover cooked rice on the stove in the kitchen while, in the living room, another argument in Dutch ensued; she slid off toward Melly in her bedroom with plates piled high with rice, topped out with several pieces of crispy fried duck. It didn't taste as good as he'd hoped, what with his nerves having destroyed his appetite.

Melly and Alex were chatting again, enjoying time alone in her room and away from Sassy's deep, hard voice when she appeared at the door.

"My food is your food, that's what I say," Sassy began. "Why did you not get some food for us? Why did you not include us? You cook for yourself and for Melly but not for us. This is not like it is in my house. Shame on you. My white is your white and my brown is your brown. You think we have eaten today? *I* am hungry and *you* have eaten."

Alex looked in all directions for an escape to these barbs, and her eyes came to rest on Melly.

"I have to say," said Melly, "We were going to go out for a meal but decided to bring it home instead."

"But now we're going out. Goodbye," said Alex, completing the swipe.

Sassy retreated to the fresh supply of heroin that Alex had brought home. It smelled like burning plastic with a tinge of sweet incense.

"You don't use heroin?" Melly asked Alex.

"It tastes horrible, no. I used to but it is no good. No." She cringed at the thought and coughed.

Alex had been coughing intermittently throughout the day. Melly hadn't noticed before but as day turned to night, it became more regular, more insistent and more helpless.

"Are you taking anything for that?" he asked.

Alex shrugged her shoulders. "You're going to need something warm for the outside," she said, avoiding an answer. "Your jacket has no sleeves and you will freeze; I have a jacket for you. Try this on."

She threw him a jacket that was clearly too small. He wondered if being offered a jacket meant he'd be expected to come back to this place at some later point. He didn't want that. He wanted to get back to town and look out for the other Alex; he wanted to dump his ruck' on his hostel bed. He wanted to be free of *this* Alex. He had things to do and he didn't want to have to come back with *her*. As much as he had enjoyed his time with her, she was no longer his main focus. There was another Alex to find and, maybe, another after that; Kenneth had said so.

"I've got to keep looking for the girl," he said to Alex.

"So I am not her, then?" she said, looking suddenly downcast.

"You are not the one I met. I know you're not her, but you could have been her, so easily, and I almost wish it was so," he said.

He went in to the living room to bid farewells; he was about to anyway but Alex ushered him forward into the room.

"Be nice," she whispered into his ear, "say goodbye to them."

Sassy cold-shouldered him; Bernard nodded warmly but quietly. Kenneth sat in the sofa, behind a mist that shrouded his very being. Melly took his hand and peered into his face, trying to locate him.

"Kenneth," he said. "You're a good man for taking in Alex and looking after her. And if I find Talish, I'll have you to thank."

Kenneth blinked an ill-defined blink and remained silent, wizened and good.

Once out of the apartment with Alex, Melly felt sorrow for the group they left behind. The conversation there had settled on the price, quality, availability and suitability of white and brown. They talked of nothing else. And while they talked and argued, they burned heroin in foil and inhaled the sickly-sweet, black fumes. Melly recalled there *was so much else* to do in life.

"Could you work for anyone?" he asked Alex on the road back to the bright lights. They had linked arms again. "What are you good at?"

"I make things; I am good at making things," she said but did not elaborate. "But I couldn't work for anyone. Once you've been working the streets, you ain't gonna let anyone tell you what to do; no way!"

They walked back to the Old Town, looking for somewhere to stop to have a drink. It was his idea but she wanted to keep walking; he wanted to stop walking and sit with her. She wanted to keep moving so that the noises in her head would not get too loud. They made it back to the Greenhouse only to find it filled to capacity with noisy customers.

Melly was getting to feel a little uncomfortable again. He wanted to close the evening and he could not afford to spend any more time with Alex. He owed it to Talish, or to her memory at least, to seek her out.

They were walking down a quiet lane when Melly suddenly stopped and looked at Alex directly.

"Give me a hug, Alex; please give me a hug," he implored.

He pulled her to him like a rag doll and embraced her fully. She gave enough back to satisfy Melly that she might want to feel his embrace, or might want to thank him for it or, even, make him feel *wanted*.

"Alex," he said, "I'm so frustrated for sex, or sex with some affection, and it's driving me mad."

She waited until his hold on her loosened.

"You'll never get sex with affection from the prostitutes in Amsterdam," she said, "You need a lover for that. Do you have a lover?"

"No, I don't," said Melly, "and I don't want one. I won't allow myself to love anyone other than my wife. I will sleep with others but they will not become lovers."

"And does it ever work out for you?" she asked, "Do you get your *sex with affection*?"

"Rarely, only very rarely," said Melly.

"Take my advice," she said, "stay away from hookers because I know what you want and you will never find it. Everyone looks for the same thing but it's not there to be found. We are all acting; we are not giving it. We haven't got it to give anyway. I hate the work I do. I close my eyes to it but it fills my head; I can't stand it."

They walked a while further, with Melly conscious of a gulf widening between them.

"Hey, come with me a moment," she said suddenly and led him to a dealer. "Have you got twenty guilders?" she asked of Melly.

"No Alex, I haven't. Look, I'm going now," he said, backing away.

"Wait for me," she called and ran up beside him, linking into his arm.

She was not angered by his refusal to buy for her and they walked slowly as far as his hostel.

"You're not allowed in here, are you?" he asked her at the door.

Alex peered in. A second-rate boogie band was playing in the bar, cymbals crashing, and high treble screeching through the PA. The bar sold beer and coffee. This evening, it looked welcoming but she just shook her head. There was nothing else he wanted to offer to her.

"Alex, I'm going to say goodnight."

"Oh?" she sounded a deeply mournful note.

"I'm going in. I need to sleep, and I need to look for Talish tomorrow. I may see you tomorrow."

"What time do you wake?" she asked excitedly.

"Me? Oh, eight," he suggested.

"I'll be here at eight," she said, offering him her cheek. Even as he kissed it, he could feel the tension and mistrust through her tightening skin.

As she wandered off, he watched her disappear from view and his heart sank. It was now one o'clock in the morning. The bar was full, and the dormitory was empty. He put his ruck' down at *C7* and kicked it under his bunk, then went downstairs to the bar. Sinking a beer quickly, he went out again. Finally, after so many hours in Amsterdam, he was free, alone, and again in search of Talish. Wasn't that why he was there?

He wondered about just how much time he had spent with Alex and whether it was, in truth, time wasted. She was a remarkable girl. There was so much she had to offer; he had seen one or more of her many sides, yet demons and ill health plagued her. Alex *was* the girl he had been writing about, not the girl who inspired it. So many things he'd imagined about her were true; the underlying premise was sound though he could see that he'd got it wrong in one significant area. It didn't make any difference how much Alex claimed that she didn't have a problem with crack and how it was possible for her to go several days without, as Talish had claimed. The fact remained that it was the singular objective of her day; the smoking of the pipe and its continuous replenishment. If the source was there, and if the means was there, then it became an unstoppable obsession. Talish, Melly thought, would not have been a willing participant to the hotel experience if she wasn't guaranteed a smoke. And her agitated need to walk would have made her restless very quickly, not to mention the restful quiet of the hotel room in which her demons would be free to run riot. Melly caught sight of those demons a couple of times during the day. Alex would suddenly grip her head by the ears and turn in on herself. At times like that, she would nudge him forward to keep walking, keep talking, and say something. Melly wasn't very good at *saying something.*

He realized, also, that she was not going to offer him physical affection and he could not offer any small talk unless it was an endearment or a charming witticism. He hadn't achieved a romantic link with her, she'd made that quite clear, and he wasn't up to confident banter. He was lovelorn. He would have loved to lie with her but it wasn't going to happen and he no longer knew how to talk to her, now that he had nothing to gain from the effort. There had passed between them, sometimes, silences in which he wished only to bask in her beauty and her potential serenity while she just craved his words of encouragement, of understanding, and of unthreatening conversation. Melly was not a good conversationalist. Even she, Alex, sometimes ran out of things to say too. *Then* it got really quiet.

Melly went out into the Old Town, freed of baggage, and a free spirit. This time, he strolled past the windows soaking up as many of the come-ons as were available. He still had enough money to pay for someone to tickle his bollocks, provided he could find someone suitable; the day had left him *that* frustrated. And he was desperate for a bit of affection. As he sifted through the girls, sorting them in his head, it occurred to him that they were, indeed, all actors in this game of make-believe. They set the ground rules, they set the parameters, and they would be what the punters wanted them to be, unless their acting had them typecast and limited to one character. And they would make the right noises when it suited them, not the client.

He remembered what Alex had said about disliking the job. Seeing his partner unimpressed was anathema to Melly's lovemaking principles.

He knew none of the window women would care a fig about him just as he would not care a fig for any of them. Not one-and-a-half seconds after climaxing; this was roughly the time it took for guilt to set in and, perhaps, half as long as it normally took him to lose interest too.

There was no joy on the street or in his head that night yet Melly was up for stimulation. He figured he'd try to touch base with Barry and Jono and the two Andies. They had arranged to meet at the Space Café *later* but, you know how it is; you look everywhere and even though it's staring you in the face, you can't see it. Melly couldn't find the Space Café; hell, he couldn't even find the sex shop where he'd seen the *orgasmatron*.

"Does everything change so quickly when priorities change?" he wondered. "Do things that were important really disappear so fast? Do we really become as blind as to ignore the obvious?"

Melly was soul-searching. The activities on the street, the deals and the wary look over the shoulder were a constant reminder of what *he* had been doing throughout the day. He returned to his hostel for another beer and a spliff. The band was still pumping boogie. It didn't matter if was good or not; it was loud; that's all it needed to be rated *good*, as it filled every corner with a shrill intensity. You don't go to places like that if you want a chat. His four young travelling companions were in among the audience, propping themselves up on elbows, sitting at a table, either melting or dissolving; at any rate, wrecked in a very Amsterdam sort of way.

"Good is it?" shouted Melly cheerfully, and patronizingly.

"Fuck, yeah," Barry answered through his glazed pinkness, "Well gone, me. Say, did you find her?"

"I found one, but she was the wrong one," yelled Melly into the noise. "I'm looking again tomorrow."

Barry looked at him, mystified, not sure if he'd heard correctly.

"Wrong one?" he yelled. "When did you work that one out?"

Melly didn't answer. He just shook his head, and gave that *nah* look that speaks volumes of *I'd rather not talk about it 'cos I'm an arsehole* and took his drink off to an empty table to sit down and review his day.

The wrong one...when did you figure that one out? Melly wondered about when it began to matter to him that Alex wasn't the one he'd been looking for.

"True," he thought, considering the depleted wad on his money pouch, "too fucking true, Barry."

He rolled up a spliff, alongside younger men who rolled theirs to remain legless. Melly rolled his in order to come down to some semblance of reality. It's quite astounding how people get differing things from smoking dope.

And he cried. Quietly, like a yawning chasm that waited to swallow him, Melly felt a bleakness, an abject uselessness, that made him panic. Something deep inside made him look at his life-clock and conclude that he was a bad, bad man, who was self-seeking, egocentric, dick-led, and hopelessly, if not naively, romantic.

What was it Alex had said? "I have a client who comes to see me. He is the wealthiest man in Europe, and he spends time with me. He has asked me to go away with him but I will not go. How can I go to become someone's ornament, to be on someone's arm? He thinks money will buy me but it is love I want. He would not give me love; I would be his possession. Still, he gives me virtually everything I need, and almost everything I want."

Melly didn't believe her then and he did not believe her now. He wanted to believe her and he knew *she* wanted to believe it too, but it was not about to happen, Alex was well aware of the requirements for an outcome to her dilemma. She needed someone from outside with the means to get her out of there and into somewhere completely new. She needed someone with whom she would fall in love. But did she have any idea what *that* was?

"I don't know what love is," she'd said, "I have no boyfriends, not any more. I am not good enough for a boyfriend. I am just nothing. And anyway, I have to leave this place soon. How I want to; how I *need* to leave this place. The friends, the people I know, they are not good for me, and I know I am not good for them. I have too many enemies now. I told you I drive men crazy. Why? They want me to go, they want me to leave them alone and go. When, oh when, will this man come?"

Melly sat in the smoky bar and watched the band playing an interminably long number, the keyboard player resigned to holding down a single note for the duration. With his index finger firmly in place, he took time to look round at the inattentive audience and, seeing no one was listening, closed his eyes and waited for the drum roll that would count down the end of the number. But he wasn't listening and missed his cue; the number ended as cacophony as each player looked to the other for new markers. Melly had not been listening either. He was sensing, too, except that he was blind to the real picture and the senselessness of his involvement. Alex wanted someone like *him* to rescue her and he was there to boast how he had imagined rescuing someone like *her*. Only now, he wasn't offering.

He was pleased that he had read to her of his imagined lovemaking in the hotel room; the point at which his own true sensibilities were laid bare. He wondered what relevance any of his scribbling had in the light of the true reality that he'd uncovered; a reality that had been shared with him so selflessly and so trustingly. Alex had trusted him with her soul and, yet, all he was interested in was whether she was prepared to have sex with him. The entire relationship he had forged with her was contemptuous and corrupt in the extreme. Melly thought about social workers and care workers who abuse their position and develop a sexual relationship with those in their charge. He knew what could drive those people who professed to care, and whose job it was to be trustworthy. He understood how corrupt some of those specialists could be. And he was playing the same game. He was offering some light yet, at the same time, snatching it away. But in snatching it away from a girl so desperately needy, Melly had little reason to consider himself to be any better than her and no better than even the lowest low-life.

Melly tried to justify his right to his three square metres of this Earth in the light of an indelible memory he'd forged when he was nineteen and truly philosophical for the first time. *If he hadn't become the person he'd wish to be by the age of forty, he had no right to be alive; if he managed to live to the year 2000, that was long enough, he'd have seen enough.* What fucking right did he now have to live? What did he hate so much about this life that made him want to wallow in its mire and still find himself unfulfilled?

Alex was a good soul, and he was doing her wrong. He knew this because everything could only be downhill from here. She knew she was up against the real Talish, a girl of whom she knew; a really mean whore, the one of whom she, too, had advised him to beware. It was Talish that Alex was keeping him away from. She was keeping him for herself, and was hanging onto him while he was in Amsterdam.

"Eight o'clock tomorrow morning, eh!" thought Melly as he went up to spread out a blanket at *C7* under which to lie, fully clothed. He wondered how much longer Alex would stay up, and if there was any likelihood she'd take a client home, and whether she'd finally get some sleep.

"Yeah, and then come round first thing to see me?" he thought, "Bollocks to that!"

Melly awoke at nine. His first move was to look out of the window into the alley below. Naturally, Alex was not there.

"Good," thought Melly. "Today, I am free of her; today I devote my energies to finding Talish."

He was apprehensive; Talish would cost. Alex had got to spend his money and she was only using crack; heroin, on the other hand, was that much more expensive and so much more frequently topped up by the user. Melly shuddered at the thought that his money was fast disappearing. He piled several layers of mild cheese between two pieces of bread, and tried to enjoy the weak coffee that the hostel served up for breakfast. Everyone else slept on, with the dormitory full to capacity. Barry, Alex and both Andies dreamed on, oblivious to Melly's need for their shoulder to cry on. Any good shoulder was worth crying on and, especially, he wanted Jean's shoulder to cry on. Alex was not the threat Jean imagined Talish to be. Melly's frustration was the threat, as was the way he was dealing with it. He wanted Jean to advise him. It's not that he wanted *a wife to advise her husband on how to get over someone he was messing around with.* He needed a friend to nod and tell him that he was still on the correct side of decency, that it was right how he was recognizing his own faults, and that she understood his frustration and his quest for a solution and for some sort of release.

"He wants his cake, and to eat it too?" taunted the voices in his head.

"No," replied Melly defiantly, "There's no cake and there's no eat; figure that one out."

Melly found Kokomo flying around under the *FEBO*, big blue letters on a huge slab of backlit yellow plastic, fixed to a building that bridged one of the narrow lanes.

"Hi," said Melly, deflecting Kokomo's initially raised eyebrow. "I'm not buying. Have you seen Alex?"

"Yuh," said Kokomo, eyeing the street, on the lookout for the plain-clothed police, while also on the lookout for a punter. "I saw her this morning. She met someone at eight-thirty to spend some time with."

Melly felt a tinge of jealousy creep into his head. She was giving it out; she was giving it. Then reality set in; she was getting money for her access to white. That's *all* that mattered.

"I'm still looking for the girl in the leather coat," he said. "Have you seen her?"

"She works at the back of Central Station," said Kokomo.

That was all Melly needed to know; he walked off, reflecting on his conversation with Kokomo. A bit like the way some people use phones... *"Hello, yes...two-fifteen...right...seven. Bye."* Brief and to the point, with no frills. When you don't trust someone, you don't involve in idle chatter. It's *"What do you want? Go!"* Nothing else. *Don't get into my space; don't get into my head.* Melly had got into Alex's head. He was like that; he was intrusive.

Walking to the station, he felt regret that Alex was not Talish. She had proved such a good role model. The real Talish, if the Sassy's word was to be believed, was going to be a desperate change. How close to the filthy girl of six months past, and how much worse was she, or could she, be? And what was he going to do about it? What was he going to say to her when they met?

It was noon and he was fast running out of time if he wanted to read to her as he had read to Alex. But he no longer *really* wanted to read to her. He just wanted to thank her for inspiring him. With the uncertain way he now felt about the book, he wondered if there was any point in talking to her about it at all; the book had got it *so* wrong.

But he did want to touch base with her. That's what it was! Whether the book existed or not, it had consumed him for months and he was out to take his heroine off the pedestal on which he'd put her. Seeing

Talish would be like allowing her to say, *"This is what I'm really like; I'm not like you imagined. I'm setting you free with a dose of reality."*

⊠ ⊠ ⊠

Amsterdam Central Station is a wide, deep building, with platforms high up above the booking hall and the Metro sunk deep below. A warren of connecting passages, some used as shopping malls, some undergoing reconstruction though still accessible, and all bathed in warm but dehumanising sodium light. It wasn't the kind of place Melly wanted to find Talish. There were too many people here, many of whom were loitering; each had their own reason for being there. At the far end of a dusty concourse, the open bleakness of the docks and the Amstel ferry, seen through plate glass, showed this was a side of the station with particular purpose. Melly walked out and looked around for the hookers but found it difficult to distinguish those who were from those who were not. One moment the windy forecourt was deserted, in the next, three leather-clad women, with lipstick thinly applied, were there looking interested in what Melly had to say. The eyebrow raised on one older woman.

"I'm looking for Alexis," he said. "Have you seen her?"

"She normally works here, but she's not around today," a woman in her forties said, her brightly blushed cheeks too red for her pale, freshly powdered skin. She gave him the kind of look that said, "Will I not do, then?" but which soon became "Oh, lucky girl she, I wonder what *he's* offering her."

As Melly walked away, back towards the Old Town, he could feel the concentrated stares of the three who gathered to confer, to discuss, and to speculate on his business and, finally, to jeer encouragement.

⊠ ⊠ ⊠

Melly stood under the *Febo* chewing on a slab of pizza. He'd seen these slabs being eaten by all passers-by and, now, it was his turn. The shredded chicken topping he'd ordered tasted like minced meat of some kind, but only God knows what was in there. It tasted bad from the start, it tasted worse by the time he was half through it and, despite knowing it was likely to make him ill, he forced himself to finish it, and fill himself with as much stodge as he could. Melly wasn't out to follow mealtimes; he wanted filling just there, and just then. He wanted Talish, and Talish on a full stomach, so that *it* wouldn't sing to her and cramp his style.

It was one in the afternoon when the tall, warmly-wrapped apparition that was Alex showed, walking towards him, her bulbous eyes downcast and saddened. She was holding her jaw, the toothache annoying her still. He stepped across her path.

"Hi," said Melly, "did you sleep well?"

Alex gave him the kind of withering look that screamed, *"FUCKING IDIOT, DO I LOOK AS IF I'VE BEEN SLEEPING?"*

"I haven't slept at all," she hissed at him. She looked angry and she looked depleted. "I've been walking all night," she said, making it sound as if it was *his* fault she was forced to do that; walking all night because *he* didn't have the decency to spend the time with her; bored all night because *he* hadn't been there to talk about things other than the next deal.

"I was here at eight o'clock, waiting for you," she said, nonchalantly, "then I met with someone and have been with them all this morning."

Melly felt his heartstrings being pulled, and felt the positive strokes implicit in her words cascading onto him.

"So, I *do* matter," he thought selfishly.

Alex grunted painfully and felt crotchety. "I am so tired," she said. "You'll stay with me for a while today? I'm so hungry; buy me something to eat."

Melly considered his options. Walking the streets with Alex would give him a visual key on the street and a chance to spot Alexis.

"You know I'm looking for *her* today," he said, "I'll stay with you a short while."

Alex and Melly stood at the junction of several lanes, at a particular spot in town where everyone and anyone who had business there, went. If you wanted to find someone, this was the place to be.

"You want white, brown, hash?" A new Moroccan face danced in and out of view.

Alex looked at Melly. "You got ten guilders?" she asked him.

Melly immediately had a ten in his hand, pulled out from the wad in his jacket. Alex looked at him severely and slapped his pocket.

"Hide that," she scolded, "Someone will take it easily."

Melly returned the look, feeling confused and naive. The Moroccan took the note and danced some more, then spoke to Alex in Dutch.

"He says that another five guilders will get me a good deal of white and some brown, if I want it," said Alex. "He wants to know if you want any hash."

"I don't want any hash," said Melly, "I'm fine."

Another five guilders was not easy to find; Melly pulled another twenty-five-guilder note from his pocket and gave it to the Moroccan. The man grabbed the money and walked back past Alex, waving it at her and then disappeared around a corner. By the time he was out of sight, Alex was screaming after him, while others in the street joined in, scowling, pained, and embittered.

"He's run off with the money," she said, "you were too quick with the cash. He saw *you* coming, you fool."

"Are you saying we've been ripped off and he's not giving you *anything*?" asked Melly.

"I'll get him later on," she snarled, "another day. I know his weaknesses; I'll fuck him up. You watch."

Melly wondered how the Moroccan had hoped to get away with it, running off with the money like that. Wasn't it obvious he'd have to come through again later to make a connection, and connect with those he'd just offended, or their associates?

Alex looked at him. "Come with me," she ordered.

Melly was happy with that; it seemed to him that since she knew the area, she'd know where to go, what to see, and what to do. He was hopeless; he only knew the coffee bars and she wasn't allowed in them, despite the expiration of her exclusion order. But they knew her business and her style. They knew it wouldn't be too long before she took out her pipe and smoked more crack in their bar and in front of *their* customers; their tourist customers.

Rizla 22 was waiting on a corner, ready to offer sympathy to Alex who was still infuriated by the broken deal.

"You, you stay with him," she said, taking Melly's arm and placing him next to the be-spectacled Rastafarian.

Rizla 22 had kind eyes and a face that looked as if there was a modicum of sanity stored deep within. He was alert, furtive, and in control.

"Cover me," he said to Melly, "watch my back."

Melly drew up close to Rizla 22 and put an arm up over his shoulder. Rizla 22, thus sheltered from the wind, took out a piece of foil from his mouth and fried some globules of the dark, sticky heroin it contained with a lighter. Melly reached over and pulled the man's coat up over his head, creating a warm, airless cavern for the ceremony of inhalation. After a long deep breath, then another, Rizla 22 emerged with his eyes glazed, and sniffled. Melly breathed out, finally, and relaxed. He was clear in his own mind that he would not yield to heroin's attraction and, consequently, had found it easy to say no. That was easy because he saw what it did. He knew his weakness for cannabis and he knew that his was an addictive personality. He knew he could easily become a heroin or a crack addict but he simply wasn't interested. As deeply as he found himself immersed in this sub-culture, no-one had forced him and no-one had even enticed him to join in. It was *their* smoke; they didn't share it with one another, especially not pipes. Each had their own supply and their own target for the day. Sassy was the one who'd said, "What's yours is mine and what's mine is yours," but what she really meant was "what's yours is mine and what's mine is my own," and that made her unpopular. Melly had never seen Sassy on the street, not around the Old Town, anyway.

Alex returned, agitated, and nodded to Rizla 22.

"You have thirty guilders?" she said to Melly.

The sad tourist gave her two twenty-fives. "You want some?" she asked.

Melly shook his head. This could not go on; she was costing him too much. Rizla 22 spat out the contents of his mouth and took out a large ball of white and looked over at Melly. Melly shook his head. Rizla 22 took a smaller bag and gave it to him along with a twenty-guilder note. The tourist marvelled that there might be some honour among thieves, and that at least Rizla 22 was not going to rip him off too. But Rizla 22 was okay. He had an intelligent face, like one of those kids at school who used to look all bookish behind their glasses and even more intelligent when they push them up their nose with the middle finger in order to see more clearly. Rizla 22 moved his glasses to see clearly.

Alex pulled Melly to her and had him go through the ritual of screening, enveloping her again as she smoked another pipe in just one or two lugs.

"We go now," she said, "let's eat."

But they didn't eat; they didn't eat for a long time. Instead, they wandered about, looking for somewhere to go. Once again, Melly's head filled with anticipation about what Alex might be thinking, about what her agenda was for him? Why did she want him to be with her when she knew he was out looking for another woman who was another user? Then, he began to understand. The longer they walked, the more it became clear to him that he was not being treated as a client at all. Alex wanted his company and she wanted him to talk to her. She was falling asleep with exhaustion and she needed rest. And yet, she needed to stay awake, to stay awake to smoke some more. She needed Melly's money; this much was plain yet Melly constantly refused to believe it.

"Last night," she said, "I went to Central Station and stayed there for much of the night. Policemen were there. They know me; they know who I am, and they take care of me. It's Danny; he's one of them. Why is he so interested in me? He was laughing with me. Do you think he likes me?"

"You like being with him?" asked Melly, "Do you think he wants to trick you? Do you think that he might be someone who can help you?"

"No," she said, "I want to know what he wants from me. We arranged to meet tonight at the station at midnight. But I am so tired," she yawned, "I need to sleep."

"Well, then, let me take you home and put you to bed," said Melly, and then checked himself, thinking about the way time had been wasted the previous day. "No," he restated, "*you* go home and go to bed;

you have a long time, many hours, until you meet with him again. You want to look your best, don't you? Go, sleep."

"No, no. I have to stay awake," she wailed petulantly, stamping her feet on the ground and hiding her head in her hands as she struggled to shake off a demon that was annoying her.

"Why won't you sleep? Why do you drive yourself to this?" asked Melly. "Are you angry about last night?"

"It's not about *you*," she said from behind her elbows. "My head is spinning with thoughts, I can't stand it. What shall I do about *him*?"

"If you see him tonight," asked Melly, "do you think he will be nice to you?"

"Maybe," she said, looking sadder still, "but if I go with him, it will all be over, I know it. I am interested in the chase but I cannot give him affection."

Melly felt he had no answer to that.

"Come, talk to me," she said, "say something."

Melly was not into small talk. He was out of ideas about what to say to her. What did she want to talk about? What was there to talk about? He wanted to get away; he wanted to buy her food? He wanted some quiet time with her and she was dragging him about the streets, vacillating, and he was so easily pissed off by people who vacillated. He remembered once in Ireland, he was hitchhiking and got to Lisdoonvarna, three weeks before the annual music festival. All he wanted was a bed for the night; some floor somewhere but, instead met Connor at eleven that morning.

"Sure," said the old boy, "Y'can sleep in my cottage; it's in the next village, but we'll wet our whistles first."

Maybe it's something about the Irish, maybe it's something about drinkers; Melly found himself accompanying Connor wherever he went that day, like an anxious hound, hoping, and waiting for a treat or a bone to gnaw on. Melly finally abandoned Connor in a bar at two the following morning and trudged the thirty metres to his cottage, alone and thoroughly disheartened. Such a waste of time and energy, all for a couple of hours sleep in a coal box, for that is all there was for a bed. And now, Alex was wasting his time, following through from one place to smoke to another place to smoke.

"Can we sit down?" he asked, seeing a wide sun-drenched piazza.

Unusually, Alex sat down with him on some steps at the foot of a Rotunda, which stood as a reminder of a wealthy commercial past. She was done walking, moving and fidgeting for the moment. She sidled up and stared at the buildings opposite impassively.

"Put your arm around me," she said suddenly.

Melly might have been hoping for some affection, or for some request for affection, but he had grown used to this particular move. Melly shielded her as she poured out another pipe and smoked again. Melly gripped her by the arm, purposely, though not harshly. She didn't cringe.

"Alex," he said, "I need to know. I'm sitting here and thinking. At what point during the last couple of days did I move from being one person and become another? I mean, am I a client of yours or am I a friend? Are you a prostitute to me or are you a friend? I'm trying to work out why we're together still and why I'm not getting anything I might have thought I was going to get?"

"Go on," she said.

"Yesterday," he said, "you asked me if I wanted to sleep with you and I said yes. I've been waiting ever since."

"When did I say that?" she said, looking up at him. "I did not say that."

"So, I misunderstood," he said. "And so, I ask myself, why am I here? There are so many signals from you I do not understand. You are such a provocative, good-looking woman. You must forgive me but I can't help but look at you longingly and lustfully. You're so gorgeous. And I don't know what to make of you. You say men want to kill you; I can understand what you mean. You're making my blood boil with lust for you but you do not see it that way. Sex is so far from your mind yet it is what I identify you with. Yesterday, I asked you to sit with me, and you would not, I kissed your wrist and you withdrew. Yet, you were entertaining me at your place until so very late. I'm thinking whether things would have been different if Sassy and Bernard had not come. Forgive me Alex, I want to respect you as a person but I cannot overcome my lust for you."

"You know," she said, quietly, "I thought exactly the same thing. You've got my thoughts completely, you understand me so very well-."

Just then, Rizla 22 showed and sat down next to Alex, asking to use her pipe.

"With him, I share. He's my good friend," she said, shielding him from prying eyes.

What they were doing was obvious. It was obvious to the public who passed them; it was obvious to Melly who could detach himself and see the three of them huddled unnaturally, and behaving suspiciously.

"See over there," said Alex, preparing a pipe and nodding at a building on the far side of the piazza, "that's the police station and I'm smoking my pipe at their door. Suckers!" She raised a defiant fist.

"Alex," said Melly, slightly panicked. He recognized the police station. "Do you want to get busted? Aren't you being just a bit, er, crazy?"

Alex looked over at Rizla 22. Like old friends working spontaneously and in unison, they drew their heads together; each raised a clenched fist and yelled, "SUCKERS!" Then Rizla 22 took off.

Melly felt he could no longer stand by and watch impassively. There was business to attend to and he was being remiss. He needed to start dictating terms and the ball was now in his court; he took Alex by the arm and dragged her into Chinatown and directly into a Thai bar. He led them in, not really registering where he was or what he was meant to do. Alex had not been inside this sort of place for some considerable time and had forgotten the form. She spoke as if on the offensive; for too long, she had been defensive, now she felt plucky. It was time to kick arse, to spend some money and get some service.

"Coffee," said Melly automatically.

"Tea," said Alex, automatically.

Melly looked at an adjoining table and realized he was about to eat Thai food.

"Yuh, mine's a tea too," he said, confusing the Thai waitress who was trying to welcome them.

They did not sit at a table as normal people sit. Alex walked towards a bench under a counter close to a coat rack. Purposely low-life and not fully exposed, it allowed her to cower from the world. It was a quiet, unimportant, and insignificant corner for Alex. It hadn't even been set with cutlery.

Melly steered her further on towards a bench that was closer to the light in this bright room. Even though it faced the wall, the counter was set with place mats.

"No eating across from one another," thought Melly sadly and sat astride the bench in order to face her.

Alex sat on the bench but with her back to the counter, her long legs stretching out to tangle with the adjacent tables. Then she took off two layers of coating and threw them unceremoniously on the floor under the counter. It was uncommon behaviour and likely to attract attention; everyone looked at them. The waitress and Alex began talking in Dutch and appeared to get into an argument; Melly didn't understand and it upset him because, here, he was not in control. The waitress turned to him.

"That will be thirty-seven guilders," she said.

"I've got money, look," said Melly defensively and then realized he was in an open food bar where, for a standard charge, he could fill his plate.

Melly relaxed and allowed his adrenaline to settle. There was a time he'd have handled all of this very differently. But this wasn't his space, it was Alex's, and he had let *her* set the pace. And, maybe, she was out of *her* depth and needed *his* help. Paranoia can be so infectious. Melly avoided paranoia like the plague.

This was no romantic meal that Melly and Alex, Melly and Talish, or any two people ever shared. Despite their jovial swagger on entering, they both went to the bar and made their extensive selection in silence; they chose their chopsticks in silence and returned to the thin counter under the wall in silence. Side by side, they faced this neutral bleakness with their legs tucked under this counter. Melly let out a few involuntary *wows* as he tucked in, but it didn't really matter because they were filling up and that was rare for both of them, especially so for Alex. After one heaped plate, Melly was sated. It wasn't brilliant food, just unusual. He wolfed his down and was left watching Alex as she ate. She had good manners; she held her soupspoon correctly, she used her chopsticks skilfully, and made the minimum of mess, until she felt his eyes bearing down on her.

"Read a magazine while you're waiting," she snapped at him with half a plate of food still in front of her.

"Ah," he said, believing that the procurement of and payment for food was the only reason he was there at all. He'd achieved that much and now wanted to get away and leave her to it. "Yeah," he announced, "I might go soon; I've got to carry on looking."

Alex angrily slammed the back end of her chopsticks on the counter and they made a sharp crack. Everyone in the room looked up again.

"Fuck you," she shouted, "you're not leaving me here alone. I was brought up properly, you know. When a man takes you to lunch, you expect him to bring you back from lunch. He takes you into a restaurant and then he takes you out of the restaurant. Idiot!"

Melly felt six years old and suitably chastised. He stayed in his seat and Alex, as if to punish him for such impertinence, ate the remaining half of her food silently then went to load up again from the bar; and yet again after that. By the time she returned with her third helping, they had both begun to mellow. The food had nourished them and they felt revitalised and better humoured.

"Is there a bathroom here?" Alex asked.

Melly pointed to a sign.

"Will you be here when I come back?" she asked.

"Yes, I'll be here," he replied.

Alex left and, after ten minutes, Melly understood that she was smoking her pipe again and doing things that women spend ten minutes alone in a bathroom doing. He took the opportunity to write out his London address and phone number on a slip of paper and slipped it into the wallet in her anorak with a brief note. He wasn't sure why he'd done this, though it had to do with her not being a threat to him and, consequently, someone he could *entertain* publicly. The substance of *not-an-affair*.

When Alex returned, she redressed herself from the undergarments outward, readjusting the lines in her clothing. If there was one thing that Alex proved then, it was that she was fastidious and meticulous about her appearance.

"As long as you're clean on the outside, people will think you're clean on the inside," she said finally.

"Are you clean on the inside?" Melly asked.

Alex looked at him but did not answer.

"Come," she said, "I'll walk with you to the station."

Melly wasn't so sure about that. He did not want to have Alex impact in any way on his meeting with Alexis. He wanted to keep the two women separate.

"This is as far as we go," he said abruptly at the entrance to the station.

"Nonsense," she said and led him to one of her known haunts, near the left-luggage area. She was not prepared to let him go.

Suddenly, the Moroccan appeared and walked past them. Melly made as if to approach him.

"He's got my money," he said to Alex with indignation. "I'm going to ask for it back."

Alex held onto his arm, forcing him to stop in his tracks.

"It's not him," she said, "he is not the one from this morning; it is another man."

Melly felt that, even in the face of the earlier rip-off, these people had short memories and that there was little honour among thieves, and other things like that.

"I'll get him another time," Alex said finally, once he was out of sight, "I'll *fuck* him real good."

Melly was placated, for the moment. She led him upstairs to the main line platforms where another connection could be made, and where it was quiet enough for a smoke. There, again, Melly refused to fund another ball for Alex.

"Okay, okay," said Alex, sensing Melly's impatience. "Let's take the elevator," she beamed. "I love the elevator."

Two floors in an elevator can be an eternity and Melly, for the final time, thought whimsically of how he might spend his last few moments with her, out of the public gaze and in complete privacy. The doors closed behind them and Alex pulled her pipe from inside her sleeve. It was primed, ready to go and she smoked it contentedly. She was, by now, looking through him, into some middle-distance with a blank expression that might well have said, *"I am tolerating you now because I no longer enjoy your company."* Melly felt used, abused and exploited; willingly but, nonetheless, callously.

"Alex," he said to her finally. "I want to know why you won't let me go; I'm trying to work out what's in it for me. I'm in two minds about finding Alexis at all now. I'm getting to hope I won't have to stay too long with her. When I finish with her, and it may take a short time, I don't know, I'll return to you. But, right now, I must go."

"Don't go." she said as the elevator doors opened and threw them back into the world

"I have to," he said, "I've nothing left to give you."

"You don't give me anything," she said, defensively.

"Is *that* a fact?" he said incredulously, "I bought you four balls yesterday, I've bought you three balls today; I'm standing here thinking, why am I buying you all your white? Why *should* I buy all your white? And what am I getting out of it? Why are you treating me this way?"

"I need your support," she said.

"And tell me," he said, "if I wasn't here, to support you, what would you do?"

"I would find someone else to support me," she said.

Melly knew this was the only answer she could give. It was the clear statement he needed to help him make a decision.

"Well fuck you, Alex! I came to Amsterdam for a reason. I was looking for someone and I haven't found them yet. And even though you are like them, even though you may be all I need to find, I must find the real one so that I can end my own nightmare, and so that I can put my story to bed. I've spent so long with you and now I can't afford to spend any more time with you. I *have* to go. We're done. We're finished."

She turned away and hid her head beneath her hair, flattening herself against a pier. Melly came up behind her, to stroke her hair forgivingly. She started up, unused to not being in control of who might touch her, and of where and of when. She gave him a look of anger, and one of desperation. Her eyes moist with tears, she hid her head again.

Melly could have walked off, far into the distance but he only made it to the other side of the pier, out of sight. There he crouched next to his rucksack, and curled up into himself, wringing thoughts of Alex out of his head and out from under his skin. He felt like crying but stopped himself; that would have been just too melodramatic.

When he was satisfied that Alex had really gone and that she had finally let him go, he set out to explore the station. In the ticket office Melly bought two rail tickets to the coach terminal. At three guilders each, it was a small price to pay for the hope that Alex might come to see him off. A girl in black loitered close by. Melly wondered if she was waiting for someone. By the time he thought of asking her about Alexis, she was gone.

Kokomo passed him and nodded recognition.

"She's gone to the *Febo*," he said, without being asked, "I've just seen her."

Melly trudged back to the Red Light district and sat down at a table in an old-fashioned pub across from the *Febo*, where everyone passed. She would pass too; she was bound to, surely. He sat a full half-hour before the barman suggested he buy a drink. They're like that in Amsterdam; unhurried, patient and unbothered. No-one was bothered with the panoramic view of the lane under the *Febo*. Framed for half its length by the pub's gigantic windows, Melly saw what Amsterdam's sub-culture was up to. He saw Rizla 22 connect with a man, peering furtively over the rim of his glasses for any prying eyes. It was like a caricature. Hopelessly larger-than-life movements and gesticulations. It was almost like farce because, not one metre away, in the cosiness of a pub, sat an audience of at least one who had not been looked out for and who, through not being out on the street, was being ignored and written out of the equation. He could have been anyone, or anyone undercover.

Melly saw Alex walk by, intently following the Moroccan who had just passed. She returned a while later and he saw her connect with Rizla 22. Then, a man who had very definitely lost control of his mind, staggered about in front of the window, shuffling two paces forward, turned and shuffled three paces back. His eyes had gone grey and dead like stone; Melly had seen this before, but not for a long time; not since the things he'd seen in London. This one was a businessman; the suit he wore had been clean that morning but, already, his piss-stains were showing through. This victim was a freshman in Amsterdam and Melly knew he wouldn't last long.

"Small beer," Melly called to the barman finally and rose to collect it.

No sooner had he resumed his seat in the window when he saw a mass of curly, auburn hair, tied back tightly on a girl dressed in a long black leather coat pass along the lane. Melly sprang to his feet and ran towards the pub door, slowing down to negotiate all the other customers who stood in his way.

Once outside, everything looked different. To start with, the girl was not there and there was no sign of her red head bobbing in among the crowd. He followed in the direction she had walked but it was clear he'd missed her. Melly returned to the pub, to his table and to his half-pint with the sip missing. He took another sip. It was six in the evening; he had only about four hours before his coach back to London. Rizla 22 passed the window again and, this time, saw him looking out and observing before peering in. A slight nod passed between them. They both knew and both were saying nothing.

A girl dressed in black passed the window. Melly recognized her as the one he'd missed at the station; the one he was going to ask. On seeing her for the second time, he recognized the sharp jaw, knew the curls in the hair, and recalled the line of her eyes. He abandoned his drink for the second time and took off, out of the pub. It had to be Talish; there was no-one else to look for because, he felt, he'd seen them all.

She was moving quickly and with some determination. Melly quickened his pace while his rucksack bounced embarrassingly on his back. Some entrance this was going to be! He slowed down so as not to run out of breath. What he had to say to her was important to him, and he wanted to get it right. But he didn't know what he wanted. Maybe he just wanted to see an old, long-lost friend, and embrace her. And he wasn't entirely sure it was her, either. He had to be wary; of that he was sure.

The first thing he noticed was that he couldn't smell her up ahead of him and the second was that from within the crowds, people moved aside as she passed. They were wary of her advance along the road; they made room for her and stood back, respectfully.

The coat was different; it was black, yes, but not the smelly, stiff leather of old. This was a leather wrap with a fur-lined hood. She wore clean, solid platform boots under black jeans. She was lean, but not bony thin, and she didn't look dreadful. She looked freshly but severely made up, alert and confident. The hair was dark, fuzzy and long. Collared hair ties, mostly red, interfered with her line. She looked attractive and she looked Middle-Eastern. She paused to scan the street.

"Time," though Melly, "time to perform."

"Excuse me," he said, standing in the gutter while she stood on the pavement, "what is your name?"

"My name?" she looked at him directly with piercing eyes, heavy with mascara. "My name? It's Alexis."

Melly felt a chill. "Is that right?" he said, pulling off his woollen hat to reveal his bald pate, "Do you remember me?"

A glint of recognition sparked in her face. She smiled a warm smile.

"Yes I do," she said, "I heard you're looking for me."

Melly, on guard, chose not to trust her. There were several Alexes; Kenneth had said so. Word would have passed down overnight and now any one of them would be out there looking to rip him off. He thought he'd test her.

"What did we do?" he asked.

"We ate spaghetti together," said Alexis, laughing.

"So far so good", thought Melly, "she's probably heard that one already."

"Where, what did we do?" he asked

"You had a car?" She was fishing for inspiration.

"Wrong, bitch. Wrong, wrong," thought Melly, untrustingly.

"No, I didn't," said Melly, "You know, we did nothing and I met you three times. You had no shoes on."

"Yes, I remember," she said.

"You asked me to buy you a drink," said Melly, "and I refused."

Alexis spoke good English; she looked and sounded healthy.

"Why did you run away like that?" she asked. "Why did you not come back?"

She had, indeed, remembered. He had found her; *at last, he had found Talish.*

"Because I had no money to give you. You were horrible then," said Melly, "You were in such a sorry state. I wanted to lift you out and protect you. So I wrote a story. It's a story about an imagined relationship between us, inspired by what I saw."

"I want to hear it," she said, "But have you got ten guilders? I want a drink. You want; we have a drink and talk? But first, I need to puff."

Melly felt he had been down this road before, all too recently. He stopped at a kiosk and bought a stick of chewing gum, giving her two fives from the handful of change.

"I came to thank you for being the inspiration for the book," he said, "and to see how you were. I came to take you off the pedestal I'd put you on. Can we talk?"

"Sure," she said, leading him down towards the Central Station. "Hey, you want to write about life on the street? You don't know nothing!"

Alexis eased up considerably. Her shoulders were no longer tight up into her neck; she relaxed and spoke, and spoke. She spoke like there was no stopping her, as if her mouthpiece had suddenly been located, cleared out and made ready for the long delivery and the long oration; she had plenty to say.

"Like, there's only a few men that I will go with," she said, "No blacks, no Arabs, no Sudanese, not Lebanese. If I don't like, I don't go. I'm very choosy."

"You're looking good," he said, "much better than before."

She laughed. "Summer?" she said. "I was in a bad way then, wasn't I? My feet were in a terrible state, I remember. But you're lucky, you know," she said, "I've just come out of prison, yesterday. Twenty-eight days. Didn't pay my fine, see." Alexis pulled out a fresh exclusion order.

"Got this only this morning," she laughed. "Smoking my pipe in public, but hey, I don't care. These are my streets, I gotta work!"

She was upbeat and optimistic. It was clear to Melly that her time inside was spent under a regime that allowed her to clean up a bit; freshly laundered clothes, and a period under medical supervision.

"Yeah," she said, "they put me on methadone for a month. They think it's gonna clean me up, but fuck, what do I care? I don't care shit."

"Do you want to clean up?" he asked.

"Fuck, yeah," she said, "We all want to clean up. If I didn't have my brown habit, I'd stop tomorrow; I'd stop yesterday. But it's not easy, you know. I'm looking; I'm waiting for someone to take me out of this. They'll come, when I'm ready."

"So you don't have a boyfriend?" said Melly, "you don't have friends?"

Alexis laughed heartily and spat heavily onto the street, ridding herself of sour saliva.

"Boyfriends?" she said, "You're fuckin joking. What? From the rabble we got in Amsterdam. Remember this one thing from me." She stopped and gripped his elbow. "In Amsterdam, you don't trust no-one. Everyone's always out to rip you off. I don't trust no-one and no-one trusts me. Where am I gonna find anyone worth dealing with in this place? Friends? No chance! And boyfriends? What's that? Once you've been on the street as long as I have, you get to hate men; you get to hate their weaknesses, and you get to despise how they see women."

"You dislike men?" he asked.

"No, I don't dislike them," she said, "I just don't see how I can ever treat a man with respect after what I've experienced with them They only want to ride you and spread their seed all over you. That's so shit.

I have no faith in men any more. Find me a strong man, yeah, with no hang-ups."

"So you're not affectionate, there's no love?" he ventured.

She laughed again. "Love, affection? You're joking. No way love; I don't even think I know what that is any more. And affection? Stop being so romantic! I haven't known affection so long, I wouldn't know if it hit me in the face. And, I wouldn't know what to do with it. I don't trust it to start. Hookers don't give affection, you should know that. It's just a job, just a fuckin' job. Like dipping in water, you hold your breath, hold your nose, close your eyes and dunk. Being with clients is the same. You do it 'cos you have to, but you have no respect for the guy you're doing it with; just in, out; you done yet? Now fuck off! Affection? Ha!"

She turned to him suddenly. "You know," she said, "I don't believe this. My time is precious, my time is money, and I'm walking down the street here with you and I'm not earning, I'm walking down the street and talking to you. I've never done that before; taking time out to talk like this. You got something about you that makes me want to talk. I love it. Go on."

"So tell me about it," he said, pouring her a coffee from the smoke shop, the one next to the plaza in front of Central Station, and the one he used first on his arrival to Amsterdam. He bought a fat ready-rolled spliff of Super Skunk. She lit it and spat.

"Fucking grass cuttings in here," she said, "No Super Skunk in this. You're getting ripped off."

In truth, Alexis confirmed much of what Melly felt. There was a hit in the grass but it wasn't as much as might have been expected, not for the seasoned smoker, at any rate. He was a seasoned smoker. Alexis was a seasoned smoker and Alexis didn't take shit. Not from anyone.

"So," she said, relaxing into an alcove, "You wanna hear? I was born in The Hague, but my dad was Tunisian and my mum is from Israel. I'm twenty-seven years old, twenty-eight next Tuesday and I've been smoking white since I was seventeen. I've been a prostitute since then, most of the time in Rotterdam, that's for ten years. You have to, to keep up the habit. And I've become very good at it. People think they know what they're getting with me, but it's all an act. That's what I do, I'm an actress. I'll be what you want me to be, then *fuck off*, but it ain't me under all that lot. I've been smoking brown since I was twenty-five. That is why I came to Amsterdam. Hmm," she said, sounding a note of regret, "I been working a lot since then."

"I know it's my problem," she said, "Only I can solve it; but at least now I'm on methadone."

She was hardened, severe, lean, wide-faced, big-eyed, tight-panted, and she looked horny.

"I wanna tell you something," said Melly. "Are you ready for this?"

"Go on," she said, "I can handle anything, shoot!"

Melly leaned across the table towards her. "I came to Amsterdam yesterday, looking for you and it's taken me *this* long to find you, and I'm off tonight on a coach back to London. I came to thank you for being the inspiration for a lot of writing and to see how you were doing. I come to pay homage and, you know, it would have been good to spend some time with you but, like the messenger who was carrying the big prize, the prize has all gone. It's all spent."

Whether she understood or not was immaterial. He was alluding to the idea that he'd spent all his money *on another* and had none left for her. Melly had also come to the conclusion that Alexis would cost him much dearer than Alex ever had. At fifty guilders a ball of heroin, this was double *her* rate of crack use. Alexis was getting fidgety.

"You know, you're really weird saying all this," she said, "You're a fuckin' strange guy; I ask you for ten guilders, you give me ten guilders; you even ask for change to get ten guilders! Anyone else, they give me twenty, twenty-five. Am I not worth any more?"

"How much *are* you worth?" asked Melly.

Her eyes widened. "Fifty guilders for me, and I know a lady with a hotel that's twenty-five."

"Would you go with *me*?" asked Melly.

"Yes I would, I'd go with you," she said without hesitation. "I like you, and I'm very good. We can have as much time as you like."

"Then let's," he said quickly.

Whore talk, sales pitch, hot air, and false promises. He didn't believe a word of it. He wanted to, though. He really, really wanted to. *Going to bang the best whore in Amsterdam!* Wow! It sounded good.

"Okay," she smiled and led him away.

⁂

Alexis was purposeful, alive, and so much a contrast to Alex. This was the difference between the drugs that either used. As he walked through the streets of the Old Town with Alexis, people stood aside respectfully; it was uncanny.

"I paint," she said, "and I write; I do a lot of things. I can do a lot of things; I don't need to be on the streets forever. What do you think I should do?"

"You could sell your work in the market," he said, "You could join a studio-."

"Hey," she interrupted, "I don't work for anyone, I work for myself; no-one tells me what to do."

They reached the *Febo*, a 24-hour automatic snack bar, full of sandwiches and cans of drink. Alex was inside, slumped against the window, looking quite upset and very wrecked. She saw them, walking together. Melly looked at her and gave her a faint smile, the kind that said, *"Look, I found her, uh"* The 'uh' part meant he wasn't sure about it all.

"I'm hungry," said Alexis, "can we get some cakes?" She led them to a bakery; it was already early evening, and the bakery was closing.

"Take what you fancy," said Melly.

Alexis picked out three ornate pastries heavily dusted with icing sugar and had them wrapped.

"I need to see someone first, to get some poof," she said, "Come with me."

Though he walked on, something in Melly froze. She was taking him to connect for her on some heroin; she was taking him along as the paymaster of her next smoke, just as Alex had done, time and time again. He knew he did not have enough to make it happen and wanted out. He would hate for a downer on his forthcoming pleasure, in the form of a pissed off Alexis, pissed off at not connecting when *she* needed to connect, at the precise moment, because *it* came first and everything else came second.

They were passing a bridge; Melly took her by the arm and settled her in against the wrought-ironwork of the balustrade.

"I want to take a picture of you," he said, moving her onto the bridge. "I want you to look out over the water and get a mood going."

"Ha," she laughed, "That's easy."

She was right. Her black clothing dissolved into the darkness of the night and left her wide, heavily made-up face and red hair ties ready to frame the severe expression she adopted.

"Anger!" she said, "That's really easy."

At the end of the shoot, Melly pulled her up close and said, "Are you ready for another one?"

"Yeah, go on," she said. She was game.

He took off his jacket and placed it over their heads.

"So's no-one can see! Pretend you're taking a lug," he said, "I want you to plant one on me."

Alexis gave him the kind of look that showed she was wary of him, in the extreme. In the darkness under the jacket, she quickly brushed her cheek up against his cheek, making very light contact and pulled away quickly. Too quickly. Melly pulled the jacket off their tryst, back onto his shoulders, and held her up close but gently by the lapels in mock remonstration. *She wasn't even prepared to kiss him.*

"You know," he said, "It doesn't matter whether we do fuck or if we don't fuck, the most important thing is the money, isn't it? And, you know? I'm thinking you'd rather not."

He looked at her, so far, far removed from the ragged waif of six months past.

"I'm not going to get the sex with any affection, am I, and that's what I really want," he said, "I want you to enjoy it and I want you to enjoy me."

"You won't get affection," she said, "Not from me."

"I want a loving body," he said.

"Then take a lover," she advised.

"No, you see, I can't do that." he said. "I love my wife too much to want to love anyone else. I don't want to *conspire* a lover. I haven't got room in my head for one."

"Oops!" said Alexis, shrugging her shoulders and making one of those, *"well, don't ask me for a solution"* looks that accompany pursed lips and wide-open eyes. Melly wondered how many times she'd heard *that* particular story. And Melly was wondering if he could change the habits of a lifetime for a prostitute in the same way that some men seek to change a lesbian's mind about heterosexual sex. *You'll enjoy it if you try it. And I'm the one to make you try it.* The non-kiss spoke volumes to this. Alexis trusted no-one, not even slightly.

Images of her from his story flashed through his mind. The wounds, the bony, cold body, the smell, and the diseases. And then, Katryn's polythene gloves, the inevitable hygiene, the sex at arm's length; perform or fuck off, perform *and* fuck off.

"And I tell you what else," he said, "I'm scared. I'm scared of destroying you."

Alexis looked at him quizzically.

"So what I'm gonna do," he said, "is give you the seventy-five and say thank you for being around. It's been good, Alexis. I gotta say I respect you too much to have sex with you. So I'm going to go now. Goodbye."

"Wow, *interesting!*" she said, stunned.

Melly slipped her a clutch of notes and kissed her paternally on the forehead. She accepted it graciously.

Was he lying? Yes, he was and, yet, he wasn't. He respected her enough to say *you don't have to do this; here's the money instead* and, at the same time, he didn't respect her *enough* to have sex with. He feared her too much to have sex with her. She didn't, of course, deserve the hurt from being told this. The image he'd created of Talish was so deeply embedded in his mind that to attempt to realize the imagined bliss was certain to end in failure; if not during the enactment, then after the climax, what with the regret and the guilt. He did not want that baggage. He did not want to tarnish Talish's reputation, such as it was. And as for Alexis? As far as he was concerned, Alexis could go to hell; perhaps *return* there. This real Talish was someone about whom he now had grave misgivings.

Alexis looked at him with an easy, warm, and generous smile.

"If you change your mind," she said, "tonight, later on, or next time you're in Amsterdam, come and see me. You're on for one."

A tinge of regret passed momentarily across Melly's brow, and then a feeling of relief that he was done with her.

"Which way ya going?" she chirped, "Yeah, I'm going that way too."

Within three paces *that way* she was met by a dealer and stopped to talk to him. Melly carried on walking and, without a backward glance, went off to search for Alex. He didn't need to go far; she was on the next corner, at the side of a bridge, sitting on the pavement swaying mindlessly, hiding under her hair. His path was suddenly blocked by a bird that swooped out from within the crowd.

"Hi," said Kokomo, "I see you found her. You got five guilders?"

"The men here beg too," thought Melly and began to wonder how men found the money to finance their habit. "Surely it's not just down to stealing and re-selling stock or buying and selling dope. And how many times can you get away with ripping someone off?"

Melly found a ten-guilder note and went into a shop for change, closely followed by Kokomo. There was a long queue of customers waiting to be served, giving Melly enough time to be grilled by his conscience.

"...You're really weird; you only give what's asked for, never more..."

"...My time is money; I can't afford to hang around doing nothing..."

Melly saw the resigned look in the birdman's face and realized he was being somewhat churlish and a bit too tight. *"The things you have to do for five guilders."*

"Yeah, Kokomo," said Melly, "I did find her and it was down to you. Here, take the ten." He should have given him more but he couldn't afford to.

"Yeah, cool man," said the birdman as he slapped Melly on the back with his wing and disappeared into the crowd.

Melly was left staring directly at Alex.

"Had your fun?" she mumbled, "Met your heroine?"

"I've finished with her now," said Melly and sat down in the road with her. "Tell me," he said, "Last night, before we went our separate ways, if I'd asked you to go to a hotel with me, would you have gone?"

Alex sighed, exasperated.

"Yes, I would have gone," she said, "but I'm glad we didn't. As soon as we sleep together, it's all gonna be over between us. I don't want that to happen. Now, will you stop going on about it?"

Melly felt heartened at her reply. As they spoke, a posse of users and street people swept past, purposefully led by Alexis. She gesticulated with wide sweeps of her arm that arrested anyone who tried to overtake her at the side. It made her look very much the controller. She didn't notice him and she didn't look his way. Alex noticed, though.

"Did you argue or something?" she asked sounding optimistic.

"I turned her down," said Melly quietly.

Alex came alive. "You didn't, did you?" she said through a dropped jaw, "She hates that. Ha, ha."

She was beside herself with satisfaction and would have laughed out loud but a coughing fit seized her suddenly. Melly held her shoulders while she settled and recomposed herself.

"What are you on?" he asked.

She looked at him then down at the ground, embarrassed.

"Brown," she said, adding quickly, "Just the once. It tasted horrible and I feel sick."

"Just the once? Fuck you, fuck you Alex!" Melly said angrily. "Not you too. You said you didn't like it, you knew it made you sick. Why?"

"I was feeling down, okay? I was just feeling a bit down," she said in apology.

"Yeah, well I can't afford to be around you any longer," he cussed. "My money's gone. You got punters to find; I'll leave you to it."

Alex hid her face under her hair and tucked her head in her arm.

"Can I come and see you off," she asked. "Are you flying out of Schipol?"

"No," he said, "I'm going from Amstel Square by coach. You can come to see me off, if you want. Look, here's a train ticket I got you to Amstel. I'll be moving out at about ten o'clock for a coach at half-past ten. I'll see you there, huh?"

Alex took the ticket and stood up to face Melly as he pulled her to her feet. He embraced her lightly, if only because she could not ease into the embrace.

"Alex," he said, "I came to find Talish and even though I found her, I wish it had been you. You've been good to be around and I've learned a lot from meeting you. I've learned a lot from meeting both of you. But *you*, I like especially. I'll see you later, yeah?"

With that, he kissed her on the cheek. Alex returned the salutation and kissed him on the cheek too. Finally!

⊠ ⊠ ⊠

Melly looked across the bridge to the coffee bar where Katryn worked. A big sign in the window advertised work for bar staff. Melly entered and spoke to a barmaid.

"Was there a curly-haired blonde here last summer; young?" he asked.

The waitress shook her head. "I've been here since September," she said, "I haven't seen anyone like that."

Melly wondered if Katryn had moved up-market, or down-market for that matter, and was now on the street herself, full-time and, maybe, working out of a window. His session with her would have confirmed in her mind that easy money was to be made and it was not dependent on tips or on working hours. Melly reasoned she had most probably left Amsterdam.

"Shit," he thought, "It's so easy to go under, here."

Around him, new faces were going under every day and every hour. Was Alex going under? He hoped not; he sincerely hoped she would not. He wondered whether her reference to Schipol was a last-ditch attempt on her part to see if he might whisk her away on a plane, off to London and off to a new life. He would have taken her but, well, it cost four balls of white, and white was more important. It *always* was, and she'd want it when she got to London.

Melly was down to his last forty guilders. Enough for a bit of food at the coach station and a bonus twenty-five for Alex when she came; a peace offering. Some peace! He sat down in the coffee bar window and looked out onto the bridge. All the faces he saw, he now recognized. All the furtive glances to the left and to the right, he now understood. And he didn't want to look any more; he didn't want to see any more. He had seen enough.

As he was leaving the bar, a man carrying a bundle of dark red roses walked in. Melly immediately bought one and carried it to his smoke shop on the plaza, outside the Central Station, and rolled a couple of big spiffs with the last of his Zero Zero. It used to be good and strong, now it only dulled him slightly. He would share the last with Alex, just before boarding his coach.

For the next hour Melly, the writer, wrote again in a notebook with his eye on the clock. The thing about writing is that time flies when you're hard at it. It was already nine-thirty when he brought his scribbling to a halt and thought of a title which he wrote on the front. He tore away to the tunnel, just outside, to the Metro station; fully paid up, it was going to be easy. Security guards at the entrance to the Metro platforms would wave him through, wouldn't they?

"You can't come through here," they said. "This is the wrong ticket."

Melly's look of disappointment was evident but it didn't cut any ice.

"Look," he pleaded, "I'm leaving from Amstel coach station in an hour. This is the only journey I'm making."

After several repeats of the same argument, they let the stoned foreigner through though, once on the platform, Melly looked at the offending ticket to see that it was for the main line train. He returned to the security guards at the entrance feeling sheepish.

"How often do the trains run to Amstel on the main line?" he asked.

"I don't know, you can go by Metro," said one of the guards.

"No, you don't understand," said Melly, "How frequent is the service to Amstel by the main-line train?"

"I don't know," he said, "I work for the Metro, not for *sneltram*. Your ticket is for the *sneltram*. Why should I know?"

Melly was taken aback and said, "I just thought, you know, as someone who uses transport in Amsterdam, maybe you know if the other line through the town has regular trains."

"Well, I don't," said the guard.

Melly considered the options. He'd left it so late that he could ill-afford the time to get to the main-line platform and wait for a train without knowing how long he'd have to wait. But that's where Alex was likely to be. She'd have recognized the ticket and known where to go, unlike Melly. She might even know when the next train was due. Either way, she would have made a decision about how to get to Amstel, either from the main line platform or from the Metro, and she'd have to talk her way though that one. Besides, Melly was not enthusiastic about running across to the correct platform in the main station to see if she was waiting for him when he'd actually arranged to meet her by the coach. The rose, in the event, would suffer trauma; flowers always come out worst during lightning dashes. He damned his own stupidity. Wrong *again*!

Melly returned to the Metro platform and caught the next train out to Amstel and the coach terminal, where he stood vigil, watching the station entrance and the huge, neon clock above it. He watched the main-line trains trundle through, high above him on the overground. There were several but not many stopped. One of the two Andies approached him, looking very glazed.

"You lost everyone?" asked Melly emptily, "So have I!"

Ten-fifteen and Melly, pacing the forecourt next to his coach, was about to light his final joint of the town, to set him up for a good sleep, when the driver spotted him.

"Come on, come on," he said, "We've got a tough one ahead and I'd like to leave early. You're the last one we're waiting for."

"Just one moment," said Melly and ran to place the rose across a bench there.

He was too far-gone to bother with notes; he was done with writing notes. If Alex were to turn up after he'd gone, she might spot the rose and wonder who or what, maybe. But probably not. The fact remains; she hadn't come and Melly was pained, mostly with regret that she *couldn't* make it, not because she didn't want to. Maybe it was the train, maybe it was the heroin, maybe it was Danny, the policeman, or maybe she had a client.

Racked with disappointed, he tossed his notebook down next to the rose. He wanted to leave it all, every single thing, behind… Entitled *Melly's Strip*, it seemed a fitting epitaph. Even ridding himself of every last thought, written or otherwise, felt oddly liberating.

Melly relaxed into his seat knowing that he'd have just one stop, the rest rooms at the French customs, where he could finish off his supply of hashish. What a trip! He'd come looking for Talish and uncovered two contrasting images of her or, rather, two realities. One represented a dark, sinister side; the other represented the pain of a sweet victim. Talish had been portrayed as the victim; the one who'd inspired Melly was hardened, assertive and in control. She would never have stayed willingly in the Sonesta hotel room unless Melly had an endless supply of heroin or crack. Once that was sorted, then the business of life and recovery might begin.

But that was the case with both Alex and Alexis. Their need for a source and the means to pay for it was *the* priority, however much they denied it. And yet, smoking it, as he'd watched Alex smoke, made little noticeable difference at the time. Over the period, he'd noticed an accumulation that would suddenly make her act irrationally, laughing to herself, arguing with herself, hurting with noises in the head, and still hurting with toothache. That's why Alex tried heroin again, because there was no getting away from the pain and the memories, especially with Melly unlocking them. The parallels he'd drawn between his relationship with cannabis and Alex's with crack were accurate but he felt shamed into believing his image of Talish was too easily controlled and too trite to be real. He'd seen the real Talish and she was formidable.

He'd uncovered both sides of Talish: the sharp and the dulled, the inviting and the uninviting, the content and the malcontent, the honourable and the dishonourable, the possessed and the dispossessed. They shared some qualities but, on balance, each had their own share of the alarming as well as the disarming.

As prostitutes, neither of them delivered sex to him; one because of a refusal and the other, because of a refusal. And what's more, *everyone felt good about it.* Within a short space of time, the opportunist lover had found how rocky the ground in the sexual playground can be and that he could not hope to deal with professionals in an unprofessional manner nor with non-professionals in a professional manner. He hadn't got his rocks off but that no longer mattered as much as it might have once. He'd met people for whom sex was meaningless in *his* context, yet who feared it more than he for all the harm it could do. And though he really yearned the affectionate body of one, he came to realize that access to it required love and he wasn't prepared to risk new love at the expense of his wife. It required trust but, in this world, in this Red Light district, no-one trusted any other. Inevitably, it had to be that way on the street.

Melly was grateful that this was not his lot in life, yet, he felt very conscious of having trampled over the emotions of one, if not both women. And still, he seemed quite unconcerned about the emotions of a third. He wondered what gave him the right to do so, in being so deliberate and helpless. Wasn't *he* the intrusive one? Didn't *he* realize he had the capacity to get under people's skin as much as they got under his?

His lot, the wife he resolved never to leave, the social hub that was the home they'd built together, and the realization that his was a safe contentment sufficient to prevent a slide down the path to maximum escape and maximum denial; that was the difference between his cosiness and the bleakness of the street. It wasn't worth throwing away for a fleeting moment of pleasure. It was as if, when he went away, whenever he did, it was in order to convince himself that there were people worse off than himself. That, in itself, convinced him never to go down the brown and white road for it presented him with stark reminders that his was a cushy number and he'd made it cushy, so what exactly was his complaint? Was it so undeserved or was it just worth remembering that it was his to cherish and to enjoy? This guilt; he was always so racked by guilt...

On this occasion, he returned home from yet another trip away; this time, he was heartened, open-eyed, upbeat, and he returned a discoverer of further truths. It felt so much better than before. He'd gone to close the book on Talish and, finding himself ill-equipped on both an emotional and economic level to deal with her many facets, was now glad to get away from her, knowing what he knew. He had managed to take Talish off the pedestal he'd built for her, yet leave her memory, somehow, alive and unsullied as a reminder of his weakness. Indeed, he felt free to slam the book shut behind him.

"There was a call for you from Amsterdam during the night," said Jean as soon as he came in at the door, "someone called Alex who burbled a lot. She said something about how she *was now ready to sleep with you*."

Melly's face reddened.

"Don't answer Melly, I don't want to hear," she hissed angrily and closed the front door behind her.

Melly's Strip

Melly opened the polythene bag of Bahamian grass and read the slip marked *Instructions for Use*, guessing they had been translated by someone abroad: "Smoke – inhale and keep insight as long as possible." He lay down and closed his eyes. This was to be the last time; there has to be a last time for everything and, as his time-line shortened, he found himself at the head of the queue.

"Next!" called the Dream Maker.

"I've come to have the dream of a lifetime," said Melly. "I've come to dream about the things I could never get right and the things I could never do. Can you help me?"

"Go on," said the Dream Maker.

"I've had enough of this life," said Melly, "I see too much anger in the street, people are callous and hurtful and I just can't… I just can't compete with them any more. The world has changed, the cities are different and I've lost touch with the present. See me, standing in the wings, watching life pass me by. I'm too scared to join in. But I want to get it right. Just once, I want to get it right. I want to be a participant, not just an observer."

"And…?"

"Show me how it might have been. Let me feel the pleasure I have been seeking so desperately. I wanted to save; let me save, if only so that I can say that I went through with it, all the way. Let me have Alexis, let me say I really knew the best whore in Amsterdam! Let me have any whore, any paid contact of any kind that might, just might, convince me that affection can be bought. I want to be numb to the cynicism that permeates this world. It's not the good old days, and it's not the halcyon days I'm after. Show me there's a life that's generous and accommodating, and I…I'll…owe you."

A tear slipped down Melly's cheek and caught in his stubble. He hadn't slept for days, he hadn't eaten for hours. He was, at this point, shortened in stature.

"It's all a bit *me, me*, isn't it?" said the Dream Maker, "Haven't you ever thought about dreaming for world peace and the eradication of pain?"

"Yes, I've done that," said Melly. "I played that one, not too well as I recall, but I've put in time looking after people and solving their problems. Now it's my turn. I'm the one who needs help; I want the inner peace in my world, I want the eradication of my pain. I want the cure, not the solution. I want to get it right, just once."

"And exploit the vulnerable?" said the Dream Maker.

"What is exploitation?" said Melly defiantly; "it means making the best use of something. If someone is there to be exploited and made use of, I'll do it. People have been doing it to me, exploiting me, and exploiting my talents, always. Don't throw the word exploitation at me with your own values attached. Exploitation is not abuse, remember that!

"And vulnerable? Tell me about vulnerability. We're all vulnerable; press the right buttons or press the wrong buttons; it makes no difference to me. We laugh joyously and cry with pain or we cry with joy and we laugh to hide pain. And if I go out to sell to you, am I to be damned for selling or are you to be damned for buying? Either we're either both guilty or we're both innocent.

"I have always done what had to be done, to get by. But I've never callously gone out and taken advantage. Okay, okay, I did between the ages of eleven and fifteen, but that's because I didn't know any better, and I never really grew up until I was twenty-nine-."

"You never, ever, grew up!" reasoned the Dream Maker.

"Well then," cried Melly, "let me play. Let me be satisfied, let me be the hero, let me save the day, let me know it's all been worthwhile-."

"Worthwhile?" scoffed the Dream Maker, "…in your dreams, Laddie, in your dreams... Now, come with me and retrace your steps."

⊠ ⊠ ⊠

The best time to catch a hooker in Amsterdam is the early morning. The girls have been busy for much of the night but in the hour since dawn, the punters have all but dried up. How many clients is it possible for a hundred prostitutes to secure if there are only seven punters walking the street? And at that time of the morning, the girls are known to get slack. Their business sense, like their candle, is burnt at both ends. Now, it's hard-sell and devil-may-care.

I'm outside De Oudekerk, looking at the girls in the windows. They're all African; they all give the come-on. "Just a minute…hello, hello sweetie…you want me?" All are dressed in white, in lace underwear or in robes, and entice with promises, all except for one who sits with her coat open, and silently massages her inner thigh.

I do a couple of tours, window-shopping along the cobbled alley and settle on the one with the softest tone. She looks trim, full-breasted and relaxed.

"You can't give me it." I can joke.

"Yes I can!" she says, "I can give you what you want. I can massage you, I can suck you."

"Can I touch you?" I ask.

"Of course, if you want."

"Can I lick you?"

"Yes, you can lick me, we can 69. You like that?"

"Can do!"

"We can fuck," she says kindly.

"I'm not sure about that." I say. I've heard this before. "What's all this costing?"

"How much do you want to give me?"

"Say a price." The ball is in her court.

"200," she says.

"No way!"

"100?"

"No!"

"75?"

"For it all?"

"Yes, all!" she says, "I'm going to wash, you wash too, then lie down."

Perfect, negotiated, settled; in all honesty and no bullshit.

"I am Frances."

I know it's a wig. She looks more fragile without it. She lies down, ebony in the red light. African rhythms pound in the background.

"I've never had a black girl. You're so firm."

There is not an ounce of fat on her. And she does it all honestly, except for the moment she thinks she has me and squeals, "another 25, I'll make you come!"

"No way," I say, massaging her.

I am good to her. I am kind, considerate; a client, for sure, but not one who is brutal or hungry. I hover over her with a vibrator that does not vibrate.

"You're so dry," I say, "Give me cream."

Cream, indeed, but she will not let the vibrator pass. Tight and closed she is.

"You're very small," I say.

She looks at me anxiously.

"It's lovely," I reassure.

She smiles and lets the vibrator slide in further. She lets me in too; not far, but enough to grip me tightly and hold me in position. I see one of her nipples is half-erect.

She is acting, and moaning on queue. She is good at this. And then, while she finishes me off, she says, "Your time is up soon. Give me another 25 and we'll go on another half-hour."

"Is it over so soon?" I say, "No! Just another moment."

She is smiling to herself as she moistens. I have made her moisten. And she makes me moisten, plentifully.

I know what to do now, now that it's all over.

"Thank you," I say.

"Thank you," she says and shows me unhurriedly to the door.

I am able to leave, unburdened after a lifetime fearing that prostitutes have no soul and have no enjoyment of their work; ladies of the night who know a sucker when they see one but I am no sucker. Not this time.

No. This, this I really enjoyed, yeah.

⊠ ⊠ ⊠

I'm out looking for Talish. Who do I see? There are so many who qualify:

Serene Talish looks Somalian; like she's come in from the East, dressed for the desert, with white shrouds billowing about in her hair and over her skinny frame. She has great style.

Manic Talish is tall and lean, ginger-haired, roller-bladed, paranoid and uninvisible to all but herself. She peers over dark specs and moves by extremes, making it clear she's being secretive.

New Talish, soft and endearing, is not yet worn down by the street but her lines are well practiced.

"I've been up for three nights. Give me another 10 and I'll have a bed for the night... Oh, are you not going to help me?"

"No, I'm not going to help you." I say. I know where this is going.

Old Talish is here. The frail, the lined and the hoarse offers a bed for the night with lots of fun. "When you've been around as long as I have been around," she says, "understand that a bed is a bed. 50 for you, eh? But first, I must smoke."

"You're tricking me," I say, "I don't want to be tricked."

Hardened Talish is dark, drawn and drab. There is a look of hatred in her eyes. It shouldn't be her, but it is. No longer leading the gang, nor cocky, she's back in the depths of despair and vulnerable.

"You know me?" I say.

"I know you," says Alexis, cursing her high-heeled boots.

"You owe me," I say.

"I know. You got a hotel? I got a room."

There are blackouts in all the windows; let there be night. The bed is for fucking. Nothing much else goes on in the shambolic apartment.

She takes off her clothes matter-of-factly and hunts for something 'light'. Her body is grubby with disgust.

"Don't look at me," she says incompletely, "let me put on this slip."

But she cannot fill it. Her breasts are no more, sunken to oblivion.

"Come, lie with me," I say.

She snuggles in, under my arm, and throws her knee over my stomach.

I close my eyes. I am holding Talish; bony and slight, and in need of help.

I open my eyes. I am holding Alexis - lean and vibrant, helping the needy.

We go all the way in every way, as only one who 'owes' does. She is open to all suggestion and gives of herself completely. She gnaws me worshipfully and chews my balls; she is astride me, and I am deep, oh, so deeply into her; she flops her chest onto my hairiness; I tweak her nipples and she tries to smile, except that she is unable to smile.

And at a critical point, as I look upon her, and as she looks down at me, I see the grey coldness in her eyes, a long distant cracked haze that numbs her from the world. She is not here.

And only after I am satisfied, only after I have kept her for over an hour, and she has kept me up for all that time, only then do I give her two fifties. She deserves more; so very much more.

"Thank you," I say.

"Thank you," she says.

"Are you Talish?" I say.

"Talish is a fantasy," she says.

Soft Talish is somewhere here. If you're lost or looking for someone, ask a policeman though it seems a bad idea to ask Danny about Alex.

"Hi, I've come to screw your woman." I am saying.

I meet the smiling one who chooses not to be Talish but remains Alex. She looks very good for having spent the last sixty-two hours eating and sleeping on the outside of the city. She's counted the hours and is now ready for a smoke. She is pleased to see me and talks wisely and with generous, good humour.

"You know you're not sleeping with me," she says for openers.

"I know," I say. There is regretful relief in my voice. After a long while, I say, "I need to talk. Can I spend some time with you?"

"Of course," she replies, "but will you sponsor me?"

I cannot refuse. I have always expected her to cost. The deal done, we walk and talk.

"You're looking good," I say. "How did it feel to get away?"

"I could do it," she says, looking at me. "I could go away now, forever. I keep meeting good people who want to rescue me. I'm ready to go!"

There is a guy, Bruno, who has adopted himself as a brother to her and moves among us jealously, disturbing our intimacy. He doesn't like the fact I'm not a client but someone more substantial. He smokes with us.

"He's a writer; he's writing about the girls in the Old Town," she says to him in Dutch.

Bruno backs off, babbling speedily.

"And then," I say to her, "you know how Talish is thin and wasted and I dream of holding her in my arms and protecting her?"

"I remember," she says.

"I have," I say.

She looks at me. "You have?"

"I have slept with Alexis. I lay with her on a bed, naked, and she cuddled in with my arm around her, as I offered her protection. And she was as thin as I'd imagined. Bony and grubby. And she did everything; she was very good, but she wouldn't let me nose around down there. That was her private place. She said, 'I don't want you to give me pleasure, I don't want to enjoy you,' But I tried to make her enjoy me. I wanted to get her juices flowing. I almost succeeded. And she took me without a condom."

Alex stops listening.

"You're onto a death wish, aren't you?" she says, "This fantasy world of yours. In this world, do people have diseases? You slept with her and with no protection? That's the most stupid thing you can do. What were you thinking? I am always clean. But she, she lives with a man who uses needles and shares needles. You don't know what you're doing?"

"I'll go for tests and treatments," I say.

"You do that," she says, "Didn't you ever listen at school? I did. It's what has kept me alive. I can't believe you would do such a thing!"

"I'm a wanker, then. Is that what you're saying?" I ask.

She places her arm over my shoulder and pulls me in close to her as we walk.

"No," she says, "you're not a wanker. You just have to stop all this. You've done it all. Now stop the madness."

"Not just yet," I say, "I've one more thing…I have a spare boarding pass for the coach to London." I say, giving it to her. "You can join me there but you'll have to take your chances on the journey because I can't be there for you; you're on your own."

"I'm ready to go," she says, pulling out her passport, and pecks me fondly on the cheek.

"Thank you," I say.

"Thank you," she says.

I await her descent from a coach to London. Her decision and my facility. I am, forever, to be her hero and her saviour. But she will not give or accept a quick fumble in thanks for she has crossed over. Her decision and my facility.

⊠ ⊠ ⊠

"Ah, bliss! Now is the time for me to die, Dream Maker!" said Melly, "or, yet, live again without guilt, fulfilled and completely satisfied. I am finally at peace with myself."

"Is that all?" the Dream Maker asked, "and what about Jean?"

"Jean?" said Melly, "I don't understand what you mean. Jean is not a part of this."

"Is she not?" said the Dream Maker, "and perhaps she could be? Perhaps she should be a part of this."

"You are mad. The time is not right," said Melly.

"The time is never right," said the Dream Maker, "if it was ever the right time, we wouldn't have pain. But you, you have to bear the pain."

"So must she," said Melly. "It will hurt her the most."

"Yes," said the Dream Maker, "Yes, it will hurt her the most. But you owe me, remember?"

The Dream Maker laughed out loud, and looked at Melly keenly. "Live or die, you decide, but quick, chop, chop; you're out of time..."

⊠ ⊠ ⊠

About the Author

Marek Nowina (pronounced NOH-VEE-NAH), born of Polish refugees in England, was educated at the University of London and now lives and works in Massachusetts. While *A Field in Arlon* is his first novel, Marek has had a number of articles published in journals as well as in local newspapers, and has worked as producer and promoter with drama groups and musicians on both sides of the Atlantic.

Breinigsville, PA USA
10 September 2009
223806BV00001B/53/P